Also by S.L.Mason

KILLING GODS

ALETHEA

CALYPSO

HERA

FATES

UNDERWORLD

ELYSIUM

POSEIDON

THESE HALLOWED HILLS

TRICK OF FAE

TEST OF FAE

THORNS OF FAE

TWIST OF FAE

TRAITS OF FAE

FATES

KILLING GODS

IV

Quick Quill Publishing, LLC

© 2018

This Book is a work of fiction.

All of the characters, organizations, and events portrayed in the novel are either products of the authors imagination or are used fictitiously. Its not about you.

Copyright 2017 Quick Quill Publishing, LLC

DEDICATION

~ 5 ~

I always think of my children while writing. They are my breath and life. The thing I will fight to the death for. Every book I write is for them and their future. Without Jack and Gillian none of this would matter.

TABLE OF CONTENTS

PROLOGUE

Pythia bathed naked in the Castalian Spring and drank the holier waters of the Cassotis. It flowed closer to the temple, where naiads possessing magical powers were said to live.

Anu

ISOLDE

Looking back, I can say, '*That's 'it'! That's the day my life changed forever*'. Most people can't do that. Of course, they can point to the year or to something they were doing around that time. But not to the exact moment their whole world turned upside down, never to return to normalcy.

Well, I can and I can say it precisely, it was the exact moment when I touched Jacques. With a simple touch, I learned that evil existed in the world and if it weren't for Tristan and my mom, I'm not sure I could have survived.

It was Tristan who blocked most of the horror out for me. He is my brother, my twin, my friend, my ally.

For a long time after Jacques, I was petrified to touch another person. Even the mere thought of relieving that experience terrified me. The last thing I wanted was to relive every moment of another person's life ever again.

Would it happen again? Could I stop it, or was it always going to be this way?

CHAPTER 1

HERCULES

"Where is she?" I demanded, whipping my head left and right while searching the Infinity Pool for her.

Isolde has to be here somewhere.

A strong hand pressed me back into the tepid water. "Relax, big boy! She's alright. We got her out hours ago. It's you we need to worry about," the woman said.

I couldn't think of her name. It sat at the back of my tongue, teasing me with the sweet flavor of unlocked knowledge. She looked like Tobias, with all that black hair and sky blue eyes.

Melinda! Her name is Melinda! She's T's great aunt.

I clung to the information. If I had enough of my faculties to remember someone's name, I couldn't be that far gone.

My chest ached and my mind raged with pain. The acid from the Nemean Lyon still clung to my limbs, eating at my flesh.

The blue light in the Infinity Pool soothed the mind. It was designed to do so. The Primordium keepers tuned everything toward health and healing. Yet, the color wasn't enough to ease the stinging affliction.

I gazed down at my chest and arms. The skin was nonexistent, while the muscle and tendons were exposed, along with every nerve ending I had. That's when my moans of pain bleed through from the background. I didn't realize they were mine. The sound cut through my agony, reaching my ears, allowing me to pinpoint the pain in my raw throat.

Soft hands cupped my cheeks and turned my head, forcing me to gaze into beautiful blue eyes, "Hercules, Hercules, listen to the sound of my voice and follow me into the dreamwalk."

Mother's tone was reassuring and strong. It revealed no fear, only a firm command.

I allowed my eyes to slide shut and let mother pull me into the dreamworld. The pain dulled and I found myself standing on the side of Olympus as if I'd never left.

"Mother?" I called into the mist, clinging to the upper mountain.

"I am here," mother appeared next to a shrine to the Goddess of the mountain.

The stone statue resembled her in posture. Its base was labeled 'Hera' and flowers were laid at its feet along with a bowl of wine and a small pile of wheat.

It was the same shrine the village people had worshiped through all my childhood. This was where Hebe and I had laid our own offerings in a hope that mother would return alive from hunting our father.

"You were gravely injured. I must keep you here for a while longer so the pool can do its work," she stated then took to her feet, cupping my chin. "What possessed you to fight them? Those Lyons kill more Themians than you can ever know. You are only a hybrid," her voice carried concern, even if it didn't filter to her features.

Her concern was sweet and irritating, all at the same time. I found my emotions falling back into old ways with the mountain in the background.

Anger rolled over me. At first, it was because of my childhood, but her neglect was long ago and for a good reason, even though I couldn't understand at the time. I pushed the emotions back into the past where they belonged. Instead, I focused on the present and the woman I'd just saved.

"I had to save her. She's Sydney's child," I supplied to hide my true reasons. "I'm a Demigod, mother. One who has now tasted the power of the Primordium Pool," I finished, leaving the ramifications of it hanging in the air.

She pulled me into her arms and laid her head on my chest.

I'm too big to be cradled like a child.

"I know, but you could have died," she stated and her tears wet my shirt.

Even though we were in a dreamwalk, tears felt real.

Whatever residual anger had lingered in my heart, evaporated. I wrapped my arms around the small form of my mother and cradled her head in one hand.

"I'm sorry, mother! I didn't mean to scare you. I only tried to save both the Lyons and the girl. Is she alive and well?" I inquired while trying to keep my emotions steady and to myself.

Mother lifted her head and stared up at me. "Yes, she lives, though, when Sydney gets her hands on her, she may wish she was dead. That is one conversation I would like to witness," with that, mother gave me a half smile and stepped back.

"She didn't know and Sydney let her in to begin with. I was very explicit when I put that lock on," I said and a new type of anger tore through me.

If Sydney had only listened to me, none of this would have happened.

"You can have a fight with Sydney if you wish, but I'm not sure the old Grecian ways will work on her," my mother laughed and twirled in place to indicate the mountain side and the life we all once lived.

She was right, of course. I could not challenge Sydney to combat. She would only call for a champion and Adrian would surely be it. It would be either him or Ares, neither of which I had a desire to fight to the death.

"The last of the Lyons will need to be captured and relocated to a secure location," I remarked, leaving my mother's statements hanging in the air, then stepped away from her reassuring form.

I'd moved beyond the petting of childhood long ago and my taste for the dreamwalk had faded with it. I only wanted to live in the real world. I sat down on a rock and stared out at the vista from the mountain, a vista that did not exist anymore.

Thousands of years and human technology would have changed it, but I stared at my glimpse of the Aegean Sea anyway, taking a new comfort in the blue of the water. I marveled at a feeling I've never felt before.

I am not alone.

CHAPTER 2

ISOLDE

The skin on my face itched and my screams echoed around the sphere-shaped room, crashing into the curved walls and rebounding in every direction. My eyes darted around the space in search of relief and someone to trust. I finally saw mom and Tristan sitting on the edge of the pool, murmuring.

"She will live!" Tristan stated to my mother and glanced down.

His eyes widened with the realization that I was awake.

"Issy, I'm so sorry! I was so busy with everything, I..." my mother choked on the words and pressed her hand to her mouth to stifle a sob.

Tristan ran a hand up and down her arm to comfort her, while keeping his other hand on my head, petting my hair.

"We were both too busy. I'm sorry, sis! If I'd only listened to you," he stopped, and his Adam's apple bobbed, while he shook his head.

I attempted to speak. I wanted to tell them that it wasn't their fault, that I did this to myself. Yet, my throat wouldn't work.

"Don't try to talk. The cat ripped part of your throat. Just lay here," mom replied, with that she changed the tone of her voice and continued, "Hera, can you please take her into a dream?" Mom coughed and swallowed back her plea. Tears welled up in her eyes again to pool at the edges.

They said something else, but the words drifted away on the mist of the dreamwalk and coalesced into another world. A moment later, I was back in Italy, walking the canal paths in Venice.

Hera must have searched my mind for a happy place to send me to.

I hadn't been back in Venice since we bought the boat, but the scent of the lagoon with the arching bridges and walkways always made me smile.

I wandered aimlessly through the walkways until I came to San Marco's square and took a seat at one of the many tables near the cafes. The birds flocked around the tourists, searching for food, while the duomo shined in the morning light, reflecting off the golden mosaics. For a moment, I drank in the rich blues of Venice, allowing the musky scent of the lagoon to lull me.

A dull ache covered my chest and part of my face, flowing down my neck. I couldn't place where it was coming from. The dreamwalk was covering the reality of my situation and the pain from my injuries.

The man from the Biodome appeared in a chair at the table next to me and I groaned.

"How did you get here?" I moaned and leaned back, crossing my arms.

He didn't look at me. He simply stared at the building behind me, unseeing.

"Oh, now that you've saved me, we don't need to talk? Are you ignoring me?" I demanded and sat forward. I leaped to my feet to stand right in front of him, blocking his view of the building. But before I could reach him, he dematerialized and was gone.

Hera must have gotten our dreams mixed up.

I shrugged, glad to be rid of Hercules '*I am a DemiGod high and mighty*'.

Instead of retaking my seat, I headed to the pier to find a gondola and a quiet ride around the city's canals. The Venetian blue of the city arrested my soul and pushed back the irritation that had welled up at the sight of '*Mr. DemiGod*'.

That man was an asshole. I recalled him screaming at me, calling me a moron. It made all the hair on my neck stand up and set my teeth on edge. I ground my jaw down on the sound of his voice barking at me and I pushed that thought away.

Odyssey is a big ship. I can avoid the Herc-ing DemiGod easily.

You don't need to speak in a dreamwalk, the dream morphs your will. I climbed into one of the many gondolas and a Gondolier thrust his oar into the water as we pushed off from the dock.

At the edge of the water, Hercules was sitting in the air, staring off at nothing once again.

Perhaps Hera is having a hard time keeping our dreams separate.

"Hera," I called but there was no answer, just the lapping of water on the side of the gondola, accompanied by the sound of boat motors in the distance.

"Tristan," I called again, hoping my brother would come and keep me company, but he didn't hear me or was too busy to respond.

I toyed with the idea of calling Emmaline, but thought better of it. Emmaline had better things to do than listen to me bitch about an asshole who saved my life.

I rolled the truth around in my mouth for a few minutes. Hercules did save my life. I should thank him, but part of me was still mad. I was aware it was stupid, but I was mad. He manhandled me and bossed me around.

He did save my life.

Daddy would say I should be grateful he was there and willing to risk his life for mine. The rocking of the boat was relaxing and the dull pain in my chest and thigh had eased. My presence in Venice brought thoughts of Daddy. A smile touched my lips and faded just as fast as it came.

He's gone and will never come back. This is just a dream that can never be.

The overwhelming loss hit me fresh. Tears threatened to overtake me and my throat closed on the realization I may live forever without him.

I closed my eyes and called forth a vision of Homeworld 10's library and Vika.

I let my once happy dream fade into the background and the past where it could remain along with the painful thoughts of Daddy.

Vika sat at her usual table, crouched over a tablet, devouring the information on a data chip. Her hair was held up in a net. They have a name for but I couldn't remember. She was always in perfect order and I envied her attention to personal details.

Mom wasn't much of a girly-girl. She was naturally pretty and didn't waste time on make-up and dressing up. Truth be told, living on a boat for eight years you learn to be less hygienic due to limited freshwater.

Part of me wanted to go back to my room and clean up, but I couldn't. I was not awake. I was in a dream coma.

The feeling of having my cheek ripped open was still fresh in my mind and for a moment I couldn't breathe. The terror of watching the giant cat leaping at me with its claws made me quake. Sweat formed under my arms and I was shaking and gulping for air.

I stamped my foot to change my body position and stop the shaking. The panic in my chest eased but the lightheadedness didn't.

The sound of my foot slapping on the floor caused Vika to look up and smile.

"I thought you guys were taking a day or two off," she said and leaned back in her chair.

I opened my mouth with a quick reply, but the smile on her face faded away and morphed into a grimace.

"Isolde, what has happened?" she demanded.

"I... I was hurt. Mom forced me into a dreamwalk. I..." my throat tightened on the words I couldn't voice. Just as quickly as the thought came, it got pushed out of the way. "I was attacked by a Nemean Lyon. One of Hera's sons saved me," I stated

Her eyes narrowed before turning back to her tablet. "I heard you met Hercules."

I snorted, "Met. That's an interesting way to put it. Do you know him?"

She pressed her lips flat into a tight amused smile. "No, but I have heard of him. All Themia knows of Hera's DemiGods. I understand he is a great fighter and tracker."

I shrugged and grabbed one of the many data chips on the table, then huffed. "More like a Herc-ing bossy, ass."

She didn't bother to glance at me, "But he did save you from a Nemean Lyon. That is a great feat even for a full blooded Themian, let alone a DemiGod."

I sighed, "Yeah, he did. Not just one, but four," I rubbed my neck. The dull ache was subsiding, but the flash of the giant cat leaping at me brought a gripping fear back fresh.

Vika set her tablet down to take me in. "Four? He killed four of the pride?" she asked.

"No. He captured two. I think he killed the other two," I squinted my eyes.

The event was still a jumble. The first two jumped into a cage. But the other two...was where everything goes fuzzy, most of it blocked out with a blue electric light.

"He didn't get the whole pride?" She asked.

"There are more than four?" I squeaked, pulling my arms over my chest protectively.

I couldn't help but place my hand over my cheek and run it down to my neck.

"A Nemean Pride consists of one male and four females. They work as a team. The females herd the prey and move in for the attack while the male leaps in at the last to finish the kill off."

The blood drained from my head and I grew lightheaded.

God, he was going to take all of them on at once! That sounds like a death wish. Why didn't he just have Ixis take me?

The longer I let the truth of the matter seep into my brain, the worse I felt. He could have gotten both of us out of there at any time, but he chose to try and save the Lyons anyway. I gulped back the fear lining my throat.

"He told me he was trying to trap them and I got in the way. Who would put such a dangerous animal in a Bio-dome to begin with?" I demanded, turning my anger away from Hercules.

Vika swallowed a sip from her water glass before replying. Her back straightened. I've seen that poise before. It was Vika's teacher mode. "Nemean's are endangered. They were discovered on Delphi and many of them were killed. They don't assimilate well into new environments. Every millennium project receives three prides with the hope that a new Homeworld can be found for them."

The truth of Hercules' actions slammed into me. He was trying to save them and I got in the way and made him do the one thing he was trying to avoid — kill them. My mouth went dry as guilt climbed around inside my chest. The dull ache from my injuries dissipated into the background as my shame overtook me.

How can I ever face that man again? He must think I'm the biggest idiot in the galaxy.

I bit into my lip to hold back anything that might decide to exit my mouth.

My eyes trailed around the room and there, sitting across from Vika, was Hercules. My mouth dried on any words I might have been about to say.

Vika moved from the table to my side, and grabbed my arm, dragging me to the very seat the hulking man was sitting in. I yanked my arm away from her, unwilling to sit on the man, wishing she hadn't touched me.

"I don't want to sit on him." I wailed.

The cry barely escaped my lips before I was slammed with visions of Vika and her life.

*****

Quiet and orderly was the only way to describe it. Her family nurtured her, helping her find her way in the Themian world.

She was the first Themian I've touched and my understanding of how Themia operated grew at an exponential rate.

Her life flashed forward to the library and her thirst for knowledge grew with her ability to research, up until the moment she stood before the High Council.

"I wish to study Pythia's final prophecy," she states with her hands crossed in front of her body.

The twelve people seated above her stared down with hard eyes and tight lips. Finally, the woman in the center seat replied, "No! The final Prophecy of Pythia is not to be used for research purposes. It is sacred. We are the keepers of the Fates and your talents are more useful in other areas."

My emotions followed Vika's as if I walked in her footsteps on a beach. I expected her to argue her point, to fight. But she simply nodded her head and quickly left the council's chamber. I held my breath, waiting for her to feel something, but the bitter disappointment never came, only the resolve to petition the High Council again in a few hundred years and to keep doing so until they granted her request.

That was so long ago my head swam with the magnitude of the ocean of time she had waited.

Vika's life was a repeating cycle of research, requests and denials. That was until recently, when she decided to take matters into her own hands. The news of Hera's rebellion and thwarting of the High Councils edict emboldened her and she booked a passage to Delphi with the intent of studying Pythia's Prophecy, even if it got her sent to Tartarus.

She didn't expect to meet Hera or my mom, but seeing my mother through her eyes changed my own view of her.

I have always found my mom to be intimidating, but she filtered it with a fierce passion and her love softened everything.

Vika's view was very different. Hera and my mother were two powerful forces and Vika's chest clenched with fear, an emotion so foreign to her she could barely catch her breath.

Vika's only power was a light control of the forces and she found patterns in data. Watching her life played through my mind, gave me a feeling of power. The fast forward of it reached the moment where I met her and I saw myself and trembled.

Vika was terrified. The three of us stood before her, asking for her to allow us an illegal use of the library and informing her of our intent to find the first Homeworld.

She dug into the reassess of her mind for the connection that she felt was there. Yet, she couldn't quite recall why the meeting was eating at her very core. She was awed by the three of us and couldn't explain why. Relief washed over her every time we left or only one of us was present.

I couldn't understand her fear. It didn't make sense to me.

*****

The vision came to an end just before she touched me, but the vision of my flesh hanging open on my body came through crystal clear. The reality of my injuries bled through into the dreamwalk, along with the knowledge.

She never saw Hercules in the room. Yet, I did. Why?

Vika hadn't noticed my reaction to her contact and I didn't feel like sharing. I was still shaken from the information download and the gruesome vision of my injuries. The silent form of Hercules had disappeared and I fell into the vacant seat in a heap.

"Your choice to work while you heal is a wise one. What do you wish to study?" She asked, brushing away my injuries as if she'd never seen them and they were simply a minor annoyance.

"Pythia spoke of the path to Delphi, and a trip out of the underworld. I want those data chips."

I'd already told mom and Hera my idea. All I had was time, so I might as well use it to prove my point. I would worry about what I was going to say to Hercules later.

This way I didn't have to think about the pain. If I wasn't going to live, mom would be here with Tristan.

They would tell me.

I clothed myself with that belief and stared down at my tablet, focusing on the information scrolling across the screen.

CHAPTER 3

HERA

Hercules only wanted to be alone with his thoughts. Truth be told, he had always talked more than any man should. Most of it was all hyperbole. So, this withdrawal from everyone was unlike him.

Part of me wanted to stay in the dream world of Olympus, but that mountain life was over and would never be again.

White mist from a dream shift blanketed me and I fell into it like a soft bed made from the underbelly feathers of a hippogryph.

The mist never cleared and instead of Odyssey, Hyperion emerged.

His strawberry gold curls bounced as if he had jumped into the dreamwalk and not appeared, "What is going on?" He demanded, as his jaw snapped shut.

Emotions I'd never felt from him swept over me, filling my being. I gulped back the flavor of rage.

"You must be more specific," I returned, standing my ground.

I hadn't heard from him in thousands of years and he forced his way into my dreamwalk. It demanded answers!

"Why are you on Alexandria?" He asked.

My emotions fed his. We were a circle, each enhancing the other's world. The last time this happened we were small children.

I had always been the one to pull back and end the loop, but not this time. I saw this for what it was – domination. Hyperion was as capable as I of dominating anyone. When we were children, I let him win. But I had lived a more challenging life then he had and I would not back down this time. Themia had no control over me.

"Nice to see you too, Hyperion. How has your life been these last few thousand years? Are my children doing well?" I returned side-stepping his questions with a few of my own.

"You know very well how your children are. You stole them! Or got Ixis to do it for you," he spat.

I faltered. "What makes you think that?" I asked, raising an eyebrow in the same fashion I'd witnessed Sydney do.

I smoothed back my hair and placed the one long curl behind my shoulder. My chiton was clean and wrinkle free.

Hyperion ran his fingers through his hair. "You do this every time we are together. My emotions run wild. I don't know how you do it, but you do," with that he turned away from me for a moment and raised his shoulders with a large breath before lowering.

"The High Council knows you took your children. They have grilled me for days and demanded I dreamwalk you for answers." Hyperion turned to face me, then took two steps and was at my side with his arms around me.

I clung to him for a moment, enjoying the feeling of being whole. I pulled back to stare up at the man my brother was, not the twin I remember.

"I know you are poking around the library," he stated in a whisper as if anyone could overhear us.

I shook my head in denial.

"Don't lie, Herathina! I felt you the day you arrived and every day after."

He grabbed my shoulders and stared me down. The desire to glance away was strong, but I stared back.

I knew he'd sensed me, I should have said something then.

"I was there," I replied. "I did take my children and you would have done it too," I snapped, then softened my tone. "You never even spoke to them."

He turned in a circle waving his hands.

"I wasn't allowed to. No one was. They were to be ignored. The High Council deemed it so. No interaction was allowed," he retorted and the truth of his situation bled through to the dream construct.

Hyperion had welts on his back and chest.

I reared back from the vision before me. "What have they done?" I cried with tears streaming down my face.

"The extraction of information was deemed necessary," he stated in a cold voice.

I shook my head in disbelief. This was not the Themian way. Torture was not how Themia works.

"They lashed you?" I asked with a trembling voice.

"Stop all the tears. Your emotions work on me like acid, sister," he closed his eyes and forced the reality of his body out of the dreamwalk only to replace it with a vision of normalcy. "They know you are dreamwalking here. They are looking for your ship. Ixis lied. They never agreed to let you leave. The High Council wanted all hybrids cleansed from the planet along with your children," he huffed with the weight of his message.

My chest heaved. Part of me wanted to rage at him and beat my hands on his chest, while the other part held me in check. However, the edge of that rage was so close and I wasn't sure how long I could walk it.

"Why? Why would they want them dead?" I demanded as the pressure in my chest grew.

"They are an anomaly that never should have been. They are searching the stars for you and the ship Ixis took. They suspect you are on Homeworld 10, stop going there," he said.

His face smoothed into an emotionless mask. "Herathina, they will kill you all. They have an almost unnatural fear of you and the hybrid you call Sydney. There is another they fear, but I couldn't glean her name. Leave this space and never return," he grabbed me and shook me.

My head snapped back with the motion, helping to shake away the fear for my children from me.

"We are not on Homeworld 10," I replied in a cold voice and a bland face.

"You have a conduit! It doesn't matter at this moment. They are tracing the faults in the crystalline circuits to keep you out of the library. They will find a way! Hera, I am sorry that I never contacted you or your children. I couldn't. Now, take your ship and leave while you still have life in you." He hugged me and faded away.

For a moment I didn't know what to do. Sydney would lose her mind over this.

Ixis lied!

I knew why he lied, but as to how he got the ship and convinced Athena, that was another question.

A question that would need answers.

CHAPTER 4

SYDNEY

The first landing data-chips weren't here. I couldn't decide if it was luck that Vika was planning on going to Delphi or not. Why would they keep all those data-chips for themselves? Delphi sounded like the hub of Themian culture, the cornerstone they built on. So, why keep it hidden?

The first landing chips were all about Homeworld 1 — Elysium or so Vika said. The truth of whether we were going to find this map Issy thought was there was a different story.

"So we are in the wrong place!" I stated and rolled my eyes, since I knew that Vika and Hera had an irritating habit of telling a convoluted version of the truth.

"You're in the right place to learn about all of Themia and in the wrong place to learn about the first landing. '*There are many who came before my death, but none shall come after it until the Fates arrive*'" Vika quoted Pythia as if we needed the history lesson and hadn't been reading until our eyes bled for the last few months. "It doesn't make any sense. If she was the first Oracle, how can there be many after her but none after her death? It's nonsense, " I sighed.

Themia's obtuse prophecies gave me a headache. I rubbed my forehead, hoping it would push the pressure away. I didn't believe in fate, unless I was fated to have a headache for the rest of my life. Then yeah, I could get that.

I bit my lip and tried not to fidget while I waited for answers.

"The first Oracle, Pythia, lived a very long time. She was the one who discovered the secret of immortality. There were many oracles that came after her, but most did not live as long as she did. They all died before Pythia. Some were acolytes, while some were full-fledged Oracles in their own right. They lived on different worlds." Vika turned in her seat to face me, placing her hands in her lap.

She looked more like an artist rendition of Plato teaching than a research librarian. Her hair was pinned high on her head with just a single curl hanging down against the back of her neck. The crossed ribbons of her dress were a subtle shade of celadon, lending to the feel of being in a museum that I couldn't shake.

"In the years just before the first Oracles demise, the acolytes and other oracles all died, some mysteriously. The speculation is that they were all murdered. However, according to the records, some committed suicide," Vika supplied, but she didn't seem convinced. Her mouth hitched to one side as if mentally chewing on the problem.

This was an enigma that kept getting more confusing the deeper we dug. I rubbed my forehead. I just wanted to find Elysium, not become Sherlock Holmes. Yet, more mysteries kept popping up and all of them centered around Pythia.

Why was she so important? Who was she before they left Elysium and did it even matter?

"Themia is and will always be. Themian society wants nothing to change ever. However, things change every day constantly, all the time. The idea that nothing will ever change is ludicrous. Change is a constant. You cannot stop it. It finds you. Turning back the tides of change is like stopping the cosmos from spinning further out from its center which is impossible," I scoffed at the entire idea. The Themian belief system just didn't work for me.

"We're capable of anything. We can move worlds, manipulate gene pools, find your soulmate. You seem to be able to do everything. You communicate over vast distances, build ships that contain entire ecosystems within them. But you can't do that?" I scoffed again.

Hera nodded and her head and stretched out her hands. "Thank you, Vika, for everything. We know what this could cost you."

Hera's presence was calming and I was thankful. I needed that sometimes. She was the mother I always wanted. Yet, I couldn't look at her that way. The mother-daughter relationship is not one of equals and I needed the upper hand to lead. Hera had already stated she wasn't the big gun, but I couldn't kowtow to her at the wrong moment. Not when everyone needed me to be strong.

"Yes, it could cost me a trip to Tartarus," Vika stated flatly.

Vika was leaving the next day for Delphi and I wasn't sure we were done here, but we had to be. I knew searching this library always had a time limit. I just wished I could be sure we didn't need anything else, that we had gleaned all there was to know from this place.

Have we sucked the marrow from these bones?

CHAPTER 5

SYDNEY

One month earlier

"What if Pythia wasn't speaking theoretically when she described how to find Elysium? What if it wasn't just a story? What if it was a map and all you have to do is follow the map to find Elysium," Issy stated, her cheeks flushed with this revelation.

She pointed her toes whenever she was pleased with herself.

Present day

"Pythia's descriptions of how to reach Elysium could be a map, but where would the starting point be?" Hera asked, moving all of us out of the library and into a dream construct for privacy.

"We have to find an entrance to the underworld, right?" Issy squeaked, then pointed her toes again in her cutie fashion.

No matter how old she gets, I'm not sure this mannerism would ever go away.

It was the first time I'd seen Issy happy since her encounter with the Lyons and Hercules. However, she had spent all her time in the dreamwalk, and I didn't know how healthy that was.

Vika appeared in the construct and I couldn't help but cock an eyebrow at Hera. We were only here, in this in-between space to keep prying eyes and ears away.

"Your human mythology about the entrance to the underworld theory is not necessarily true. We have gone over it. That was added later as a purely human idea. It is not what the Oracle said at all. You don't have to find an entrance to the underworld," Vika remarked.

Issy nodded her head vigorously in agreement as if she knew that already.

"Then, what do we have to find?" I asked, smacking my lips together dryly.

I fiddled with my sheet like dress to pass the time. All that supposition was eating at me. I used to love reading and research, now that love had been replaced. All the while, a driving need pressed on me. It was the need for action which was overwhelming my thirst for knowledge.

I thought that once I found the island it would go away and actually for a little while the pressure fell into the background. But ever since I moved the ship to Homeworld 10, the triple starred system pulled that desire back to the forefront, making my urge for forward momentum eat at me anew.

"The Oracle says you must follow the five rivers into the underworld. First, you must find and pay the ferryman. He will take you down the rivers safely," Vika explained.

I shifted on my feet, even though my feet couldn't hurt since what I was experiencing wasn't real. It was all in my mind.

"You mean the river Styx?" I asked.

"The five rivers, each representing something different. Styx is just the most well-known," Hera remarked absently.

She too had become restless. Her statuesque manner was replaced by fidgeting, while her eyes were darting to mine, then Issy's.

Hera told so many humans about the river Styx it became a myth, leaving humans to believe that it was really the only river you had to travel to reach the underworld.

"Are they real rivers?" Issy inquired with her lower lip between her teeth and her greenish blue eyes brightening with hope.

Vika piped up, "I don't know," then turned her attention to Hera.

"How do we find the ferryman?" I asked the next logical question in an attempt to move this session along. "And don't we have to give him something like two pieces of gold?"

From all the books I'd read, Greek Mythology was one I skimmed more than read.

"Yes, Pythia said we would need two circles of gold for a trip down the river," Vika stated.

It was clear that the wheels in her mind were working overtime. She looked at Issy, then back at Hera, before her eyes landed on me.

I huffed with irritation and charged on. "Hera, when you told your stories of Elysium and the underworld, you obviously told someone that the way to get there was through a cave. I mean, several of the stories talk about heroes entering the underworld through caves, and reaching the river Styx," I urged her on for the answers that were, oh, so slow in coming.

Hera stopped clenching and unclenching her fingers, "My mother always insisted that to reach the underworld, you must first enter a cave. The cave of the ferryman," she looked at Vika for confirmation.

Vika waved her on without interrupting. Her interest in the human world's version of Themian stories over road her purpose in being here in the first place.

"Jorhan asked me if that cave was the entrance to the underworld. I told him that I didn't know, but I'm not sure he believed me," Hera ran one hand up and down an arm.

I had never heard her speak of Jorhan, yet, her body language implied she was comforting herself over something.

"Jorhan loved the story of reaching Elysium and the underworld. It was his favorite. As a boy, he harassed me to repeat it over and over again. My youngest son, Hercules, also asked for the stories often and I know he repeated them many times on his hunting trips. Although, judging from human mythology, I assume Hercules told many people 'he' went to the underworld," a sad smile touched her lips.

Issy stiffened at the mention of Hercules, then she laid her hand over her cheek, letting it slide down to her neck.

I gulped back the vision of her face and neck ripped open. Just her hand movement was enough to bring it back to my mind. I couldn't imagine what she was thinking or feeling.

"I have a lot of preparations to make before my transfer to Delphi. I only came to inform you that I would be unavailable. Hera can you release me?" Vika asked, then faded from the construct.

Hera didn't miss a beat as she continued, "The rivers eventually lead you to the gates of Hades. These gates are defended and protected by Cerberus, the three headed dog," she droned on with her tale of the underworld.

I only half listened.

"If Cerberus notices you or you attract too much attention, he will destroy you. You cannot attract Cerberus," she stated it as if a three headed dog was going to be a real problem. "Then you pass through the gates of Hades and on to the plains of judgment. Once you've made it through the planes of judgment, you will arrive at Hades' home."

Issy stared at Hera with wide eyes and an open mouth, drinking the story in. If my life had been different, I too would have been the same when I was younger.

"Then, you will be brought before Hades to be weighed and measured. If you are found wanting, Hades decides your punishment. Bla-bla..." I moaned.

Hera cut me off, "However, if your heart is found to be light as a feather, you pass on to Elysium," she smiled as if it was just another children's story and nothing more.

Elysium, sometimes known as paradise and a place of tranquility, but also as the home of heros and of those pure of heart. All these ideas had been implanted into the human psyche. Reaching Elysium is equal to reaching perfection. Even though everyone wants that perfect outcome, it does not mean it is available.

It could very well be that Elysium is nothing more than an idea, an ideology, a place the mind goes to when it needs to believe in the balance and perfection of the world. A place you seek when you're disheartened by all of the evil that you've witnessed.

I had to take into account the chance that this was all a fool's errand, that I was toying with all the lives on Odyssey.

If Elysium was a real place and not just an idea in Greek mythology that was passed down by Hera to her children or something that Themians taught as their original Homeworld story, a place they all came from, then the story of how to get to Elysium had to be real.

Is this the trail that the Oracle took to find Delphi in reverse? Is it the map she left so that we could get back to Elysium? And if they left, why would she leave a path back to it?

Issy jumped up and burst at me, "Elysium exists! It's not something Themians tell each other! You know that the Oracle wasn't the first and last of the pre-sentient!"

Her outburst told me that I was letting my mental walls slip, so I quickly re-enforced my mind, blocking everyone but Adrian.

"How do you know? And I don't want to hear about how you feel it or how you have faith in it or any of that nonsense. Themians are all scientists. They deal in truth. Yet, you and I are reading about ancient tales, Themian fables. So, tell me. How do you know?" I demanded, staring Hera down.

I started this, but I needed to hear that she agreed with me. To tell me that Isolde's idea wasn't mad and I was not insane for listening.

Hera straightened her back and shoulders, then leveled her chin before gazing at me. She was preparing to answer. I could feel her organizing her mind, lining everything up so it would come out in the proper order.

Themians were organized. They didn't like to speak out of turn. They did not have emotional outbursts like humans.

The construct around us changed from the misty white of a foggy day to a bright white sunlight. It was almost blinding with the color of the star overhead. I raised my hand to block the star's rays and shade my eyes.

"Everything I've read says that Themians arrived at Delphi on a ship." The construct changed and the shape of a ship formed in the distance in the sky. "A ship capable of traversing the stars. It was the first ship of its kind."

As Hera spoke, the bright sun disappeared and was replaced by the black void of space. The three of us floated weightlessly in the cosmos. My breath was taken away with Hera's ability to turn her story into a virtual reality experience. Hera came across as being mild and weak, but her power over the mind blew me away. She could make you see and believe anything she wished.

"They were floating in space lost and adrift. Their shifter had become ill. There were several entries about him missing something. When the Oracle entered the ship, she was listed only as Pythia, a very minor young woman with no parents. But something changed. When the first shift was over chaos ensued, she had a vision that told her where to go. It was Delphi. So, she took control of the ship and saved everyone."

The scene changed again and we were floating over a golden world. Off, in the distance, was a white star three times the size of Earth's sun.

"She wrote down the directions to reach Elysium, but claimed we would never be able to go back. Most do not know why."

Once again, we were back in the foggy indistinct construct of the dreamwalk's in-between world. Hera's story was over, giving me no more answers than I had before.

I found the restlessness that had plagued me falling away as we worked the problem. I didn't want to stop. I pushed my hair out of my eyes and forced one lock behind my ear.

"The ship, it's there, on Delphi? Where they landed it?" Issy asked in a low voice filled with hope. She had pounced on the one detail I had overlooked.

Hera tipped her head down, "It's described as being the first city. They used it for housing and for shelter. For everything actually."

"Did it disappear? Do you know where it sat?" I demanded.

"The greatest city on Delphi is Abydos. It is also the oldest with the largest population. I do not know if that is the landing place, but there are notes in the records that say they went forth from the landing place, leaving the safety of the Old Citadel," Hera opened her hands as if she didn't know anymore.

The name of the largest city on Delphi threw me. I wasn't prepared for an Egyptian name in what sounded like a Greek world.

Who am I kidding? It's all Themian, isn't it?

"They left it behind. Why?" Issy scoffed a little too loudly. "If it was a city, their shelter, why would they suddenly leave it?" Issy began pacing.

Issy had never been a pacer and I watched with wide eyes as she walked. It looked more like a man's stance than the young girl I've raised.

"The Oracle led them to a land of milk and honey," Hera shrugged, unable to offer a better answer.

Her text book responses were wearing down my last nerve.

"She's some kind of Messiah's, like Jesus?" I snorted, shaking my head in disbelief, dusting the misty fog of the construct away from my body.

God, I wish there was somewhere else we could have this fete.

The milk fog of the construct was itching my last nerve too. To be honest, very little wasn't irritating me at that point. I rubbed the bridge of my nose and squeezed my eyes shut.

"I'm assuming that by Messiah you mean spiritual leader?" Hera replied then ran her hands up and down her arms as if she was cold.

I cocked an eyebrow at her. She shook her head and waved my concern away.

Sometimes, when I looked at Hera, I could see the ancient woman living inside the youthful body. Her eyes spoke of a long-carried pain, which I could feel almost as if I was connected to her. I couldn't help but shiver at all she'd faced.

"Other than finding the planet, was the Oracle some kind of savior?" Issy asked, chancing a glance at Hera and then looking away. Issy's excitement suddenly cooled with the mention of religion.

"They revered her almost like she was a God amongst our people. She was a great leader. She established the first High Council, claiming that no people should be ruled by just one person but led by many. She explained that was the only way to create balance in any society. She also said the rulers should be the oldest and the wisest of the group. By her rules no one should lead for more than 100 years. Furthermore, no person can qualify to be part of the High Council more often than once every thousand years."

Hera changed the room into a council chamber and the three of us stood before the dais which was covered with twelve backless chairs.

Hera's voice echoed around the cavernous room as she continued, "She said it was the only way to help keep people honest. She said that becoming a leader of the people and returning back to them is the only way to be in touch with them. She proclaimed that anyone who views themselves above everyone else will become a tyrant and destroy us. She refused to take a seat on the High Council and instead stood as an adviser. She had no vote. She simply offered her counsel and wisdom."

Issy grabbed my arm in expectation for more of the story because that is how it felt listening to Hera talk about Pythia. It was as if it was just a story and nothing more.

The vision shifted to an infinity pool, "She also helped us discover the primordial waters. All the water that had come with them from Elysium was in the original Citadel. There was some kind of a plague. It spread through the people and they discovered that only the waters from Elysium could save them. All those who did not drink the ambrosia of life soon died."

My head pounded with the visions she peppered us with. Thousands of people dying of a nameless disease and being offered Elysium's water to live.

"Those who took part were energized and regained health again. The Oracle worked with the greatest minds and helped create the primordial bath which later became the infinity pool, to reproduce this ambrosia. All who partook of the primordial waters, never felt ill again. Additionally, they became more."

A vision of the statue on Alethea appeared, only it was not a statue because it moved. He was a real man, someone she knew. His golden hair hung over his shoulders like a lion's mane. I stared at the God-like man in awe. His lips moved into a smile and I found my hand touching my own lips.

Everything about the golden-haired man entranced me. I couldn't shake the feeling of deja-vu. Something about him was familiar.

"What do you mean they became more?" I demanded as my mouth hung open at the sight of this man.

CHAPTER 6

ISOLDE

The vision of the golden hair Themian quickly disappeared. My mother stared at the vacant space as if she was puzzling over something. I reached for my mother's mind to hear her thoughts, but she had gotten better about shielding herself from my mental trolling.

"Their shifter was the most powerful person on-board and he was also the first. How come it doesn't say what his illness was?"

"When a shift occurs, the person who performs the shift doesn't just move you through space from point A to point B. They move you through time and space. They pull you out of the normal space time and thrust you back into it, but in a different location," Hera flashed from the rings of Saturn to the nebula we hid in near Homeworld 12.

The scene change was no different than having someone change a slide in a planetarium. "They do it instantaneously. You are in a quantum flux. You're not in real space or real time. You are in between. When this happens, your entire body is, but also isn't. When the first shifter moved them from Elysium to the point they thought they were going, something happened. They had never traveled beyond their own galaxy."

Hera was still manipulating the construct, flashing pictures before us to explain the mechanics of Telekinesis to our childlike minds.

I normally would have burst at her over it, but I really didn't understand how it worked, even though Tristan had tried to explain it to me several times.

It made my head ache. I have never been great at math and science-y stuff. I looked at mom. She was biting her lip. A smirk curled the side of my mouth.

It's good to know that I'm not the only one having a hard time. Mom, who is the know-it-all, was stumped too.

Hera's explanation of the first Themians trip came across like a fable or a revolutionary tale.

"Every person on the ship had taken a chance. They might be moved into a star, reappear in a nebula or not reappear at all for that matter. Every one of them took that chance for a reason. Unfortunately, none of the personal logs survived, so all we have is speculation," Hera finished her history lesson.

She took a breath and I jumped in, "I felt the pressure changing around my body. Just like going up in elevation in an airplane, my ears became clogged and my vision blurred slightly like the world became unreal. The world was real and yet transparent. It was there and not there. Then, there was suddenly a pop and everything snapped back into focus," I snapped my fingers as loud as I could.

"The pressure change you felt was your body being pulled out of space and time. On the other hand, the fuzzy fogginess or blur, was in-between space and the pop was the real space and time. Those feelings aren't the same for everyone. However, your description is about average," Hera nodded her head in approval.

She had just run so much information at me, I wasn't sure I'd remember it all. The Oracle was young and unremarkable. Then, they jumped through the space-time continuum from one place to another, landing at an unintended destination, only to have their shifter suddenly become ill.

I scratched my head as if to stimulate my brain matter. My nervous tick was a dead giveaway to Tristan. If he were here, he would have teased me by saying '*don't hurt yourself Sis.*' I huffed and blew air out my nose.

The Oracle arose. She became.

My mother was a strong believer in evolution. She deeply believed that the weak die, while the strong rise up to meet the challenge of their new environment.

From what Hera told us, it sounded like everyone might've been affected by the shift. The Oracle rose to the occasion, she faced it and evolved.

There must've been something about her that allowed her to evolve.

I didn't believe evolution happened by accident. And yet, the record said she was unremarkable, she didn't even have a last name. figuring out the mysteries of evolution wasn't my thing, and never would be.

I'm not here to discover how my mother became what she is or why I am the way I am.

The Oracle was unassuming and she led people quietly without using force. They willingly followed her and listened to her wisdom. That by itself was remarkable.

There has to be an answer here somewhere.

"Isolde," my mother's voice broke me out of my rumination. "I think your decision to visit Delphi is extremely wise. You're right. We're not going to find the answers we're looking for here. They only lie in Delphi with the first landing. This is why we need to find the original Citadel–move the ship!" My mother whispered.

"Wake up now, Isolde! You have to rest. We will be spending a lot of time on Delphi and you will need to be strong," Hera ordered.

She pushed my shoulder as if to urge me through a mental door.

My eyes fluttered open meeting Tristan's clear blue eyes. "You've awakened early. Hera's still not awake. Did she release you from the dream?" He asked.

I glanced around the room Hera had allocated for the dreamwalking projects. There were several people still laying on the dream couches. Their faces were wiped clean of all worries and I must confess that I envied them for that peace.

"No, we've learned all we could. We need to move the ship. We must go to Delphi. All of us."

Tristan laid his hand on my shoulder and in a flash we were in the shifting room.

"Adrian, mom said we need to break orbit now. We need to go to Delphi immediately. There is no more waiting."

*****

Just like that, my belly dropped like I was in the front seat of a 4G roller coaster. The licking heat of flame blasted across my body and the shifting room disappeared from my sight. Through panting breath, I witnessed flames and heat scorched its way down my throat, burning my lungs.

The blast pushed all moisture from my eyes. I whipped my head left and right, searching for Tristan or Mom. They weren't there, wherever there was. I stared through the crystalline glass of a shifting bridge with flames licking at the edges.

Someone was here with me. A large hand grasped mine. I wanted to see who was attached to the mystery hand. The vision refused to grant me that one answer.

The window on the cosmos showed a battle, thousands of ships in all shapes and sizes winking in and out. The brightness of lasers and explosions littered the void, and lit the dark side of ships. One of the ships looked like Odyssey. I screamed as it exploded.

*****

Ixis voice cut though the vision. "It will be done. I have not visited Delphi for many years. Will Vika be meeting us there?" Ixis turned to face me.

I stepped back and choked on my response. My knees buckled and Tristan grabbed my arm to hold me up.

"Yes. Someone must wake Hera from the dream. We need to gear up," I coughed.

Mom appeared and asked, "Why?" She moved closer.

"For war, Mom. I think we may be heading into a war." A tear found its way down my cheek.

She stood there stiffly, shifting her eyes left and right. Adrian opened his mouth to say something. I had not yet resigned myself to him being my mother's boyfriend — mate. He was not a man of many words, but when he did speak, it was always worth paying attention to whatever he had to say.

"You believe there is a war coming?" he asked, enunciating every word slowly.

"Aren't we bringing one, just by showing up?" I asked and swallowed back the terror from the vision.

I don't know why, but somehow, I knew it was true.

Hera glided into the room through one of the arched entryways. She came and stood beside me. I nodded to her.

"Isolde may be right. We may indeed be bringing war to Themia and the landing site. It is the most sacred site in all of the Themian world. It has been lost, so if we do indeed find it, they might consider our visit a sacrilege. We must prepare for all possibilities."

Hera's answer articulated what I could not. I threw her a tight smile. I wanted to tell them what I saw, yet a dry heat still burned behind my eyes.

"Tristan, please go find out how many hybrids have military training of any kind. I don't know what Issy found, but I do know that whatever it is, if it's going to bring war, there has to be a good reason," Mom ordered then glanced at Adrian.

Their quiet side play wasn't lost on me.

CHAPTER 7

HERA

Isolde's pronouncement frightened me. I couldn't leave the shifting room fast enough. Forcing my feet to maintain a steady pace was a chore. As soon as I entered my quarters, I sat in the nearest chair and entered the dream world.

Hyperion appeared in our childhood garden. He faced away from me. His shoulders were tight with worry.

"Did you pull me here to further implicate me in your crimes?" He demanded, whipping around with such force, making his golden curls bounce. It was the force of his stare that froze me in place.

I opened my mouth to speak but the words wouldn't come. I lowered my head in defeat. "No brother, I came for council."

"I have given all I can give. Herathina, my family is in danger over this. Mother and Father are locked not only on Homeworld 10, but they cannot leave their home. I can only leave to work. Our homes have been altered so we may not dreamwalk anyone. My mate is on Homeworld 10 with our parents," he spoke in a low matter of fact tone and changed the construct to reflect the sitting room from our childhood.

I fell down into one of the chairs.

"Why? Why do they treat you and our family this way? The hybrids are not a threat to Themia or anyone else," I cried.

I took in the family space. Hyperion's memory of it was unchanged from my own, with all its clean line and quiet order. The comfort I used to glean from this space was lost on a whirlwind of emotions.

"If I had those answers, I'd be on the High Council myself. Why are we here, sister?" he asked, taking the seat next to me, taking my hand into his.

"One of the people on our ship is a seer. She thinks war is coming," I stared down at our clasped hands, hoping my fears were unfounded.

"There are no seers. The Oracles are all gone. It is just the fears of a young one's mind. You shouldn't take it to heart. Helios is the same way," he replied.

I glanced up at him, "Helios fears?" I asked quietly, my mind racing with the implications.

He could be an empath like me.

"Yes, we have tried to keep it quiet, but his emotions bleed out, much like your own do," Hyperion smiled with pride when speaking about his son.

He slicked his hair back from his face, pushing all the way to the nap of his neck, then mentally added a tie to hold his curls out of the way.

I smiled at him. He had always worn his hair in a tight tail. It was a reflection of his tight control over himself and his world. I reached out and smoothed a disobedient curl into place.

"Herathina, keep the Hybrids away from Themia at all cost. The High Council is deliberating pulling all millennium projects back to protect the Homeworlds," Hyperion said.

"That would ruin hundreds of thousands of years of work. We are only one ship, not an armada. This isn't the same as the Great Division. That is not logical. We are not trying to take over Themia and the Universe," I retorted then shook my head to regain control.

I glanced out the window to take in the red glow of Homeworld 12's sun. The rosy color gave all life on this planet a softness. I longed for that, knowing it could never be mine again. A long-forgotten sorrow came with it. For thousands of years, I buried all of these emotions and focused only on the reunion with my children. Facing these long-suppressed feelings did nothing more than distract me from my mission.

"I am sorry. I should not raise my voice. You are not to blame," I murmured. "If they have blocked all connections, then how have I managed to reach you?" I asked the one question, I should have asked from the beginning.

He chuckled under his breath. "I don't believe they can hold you back from touching anyone you wish to reach. I am at home."

He shook his head and his eyes danced with merriment. The light I had always bathed in shone from Hyperion. To be in his good graces was to walk in a world illuminated by a golden sun. His very presents made the flowers around you blossom and give off such sweet scents.

"I could bring your mate and children in," I offered, then mentally reached out to touch their minds. All were easily reachable with no resistance of any kind.

"No, it would only bring suspicion if discovered. Helios and Heliades would eventually give it away." He approached me in an attempt out to cup my cheek but thought better of it. "You always calm the tides in my mind, sister. If the High Council does decide to fortify the Homeworlds, I will contact you somehow," he assured me.

Part of me wanted to hug him, but Hyperion would not welcome it. He always preferred to keep everything at a distance, touching with hands and eyes alone.

"I will keep an ear out for you," I smiled back at him, using the Terrain term for listening.

He squinted for a moment before understanding dawned over his face.

I ended the dreamwalk and sat staring out into the cosmos. The stars had shifted from Alexandria to Delphi. Part of me hoped this trip would be quick, but the other part dreaded going down there and, truth be told, I burned to get away from this world.

CHAPTER 8

ISOLDE

Abydos was as hot as a blast furnace. The moment we popped out of the shift, all my moisture was wicked away. My eyes grew scratchy and my lips smacked, while my tongue searched for the saliva that was there a moment before.

I used my hand to shade my eyes from the blaring star in this system. The light, almost sheer, fabric which was covering my body did little to cut the blaze. All of this was coupled with the thick orichalcum bands around my wrist and the heavy earring in my ears and the five-inch-wide collar Hera insisted I wear was a burning band of metal around my neck.

At this rate I'm going to die of heat stroke before I find the underworld.

Glancing around, my eyes moved over my mother's form. She actually looked more like a cross between Cleopatra and Nefertiti. Her braided wig brushed her shoulders and every move of her head created a metallic clinking sound as the golden colored orichalcum beads tapped against each other.

Hera moved into my line of sight, blocking out the vision of mom and her super-hot eyeliner which traced back into her hairline. The smirk that had taken up residence on my face was quickly washed away.

Hera was wearing an almost completely see-through dress that ended just under her breast and was tied in the back. The only other adornment was her collar which covered most of her chest but leaving half of her breast exposed.

I quickly looked away as heat stained my face. Being told something and experiencing it for yourself are completely different things. Even though Hera told me that Delphi was different and people here held closer to the old Elysium ways, meaning that there is no need to cover the body since it is beautiful, the sheerness of my own dress embarrassed me, making me wish we had dreamwalked in and not shifted down.

"I changed our bracelets to reflect the Delphian style. It's heavy but we want to blend into the crowd while we search." Hera held her wrist up to reveal a clunky woven beaded band with a scarab set in the center. Between each set of beads there was a band of orichalcum they worked as conductor for the crystalline technology to run its power through.

I fingered my own, to find dark heavy jewel tones of green and a milky yellow scarab. My mother's was made with all fiery red beads and a black scarab.

The bracelets seemed to suck up the heat, as if that was its power source.

Though we stood in the shadows of an alley, the bright reflection of the stars light off the side of the limestone colored buildings, blinded me. Unfortunately, the heavy eyeliner did little to cut down on the glare and the longing for the shadows and night overwhelmed me. I never thought I'd wish for the darkness of the spatial void over the light of a sun.

"Let's move into the avenue and mingle as we find our way to the hall of records," Hera suggested and stepped towards the sound of civilization.

My mother moved to follow and I too found myself in step with the two of them as if pulled by an unknown source.

We passed darkened openings into buildings and I caught the flash of light off of glass windows set deep in the side of the building. Doors too were set back at least three feet from the outer walls, as if to keep the blinding star from beating its heat inside the structures.

Many women walked the streets with their breasts exposed to the harsh rays, while men wore only the Egyptian style kilt with heavy pleats. Their chests too were exposed, having nothing other than the large collars hanging from their necks. Some men had shaved heads, others sported a single braid.

"What is with the braid?" I whispered to Hera?

"They follow the cult of Hades," she replied without looking back.

I gulped and drifted back behind my mother. Mom chose that moment to snicker under her breath. She didn't believe in any of this. It was her default setting.

I can't understand why she's going along with this crazy hunt if she doesn't believe it.

<Because I believe in you.> Mom remarked.

<Both of you are too loud. If you keep this up we will be standing before the High Council of Delphi in as much time as it takes to shift.> Hera barked.

We all stopped walking. Hera turned and grabbed my bracelet and tapped the beads in a pattern. The scarab lit up and pulsed before turning dark again. She repeated the same process with my mother's then gave us a reassuring smile, squeezing mom's hand.

The avenue ended in a plaza boarded on three sides by a building with the title '*Sesheta Scriptorium*'.

"This is the archive of Delphi - the Sesheta Scriptorium," Hera remarked, enunciating it She-a-hat.

She continued across the bright square to the towering columns, holding up a limestone roof beyond the point of a pyramid loomed. The closer we got, the less the building looked like stone. Instead, it took on a yellowish crystalline effect. Other than the color, it had the same quality as Odyssey.

We passed under the columns and into a courtyard with a single statue in the center. It was of a woman covered in a leopard pattern dress and a crescent shaped diadem with 7 rays of light rising out of it.

I had so many questions but this wasn't the place. Our steps carried and rebounded off the flat walls all around us. Our voices would have too. I coughed just to check. Indeed, it echoed around the space and immediately my mother threw me a dirty look over her shoulder.

Hera led us deeper into the complex and into rooms filled with a type of scroll. Finally, we came to a room with a familiar figure who was hunched over a holo screen, tapping the table next to it.

"Vika," I squeaked.

"Awe, you made it," she smiled and looked us up and down. "I see you have taken to the Delphian ways."

Her clothes were still the style of Homeworld 10, wearing a short tunic with a belt.

My mother laid her hand briefly on her collar and replied, "Yes, well, when in Rome."

Vika's face remained blank at the quote and I laughed. "It's an Earth saying. It means '*When in Rome, do as the Romans do*'," I supplied and cocked an eyebrow at her.

A slow smile peeled across her face and she nodded her head in understanding. "Yes, it is best to meld with your environment. I only brought Alexandrian style clothes and I see no need to change. It is an afterthought, but if I stay here on Delphi, perhaps I will take up a new style."

Her attention lingered on Hera a little too long. She cleared her throat and charged in, "The only cave or cavern I've ever seen makes reference to the Oracle's final resting place. It is said that she was put into the cave under Mount Parnassus. She also asked that it be marked." Vika flicked the holo screen to a different tab to display a page full of writing. "And I understand that it was decorated with the Elysium glow. The shifter of the time moved around stones to block the cavern so that her rest would not be disturbed by robbers and thieves." Vika moved the holo to a drawn picture of an ancient alcove with a woman's body lying on a stone slab.

"I thought that Themians were perfect and didn't have crime," I snickered then covered my hand to smother the sound.

<Isolde, your infantile sarcasm has no place in this discussion > Hera chided.

< Sorry, Hera. Themians present themselves as if they're perfect and yet so far I haven't found anything about them that's perfect. Other than having really cool powers and the ability to move stuff around, it just seems that most Themians are arrogant and full of themselves. > It came out harsh and I didn't mean to sound that way, but it's harder to hide your true feelings when you use your mind.

<That is only how it appears to you.> Hera remarked and turned back to Vika and her research.

"Where is this cavern under Mount Parnassus? I mean it's here on Delphi, right?" Mom demanded, then swallowed and bit her lip before taking a deep breath

"Outside the first city, I'm sure. By more than 300 leagues away. Actually, the texts referred to a long journey to remove her to her final resting place, one that she had already prepared," Vika remarked and changed the holo to a different book filled with writing.

I glanced around the room, taking in all the shelves of scrolls and a few bound volumes of books. Most of them held placards with numbers, names and a bowl.

My attention was drawn back to the conversation by my mother's irritated voice. "Okay, so somebody has to know where it is. If she prepared the location, there must be some record. Work orders, stuff like that. Nothing gets done without a butcher bill.”

“Yes, there are records. Most artisans and workmen of the time paid homage to the Oracle,” Vika said as a matter of fact.

Hera let out a dry laugh, “We keep going round and round with the answers right in front of us. How do you find the entrance to the underworld? How do you get there and how do you find Elysium? All these questions when it’s actually pretty simple.”

She crossed her arms like my mother did when she knew the answer and was waiting for you to get it.

“Okay, Hera, if it's that simple then what’s the answer? And what’s the point in letting us rant on for the last few minutes?” Mom demanded, ringing her hands in the air.

The pressure to move forward bled over to me. However, no amount of tinkering with bracelets was going to dampen mom’s mind bleed.

"Vika, bring me an old map!" Hera instructed, then took a seat at Vika's table and waved to my mother to follow suit.

Vika crossed the room and went out an arched doorway. I trailed behind her. Curiosity was too much for me. I guess that maybe this has been my problem all along.

Curiosity killed the cat.

She entered a new room with the entryway marked by a giant star. I meandered behind her only because everything in the room was so distracting. I did not realize the library on Delphi was going to be so immense. I guess being the first on a new Homeworld meant that you gather a lot of shit for the shelves.

I glanced into the room she occupied. The walls were filled with an interesting plastic type Themian paper. She didn't stop but continued deeper into the space.

The only real light shot like beams across the room from windows high up on the walls. Each beam landed on the floor as a square of enlightenment with motes of dust floating through them.

"Keep up, Isolde! I don't want you to get lost. Here is where we store maps and star charts of every world we have ever been to," Vika offered and waved her hand to indicate the entire room.

The scriptorium's rooms were cool and my jewelry had lost its warmth against my skin. Goosebumps rose up with the realization of where I was.

"This is a hall of intergalactic maps?" I whispered in awe, whipping my head left and right to take in the sheer size of it all. The shelves rose up into the high-ceilinged room, making me wonder how I could reach the top shelves.

"Yes, they're all digital, of course. We keep the planetary maps in a flat version also. I find it's just easier sometimes when you're on a planet versus thinking about it in a three-dimensional method. Moreso, intergalactic maps look different than when you're actually there. Sometimes, viewing a map in two dimensions versus a three dimension actually allows you to make the jump to the three-dimensional thought easier," Vika stated as her tunic swished back and forth with each step.

I smiled to myself at her constant teaching. Her wealth of knowledge outweighed my mother's. Notwithstanding, I found her comforting. I loved her story telling way of sharing things.

"Is that how your people learned to think about the Universe?"

"No, I'm not an astro-cartographer. I leave those things to the greater mathematical minds. I studied science and history, knowing information from your past makes you more powerful than just knowing how to get from one world to another."

She turned down a new aisle and continued on following a path I still couldn't figure out.

"Yes, but in this case we may need to use all of it mixed together to actually solve the riddle of Elysium," I said, keeping my stride just behind hers, minding my feet so as not to step on her sandals.

"How messy the inside of your mind is. It's your insatiable curiosity I find refreshing and amusing," Vika chuckled. It was a new sound which came out deep and throaty.

We must have passed about 53 shelves before she turned left again and began walking some more. I was beginning to wonder if maybe staying with Hera might not have been a better idea. I thought this would be a little jaunt and not this long trek across the library. Mercifully, Vika stopped and reached into a shelf, pulling out 12 scrolls along with two bracelets.

"What are the bracelets for?" I asked a little out of breath.

"The scrolls are two-dimensional and the bracelets are three-dimensional," she offered then continued, "Every shelf has both." Vika stopped moving and stared at me intently. "Are you okay?" She inquired.

"Yeah. At least I think I am. I feel out of breath and I don't know why," I said and placed my hand on the heavy collar hanging around my neck.

The muscles in my legs tensed and for a moment my body moved into a fighting position, before I righted myself.

"The gravity here is close to Earth's gravity, so you should not feel any additional pressure or strain," she stared at me assessing.

I closed my eyes and for a moment I was back on Odyssey in one of the sparring rooms, staring at Uncle 'T'.

The vision disappeared and the pressure on my lungs eased as if it never was. I shook my head and laughed the momentary lethargy away.

My eyes were fixated on the bracelets, "You grabbed two bracelets and we have twelve scrolls," I remarked, hoping to draw attention away from my vision spell.

"There are only two of us, so we only need two bracelets," she stated as if it was the most obvious thing in the Universe.

"The bracelets have everything on this entire shelf?" I ventured, glancing up at the additional shelves in this section.

"It wouldn't make any sense to only put just one map on a bracelet. The bracelets can carry an infinite amount of information. We're trying to scale it down to just this area or just the specific subjects. They only put the information from that section on the bracelet," she replied and turned to head back the way we had come.

I couldn't let it go. This wasn't like typing in a query on the Internet. "What if you wanted to cross reference it with something else?"

"The bracelets are designed for cross-references," with that, her tunic swung slightly with her hips as she moved away.

I rushed to catch up. The last thing I wanted was to get lost. "Good, because I'm pretty sure that nobody's thinking Elysium is a real place anymore or that a trip to the underworld can happen," I remarked as my eyes landed on a standing desk that peeked through an aisle of shelves.

"Your words ring of truth, Isolde, but that doesn't mean that someone wasn't looking and didn't survive or that they simply decided it wasn't worth looking for anymore. The other choice is that they used the information to enrich themselves. Themians were once very greedy, obviously," Vika was so withdrawn from it all.

I'd seen inside her mind and the only passion she seemed to carry was for the search of Pythia's Prophecy.

"Yeah, somehow I don't think that anyone's gonna pay someone else to keep quiet about Elysium and the underworld," I added under my breath.

"Isolde, you're very young. Themian people changed a lot in the 2 million years we have been here in this portion of space, exploring. I will say this for your question. With the infinite number of answers, you are right. Just as Occam's razor could be correct, the simplest answer is usually the correct one. It is more probable that no one looked in the fashion we are looking right now. However, that doesn't mean that someone didn't try," Vika left it hanging in the air and it grew like a morbid rot.

What if someone did try and died?

"Vika, how long have you been looking for Elysium?" I asked with my breath catching in my throat over the answer.

"I actually wasn't looking for Elysium," she replied, evading the age question. "I've just been studying the Themian origins. Mostly, I'm studying the Oracle. What I don't know is where Hera is going with all the Elysian research," she sighed as if an egg had dropped on the floor and cracked open, leaving a golden sticky mess.

"Well, let's just get back to Hera before I need a nap," I moaned as my sandals slapped the stone under our feet.

She tilted her head back and let out a hearty laugh.

We returned to the private study and set the scrolls and bracelets on a table. As soon as we entered, Hera went to the entryway and waved her bracelet over the doorway, closing us in.

< Both of you, put your blocks up! What we are about to do is very important, so we cannot risk being overheard or spied upon. > Hera instructed and rolled out two maps on the table, and began searching them.

Placing my mental walls in order, I only left two conversational pathways between my mother and Tristan. Mom moved from the chair to stand, leaning over the table to take in the maps.

Hera first opened a map of the city with some of the outlying area. She quickly closed it and set it off to the side, shaking her head. The next one was a map of the new Citadel along with the underlying sewage systems. She let that go also, allowing it to roll closed. She opened several more letting them snap closed in frustration.

<Vika, what do the records say about the building of her final resting place?>

<Only that Sesheta held Pythia's hand to stretch the cord and set the cornerstones of Pytho, the home to the Oracles.> Vika remarked

I bit my lip, then forced myself to stop.

<Who is Sesheta?> My mother broke in and took over the conversation.

<She is the teacher. She divided the language of Elysium into many. She organized all the records ever made after the building of this city. She designed the architecture here and on many other Homeworlds. Her understanding of mathematics helped raise the first of the new shifters. She was the keeper of all knowledge. Through Sesheta you will never be forgotten, for she would keep the record of your life, thereby giving you eternal life.> Vika spoke with great awe of the woman.

My mother shook her head and bit her lip, <Great! Another polymath genius. How many do you guys have?> she stopped and looked at Hera and Vika before continuing <What? Did you all take smart drugs?>

I snickered at my mom's sarcasm.

< Maybe, if we just look for Mount Parnassus we would find her resting place.> Hera remarked and opened the eighth scroll.

It wasn't just a map of the city. Actually, the city was marked with a relatively small dot in the center, labeled as 'Citadel'. It also showed a great deal of the outlying areas and most of this side of the main continent. There were no mountains, only notations of plateaus and hills. But no mountains, not a one.

Hera moved her finger in a circular motion. Outside the city there was a small notation. It resembled an old zuggernant and it was marked with a word I didn't recognize. It said 'Oracle' something, but I couldn't make it out.

< Hera, what is? > Mom asked, leaning in to squint at the tiny writing.

< It is Pytho's Home to the Oracles. It is the place where she trained other oracles. The Oracle was murdered in the city and it took them many days to take her out to the final resting place she had prepared. The only building project we know for a fact that she was 100% involved with, other than the Citadel, was Pytho. > Hera rubbed her forehead.

< Yes, she designed everything about it. Sersheta said that she points the way to the Oracle.> Vika added.

I looked at each of the women in the room, then snatched a bracelet, dashing out of the room. My feet slapped the stone and my breath grew ragged. I slid across the floor, turning a corner then had to hop to keep my balance. As I came to the grand courtyard, I grabbed the side of a column and rounded it, heading straight for the statue before coming to a sliding halt in front of her.

She had been carved with a large heavy wig. The ends of the braids were sculpted with beads and each bead in-turn carried a design. I could now make out the details of her dress. It wasn't a dress at all, but the skin of an animal. The head hung down her back and its eyes glittered. The paws of the feline created a single strap over one shoulder. The stone rippled at her side, only to reveal the way the cat's skin had been stitched together into a sheath dress for her. Finally, the bottom hem was edged with two hind paws and the tail was trailing down around her feet.

I was in awe at the statue. Not only was it a work of exquisite beauty, but the craftsmanship was impeccable. In one hand she held a tablet and the other a stylus, which was raised as if to write on a wall that wasn't there. Her eyes stared off into the distance through the blinding Delphian sun.

I climbed the pedestal to find I was the same height as the actual statue. I stared briefly into shining whiskey colored eyes with a tar black outer ring.

Sesheta had been a beautiful woman. The emerald green eyeshadow that colored her eyelids only brought that point home.

She held her tablet on her hip to the side, creating just enough space for me to stand in her embrace. I turned around and allowed my head to line up with hers. I slipped the library bracelet over my right wrist and lifted my arm in line with Sesheta.

The sound of feet meeting stone came around a corner and were followed by a gasp.

"Yes, that's it!" My mom urged me on.

"Show me the terrain!" I ordered the bracelet and a map blazed to life before my eyes.

Her stylus pointed out of the city into the desert surroundings.

"You will never get an accurate location that way," Hera remarked and slipped the other bracelet over the statue's wrist, ordering it to turn on.

The overlay from one holograph to the other was dizzying. I pulled my bracelet off and the display instantly disappeared.

The entire courtyard was alight with the outlines of hills and valleys, stretching out beyond the horizon. I squinted to block out the blaring light from Delphi's star.

Without regard the blasting heat returned, giving me a burning need to retreat back into the shadows of the pillars and the cool air of the scriptorium.

*****

"I don't want it on any maps," the woman stated.

It wasn't a plea. She was staunch in her orders.

"Everyone here already knows where it is. Who would you be hiding if from, Pythia? The next generation?" Sesheta asked, irritation coloring her retorts.

Pythia crossed her arms to hold herself as if someone had walked over her grave. "The future is never what you think it is. Sesheta, do as I ask! I will carve your statue myself to perfection," Pythia uncrossed her arms and let them fall to her side and sighed in resignation. "The Fates will know what to do when they arrive."

"Fate cannot change memories or the face of a world. Nothing you do will hide the alethea from our people,"

Sesheta retorted but continued drawing the layout for a courtyard.

"The Fates will change everything. They will reveal the alethea or the truth to our people, not hide it. Refrain from using the old words. I despise everything Elysium stood for, as do you. If I never hear my native tongue again, I would be happy for all my days. The statue will point the way, and only the Fates can decode what it points to."

"Even if we can do it, leveling off a mountain will not hide anything," Sesheta scoffed.

*****

The vision faded away, leaving me shaking. Somewhere off in the distance was what Pythia was trying to hide.

Alethea - the truth. You can never keep the truth a secret. Eventually it comes out.

I stared straight ahead into the holographic terrain, looking for a mountain that wasn't there.

"How do you get this thing to draw a line or something?" I asked, tapping the beads around the statue's wrist in frustration.

Vika stepped up and tapped in a sequence, "Point with your left hand on the hologram and tell it what you want it to do," she instructed.

I stared off into the distance at the holo and pointed at the tip of the stylus, "Draw a straight line around the planet, following this point of angle."

A bright blue line appeared with-in the hologram, stretching out ahead of me and returning to the stylus tip from behind.

"What's your guess, Issy?" Mom asked, moving into my line of sight.

"Somewhere along this line is the underworld," I shrugged and moved my focus back to the bracelet, "Save changes!" I instructed," with that, one of the beads blinked and the holo disappeared.

I slipped the bracelet off the statue's arm and into my pocket.

CHAPTER 9

SYDNEY

The terrain markings on the map hadn't been explicit in the courtyard. Nonetheless, standing in the dim library changed my perspective. Without all the blinding white light from Delphi's star, I could see the elevation changes.

The terrain was not as varied in color as Earth was and my longing for the blue of the ocean or green of a tree hit me. I missed them all, mostly I missed the water. I missed the slapping sound of waves under the twin hulls of Calypso, rocking me to sleep or the blast of salt flavored air, pushing my hair back and filling my ears with the white noise of the wind. The pull of the sea still sung its siren song in my blood, and even here, I could hear its call.

If I closed my eyes, I could point in the direction to the nearest body of water, waiting for me to control it.

I bit my lip to focus on the holo-map, floating before me.

The blue line intersected many hills and valleys but no large bodies of water. Other than dry river beds and a few bubbling springs, the line crossed nothing of interest.

Reading three dimensional maps was not my thing and I still loved the feel of a real map under my hands. I leaned over the table with the 2D map and worked out the exact angle of the line Issy had drawn from the holo.

It crossed a section with a high elevation on one side and a low valley on the other. The map listed Pytho as a tiny dot right under the Sesheta line. I bit my lip again and grabbed the bracelet. It immediately lit up. I tapped the beads several times to code in the map number, holding one wrist out. Using the other one for navigation, I moved it to Pytho. It was amazing. Right there, in the cliffs, there was a sanctuary.

<Mom, are you seeing what I'm seeing?> Issy asked.

< Yes!>

"I dreamt that the three of us were there, at that temple," Issy remarked to no one in the room.

Vika squeaked, "You dreamt what?"

"I dreamt that Hera, my mother, and I were there. Wherever this is, the three of us arrived together there," Issy stated as if it was a foregone conclusion that we would arrive just as she'd dreamed.

"You dreamt that all three of you would arrive at the training ground of Oracle's together?" Vika moaned and took a step back, knocking a few scrolls off of the table as she went.

She jumped and screeched with fright at the clattering of a bracelet hitting the ground.

"Yeah. So?" Issy scoffed and her collar jingled as she moved.

Vika's lower lip trembled and she asked: "Which one are you? Are you Klotho, Lakhesis, or Atropos?" her frightened eyes darted from Issy to me, then Hera, and back again.

"I don't know who Klotho is and no, I am not her, whoever that is," Issy replied in confusion, shaking her head.

I moved closer to my daughter, angling my body in front of her. Vika's sudden change scared me. There was no way I was letting a glorified Librarian hurt my child.

Vika took three more steps back, moving to the door.

"Vika, wherever you're going, you cannot abandon us now. Whatever you know, you must tell us," Hera said and moved toward her at the same time.

"I cannot... I cannot be part of this," she moaned.

A flash from her mind filled mine.

Her eyes darted like a wild animal on the run from a beast intent on eating her. Her fear ate at her. She wanted to run.

"Be a part of what?" I asked, "Don't get your panties in a wad?"

Deflect! If I can get her to think about something, anything. Maybe the stress has been too much for her?

"Whatever you think is going on here, we can't help you or change anything if we don't understand ourselves,"

Hera stated, becoming the voice of reason. She then lifted both her hands in a gesture of surrender.

<Mom, she's terrified. Fear is pouring off of her. She is acting like she's seen the devil or something.> Issy remarked and moved out from behind me.

<She's gonna make a break for it.> Tristan informed me.

Hera announced, <We can't let her go. Wherever it is, she's planning to go. Our lives depend on anonymity.>

I flashed Hera a glare. She knew something and I wanted to know what it was. Whatever was terrifying Vika that much I needed to know.

Hera and her secrets will have to wait for another time.

<Tristan, take her! > I ordered.

<Yes, Mom. >

Vika disappeared along with the sheer terror she carried within her.

"Whatever she might have told us, she won't now," Hera shouted and turned away from me, smoothing her wig and tilting her head up and down to compose herself.

My eyebrows rose to my hairline. "Hera, she was gonna make a break for it. Something she heard scared the shit out of her. We need to know what she knows before she reveals us to the Themians," I retorted.

Ugh! Isn't that what she meant? How can I be the only one who sees that?

I groaned and rolled my eyes. "We can't afford anyone knowing we're here."

Hera faced away from my searching gaze. "You're right, of course. It just goes against all I believe in to abduct her against her will," she coolly replied, moving to pick up the fallen bracelet and scrolls.

She stacked them on the table and rolled up the rest, all except the one I'd drawn a line on. That one disappeared from her hand with a shift.

I narrowed my eyes at Hera, "Are we really abducting her? She asked to come with us. She came here to help us and now she's the one who is suddenly backing out. What did Issy say to her that scared the shit out of her? Something about all three of us going someplace on Sesheta's line? How is that terrifying?" I was pacing again.

The forward movement wasn't enough. I wanted to press on and quickly. My need pressed in from all sides.

"I don't understand either, but I think we're going to need a few more people before we go anywhere. Abduction is just another way of saying 'prisoner' and I won't be a part of imprisoning anyone," Hera stated and crossed her arms.

I sent a vision of the maps to Ixis, Tristan, and Adrian so they would know where we were going.

Not exactly sure how we were going to pull this off, but a forgotten structure on a desert planet can't be that much trouble, can it?

<I put her with Melinda. She won't be able to contact anyone. She's confined to that section of the ship, in the mental ward.> Tristan offered to calm everyone down.

<There are no mental patients there now. We don't even have any more criminals, so really she's just in the lab ring.> Issy remarked

Great! She's a lab rat.

I rubbed the bridge of my nose and squeezed my eyes closed.

<I would rather be a lab rat than a dead rat.> I stated to end the debate because I was sure that the kids would go on bickering for at least thirty minutes if I were to let them.

<When you put it like that. Yes, I would much rather be a lab rat than dead. At least a lab rat has the hope of escape.> Hera replied in her dry Themian manner.

I knew what she was actually saying. She'd been trapped, and as long as she had hope it was better than death.

I tilted my head to her in understanding. She returned the quiet acknowledgment.

I won't keep Vika against her will forever. Just until we leave Delphi. By then, it wouldn't matter what Themia thought. We'd be gone.

Tristan's mental laughing over the lab rat comment was more than I could bear. It was like the cackle of an old woman. It bled over into the pressure change and the next thing I knew, I was standing on the bridge in the shifting room.

"We found a Temple." I stated to the room.

"Yes, but all of the books or records stated Pythia was placed in a cavern. A cavern implies a large underground space with a vaulted ceiling," Hera remarked while whipping the heavy eyeliner off her face, which smudged the black coal down her cheeks, but she didn't seem to care.

"The big question is this. If it's in the building, is the building built in front of it or directly over it? The Temple meets the side of the cliff seamlessly. You cannot tell where the entrance to the underworld or cavern could be," I added.

"We could send in a recon. It may not even be part of the temple at all. What if it's close by?" Issy suggested and shrugged.

"No. The Oracle said there would be no new oracles until the fates arrived," Hera replied.

The pit in my stomach turned to acid.

I hate this fate crap. I can't trust this trip to a recon team. If it's got to be, it's got to be me.

CHAPTER 10

ISOLDE

"Who should we take with us?" I asked though I was sure mom already had a plan.

"Tristan and Adrian. No one else," mom replied, pushing the black wig from her head and pulling the heavy orichalcum collar from around her neck. A moment later, she was in jeans and a t-shirt.

"The most powerful weapon is the ability to move quickly. I can only push people out-of-the-way. Tristan and Adrian can move all of us out of the entire system," she continued, justifying her choices.

"We need a rallying point," Hera muttered through her face, scrubbing.

"We don't need a rallying point. Our rallying point is the ship," mom replied, removing her arm bands and earring.

She never touched her makeup, though. Part of me thought maybe she liked it.

"Tristan can't move stuff that far?" I blurted out and heat reddened my face.

I didn't like the way I sounded. I wasn't knocking Tristan down, but that is how it sounded.

"Thanks for the vote of confidence, Sis. Yes, I'm actually the one who pulled you back from the planet, to begin with," he barked at my lack of confidence.

"Sorry, I didn't realize you are now the moving man," I murmured, hoping my blush disappeared as fast as it came.

"Matter is matter. It doesn't matter whether you move somebody through space or matter. It doesn't matter. Ha! That's a teleportation joke," Tristan shrugged and guffawed at his own wit like a big dork.

"That must be the worst joke I've ever heard," I remarked in a droll tone, while rolling my eyes.

"I know. That's what makes it so funny," he returned, pulling the bangs in his eyes then finger-combing them back.

Honestly, my brother was such an overachiever dork.

I sometimes don't know what to do with him. 90% of the time he's too serious and the rest of the 10% when he decides to cut loose and be funny, he's an idiot.

"I want to see a full map of that area. It has to be modern-day and not old," mom ordered, staring into the open space over our heads in expectation.

A three-dimensional hologram appeared.

I always enjoyed watching science fiction movies. We read a lot of books and mostly watched movies on the boat during big ocean crossings. Truth be told, I spent most of my time daydreaming instead of watching TV. But when you see a real three-dimensional hologram floating in a room above your head, and most importantly, when you can walk around and inside of it, then point at the different places of interest it's a new level of cool.

"Can we use our abilities to test and look for underground anomalies or anything like that?" Mom asked.

"No. The materials they used to build the old temple were of an earlier composition. The temple has a design to block all our abilities. What we have now we can choose specific areas with ability blockers. Also, we know how to turn on and off fields for that. But that structure blocks all abilities except, apparently, the Oracle's. I think she figured out the proper frequency for it and did it on purpose. No one can shift through that and create havoc within the school.

"Maybe that's why she was murdered in the city. That was the only place her attacker could reach her," mom remarked, then crossed her arms.

Every time someone brought up Pythia's death, my mother froze.

"But if she knew she was going to be murdered in the city, why did she go?" I asked, wanting to get it out there and maybe, taking mom's edge off.

"You know, Isolde, that's an excellent question. If you knew you were going to die, why would you go to meet your death?" My mother had a smirk on her face.

She always had a quote from something she read that seemed pertinent. It was one of the most irritating facts about her. She was a constant know it all. Although, I had to admit she was pretty smart.

"You're talking about the merchant of Samara who went to meet his death," I remarked and rolled my eyes just in time to spy Hercules standing in one of the archways, staring at me.

He caught me and winked. I pursed my lips and turned my attention back to my mother and her 'unschooling' moment.

"Do I want to ask?" I scoffed.

Adrian snickered from across the room, shaking his head, "You know that she's dying to tell us. Just give her what she wants, so we can move on with the rest of the day," he strolled over and kissed my mom on the temple.

She returned the act with a smile and turned her full attention to the rest of the room.

"What are you talking about? *Dying to tell you*. Okay! You are right. I am dying to tell you," she smiled and continued "So, a merchant lived in Baghdad and saw a man across the way that was very shocked to see him. When he confronted the man, the man was Death, and Death said, 'I am surprised to see you.' When the Merchant asked, 'why?', Death returned 'because I didn't expect to see you in Baghdad.' The merchant was so scared by his encounter with death that he packed up all his worldly goods and left Baghdad that very afternoon, ending the day in Samara. However, when he got to Samara, he ran into the Death again, so he asked, 'why were you surprised to see me this morning in Baghdad?' Death replied, 'because I knew I had an appointment with you this evening in Samara,'" Mom finished.

"What? You're sayin is the Oracle's death was inevitable? That no matter what she did, she would've met her fate?" Emmaline scoffed and tilted her head to the side in thought. She then narrowed her eyes while studying my mother.

"Well, maybe she just had a vision of her death, but she didn't see any of the surrounding information to explain who had done it or why," I offered, itching to get out of these Egyptian clothes and throw on a nice pair of yoga pants and a tank top.

"No. Or maybe, she saw her own death, thought it would happen in her own Citadel, went to the city to get away from it but didn't," mom offered, yet her brows pulled down.

Pythia's death got to her.

"Oh, mom! Please stop! You'll give me a headache, honestly. It's the whole chicken and the egg scenario, and it makes me crazy. Only you would remember some archaic story about a merchant in Baghdad meeting death," I moaned then glanced back at the archway to see if Hercules was still there watching me.

He wasn't. Instead, he lounged in one of the floor chairs, with one leg thrown over the armrest and his head resting in his hand with an index finger pointing up and his thumb extended into his hair.

He was staring at me with hot eyes and that wasn't the most distracting part. He was clothed in only a fabric skirt of some kind with a leather striped kilt over the top and leather crossed straps on his chest.

Hercules was utterly covered in muscles. His honey-blond hair hung over his shoulders in a devil may care fashion that worked for him. My mouth went dry and for a moment, I wanted to talk to him. However, my head was muddled and the murmur in the back of my mind roared to life.

He winked at me and I snapped out of it. I closed my mouth and turned back to the work at hand. Pushing the noise in my mind away, I stared the holo in the air down.

I glanced down at my dress. It was sheer and suddenly I realized why Hercules had been staring.

I'm practically naked.

Heat stained my face. Part of me wanted to cover everything with my hands, while the other part was on the verge of dashing out the nearest archway.

<Need some brotherly help?> Tristan pipped in without all the usual joshing.

<Yes, please, Trist.> I pleaded and a second later my see-through dress became a Themian chiton.

I shot Tristan a '*thanks for the help, but couldn't you have picked anything better?*' look. He simply smiled and shrugged. I turned back to the three-dimensional image in front of me. It wasn't just a hologram of a monochromatic map. It was in full-color. Everything was like the flat picture I'd seen before, yet something burned wrong. I couldn't put my finger on it.

Maybe, if I just stare at it long enough, I might.

"Is there something strange about this hologram?" I inquired to the room, and no one in particular.

"Other than the erosion of time, nothing immediately jumps out at me, screaming 'here I am'," Hera remarked with a smirk.

She hadn't bothered to change her dress, despite her breasts still being exposed for the world to see. I actually noticed Tristan ogling them, before he quickly looked away.

"I see you picked up some human sarcasm. I guess all those years amongst humanity weren't completely wasted," my mom said with a half-smile of approval.

She loves to dish and take it.

"Of course, it wasn't a waste or I certainly would not be here and neither would you or your children," Hercules interjected, turning his beaming smile on me, before nodding to each person in the room.

Hercules dwarfed everyone, including Adrian and Tristan. He was a Herc-ing man. However, Adrian gave him a once over anyway. I caught Tristan thinking, '*the bigger they are, the harder they fall.*'

I am usually the smallest woman in the room, so size is something I keep my mind on at all times since Jacques.

The slapping of sandals pulled my attention away from Hercules only to have my eyes land on the most blindingly beautiful woman I've ever seen. She was a picture of femininity with delicate features and curves to die for. Her honey-blond hair framed her face, hanging in ringlets down her back, while her hips swayed with each step as if she floated across the room. She approached and laid one hand on Hercules' shoulder, then leaned in to whisper in his ear.

A soft smile spread over his face as he stared down at the floor. With that, he whispered back and she drifted out of the room.

A fire raged over me and I couldn't say why. Her touch was intimate and familiar, making me want to snap her perfect little fingers off. I shook the thought away. Instead, I focused on the holograph and the puzzle I'd decided was our best chance of finding Elysium.

Whatever I felt about Hercules, I had better things to do.

I reached down and keyed my bracelet to the three-dimensional image from Seshate. A second later, the old holograph popped up. I moved my arm around to try and align the two images, but I guess I was fidgeting because they just didn't seem to line up.

"If I could get this goddamn thing to overlap!" I murmured, flaring my nostrils in frustration.

"Isolde, do you really have to take the Lord's name in vain?" Tristan chuckled, joshing me.

I didn't reply. I just shot him a '*go die on a stick*' glare.

"Tristan, honestly," my mom remarked without looking at either of us.

She then cross stepped inside the two images examining the details.

"Ixis, condense the data from the bracelet on to the mainframe and overlay it for us," Hercules ordered.

The image immediately condensed and disappeared. Ixis took the bracelet from my wrist and lowered it down onto the cylinder on the center podium. The room instantly lit up with the two holographic images overlaid.

One of the images showed the valley with the new building shadowy over the top.

"Is this a modern-day with topography and everything?" Tristan asked. He always used those big words, "This is the exact image of the surrounding school area as it looks today?"

Tristan toggled between the three images until we had skeletal outlines of everything.

"There's no ground penetration?" Adrian asked, running his fingers along the floating lines of the school building.

"No, I believe not," Ixis replied while studying the main control panel.

The hologram nagged at me. I closed my eyes to picture in my mind what I'd seen in Seshate's plaza, adding pieces from my vision. I rolled my eyes behind the closed lids, searching my mind for the difference. I mentally surveyed the cliff face and the roof-line of the temple, then I traced the upper edge of the valley from one end to the other before it hit me.

Water!

The first image had a river which was gone in the second one.

"The terrain doesn't look as altered as I would expect. I mean it's 2 million years, so there are a lot of changes. What I am trying to point out is: where did the river go?" I asked and looked around the room. "The cavern is nothing without the rivers.

"She is correct. In the first image the map shows a river that doesn't appear in the second one. Also, the valley seems relatively unchanged for 2 million years worth of erosion. The river has not been there to cause any. Otherwise, the canyon should be cut much deeper," Hercules supplied while standing with his arms crossed and legs wide next to me.

I glanced at him out of the corner of my eye.

Why is he so helpful?

"Good eye! That is right. Does anyone know what the name of the river is?" Ixis asked while coolly examining the holo.

"Why?" Emmaline wanted to know and scratched her head.

<Vika might know.> I commented to Tristan.

Ixis manipulated the projection for a few moments, then separated the two images. They reappeared side-by-side. I nodded to Tristan.

A second later, Vika appeared. "You can't keep me here against my will," she shouted at my mother.

Hera approached her and that made her cringe back.

"Don't touch me! Please don't touch me. Please," she whispered. "One of you carries with you the touch of death."

Vika cowered back against the wall. I glanced from my mother to Hera, while mom tilted her head at Hera.

Hera began, "Vika, you've been accommodating and you are Ixis' friend. We have no desire to hurt you. You don't want us to touch you, then we won't. We do understand what fear is."

My eyes ran over Vika. She pressed herself firmly against the wall. Both her hands were hugging an elbow. Her body was shaking, her eyes were wide and wild, looking both ways. She kept darting from me, to my mother, and Hera, then back.

"Tristan, are you picking anything up from her?" mom asked and moved closer.

"No, she slammed the walls down. I can't find a way in. That's not my specialty. Mom, Hera, looks like you guys are up," Tristan offered and stepped back to the control panel.

"I cannot. I only did it the first few times to save all of you. I cannot do it again. I'm sorry. Sydney, there is a reason why I wanted you in charge. I cannot make the tough choices. I know this about myself," Hera stated with a morn.

My mother set her shoulders with resolve. She always moved in a certain way once she made her decision. She lifted her chin and I knew she was about to make a move.

Adrian moved to her side and she looked at him, searching for a moment. He gave her a gentle smile, so she turned back and faced Vika.

"I don't want to do this. It's a terrible invasion. Vika, please tell us everything you know. Otherwise, I will be forced to invade your mind and you may not come out the same on the other side," she stated.

I bit my lip and felt the warmth of someone standing close by. I glanced over, expecting to find my brother, instead it was Hercules.

"Domination," Vika blanched.

She stilled. Her whole countenance was one of acceptance. Her eyes lowered to the floor and when she looked back up she spoke, "There shall be no new Oracles until the Fates arrive. I can help you and I will, but please don't touch me. All this time I've spent reading about history and the great things that other people have done, knowing that I would never be one of them. That I would always be a lesser Themian, reading about greater ones." Her body trembled and she swallowed before continuing, "Three women. The Oracle spoke of three women. She knew from beginning to end you would arrive. '*There will be no new Oracles until the Fates arrive.*' She didn't mean our fate is a predestined notion. She meant three women! She always spoke to the three."

Vika pulled her frightened eyes from the floor and took a deep breath. "'*The first, the one who wove the law she created you, woven with our genes*'," she cited and then clarified for all of us to understand. "Our genes are like threads. Spun, and twisted together. If you look at the Themian genome and the human genome there's very little difference. Both of them are twisted exactly like spun yarn."

Her eyes darted to Hera, "You are Klotho, for you wove our genes into the cloth of humanity." She lowered her eyes away from Hera in fear and glanced up at me. "The second fate measures the cloth. She has the ability to evaluate. She knows your worth. She knows if you added value or have taken it away. She knows if you deserve punishment or happiness. She knows everything," her eyes fell on me, "You are Lakhesis. You don't touch people because you'll see every moment of their lives. You know exactly who and what they are simply by touching them. I saw it when you touched me in the dream walk."

I didn't tell her that and my heart rate skyrocketed.

The true terror didn't come until she laid her eyes upon my mother. "You are Atropos, the cutter. You take the measured thread of their lives and you end it. You have the ability to control and dominate anyone. You can tell them to kill themselves. You're the one who has the final judgment, the final say, even now. It is said that the 3rd fate can kill you with a thought. All she has to do is touch you. Maybe, it's not a physical touch. Maybe, your touch is simply a mental one," Vika's teeth chattered and her shaking grew as did her eyes.

A low moan escaped her lips and she curled down on herself.

My mother's eyes grew hard. "So, you think I'm the harbinger of death? That I am some kind of evil demon? What have you done to deserve my touch of death? Why would I want to kill you?" She demanded.

"Mother, she hasn't done anything," I cut in, then snapped my jaw shut at the truth of my words.

"You're exactly right, Isolde. She's done nothing. She admits that she's done nothing, but sit in a library and read about better Themians, never partaking in real society or contributing in any meaningful way," mom's head whipped back to Vika, "Only sitting around on your ass doing nothing, while your people manipulated the Universe, the cosmos, how they've seen fit. So, yes, maybe I will be the harbinger of death for you," my mother barked.

I'd never seen her turn dark so quickly on anyone.

"Maybe, I will cut your life to a proper length. Living forever shouldn't mean that you can sit on your ass and do nothing or that you can run around, playing God over everyone," her voice rose and the jewelry she'd taken off shot across the room, hitting the opposite wall and shattering into a thousand pieces.

Vika was really cowering now. It was as if every word from my mother's mouth was a slash and every muscle flexed in her body.

Adrian put his hand on my mother's shoulder.

"Are you killing or pronouncing judgment? Let her go," he urged in a low voice.

My mother stared up at him in bewilderment for a moment, then she nodded her head and turned to stare at Hera.

"If you want to stay with us, stay. Apparently, Atropos has passed judgment on you and you survived. You can stay or you can go to preach doom and gloom to Themia. It's up to you. I won't stop you."

Hera raised her hand to her mouth as if to stifle a sound, then quickly snapped her jaw shut.

My mother continued on as if she hadn't heard her. "As a matter of fact, I'll have Tristan move you wherever you desire," she scoffed and waved a hand.

I wasn't sure what had set her off, but Vika's terror was palpable in the space.

"I will stay with you. I passed the judgment! I never thought to be judged. I feel better," Vika sniffed, "I promise. I will not waste my time anymore. Whatever you're doing, I am with you. You're right to say that Themians have wasted everything that they've been given, wandering around and manipulating the Universe. I sat reading about it, revering it. Having been judged by the three fates and survived made me think that maybe, I could be a historian and keep records for you. Use my talents in a useful way," she faltered, her face searching the three of us for confirmation of acceptance.

Emmaline walked over and took Vika's hand. "Let's get you settled in a room. Trust me! I'm not gonna hurt you, no matter what you think. The three of them might be a little scary together, but Sydney let you go. I'm pretty sure she's keeping you around for good reason." Emmaline's ability to ease emotions coaxed Vika out of the room.

Emmaline glanced back at me with a look of irritation. She might have been an empath but she really didn't have tolerance for bullshit. I was sure that when she got back we'd all get a mouthful, ear full or mindful from her.

It seems like everybody can talk in my head.

I watched the two of them drift away. My belly rolled, making me wonder what had just happened.

"We need to find out where that is," my mother stated and pointed at the river.

"You want us to scour the countryside looking for a river that existed millions of years ago but doesn't seem to be there now?"

"We should be looking for where it came from," I replied and the flopping in my belly eased.

"I think Issy has something. I think she's right. River's don't just disappear. It had to go somewhere," Hercules said.

Ixis fiddled with a few more nob's zooming out from the Temple, following the river. It started further back on the rock-face, almost as if it just bubbled right out of the rock.

Maybe it was just a river after all.

"That doesn't look like the mouth of the river. They usually start with a small trickle from a higher source," Adrian remarked, tracking his finger along the holo image. "No spring? Rivers rarely spring from the side of a mountain. That means there must've been an underground river that broke the surface there. My father would have known. He was the outdoors person," his voice trailed off.

Adrian didn't talk about his parents, so I was surprised he'd even mentioned his dad. They died 30 years ago. For a Themian it was just barely a blink of an eye, but for me, no amount of time could quash the pain of my father's death.

A part of me reached out to him. Losing a parent sucks. However, losing both at the same time. I couldn't even imagine how that felt.

I returned my focus on the map. It didn't show a cavern. The water flowed directly from the rock-face. What the new map showed was a white section of the rock-face that didn't look any different than the rest of the cliff.

"I guess the question is 'do we go to the Temple or do we go to this rock-face?'" Tristan asked, turning away from the holo to face the rest of us in the room.

He'd crossed his arms and stood with wide legs in a stance similar to Hercules, but with more swagger.

If that was possible.

"No. We have to go to the Temple first. When I say 'we', I mean mom, Hera, and I. The three of us have to go together. We have to go there first," I said as my vision played in my mind.

That is the way to go.

"Because of your dream?" Hera asked, moving away from the hologram.

She picked up a light shawl and draped it over her shoulder, covering her breast and tucking the ends into the top of the dress under each breast. The stiff fabric angled out from her shoulders, giving it an angelic effect.

"Yes," I replied undeterred, then scoffed. "As if three women never went to the Temple together before."

"They didn't. Women don't go to the Temple in groups of three. It's a rule. You may only arrive at the Temple alone and you're only supposed to go to the Temple if you had a dream about it," Vika supplied quietly.

That explains why my dream about all three of us going together scared her shitless.

*****

Seeing my mother dressed in a chiton all belted with her hair piled on the top of her head and her blue eyes flashing, made me think of a Roman Goddess. Tristan, on the other hand, wore short belted tunic and sandals.

However, Adrian was the one who took my breath away. I suddenly understood why mom was in love. He wore a fabric kilt, similar to Hercules', and had crossed leather straps on his chest. A sword hung from his belt, while his sandals were laced up his legs. It was hard to believe he'd been born in the modern world.

Truth be told, Adrian was probably one of the hottest guys I'd ever seen. He was tall, strong, and had piercing blue eyes that stared right through you. He made you feel like you didn't exist and you're his whole world at the same time. When he looked at my mom, it didn't matter how much of the Universe existed. He only saw her.

"I'm ready. Everybody else ready?" Tristan asked then rubbed his hands together with glee.

"Yes," I replied somewhat grateful I was wearing a chiton already. I didn't need to change.

Why mom changed, I don't get.

Hercules caught my eye and opened his mouth to say something a moment before Tristan blocked my view.

My brother came and stood next to me, grabbing my hand. Whatever we were walking into, I had no doubt Tristan would be there to help me. I turned just in time to smile at him before the air pressure changed, becoming cold followed by the popping sound. A slight pain in my ears and we were there, standing just far enough away from the Temple that no one would notice we had appeared.

CHAPTER 11

ISOLDE

The edifice of Pythos looked vaguely familiar. All of the stone had the same golden yellow color as Abydos. That actually made sense because the surrounding area was dry and there were sand dunes nearby.

The entire area was a dried husk of an old woman waiting to bite you or cut you with her sharp tongue. Several creatures slithered around like snakes.

Just our luck. They'd all be poisonous vipers.

I glanced over at my mother. She carried a glow of wonder with her lips slightly parted. The combination of a

Greek chiton, Egyptian heavy eyeliner, and metallic green eyeshadow set off an other worldly effect, transforming my mother into a Goddess. I'd always thought my mother was beautiful, but today she took even my breath away.

The magic bubble burst as she bit down on her upper lip, while her eyebrows pulled down in concentration.

"Mom, you know something, don't you?" I sighed.

"You're kidding right, Isolde? Mom always knows something we don't," Tristian said and my eyes locked with his as we both snickered.

When it came to information, my mother was better than an encyclopedia.

"Do you know what we're looking at?" My mother replied, ignoring our side conversation and indicating the expanse of the building.

"Yes, it is the Temple of Pythos, the training grounds for the Oracles," Hera remarked in her school teacher tone.

Her matter of fact statement irked me.

Mom snickered. As Adrian quirked a knowing smile, a sparkle glinted in his eyes.

"Have you never seen a building like this before?" My mother inquired, glancing from Tristan to me.

Now, I was really irritated.

Mom turns everything into an educational opportunity. Obviously, she knows that Tristan and I have seen this. We graduated from school but for some reason the life lessons never stop. Ugh!

I turned my attention back to the structure before me and the puzzle my mother forced on me.

It was a giant linear building which rose up from the floor of the valley at least five stories high. The architecture gave it the appearance of being long and lean. It sat back against the cliff which towered above us enough to block the sun from our eyes.

Nothing about this building said 'Greece' to me. A long ramp of tiered stairs extended out to greet us. They were wide and deep with a low rise. The stairs rose up and ended at a palisade that went all the way around the exterior of the main complex. The building edifice rose off of pillars that carried a distinct style, that tickled at the back of my mind.

I snuck a glance at Tristan. His face blanched.

<You thinking what I'm thinking? > he asked in his deep solemn tone.

Tristan had already figured out mom's puzzle but didn't want to give it away to me. He was always so quick. Next to him I felt sluggish and stupid.

But then it struck me, < The pillars look like papyrus plants.> I mentally squeaked.

< Yes! > Tristan replied and his tone had changed to a joshing laugh.

The blood drained from my face.

"If you stop thinking about it as if it was ancient Greek architecture, what architecture immediately comes to mind?" Mom prodded again, a knowing smile creeping up her face.

"It looks Egyptian. I know that Temple complex but I don't know the name," I huffed as Tristan winked at me.

He knows! I hate that about him. He's as bad as mom.

"It's the mortuary temple of Hatshepsut. That's what it looks like."

Tristan the smarty-pants.

< I heard that! > Tristan retorted.

I mentally groaned. < I don't care. > I sang back to him.

"Very good, Tristan!" Mom said. "It's an Egyptian Temple. So why would the Oracle build a temple that looked Egyptian?" She stared at the golden stones with a half-smile.

"You've seen Abydos. Everything is built in this style," Hera stated.

Every head in our group must've swiveled towards her. My own whipped around, as I locked my eyes on Hera. Her eyes darted from one face to the other in return, leaving only Vika out.

"Were you not aware?" she inquired.

"Aware of what?" Adrian asked in his calm cool voice.

"Egyptian culture. Themian culture. That the whole planet is like this?"

"The whole planet is Egyptian?" Mom squeaked.

"No. The whole planet is Themian. Egyptians just resemble the Themians from Delphi," she continued examining the sandstone. "This construction predates our white crystalline style. Remember how I told you that the buildings on Delphi were different from the buildings on all the other worlds? On all the other worlds everything was built white like our ship. But, as you can see, the architecture in Abydos is yellow or golden."

Hera has lived so long between both the human and the Themian worlds, I think she forgets who knows what anymore.

"Sandstone?" I shivered.

Mom was always going on about how humanity didn't know how the Pyramids were built, explaining how some of the stones were strange. But sandstone was a far cry from aliens, wasn't it?

"No. I mean, yes, it would resemble sandstone but it's a different composition. It works similar to the white crystalline. The only difference is that this composite blocks all abilities. Her Temple was built in the older style," Vika filled in and moved to the line of enormous statues which were leading up to the stairs.

"Are the original Themians, the ones on Elysium, are they Egyptian?" I inquired and held my breath for the answer. My intellectual curiosity was getting the better of me.

"No, I don't think so. No one knows what they are. Egyptian, as you call it, or Greek, they are all Themian or Elysian, depending on which way you see it," Hera remarked while running her hand over an etching in the stone.

"Who was from Delphi on Alethea?" Mom demanded.

I internally smiled. Mom always needed answers. She was always looking for more input. Her thirst for knowledge was as hungry as a black hole in space. She was always chewing on something new that entered her sphere of space.

"Isn't it obvious? Osiris and Isis were both Delphian," Hera stated.

I put my hand to my mouth pulling on my lower lip to stop myself from biting it. It was a nervous habit I'd picked up from mom and had developed into more.

Egyptian culture is Themian culture.

I began pacing. All this information was going to take me about 15 minutes to wrap my head around and I didn't know if mom and Hera would give me the time to do that.

The site was abandoned or at least it appeared abandoned. Most of Pytho was dilapidated with age and weather worn. The yellow stone threw back a lustrous light under the Delphinian star. Everything had a normal air of neglect, along with the silence that usually comes from being forgotten.

Deep scarring and fissures lined the front edifices of each rise. Several statues lining the walkway had parts of their bases missing and while cracks ran through the sides. Every one of them wore an Egyptian headdress which carried the Viper Uraeus in one form or another. Some had wings and other feathers. There was one that had horns and a giant disk. The names on the bases had been carved but only faint portions remained. Be that as it may, none of the statues carried a crook or flail.

While they appeared Egyptian, they're features were wholly alien from the Egypt of Earth. The curve of a cheek or the shape of a nose were totally different and the lips were well formed and defined with high peaks. The eyes lacked the narrow almond shape of Earth. Instead, every set was different. As was every face, as if being Delphian had nothing to do with race. It was a culture.

Each statue had a bracelet on the right arm in various configurations. Some resembled the scarab, others a hippopotamus, while others carried the relief of a jackal head. The statues themselves had human-Themian bodies, but the heads, just like on Earth, were the outline of animals or creatures. The Egyptian highlighting around the eyes, along with traces of bright colors on their eyelids were all that was left of their former glory.

Most of the statues were the normal hawk or jackal. One actually made me shiver.

It was a man dressed in the Egyptian style with a human head. His hair hung down in thick tight ringlets from his head. Part of his beard was flecked with bits of reddish pigment. Most Egyptians or Delphinians were clean shaven, but this man, even on his arms, had small details resembling hair. I shivered as I stared into his hard eyes that still carried the hint of blue pigment.

He had the traditional front leg extended as if stepping. That was an indicative of all Egyptian/Delphian statues. However, his leg wasn't a leg. From the knee down there were gears and support bars. It was a prosthetic.

"You like the statues," Vika remarked, making me jump.

"I find them interesting. It's like a picture into a forgotten world," I replied.

I couldn't tear my eyes from the statue. I continued to examine him. He was wearing two bracelets but they were nothing more than torcs with flat disks attached to them. They were etched with symmetrical flower petals.

Overall, this statue was the least Egyptian of them all. It tickled my brain pan.

I've seen something like it before but I can't place where.

"Who is this statue of?" I asked then began searching the base for a name.

"I don't know," Vika remarked, dusting sand away and digging with her hands across the base.

It was ridged with markings worn down over the ages. Time didn't change the evidence before us. Whatever it once said was gone, chiseled away on purpose – erased for all time.

I glanced back up at his hard stare. Whoever he was, the only thing left of him was this statue.

Not even a name.

That is the truest death of all. To be forgotten.

"Hera, if everybody reveres the Oracle Pythia on Delphi, why is this temple in ruins?" My mother asked, running a hand across the nearest statue as she passed, as if by touching it she would absorb the information it had once carried.

"The Cult of the Oracle is supposed to take care of Pythos. It's under the acolytes' domain," Vika shrugged, but worry tugged at her features as she lingered behind us.

She was close enough to hear our words before the wind whipped them away, but far enough to make a break for it if things went south.

"Adrian, Tristan, can you guys hear anyone?" Mom asked.

Tristan shook his head. Adrian's eyes were closed and the pressure of his mind reached out, tickling my psyche. I slammed my walls down in my mind. The last thing in the world I wanted was for my mother's longtime boyfriend/mate, once a dead guy, to poke around in my head.

After a few minutes the pressure ceased and Adrian opened his eyes.

"There is something here, though I don't know what it is. There are layers upon layers, wall blocking and I don't mean physical walls. Just layers upon layers of something," he replied, rattling his finger in his ear, as if that would clear up a sound you hear with the mind.

I snickered.

"But there is someone here. At least one someone?" Mom asked, though I was sure she knew the answer.

"Yes, beautiful girl, there is at least one mind here. I can't reach it. It's asleep. It's there but not there. I can't place it." He shook his head.

Great! Adrian's about as clear as muddy waters.

I looked over at Tristan and he reached out and grabbed mom by the arm, "You and Adrian go right. Isolde and I will go left. This way we will swing around the outside of the temple complex."

"What if there're traps all over the place to stop invaders like us?" I ventured, looking down at the stones under my feet.

Tristan laughed, "You're worried about that? You got me! I can teleport us out of harm's way, anytime, anywhere." His smug smile made me want to smack it off his face.

Tristan liked his new power a little too much. This new Tristan just didn't sit well with me.

The low rise of the stairs partnered with a deep tread meant that every step we took in the upper direction. It took ten steps to reach the next rise, making it an exhausting slow hike.

The heat morphed the air on the stairs at the top, creating the illusion they were moving.

"Can't we just shift up to the top?" I moaned, pushing the sweat on my brow away from my eyes.

"I don't wine, Issy," mom ordered, pushing a new bead of sweat from her brow leaving her perfect makeup behind. She carried herself as if she owned the Temple we were approaching.

Cleopatra was Greek and Egyptian, modern depictions of her, dressed her as an Egyptian. However, on our trip to Cairo I'd seen her in both Greek and Egyptian. My mother wore that mixed style like she was the Queen herself. I must admit that I envied her self-assurance.

"Do you really need to advertise to everyone who and what you are? What if we're being watched? Adrian doesn't hear any other minds. You don't know what or who is here. What if that is the technology is the reason, he only senses one mind? There are a 1000 and 1 different reasons why using your powers is a bad idea," she glanced around at everyone, "If I were you, I would make sure I have all my mental shields up. We'll walk," she directed the last sentence at me.

That's rich, her telling everyone to make sure their mental shields are up.

Tristan locked eyes with me again.

< She's no fun. > I huffed.

< But she's right and her logic is sound. > he returned.

< How did you go from being an arrogant egomaniac to logical know-it-all in two seconds flat? >

< Because I'm brilliant.> He chuckled.

I wished Tristan would just fuck off. Well, most of the time.

He released my hand and we took the stairs as quickly as we could like children. I was still a child, sort of. I was 18 and half, and according to Themians I was still a toddler. I've had so few chances to be a kid in the last year, I took this one with glee.

Reaching the first level, I expected more statues or other carvings and maybe a few urns. Instead, there were piles of sand everywhere, carried here by the wind and trapped by the rock walls.

From a distance, the giant statues that held up the edifice of the upper Temple complex had looked close to the stairs, but in truth they were far away and more massive than you could possibly fathom. There were pieces lying on the ground, mostly faces and heads. There were also cracks in some of the supporting pillars, as if the area had seen some seismic activity and the natural fissures in the stone broke off with the shifting pressure.

To the left, where parts of the Temple had broken away, there was no longer a guard railing of stone around the palisade. In the opposite direction, the right-hand side seemed safer at a glance, but Tristan grabbed my hand, pulling me along.

Left it is.

"Why did you choose the left-hand side, when the right looked safer?" I asked as he dragged me behind, making my dress flap in the hot air.

"Where is your sense of adventure, Isolde? Where things are broken, we may be able to see inside." He tapped his temple as if his brain power was without bounds.

I snarled the side of my nose at him, "Yes, sure we could see inside. But it can also crumble down from underneath and we could die. So, it doesn't really sound like you chose the better side," I scoffed.

Pulling my hand free, I pushed a fresh bead of sweat out of my face.

"Well, then don't let go of my hand," he said and snatched my hand back, holding on tight. "If something starts to fall, I'll teleport us back to the stairs where we know everything is fine," Tristan clicked his tongue and winked at me.

For a moment I forgot what I was going to say.

Tristan has never done that before. Why did he wink?

I sputtered, "Sorry, I guess that sounds reasonable. I shouldn't be such a nervous Nellie. What do you want me to do?"

"Open your mind! Feel! Where there's people, there are emotions," he replied.

"It's a nice theory, Tristan, but remember Themians don't feel. And we're trying to block off everything about ourselves so the human 'feeling disease' can't infect anyone," I said.

The stones before us were riddled with cracks and fissures, ranging from a hair's breadth to a foot or more.

"I guess, but you never know unless you try."

With all the damage to the temple the crystalline connections may be broken. Even so, my brother is an insufferable know it all.

Opening that part of my mind was like opening an eye to see. Mental abilities are the third eye. Sadly, most humans have no fucking idea, but it is a source you open yourself to. It is as if you are only a grain of salt in an ocean of feelings, intangible emotions wash over you, immersing you in them.

I could only take so much before I have to close it. It was the only way to stop being inundated. If I didn't, I would be overrun.

Centering my mind, I took a deep breath and reached for that place, the one where everything pours in. I slowly opened it and I pictured myself as a Jasmine flower, opening at night.

First, there was nothing but Tristan's hand yanking on me, so I let go.

"Issy, we need to keep going," Tristan said and pulled my arm to reinforce the need.

"No, we need to stay here a minute."

It was there, but the nagging was just out of reach, so deep in the ground I understand how Adrian found it.

His description of layers upon layers were more like a wall. It was as if he was buried alive. The emotion was one of utter terror. It filled me. Suddenly, my body was frozen. I was staring straight ahead, locked in place. My mouth opened for a scream to escape, but it never did.

Fire raced across my face, as the vision cleared my sight. I stared up at Tristan who was screaming at me, "Close it off! Close it, Isolde!" He raged.

I blinked and quickly tried to shut off the section of my mind, but it was as if a hurricane was pouring through. Threatening to rip me away from this world and drown me in another.

I never should've opened it.

Two voices spoke in unison inside me, < Push!>

The three of us pushed it closed and the storm died.

I blinked and found myself standing between Hera and my mother, "What happened?" I demanded, whipping my head around for answers.

Hera placed her hand on my shoulder "You were being dominated."

Hearing her words, my mother paled.

"Whoever's in there is terrified and alone. He wants something," I replied.

"He wants something from you? '*He*' doesn't even know you!" my mother retorted.

Her hackles rose to meet whatever new threat had reached out to greet us.

"It's not so much that he wants something from me. He needs something. He can give us what we want as long as we give him what he needs," I said weakly.

It didn't make any sense to me. I tried to dust my clothes off. My legs itched from the sand caked on them, but instead of clearing them, I patted the back of my head to get the sand out of my hair.

"Thank you, for clearing that up, Isolde," my mother replied and wrapped her arms around me more to reassure herself than me.

I let her do it and I sunk into the warmth and safety the embrace offered.

"Mom, he isn't behind the walls. It's like he's imprisoned or captured or buried." The muscles on my forehead pulled down in frustration, "He's being held hostage somehow."

"Well, there's only one way to figure that out. We just have to go in there and find whoever this person is," Tristan intervened.

"Thank you, Tristan! Brilliant, truly a brilliant plan. Let's just rush right in there and find whoever this terrified, buried person is and figure out what he wants, then give it to him. Fabulous!" Mom retorted, petting my hair back from my face.

Tristan shook his head but didn't reply.

What just happened to me was probably the scariest God damn thing I've ever experienced. It was like being in an emotional black-hole which sucks everything away.

"Well, whatever you're gonna do, let's get it done before the sun goes down. Sydney, you and Hera stay close to me. Tristan, don't leave your sister's side. Vika stick close to Tristan. And Tristan, that was fast thinking, so good job," Adrian said.

Tristan was actually surprised, happy and proud. It was as if Adrian's words really mattered. It was like when dad used to praise him.

Adrian was an interesting bird. He'd always been there but we didn't know it. He was living all our lives with us but not actually being with us.

I felt the love between him and mom. I didn't have to open myself up to feel what he felt for my mother. It was something I'd never experienced before, an all-encompassing emotion. She was his whole world, everything he'd ever wanted and dreamed.

She speaks, he listens, he speaks, she listens. It is like the gravitational pull of two stars.

Sometimes I found myself a bit jealous. The pull of Tristan's hand brought me out of my revelry as we approached the giant statues of the edifice.

The whole scene felt wrong. "Stop!"

My mother and Hera turned to look at me. "What is it? Do you feel something?" mom asked.

"Yes, this is wrong or backward somehow. We're all...the three of us...we should walk in together, while Tristan, Vika and Adrian follow behind us."

"The three of us?"

"Yes, the three of us abreast, holding hands. We need to walk united, together. That's what I saw."

Hera instantly took my hand.

Adrian stepped back, moving his arms as with a slight bow. I stepped in front of him. I had Hera on my left and my mother on my right.

I guess maybe Vika was right. I am the one in the middle.

As soon as we passed under the colonnade, the light inside the temple was lit as if by a flame. For a moment, I was blinded by a piercing blue light.

There, in the middle of the inner sanctum, was a statue of a woman sitting on a golden brazier which was held up by three legs. I wanted to stop and examine the statue. It was the same woman as on several of the pillars outside. She was beautiful. Her eyes were dark and enticing but sad. She carried the world on her shoulders and she hunched with the weight. She stared unseeing down at the brazier into the smoke that rose from it.

The lights led deeper into the temple complex and I needed to follow.

CHAPTER 12

ISOLDE

The entire room was aglow. Nothing about it was dilapidated or forgotten. Twelve veiled women filed out all into the center of the room stopping next to the statues of three women holding hands.

"The Fates has finally arrived," a woman's voice announced.

I was aware that she said a few other words, but for the life of me I didn't hear anything. I had eyes for nothing but the statutes in the center of the room. They resembled the statutes found in the rotunda of the library in Alexandria. However, instead of the heavy veils, their faces were in full view and I couldn't tear my eyes away.

The face of the woman in the center was mine. Even the sandals on my feet were reflected in the crystalline stone before me.

I gulped to wet my mouth, but it did nothing to ease the dryness. I quickly glanced at the other two women. An exact replica of my mother with her double pearled necklace stood to my right, while the statute to my left was of Hera, in her Egyptian dress with her breast exposed for the Universe to see.

It is us! It is the three of us right down to the clasping of our hands.

I released my mother's hand to touch my hair. The style was still dressed for our trip to Abydos.

My heavy black eyeliner trailed off into my temple ending just before my hair. The wrist on the statute also had the heavy scarab beetle bracelet Hera had given me this morning.

"What the hell is going on? Hera?" Mom demanded, hardly able to turn her head to the side.

"Vika had a good reason to be afraid," Hera replied while her hand touched her lips, tracing the outline in both wonder and horror.

The first of the twelve women stepped forward.

"I am ready. I will face the trial," a woman said with trembling lips.

Her soft brown eyes were pinched in the concentration. She took a deep breath and her nostrils flared. She then gazed directly at Hera.

Hera laid one hand on her shoulder and a spark flashed along with a whiff of ozone. Pulling her hand away, she said, "You may pass."

Hera sagged as if a weight was gone. The girl turned and presented herself to me.

"I offer myself for judgment," she stated, staring deeply into my soul.

Or was I the one staring into hers? Against my volition, my arm rose and my hand settled on her shoulder. In just a moment, her life bloomed before my eyes. Every second played like a movie. I saw her kissing her first boy, keeping a secret for a friend, the moment she discovered her vocation and came to the Temple. She had honored her vow and kept her to her oaths, but her time was not yet.

A cloud lifted from my eyes and I was myself again. I removed my hand and lowered my arm.

"Your time has not yet to come. Step back," I stated in a flat voice that I didn't recognize.

She moved back into the shadows. The next member of the group stepped forward and Hera immediately touched her shoulder but there was no spark.

The woman lowered her head, "I've not been found worthy. Forgive me, Fates! I was wrong."

She stepped back, turned away and left the sanctuary without another word. I wanted to turn and speak to her. However, something else had control of my body.

The next woman in line stepped forward. Her catlike green eyes darted to each of us and a small knowing smile pulled at her lips, "May the Fates find me worthy for the long journey ahead," she said.

Hera's hand rested upon her shoulder. There was a small spark and it smelled of sulfur. With that, Hera said, "You may move forward."

The woman immediately presented herself to me and once again, my hand landed upon her shoulder. But instead of the peaceful life of a kind soul like the women before her a vile scene played before my mind's eye. My fingers dug into her shoulder, deep between the bones and muscles to hold her in place.

Evil, scheming, and conniving, lined every moment of her life it was like acid. I wanted to puke.

She was disgusting to the bone. I gritted my teeth as the many scenes played for me. She purposely injured her sister to win a race and poisoned a lover over his mating to another. She kicked her mother's pet to death to get rid of it. The vision of her life played before my eyes and I panted with the weight. It reeked and burned my mind. I couldn't shake it off fast enough.

When the fog fell from my eyes, I heard the words come out of my mouth, and knew they were a death sentence, but I could not stop them, "Your time has come."

She stepped in front of my mother with a broad smile scraped over her devilish face. My mother did not lay a hand on her shoulder. Mom wasn't so benign, she put her hand to the woman's forehead, covering the third eye.

The girl released a blood curdling scream and shook for a moment as blood seeped from her eyes, ears and nose. Before her eyes rolled back into her head, she fell to the ground dead as a doornail.

Bile climbed inside of my throat and the taste burned like the acid of her life in my mouth. My only wish was to bend over and retch. But I couldn't. I was incapable of saying anything or moving from my position.

I barely had time to take in what had happened when another woman was already in front of Hera, "May the Goddesses find me acceptable."

Hera touched her and the spark wasn't there. I was relieved.

It was my turn again. I never wanted to touch another person. I watched how she quietly turned and left the sanctuary. As the next girl approached.

"Klotho, I have lived my whole life for this moment, knowing it would come in my generation. Please, find me worthy!"

Hera laid her hand on her and immediately there was a spark and whiff of ozone. The woman walked toward me and dread filled my belly. Yet, I was frozen in place like the statue I faced, unable to move. Robotically, my hand landed upon her shoulder, and every moment replayed.

She was good and pure. Her life was dedicated to helping others. It was the sweet taste of honey mixed with the nectar from a flower. The words came from my mouth as they filled my mind. "Your time has come."

She moved to stand in front of my mother. I trembled as my mother placed her hand upon the woman's forehead.

Instead of falling down dead, there was an internal battle between the two of them. Their bodies locked in place, shaking with sweat. Drops of sweat were forming under the woman's chin. My mother was frozen like ice, never wavering, never moving, as sweat trailed down her temples.

Finally, the girl closed her eyes and opened them again. They had changed color. They were blue-green like mine.

"You have gained a new level. You may stay," my mother stated.

She bowed her head and took a position next to her friends.

I cringed inside as each woman in turn came to us. Terror ate at me, with each life I lived and watched it die. When it ended, four were laying on the ground and three remained. Only three in total had passed my mother's death touch.

The force holding my body released and I fell to the floor, sobbing. A warm mind encircled me and whispered.

<Those lives weren't yours. You didn't cause their deaths. They made those choices. Let them go.> The warm voice was gone, leaving me alone with my thoughts.

I choked back my sobs to find my mother and brother holding me. Mom kissed my hair while petting it back. Tristan hugged me from behind like he always did. I heaved a sigh to clean the horror from my mind, looking around at the three remaining women who approached us.

"What you seek is this way," the first of the judged stated.

There were no words to describe what I'd just seen. The remaining women dragged the dead bodies away.

Most of the unworthy left the sanctuary but several remained, "We will stay and attend to the temple and the new Oracle. Do not worry over the mess."

There were no tears, only a firm resolve.

Each one of the dead had been willing to murder, steal, and harm in any way necessary to achieve their desires. Each had hoped to become an Oracle, but all failed.

The first girl who had passed our judgment turned to the three of us, "My name is now Pythia. You may call me that since you have found me worthy. My sister Oracles and I, will maintain the sanctuary and bring it back to its former levels, helping Themians find their way back to truth and righteousness, for it is quite clear that all have lost their way."

My mother vigorously nodded her head, "Show us Pythia's burial cave."

"The only entrance is this way. None can open it, even though many have tried. They wish to bring back the river, however the river is gone and will never return." She took us to the very back of the sanctuary through many rooms, past colonnades and pillars.

"This is the room of the prescient. This is where the Oracles provide divination. If you wish. I can divine for you, now that I've passed the Fates. I can see anything you wish to look for."

My mother raised her hand palm out, "I don't want to know my future. It's not predestined and you cannot tell me what it is. Nor do I wish you to read anyone else's. Never tell anyone of their future only point them in the right direction. Divining someone's future pre-determines their life and I don't believe in predetermination."

Pythia replied in shock, "But you are the Fates. Everything you do was predetermined a long time ago. Even your choice of me."

"I don't care. My life is my own! What I choose to do with it will be my choice and not because someone else told me a prophecy," mom snapped.

"Nonetheless, I must prophesy for you. It is the only way for you to move forward," Pythia returned and remained stationary in her stance.

"Mom, obviously she's seen something and she wants us to know what it is," I interjected, hoping that my mother would get over her *I don't believe in fate crap*.

"You go ahead and listen to her drivel. I'll stand here and wait," mom retorted.

I looked at Adrian but he shook his head and stood next to me, then leaned down to whisper in my ear.

"Don't worry, Isolde. Your mother doesn't believe in prophecies or fates but I do," with that he winked at me.

No wonder my mother's in love with him.

Tristan moved to my side. I knew that this was a society of twins and that everyone here was born a twin. But on Earth it was not as common. The pull of my twin constantly being there, it was comforting and annoying at the same time.

The new Pythia stood over a golden disk which was supported on a three-legged tripod, all made of solid orichalcum. One of the Oracle's sisters brought a torch along with some cone-shaped items. They threw the cones into the disk and laid the torch on top of them. Pythia blew on the cones until a trickle of smoke rose from the center of the disk.

The new Oracle leaned over and with both hands waved the smoke into her face. She stared down at the disk and brought the smoke up to her eyes, carrying it down to her mouth and nose over and over again. A cloud of smoke lingered over her form and slowly filled the cavernous space. The sickly-sweet scent rocked my senses and burned my eyes. I breathed through my mouth to kill the scent, but it permeated everything.

Finally, the new Pythia straightened to take us all in. Her eyes were glazed over white. Her irises were gone and she spoke in a strange voice.

"The only path to the peace you seek is with the sacrifice of two gold circles. If you do not pay Charon, you will never find your way. All you know depends on the many steps in your journey. The unforeseen is never an end, only a chance to learn."

"Charon?" Tristan asked.

"Tristan, I really wish you would have paid more attention. Charon, the ferryman, whom you have to pay two gold coins," mom scoffed, shaking her head in disbelief.

"No, mom, she said two gold circles, not coins," I corrected and she flashed me a cocked eyebrow stare.

"Circles, coins, the same thing. Anybody have two gold coins?" Tristan asked the room. Everyone shook their heads.

The new Pythia replied, "We had no need for such things here in the sanctuary."

"Tristan, think! Is there anybody on the ship who would have something like this?" Mom asked, then waved some of the smoke lingering in the room away from her face.

Tristan shook his head raising his shoulders with his hands up, "I don't know. I mean, we could ask," he offered, then took on a faraway stare.

"I could go to the city and see about procuring a few gold coins," Adrian offered.

Mom shook her head. She was simply unwilling to let Adrian out of her site for a moment. On the ship it didn't bother her, but since we hit the planet, she'd become twitchy about all of us.

"We don't have time for that. If it's all fated as the Oracle says and Charon will not give us what we want unless we give him what he asks for, then fate will have to provide us a way," she snickered at her own joke.

Mom was trying to prove fate couldn't be involved, even with everything that happened in the last few minutes.

I was at a loss as to how my mother could still be in doubt. I glanced back at the three statues of Mom, Hera and I. The details down to my windblown hair was too much for me not to believe.

The new Pythia nodded her head in acquiescence and led us back to a narrow alcove. In it was a statue of the original Oracle. She pulled a lever and a stone rose from the back. The mouth of the hole revealed stairs that spiraled down into the planet.

"Well this isn't creepy, familiar or anything," mom drolled.

"You're right, Sydney! It reminds me of the entrance to the catacombs in Spain," Adrian didn't need to speak out loud, he probably did it for our sake.

"You will find much of the architecture on Terra to be similar to the architecture here on Delphi. After all, Poseidon was from Delphi."

My mother froze and so did Hera.

Hera asked, "Poseidon is from Delphi?"

"Yes, of course. I expect he would have mentioned it at some point. After all, he knew the Oracle best."

The usual press of everyone else's mind in the back of mine was light, but turned into a roaring cornucopia with everyone talking at once.

"Just speak out loud. There's no point in everybody saying it inside my head," I moaned.

"No, Poseidon never said he was from Delphi. He was my father's best friend. He never mentioned where he was from or that he had met the Oracle ever," Hera's mouth hung open and her eyes widened.

"Of course he met the Oracle. She was his mother," the new Pythia replied in a matter of fact tone that all Themians used. I would normally be irritated over it, but somehow the information overwhelmed my knee jerk reaction.

"You mean she was his mother? But she died over two million and a half years ago. I thought the Oracles were virgins," my mother scoffed, shaking her head and waving a hand.

"Virginity is not required to be an Oracle only the ability of prescient. The idea of virginity must be a human construct. Oracles were women. Many remained virgins until they mated. Many never mated," the woman remarked.

Vika's face was a mask of concentration as if mentally taking notes.

"If she was his mother, then he would've known about all of her prophecies," I said.

This brought a whole new rabbit hole to run down.

Did he know Earth is where the Fates would be found?

"Of course he would have. He is the best Themian scholar on the Oracle," the new Pythia showed no surprise nor excitement.

"Why would he run around joining projects? He could be here practically living like a God himself. He didn't need to go to Earth for that?" Hera burst and the irritation flooded the room, turning the energy sour. Her question carried a disquiet in her mind.

"We are not privy to every prediction. I know his mother scryed for him just before she died. There are no documents on what she saw. He was her only child that lived. It had nothing to do with this journey," Pythia indicated the opening in the floor, ending the conversation over what Poseidon did or didn't know.

The magnitude of what she was saying about Poseidon living more than 2 million years was enormous. He was the only son of the Oracle and she gave him a private scrying, yet he still went to Earth and watched his human wife and children die. Clearly, she didn't tell him about that.

Perhaps he has no idea that we're the Fates so there's no reason for him to fear us, is there? But he must have seen the sculpture in the main room and there is no mistaking Hera for one of the Fates, is there?

The stairs lead down in a constant swirling and curling that made me dizzy. Between the bluelights and the twisting of the stairs I became disoriented. There were no symbols on the wall so there was no way to know which direction we were facing.

"How deep does this go?" I asked then gripped Tristan's hand tighter.

Other than the eerie blue glow there were no light sources. The blue light did nothing more than hollow out faces and deepen the shadows, creating a deathly effect.

<We look like zombies.> Tristan remarked and I mentally giggled in agreement.

"The path to the underworld is never an easy one. Are you willing to follow it to the end?"

No one spoke this newly minted Oracle was interesting. Her statements gave off the feeling of an otherworldly knowledge. When we arrived, she was a normal – Themian. Facing Hera, Mom and I, changed her. I shuffled through the information I'd seen when I touched her and none of it gave any indication she knew anymore about the underworld than we did.

Did the process of being judged by *'The Fates'* change her? Part of me wanted to test that theory and touch her again but I dreaded the mental roller coaster of memories.

What if facing us had changed her? What then?

The circular turn allowed my mind to wander to places I didn't want to be and a flood of relief came over me when the stairs finally came to an end. We had arrived in some kind of an octagonal cubicle, with several tunnels leading off in different directions.

"Now, you must choose," the woman waved at our choices with no indication of a preference.

"Choose, why? There's like seven different pathways here."

The pressure of the room moved my mind to start working on the problem.

Her voice was warm but indifferent. "All of them may be right, yet only one of them may be right. Perhaps more than one is correct."

She was so helpful. Not!

The tunnel led off the main vestibule like the spokes on a wagon wheel.

Can you make a choice like this with eenie-meenie-miney-mo?

I stepped back so that my back was to the stairwell. The spokes appeared more like the rays of the rising sun.

"Which direction points up on a heptagram?" I asked, letting a picture of the rooms layout set up in my mind.

"You mean a pentagram, right?" Vika asked, running her fingers along the smooth walls in awe over the workmanship.

"No, a heptagram is a seven pointed star. Which way points out?" I asked again.

A smile broke across Tristan's face as it dawned on him.

"I think she's on to something. There's always two points at the bottom, just like feet to stand on," Tristan gave his rushed reply.

"Yeah, so the two at the bottom are feet. That would be the bottom and we don't want to go there. I think we will each have to take our own pathway."

"What are you saying?" mom asked.

There was nothing in the room for mom to mentally lift but the pressure around us changed with her tone of voice. She was scared and there was nothing I could do about it.

I gulped, "I'm saying that Tristan and I are going through the head of the star. I think you and Hera need to choose your own path," I released a huff of air, I didn't even realize I'd held.

"Why are you choosing the head?" Adrian asked in a calm voice to ease the tension then snaked his arm around mom's waist to settle her down.

"Because the top is like the head of a human being. The brain is where all thought and reason happens. That, to me, seems like the most reasonable path. When I judged those girls, I was in their minds…," I shrugged helplessly to explain it any other way.

"Adrian and I are going to the right," mom said, "My right hand was the one I used to touch to their foreheads when I judged them," she bit her lip and tilted her chin up a tad.

She always did that when she'd made a choice of which she wasn't sure of but would stick to.

"I touched everyone on their shoulder with my left hand. I'll go to the left alone." Hera took two steps with her shoulders squared.

"You shall not go alone. I will go with you. No one should travel to the underworld alone," Vika remarked and moved to Hera's side and a small nervous smile passed between them.

I nodded to Tristan and we stepped forward to the entrance of our chosen path. It didn't look any different from the entrance to the cave on the island, only there were no markings.

"Tristan, what does this remind you of?"

I was terrified this wouldn't be like the cave. There it was all for fun. We thought we were safe. I didn't know other worlds existed or that we might be part of them. Now…

"Yeah, I was thinking the same thing. Think it goes downhill?" His lips curled in a half smile.

I knew he was doing it for me. Tristan couldn't hide how he felt. His mind was assessing every avenue.

"Don't know. Are you ready to find out?" I asked.

Yeah, keep it light.

"Never a dull moment with you, sis. Lead on. I got your back."

I glanced back over my shoulder to my mother. She nodded her head. Her lips held a firm line and her eyes pleaded with me to come back to her. However, she turned to Adrian, they clasped hands and walked through their chosen archway.

I grabbed Tristan's hand and we both departed the room.

At least we can go back if I'm wrong.

After a few steps, a grinding sound echoed down the tunnel. I turned around to see a stone lowered in place. We were trapped.

Wrong again! Fuuuuck!

I stole a glance at Tristan, "Well, I hope you made the right choice, sis. It's not like we can go back the other way." He squeezed my hand in reassurance.

"Oh, ye, with little faith. I know I made the right choice."

I hope I did.

My mouth involuntarily bit my lip and I moved my hand across my face to hide it.

Great, it's like a horror movie.

You know the ones where they say '*don't go down that hallway*' but you go and then someone dies. Then they say '*don't go to sleep*' and someone does and dies. It was like watching that movie '*Scream*' where everybody did everything stupid.

"Well, look at it this way, we don't have to worry about anyone dying during sex. We're related," he chuckled.

"Disgusting, Tristan! But somehow relieving, I guess."

I didn't look at him, but I was sure he was laughing.

"Well, unless I run into that hot Oracle chic again," he added.

I shoved him with my elbow "Do you like her?" I asked as we moved down the long hallway.

"She was good-looking and intelligent," he shrugged as if checking out someone who can see the future was an everyday thing.

"Tristan, she is an Oracle. She probably already knows," I snickered.

Joking kept my mind off of everything that had happened.

"All right. The walls are well lit. At least, we won't be stuck in the dark, like in that cave on Atlantis," he murmured, then bumped his shoulder into me.

I rolled my eyes at him, "Didn't Hera call it the Primordial Chamber or something?"

"Yeah, it was Atlantis! It's kind of cool if you think about it. We discovered the lost resting place of Atlantis," Tristan stated.

"Actually, we didn't discover Atlantis at all. It was never lost. If you want to get technical, the only human who ever discovered Atlantis was Ponce de Leon and he's been dead for 500 years," I remarked, shoving him back.

"I guess it really was a human who discovered Atlantis," Tristan said and released my hand to run his through his hair from back to front. When he reached his bangs, he pulled them to stand up straight.

"If we find our way to the underworld, or Elysium, we would be the first hybrids, human or even Themians who have visited the Homeworld in well over 2 million years!" I stated, even though the thought was not a new one. However, it was the first time I'd said it out loud.

"I look forward to it," Tristan barked.

What if there are booby traps?

"Tristan," I ventured then smoothed my chiton to keep my hands busy.

"Yeah, I know. I just thought of it too. I don't think there are any booby traps. The walls are completely smooth and so is the floor. They probably dug these with lasers," Tristan pointed out the obvious.

Although, it did nothing to ease my fears. There had to be a catch. Mom was always looking for one. She always said *'there's no such thing as a free lunch. Everything comes with consequences.'*

"Well then they didn't dig it. They cut it," I retorted.

Tristan liked being right and I liked pointing out the holes in his theories.

"Okay, touché! They would've cut it with lasers. It does look cool," he said and ran his hand over the wall as we moved.

The light dragging sound of flesh over stone filled the empty space where our voices ended.

"Do you hear something?" He asked after a few minutes and cocked his head to the side to listen.

A white background noise took over where the noise from his hand left off. I glanced over at Tristan and both of our minds immediately screamed *'water'*.

It sounded like a lot of water. My eyes whipped down to the floor. A vibration moved through my feet causing the lacings on my sandals to tickle the side of my calf. After living on a boat for ten years, the fear of water wasn't as acute. We'd learned to move past that.

Unless you get caught inside the hull if the boat went down, you didn't have to worry about drowning. Also, we had life vests and a special lifeboat.

On the other hand, this was an underground tunnel and the entrance was closed by a big stone block.

I pushed the anchor weight in my belly to the side and turned around to glance behind us.

"Tristan, can you just start shifting us down the hall?" I asked. The shivering in my belly made my voice tremble.

"Good idea. Give me your hand," he replied.

As soon as I touched him, we shifted. The unmarked walls made it impossible to tell how far we had gone. The pressure from each shift grew in my ears and I was becoming disoriented.

Tristan shifted us again and I stumbled forward. My inner ears quaked in agony. Tristan caught me before I hit the floor and held me to his side.

After twelve hops, I groaned, "Tristan, stop! I can't go another round."

Nausea climbed up my throat and threatened to spill out onto the smooth stone floor.

"You want me to move the air around us with us? It'll keep your ears from hurting," he replied and hugged me.

"You can do that?" I gulped, pushing acid back down my throat. I opened my mouth to pant the taste away.

A boyish grin covered his face. His cheeks curled, then lit up red, making his eyes twinkle, "It's easy. Think about how we take everything with us."

"If it'll save my ears, go for it. And don't ever move me the other way again."

He grabbed my hand and we hopscotched again. This time there was no pressure change.

"If this is how shifters really travel, this is the only way to go. And I would never walk again," I marveled at his ability.

He chuckled and shined in pride.

Cold water creeped up over the edges of my sandals to engulf my feet. The white noise of water pouring into the tunnel had grown. Not long after we were ankle-deep in water.

"Faster, the water's rising," I squeaked.

Everything blurred. We must've gone several miles before we came to another wall. The tunnel ended in a giant stone block. I searched the edges frantic to find a seam or handle of some kind. Tristan began pushing and I joined him but the stone didn't budge.

<MOM!> I mentally shouted.

There was no reply. The only mind I could hear was Tristan's. My eyes darted to his. They were as large as a dinner plate.

"Tristan, can't we just shift to the other side?" I asked while scrunching my eyebrows together.

"No! I need a picture in my mind of where I'm going or we could shift into the bedrock," he moaned and slammed the side of his fist into the rock.

<MOM!> we both yelled at the same time, but other than each other, there was nothing.

Vika said that the material they used blocked abilities. The Oracle wasn't going to make this easy for us. I internally groaned.

I looked at Tristan and he asked, "What do we do?"

"I have an idea," I whispered and quickly glanced around the empty space, searching for anything else.

The cold water was climbing fast and my knees were covered.

"Well you better act fast, whatever it is," Tristan returned, then leaned back against the smooth wall.

I pushed the loose hair out of my face and licked my lips. "Whoever's mind Adrian and I touched, that person is somewhere here. Can you get a picture from them?" I asked and raised my eyebrows, hoping it could work.

"Oh God, Issy. I don't want to go there. Adrian's '*he's there but not there*' information is not enough to penetrate the walls," he retorted and pulled his bangs straight out from his forehead.

"We will be dead if we don't find a way to get the fuck out of this tunnel," I yelled.

The cold water had climbed above to my knees and kept rising. Panic set in when my fingertips skimmed the top of the water.

"I can't reach mom," I moaned and covered my mouth with my damp fingers.

"I know. I can't contact anyone either," Tristan replied and pulled me into a hug.

I'd come into this world with my brother. At least we'd be together when we went out.

I gulped back my regrets and squeezed my eyes closed.

CHAPTER 13

ISOLDE

The water wasn't the only thing rising in the room. Panic grew inside my chest like a balloon with too much hydrogen, flammable and ready to burst.

"We could go back to the sanctuary? You could transport us there, couldn't you?" I asked desperate for it to be true.

"Yeah, I could shift us there, but what about Elysium?" Tristan asked and loosened his hug so I could look up at him.

"We need to live, Tristan. I don't want to die in this tunnel, surrounded by water," I yelled.

"Let's wait until the water has filled the room. If we haven't figured a way out by then, I'll shift us to the sanctuary. Okay?" he asked and stepped away from me to run his hands along the wall where the tunnel ended again.

"No," I returned, running my wet hands over my hair and down my face.

Tristan grabbed my hand and stopped moving. I waited for the cold of the shift to envelope me. It never came.

"I can't!" Tristan said and released my hand.

"What do you mean you can't?" I demanded.

"I can't. God!" He smashed his fist into the hard-stone wall. "Remember what Vika said? Pythos was built with an older style of crystalline tech. That means no shifting. In or out," he shouted and his Adam's apple worked up and down as he scrunched his eyes closed.

"We have to figure it out," I mumbled.

I went back to frantically searching the walls. I glanced down at the water and over to Tristan.

<It's okay. I know we can figure this out.> Tristan tried to reassure me.

"What did we do at the cave?" Tristan muttered. He rubbed his hands up and down his arms to keep the cold at bay.

"We went in the water, swam and apparently made ourselves immortals," I remarked.

The simple thought of swimming sent a shiver up my spine. The water in here was freezing and my feet were numb.

"No, before that. At the entrance of the cave. You threw water on the wall remember?" he barked through chattering teeth.

"Yes, I sprayed some water on the wall and shapes appeared." My eyes went wide with the realization. "Letters appeared!" I remarked and immediately started splashing water on the wall with my hands.

Tristan joined in but didn't bother with his hand. He kicked water up on the wall. Indented shapes began to form.

"The wall has a coating on it. Some parts of it are disintegrating," I pointed out excitedly.

"Yeah, stop talking about it. Kick more water up on the Goddamn wall, Issy!" Tristan shouted over the roar.

The water level in the room was already half way up my thighs. I took the wrap Hera had given me for my shoulders and started using it to scrub the stone.

Something was forming. Tristan took the belt of his tunic off to use the handle as a scraper to remove the gypsum like film.

"They put some kind of a plaster over the top. It's water-soluble, I guess," Tristan said.

I was furiously scrubbing and praying we'd get it done in time. The water was rising rapidly. Several shapes began to take form, none of which I recognized.

"Tristan, do you have any idea what those are?" I cried frantically to uncover more.

"I can't tell if it's Greek or astral symbols," he replied while kicking and scrapping.

One was a circle with the dot in the center, another looked like the sign for Taurus. Another one looked like an Egyptian cartouche. There was a fourth that simply looked like a mess of little triangles indented into the wall. I stared at them for a few minutes and it dawned on me.

"Tristan, these are symbols of different languages," I stopped scrubbing and ran my hand across the indentations.

"Do we have to pick one? We can't read any of those languages," he scoffed.

"I can't read Egyptian or Sumerian, Mesopotamian, Greek or ancient Greek. But the circle with the dot I get."

"What about it?" he barked and kept scraping.

"That's the astrological symbol for the sun. Our sun!" I retorted.

I always read my horoscope. Tristan made fun of me for it. Apparently, by staring at the line of astrology symbols, I hadn't wasted my time after all.

"Pythia could have picked any language. She wouldn't have any idea what language we would choose. Sumerians, Egyptian or Greek. So what?" He yelled, then stopped slashing and slammed his fist into the stone over the top of one of the letters.

"Haven't you been listening, Tristan? None of those are from Earth. They're all Themian. We have to choose this symbol. That's actually a living breathing language that's used on planet Earth now," I took a breath and for the first time since we shifted down here it was an easy one. "You speak four languages. I speak three. But the astrological symbol for the sun didn't exist when Pythia had this made."

"I know for fact we can't read the rest. I guess the simplest answer is always the right one. Push it!" he grabbed my hand and raised it to the circle with a dot in the center.

"I got us into this mess," I murmured.

I extended my finger and turned my head away, scrunching my eyes shut.

"Damn right. If I die, it's your fault. At least we will still be together," with that he shoved my finger into the symbol.

The outer edges gave way and it receded into the wall. My finger extended far into the recess. The cold water had reached my chest and I shivered along with Tristan. His teeth chattering in my ear.

A deep rumbling, followed by a grinding noise, filled what was left of the air in the tunnel. The water churned around us.

"I think something is happening," Tristan muttered, lifting me up to keep my head above the water.

I breathed out a cloud of moist warm air as did Tristan.

"I love you," I stated and gulped back the lump in my throat.

My teeth tapped out their own message of fear.

"I love you too, sis," he wrapped his arms around me.

My feet left the floor as we floated up with the rising water. "What about mom?" I whispered.

Tristan sniffed, "She will tear this place down looking for us."

I smiled at him. Mom would level a mountain.

The water around us danced with vibration then began receding. The symbol covered stone slowly pulled up into the ceiling disappearing from site. Water rushed out with the new opening and we flowed out with it. We both landed in a puddled pile coughing.

The air tasted stale. Tristan put both hands on either side of my face and kissed my forehead.

"I'm not sure anymore who's the smart one. If it was up to me, I might've chosen an Egyptian one. Then we'd be dead." He rolled over and laid back on the wet stone.

"We're twins. You're half of me and I'm half of you. We need each other."

I threw my head back and laughed, taking a moment to enjoy the stale warm air. I laid back on the stone and shut my eyes.

"Don't say anything. I want to enjoy this moment," Tristan remarked.

"Then stop talking," I retorted with a giggle and a sigh of relief.

CHAPTER 14

ISOLDE

The room wasn't as well-lit as the hallway had been. The blue light reflected off the water and made it seem brighter. The floor was damp and sloped downward. I sat up just in time to watch the last of the water trickle away.

I glanced over at Tristan, "You are right. It is a test."

"Yeah. Unfortunately, being right isn't always what I want. In this instance, I would have been just as happy to be wrong," he muttered and pushed up from the damp floor to glance around at the space we found ourselves in. He squinted at me as if staring into a bright light and a half smile quirked the side of his face.

"Good job, sis!"

I pointed my toes and smiled back at him, "Thank you."

The cave wasn't cold and we wouldn't have frozen to death, if we weren't already wet.

My eyes adjusted to the dim light. The outline of two other cave entrances formed out of the gloom. All three lined the same wall.

I slowly took to my feet and grabbed a corner of my dress to ring it out. Water dripped from every edge of it as it did from my hair. I squeezed out as much as I could, but it continued to form drops and run down my back, causing an itching sensation. The shawl was discolored and looking worse for the wear but I snatched it from the floor and twisted it as tight as I could to get rid of every last drop of water.

"Can you hear them or contact mom?" I asked Tristan.

I was hopeful. We almost didn't make it through this 'test'. I didn't want to face another without mom and Adrian.

"No. It's a whole lot of nothing out there," he murmured and took his tunic off to stand in his undies and ring the water from the fabric, before slipping it back on.

"Does it make it any warmer?" I asked with a shiver, wishing I could shuck this dress and do the same thing.

"If you want to ring your dress out just tell me to turn around, Issy. Don't stand there worrying over it," he said and turned away to stare at the wall with the three arched doorways.

I quickly pulled the dress over my head, working as fast as I could to get rid of the water. I wiggled back into my chiton. It still leached the warmth from my body, but grew warm in the places that clung to me the most. At least the dripping was gone.

My creature comforts were the least of our problems and I moved to join Tristan who was staring at the wall.

There was no apparent mechanism to move the stones that were blocking the other arches. I moved to one and Tristan to another. Other than the obvious arches cut into the stone and the slab behind it, there were no symbols or devices of any kind. The tunnel on the other side we'd come through was much the same.

"Anything over there?" I called out.

"No, there's nothing and there's no water left. Is your shawl still wet enough to rub the wall down?"

He searched the floor for a few minutes before he found his belt and began using the buckle to scrap the stone slab in front of him. I picked my damp shawl off the ground and began rubbing the stone wall in front of me. I didn't want to go back in our tunnel for beer or money.

"It looks like we have to push on ahead," I remarked.

Odyssey is relying on us.

"Why seven tunnels if there were only three that worked? What if one of you guys took the wrong one?" He asked while scraping one of the stone doors.

"I don't think the right people would take the wrong path," I didn't want to say it was fate, but well, maybe it was.

"You are certainly more optimistic than I am. She could have just had the three. Why add the other four? Where do they go?"

Tristan had something there. "Well, whatever it is, I'm sure mom will figure hers out. Hera is brilliant and she's lived this long. If the answer for their tunnel is anything like ours, only someone who had lived on Earth could figure it out," I remarked as the truth hit me.

We are the only ones who could have figured it out. We are the only ones who've lived on Earth.

"Yeah! Betcha it will really chap mom's hide when she realizes hers was just for her. She hates that predetermination crap," Tristan snickered and stopped scrapping.

"It will hit her hard."

He turned away from the stone monolith and ran his fingers through his hair from his neck to his eyebrows and pulled on his bangs. It always made them stick straight out of his head.

He raised a hand and indicated he should move and headed deeper into the cavern. The walls fanned out away from us. The further we got from the outer walls, the dimmer the light was. It was difficult to make out the sides and I glanced behind to assure myself we were heading in a straight line.

"Hey, Tristan, want to hopscotch?" I inquired, hopeful to save my feet.

"What?" he asked, keeping his eyes pointed into the gloom before us.

"You know, shift us further along," I pointed into the darkness that was creeping up on us.

"No, for some reason in here, I don't think we should," he replied and shivered.

His voice echoed and the reverberation of sound was new.

We kept walking. The slapping sound of our sandals filled the enormous space.

"Is it just me or is it getting darker?" I asked and shivered.

My dress was still damp and cool, but not enough to raise the hair on my arms. Yet, I shivered and I couldn't explain why.

"It could be the gloom and we're getting used to it. I think it's getting darker."

Tristan reached for my hand. The light had reached the point it was necessary for me to hold on.

"Trust the Oracle to make us jump through hoops?" I remarked.

Tristan jumped in the air, pulling my arm up with him. I giggled to throw off the tightness in my belly.

"Well so far she is making us walk a lot, maybe she just wants to make sure we are not fat and lazy," he laughed.

In the dark, I could just make out the curve of his cheek when he smiled. The lack of light closed in on and me like the dark of space. I've never been afraid of the dark. The dark was just the same without light. But that was on Earth, where I knew about the plants and animals.

I couldn't keep the visions of mythological creatures from playing through my mind. The movie 'Clash of the Titans' with the giant scorpions or Medusa ran around in my imagination, filling the dark spaces. Before I could stop myself, I shivered. Tristan squeezed my hand in support, yet I couldn't shake the growing fear burning in my belly.

"Where do you suppose this cavern goes anyway?" Tristan asked the obvious.

He was filling space, to push back the darkness and keep us both cool. Unfortunately, it wasn't working for me.

"I don't know. It's as big as the Dallas Cowboys football stadium. Wasn't that the largest stadium in the world?" I replied.

My free hand fidgeted with my dress and the shawl I had wrapped around my shoulders.

"No, it was the stadium they built in Sydney, Australia for the Olympics," Tristan said and squeezed my hand.

We both fell silent talking about football stadiums and the Olympics. It hit me again.

We are never going back there. We aren't allowed to go back. From here on out, everything will be strange, unusual and different.

A lump formed in my throat as tears pricked my eyes.

I'll never see a ballgame again or watch basketball.

We didn't really watch it to begin with, but now I would never have the chance. It would always be one of those things I didn't do. "Is there anything about Earth you really miss?" I asked.

"Yeah, I miss real beef. You know, all that synthetic meat protein crap they serve on the ship's is not the same. Also, artichokes," he replied and swung our connected hands in the air.

"Artichokes are you kidding me? Artichokes?? Ugh! I don't miss them at all," I retorted and stuck my tongue out.

Even though it was dark, I couldn't stop myself.

"It's not like it really chokes you. It just stabs you while you're preparing it," he laughed and poked me with his index finger in the side.

"I don't like food that attacks me," I scoffed and lifted my chin, even though he couldn't see it.

We both snickered. Dad always made us cut all the thorns off the artichokes. They stabbed me every now and again.

I'll never eat them again.

Dad was the only one who could get me to. I missed dad. I guess I would always miss him.

A dull aching formed in my chest. I wonder if this was how mom felt for all those years when she thought that Adrian was dead. I wonder if she swapped that ache from Adrian to dad?

"It's official. I think we're in the dark. I can't see anything anymore," Tristan announced.

Something told me he was listening to my thoughts and this was a ploy to end the morose musings.

"I wish we could grab something that would make light," I released his hand and stood still.

"Okay. Be quiet for a minute and I'll see if I can shift something in here"

I waited patiently. Tristan issued a huffing noise. I laid my hands on his shoulders and a painful shaking began. The muscles in his shoulders bulged and grew hard with tension. Finally, he released it and his whole body was damp with sweat.

"I can't. Something is blocking me. Must be the building," he heaved to catch his breath.

"So, you could shift within the tunnel but you can't shift anything from outside. Vika said —" I began, but Tristan cut me off.

"Yeah, I just figured, if I was here I might have been able to move something and she just said that, we can't shift and…Well, I'm an idiot and should pay more attention."

"It was worth a try. I mean not all of her information is correct. It could have only been in the temple and not down here. I don't think anyone has been down here."

Tristan was right. No ability would help us. We would have to find our own way through this underground labyrinth.

We had to be walking towards something. So, I closed my eyes and opened the part of my mind that allowed me to contact other people's emotions.

I couldn't feel mom, Adrian, Hera or Vika. Tristan's anxiety mixed everything up for me. In the midst of that was a little thread of emotion. It was like a string that was tied back to the owner.

The string of emotions was defined and different. I was able to separate them out, leaving Tristan and someone else.

Opening my eyes, I grabbed Tristan's hand and moved forward, pulling him along with me.

"Are you gonna let me in on where we're going?" He asked and his voice cut the thick darkness.

"No. I mean, I don't know. We're following an emotion," I replied.

Tristan didn't say much after that.

Like a spider seeking the prey trapped on my web, I followed the strand, looking for the wiggling fly. The closer we got, the stronger his emotions became and more I had to close it off, filter it, condense it. *He* was bursting with a whirlwind of feelings, all desperate for freedom.

"Maybe we've been going about this the wrong way," Tristan ventured, "Almost all Themians have control of the forces. I have never tried to control the forces. Have you?"

"No, I can't. I know this about myself," I replied.

He was making conversation and I was trying to concentrate.

"We both know mom can move earth and water. I have seen her use wind, but I've never seen her pull fire. Maybe we should try and make fire," he continued, muttering to keep it from echoing around the space.

"How do you suppose you'd even use fire? Wouldn't you have to know you could first? Why wouldn't you be able to use water like mom?" I asked just to get him to think about it and shut up for a few minutes.

"I don't know, Issy," he scoffed under his breath.

"I want to keep following this emotion. I'll keep using my ability since we can't use yours while you try to conjure fire," I muttered, keeping my feet lifting and lowering at an even pace.

God, I hope I don't trip on anything.

"Why can't I put my hand out and snap my fingers and make fire appear?" he asked.

"What, like some of the superheroes?" I giggled.

My hand covered my mouth to stifle the laugh lodged there. I shouldn't have laughed at my brother.

It could work!

Then, I snickered out loud.

"I guess so."

The sound of Tristan snapping his fingers over and over again became obnoxious and comical at the same time. He reminded me of the kid in Mary Poppins who couldn't snap to clean up.

The sound of fingers snapping echoed. The mirth I felt only a second ago vanished, only to be replaced by dismay. I pulled my lip away from my teeth to keep from biting it.

What if there was something out there in the dark? What if it heard us?

The darkness plays tricks on the mind. It's a form of sensory deprivation. The mind will fill the emptiness with whatever it can dream up and my dreams were not always my own.

The nightmares of 14 other people rolled around in my head. The anxiety and terrors they lived with, I had to endure now. Each had their own fear of the night.

I mentally clung to the strand of emotion we followed, as if it was a lifeline to sanity which was pushing my trepidation into a mental box and closing the lid.

"I don't think the snapping is working. Maybe I should try something else," Tristan murmured.

"Maybe you just have to think about what creates fire like. Friction?" I replied, trying to keep my mind on anything but the scenes playing behind my eyes.

"Issy, that's a good idea. I mean snapping my fingers will create friction. But I don't understand exactly how that works with Themian forces. Maybe I need more friction? Can we stop walking for just a minute," he asked.

My arm pulled at his, so I ceased all forward momentum.

He released my hand and the sound of two pieces of flesh slapping together over and over again filled the air. However, nothing came of it and after a few minutes the sound changed.

The sound of skin rubbing against skin replaced the slapping noises which were followed by a glow. It was low, almost imperceptible, but it was there.

"Tristan, I think you're doing it. I can see a difference!" I breathed with excitement.

"Yeah, me too. It's not a flame but it's something," he laughed, as the rubbing sound increased.

"Slap your hands together again. Maybe you just haven't reached the point of ignition," I replied and grabbed his arm in my excitement, changing the rhythm.

A large smack and some brisk rubbing. Tristan pulled his hands apart to slap them again and a gorgeous ball of fire exploded to life between his hands. The flame illuminated our faces and Tristan glanced at me with a wicked smile before turning back to his flames.

"You're a magician," I whispered in awe.

"Eat your heart out, Marvel! I have created fire," Tristan yelled.

We both burst into laughter. I pounded my fist into his arm with excitement. The heat from the flames warmed me. I basked in its warmth, enjoying the way it pushed back the seeping cold of my damp clothes.

"What do you think actually ignited it?" I asked.

Hopefully I can use the information to find my own control of the forces.

"I thought my hand was suddenly on fire. It was like I created enough friction for the world. I don't know! I'm not even sure I can do it again," he remarked, then turned his right-hand palm up.

The fire ball floated above his hand, resembling a fiery orb. His other hand touched me and the heat radiating from his palm instantly dried my dress everywhere he touched.

"Now, you're a human clothes dryer," I snickered.

"No, now I am a Demi-God!" he replied in his deepest radio voice mimicking Hercules.

I elbowed him. I didn't want to think about Hercules and all the Demi-god nonsense. Tristan quickly moved his hand over his clothes and my own, drying them out along with my hair.

I smiled my '*thank you*' at him and he shoved me back and remarked in his best Aussie accent, "Because that's what Heroes do."

I rolled my eyes and the fire flickered.

"Don't let it go out!" I squeaked since my fear of the dark and the night terrors were still lingering in the background.

My eyes flicked around the cavern. The walls had closed in on us as we were walking. It was a much smaller space now. It was more like a large ballroom. The light caused the walls to twinkle, reflecting the crystalline technology embedded in them.

"Move your fire over by the wall," I instructed him.

We stepped closer. There was a delineating mark that edged an entire section. It was like a tile saw had cut out at that exact spot. It appeared on both walls in the same place. Other than that, they resembled rock, without any other defining characteristics. The crystalline starlight features sparkled and our motion gave the illusion of outside movement.

We examined the seam line in the wall, but it appeared to be nothing more than the changing of a tool bit.

Perhaps the laser needs a new battery?

The fire went out and I squealed. Tristan snapped his fingers and the flame burst to life again, illuminating his face and the wicked grin housed there. I punched him in the arm.

"You know, for someone super smart, who can move through space and time, you're a big dork," I shoved him again for good measure.

"Yes, but I've created fire and now have brought you light so you will pay me my props and give me my respect!" he chuckled at my discomfort.

"Let's just keep walking firefly," I responded with a slight smile playing over my lips. "Just because you have the ability to make fire, it doesn't mean that if you pissed me off, you can light me on fire. I'm one of the Fates! We still have to figure out what the hell is down here or how to get out."

"I think that this is some kind of trial and error where they try to fuck with us every step of the way," Tristan quipped and bounced the fire ball from one hand to the other.

"Yes, it probably is," I mused.

Staring at fire makes splotched appear in your sight and I didn't want to be blind-sided just because the power of fire fascinated me. I blinked to clear my sight and took Tristan's free hand. Fire or no fire, my brother was my best defense against anything.

A large object took shape in the distance. It made me catch my breath.

What if it moved?

Tristan squeezed my hand and we slowed our pace, as he dimmed the fire in his hand.

CHAPTER 15

SYDNEY

Part of me was still in shock to see Adrian alive, looking not much different than last time I saw him. My mind still reeled from the changes caused by going into a pool of water and coming out 30 years younger and half alien. I was more Themian than human now, but then again, maybe I always was.

Hera said I was the culmination of thousands of years of genetic breeding and so was Adrian. I had a feeling that I was really the one they were talking about, but what was she really aiming for?

Would Adrian have mated with anyone else if I didn't exist?

I never believed in Gods and Goddesses. Now, the more I was seeing, the less I believed. I just wondered sometimes, if there wasn't something out there, picking and choosing for us.

However, my mating happened to Adrian. He was exactly who I needed, where I needed him to be at the time I needed him the most.

That begs the question. If he hadn't disappeared in the tsunami, where would we be now?

I didn't know if we would've gone to the island. I didn't know if I would have bothered to look.

The blue of the lights always turned my thoughts inward, making me contemplate my choices. The grip from Adrian's hand tightened, bringing an emotional wave of fear with it. A rush of water covered my feet, bringing a leaching cold that only water is capable of.

Looking down the tunnel, I searched for the end. I was looking for a way out, a T, anything. Adrian didn't bother to ask what I wanted to do. His fear drove him to run, dragging me behind him.

"Adrian, you won't drown. I won't let you," I yelled to dig through the fear and reach his mind.

But all I could see was the giant wall of water that consumed him a moment before his leg was broken. His visions from the tsunami filled his world and invaded mine.

Minutes raced by and my heart raced with them. Adrian's feelings had taken over and I could barely sort between reality and memory.

The pounding in my chest reached a crescendo as the raging screams from Adrian's past rang in my head and my throat. My own memories of the past overlaid with his. I was reliving both sides at once.

I gulped back the bile rising in my throat as the sound of his leg snapping filled my mind. The phantom pain was a punch to my stomach and I stumbled into a wall, only to be dragged further down the tunnel.

I panted, "Adrian, stop, stop!" But the visions kept coming. "It's over! You aren't going to die in this cave," I screamed, yet he couldn't hear me. His terror was all he could see.

The arch of the tunnel formed out of the blurry sea of blue. It was blocked.

Standing at the end of the tunnel, I saw how the panic rising in Adrian's eyes was matching the rising water around us. Adrian never stopped. He began beating his hands against the stone, shouting out my name.

I grabbed his hands, but he was too strong and pulled from my grasp.

"When was the last time you were surrounded by this much water?" I asked, swallowing my own fears.

I couldn't fight him and win with the emotional connection, but I didn't want to cut him off either.

I quivered with agony and shivered from the water leaching my body heat. My teeth found my lip and I bit it. I did it for no other reason than because the pain was my own and not his.

I glanced down at the water. It was up to my thighs and Adrian was thrashing in it, kicking to keep it at bay.

Entering the house in my mind, I closed the door between us, shutting Adrian's terrors off. I sucked in fresh air for a moment and revealed in the freedom from those memories.

The leather harness he had strapped to his chest was the only thing I could get a grip on. With one hand I held on to a leather strip and the other I slapped Adrian across the face.

"Who am I?" I screamed.

Huffing through the exertion of running and screaming for so long, I shook my hand to lighten the sting.

He didn't respond. I raised my hand and crashed it again into the side of his face.

"When was the last time you were in this much water?" I shouted.

I bit my lip. His head was whipping around, searching for God knows what. He didn't see me or hear my questions.

I raised my hand again.

"The tsunami," he yelled, running his hands along the walls, searching for a way out.

I released the leather strap and pulled him to me. "Calm down! We just need to figure out how to get out of this tunnel," I said.

Using my mind, I pushed the water back, creating a bubble of dry space around Adrian and I.

We won't drown here, but we might suffocate.

Adrian's ragged breathing slowed and the terror that had engulfed him receded just like the water I'd push out of the way. He held onto me and a whimper escaped.

"I was back there," he whispered with a raw throat.

"I know, baby, but we aren't there now." I pushed his hair out of his eyes, "I need you here. The kids need you here. The past is over. We can't change it and there's no reason to relive it," I smiled tentatively at him and he returned it with a wane smile of his own.

"We need to get out of here," I stated and indicated the stone wall in front of us.

There were a few bloody splotches. I ran my hands down Adrian's face to his arms and his hands. Both knuckles were scraped. The wounds were superficial and the blood was already clotting. I kissed each one.

"It's nice to know you would tear down stone to get what you want," I joshed him.

He heaved a shuddering sigh, "Yeah, I didn't think it was stone. I thought it was water."

He pulled me to him, laying a quick hot kiss on my lips. I opened my mouth to allow it to deepen. It filled him with a feeling of safety and I could never turn that away. He pulled back and held my face in his hands, to assure himself I was real.

"Well it is definitely not water, and without a laser drill, we are stuck here." I didn't want to mention the word 'death'.

"Why don't I just ask you how to find the answer?" Adrian remarked, then sniffed and took a deep breath to cover the hard edge of a cry.

"Yes!"

It was too easy. But Adrian asked and the vision filled my mind. Immediately, symbols covered the stone, so I began scrubbing. Finding the answer wasn't the way out and I worked my frustration out on the rock.

I only know what I'm asked. Yet information is power.

Adrian scrubbed alongside me in silence, using the edge of his tunic. Slowly but surely, we uncovered the line of symbols I'd seen in my vision.

They were all a little different. Some were astrological, mythological, others looked like alchemy symbols. None of them equaled anything as a way to get us out of here. It was nothing more than gibberish.

"This one here looks Greek," I remarked and continued scrubbing.

"Yes, and this one looks Egyptian. That's a feather which is a sign for Thoth. And this looks Sumerian." Adrian's attention was erratic, jumping from one section of writing to another.

The desperation in his voice broke my heart. Adrian never complained and he never once let on how harrowing the tsunami had been.

"This circle with a dot in it reminds me of the astrological symbol for the sun sometimes used in Wicca," I trailed my finger down along the wall, searching for a defining factor, something that could give me a clue to opening the door.

"Or it's Greek. Isn't Theta an O with a dot in it?" he asked.

"No. Theta has a horizontal line, not a dot," I replied and kept scrubbing.

"Egyptian and Greek are all based on Themian culture. But Sumerian, why is that here?" Adrian placed both hands on the wall on either side of the writing as if contact was all it took to decipher this riddle.

I noticed the little push he gave the wall.

I remembered the statues we saw in front of the Temple. One was similar to the Sumerian style, Mesopotamian maybe.

"They are all Themian," I replied.

It was the only conclusion that made sense. I tilted my head to the side, hoping that changing my perspective might give me an answer.

Alchemy was the study of transmutation. It was all about turning iron to gold. But why were alchemy symbols on this wall? Or the Wicca one for that matter?

"What do we do now?" Adrian asked and glanced at me. His question carried a double meaning.

The answer came but didn't make any sense. The vision showed me pressing a triton. It was the symbol for Neptune. I shook my head.

Romans changed the name. It is actually the symbol for Poseidon.

That didn't make any sense at all. On this wall of languages, why would a triton be the answer? I've never met Poseidon. It would make more sense if Hera had pressed it.

"Sydney, stop pondering the answer and push it!"

Fear had clawed its way into Adrian's voice. I shivered with the leaching cold of the water. I'd forgotten to hold it back and it was quickly rising again. From my waist down, the cold water clawed at me.

I glanced at Adrian and without hesitation I pushed the Triton. The reason why would have to wait for another time.

CHAPTER 16

SYDNEY

Whatever mechanism was operating the stone door, slowly worked, raising the stone and releasing the water, removing our chance of a watery death.

Adrian moved in front of me and braced himself in a fighting stance with a dagger in one hand. His other hand was open as if ready to grab on to something.

"What do you think is beyond the door?" I asked, watching the monolithic rock disappear into the wall as my insides quivered.

"I don't know. Whatever is trying to drown us on this side, is probably trying to kill us on the other side too," he remarked then rubbed his free hand on his tunic, looking for a dry spot.

His eyes softened for a split second, before he turned back to whatever was on the other side. The higher the stone got, the faster the water flowed. Eventually, the water was gone, leaving the ground slick leading out into a large cavern.

There were the same blue glowing lights in the next cavern. Off in the distance, something moved, but from where we were standing, it didn't appear to be very large.

Then again, looks can be deceiving.

I gulped back the fear that climbed my throat. I couldn't see exactly what 'it' was. However, its movements were as smooth as the tunnel walls.

<Check the walls. See if there's any way to open the other tunnels.>

<What the hell is that thing?> I asked, reluctant to look away from this new threat.

<I don't know, but we don't want to attract *its* attention before we're ready.> Adrian responded, cross-stepping between me and the new threat.

I slowly turned my back on the 'thing' and began searching the cavern wall behind me. There were two other entrances from ours. The ground in front of the third was wet as if someone had already passed through. The other was dry. And both were closed.

A moment later, the sound of stone grinding on stone broke the silence.

"Adrian, a tunnel is opening," I whispered.

Why in the fuck didn't I bring a gun?

I squared my shoulders and stood as tall as I could.

<I can't turn my back on whatever that *'thing'* is. Put your back to mine, whatever comes out of that tunnel better be very friendly. Do whatever you can to destroy it until we can swap places.> Adrian replied.

I tried to draw the wind to me, but instead of a howl all that came to me was dead calm. I bit my lip and gulped, then closed my eyes for a split second. The stone inched up enough for me to see underneath it, all I saw were two sandaled feet and the hem of dresses. I heaved a deep sigh.

It was Hera and Vika. "Where are the children?" Hera demanded as if they were her children and not mine then ducked under the stone as soon as she could fit.

"I think they already passed through here. They are not our biggest worry at this moment in time," I replied and quickly turned to face the '*thing*' off in the distance, pushing the thought that the kids might have already met the '*thing*' away.

"I think you have a problem," Vika remarked in her typical unemotional tone.

I rubbed my temples and glared over at her.

Why can't she act like she is part of this team?

"Thank you, Vika. That's putting it lightly. Why is it that we have a problem? Why don't you have a problem too?" I retorted.

Adrian had another dagger tucked in his belt. Part of me wanted to grab it and hold on, but unfortunately, I didn't know how to use a knife for anything but cooking.

Note to self: learn to fucking defend yourself.

"I only came along as an observer. I cannot defend you," Vika remarked.

I rolled my eyes at her.

How in the fuck is that going to work if it kills you?

"Great! Then, maybe we should use you as cannon fodder," I retorted.

Adrian shushed me, and I gulped back my next snide remark.

"If my death will further your cause, I would be happy to lay down my life in your stead," Vika hovered behind everyone.

She wasn't cowering, but the word coward played on my lips.

'I would gladly lay down my life for you.' People say shit like that, yet no one ever means it. However, she said it with a certainty that made me believe this creature could be beaten without violence.

I wish she was more forthcoming in her ideas.

<I agree if she has some ideas on killing this thing, she should definitely speak out or I will sacrifice her too. > Hera informed me.

I was taken aback by her blood thirstiness every time it cropped up.

"Vika, you seem to know what we're up against. What do we do to kill it? Is there a trick we can use to get around it?" I asked.

Before Vika could answer, the creature emerged from the gloom and all thought froze with the realization of what 'it' was.

The main body resembled a komodo dragon in shape, but the size was to the hundredth power. It had nine heads and each one hissed and flicked its tongue. The heads whipped around to taste the air and inspect its surroundings. Unlike most reptiles, its eyes were forward facing and it turned its head more like a human than an animal.

Its gray skin gleamed with an iridescent shine. I'd never seen a snake with skin like that.

"It's a hydra," Vika pointed out. "You are searching for the entrance of the underworld. Naturally, it's defended by many guardians," she kept hovering in the background.

As if that will save her.

"Well, that's just fucking great! The entrance to the underworld is defended by guardians? How many fucking monsters aka guardians are there?" I demanded, hissing it through my teeth.

"At least eight that I know of. That doesn't mean you'll encounter all of them. This one might actually be the only one you encounter. They wander the rivers and entrances of the underworld, seeking food and amusements."

"Amusements? What are they looking for? A comedian for a stand-up show, a board game to play, or is it dinner theater? We make a sad attempt to kill them and then they eat us!"

The fear for the kids raged to the forefront. I frantically searched the ground and walls afraid I'd find blood. My nostrils flared as tears pricked my eyes. The pressure around me changed.

If there was anything in this cave it would be flying by now.

"In the case of the hydra, I highly doubt she's looking to find companionship or to play a game. Her preferred method of amusement is fighting," Vika replied with her hands gripping her elbows.

"So, how do you recommend we get by her if her preferred method of amusement is fighting." Adrian asked to cover for me since I couldn't voice another question, without losing it.

"I'm afraid that the only way to get by a hydra is to kill her," Hera said, re-wrapping her shawl over her shoulders and binding her breast.

I used to like Vika before. Now, not so much. Captain Obvious offered nothing in the way of help.

"Adrian, are you able to kill this thing?" I asked in a low voice.

The fear of loss was clawing at me.

Where are the kids?

I opened my mind to reach out to them, but there was nothing there.

"It would have been nice to have Hercules right now," Adrian stated and pulled the dagger from his belt.

"Hercules never killed a hydra. The story of killing a hydra was about Arilon. My son retold it with himself as the fighter," Hera said and twisted her fingers together in shame.

"What? We should go drag his ass down here so he can do it for real. Who runs around telling stories about themselves and taking credit for someone else's battles? Honestly! Hercules is supposed to be a big bad Demigod! Now, you're telling me that he was just a liar??" I almost screamed, through gritted teeth.

"He did do some of the feats in the stories from Earth, though not for the reasons earthlings assume. Although, he didn't kill the hydra. The hydra was killed by one of the Oracle's followers, here on Delphi," Hera stated and looked away.

She has always known he lied and said nothing.

I rubbed my fingers into my temples. Separating fact from fiction was tough enough in the real world, let alone the mythical one. My terror over the kids only grew.

Adrian replied, "This Arilon guy killed the hydra by stabbing it in the heart, right?"

"Yes, you must stop one of its hearts. It has two. Oh, and it spits acid," Hera continued.

Great! We don't have a sword. We're trapped in a cave with hydra and the only person who has killed one, was an old friend of the original Oracle who lived well over 2 million years ago.

"The hydra is indigenous to Delphi? Is it a native creature from here?" Adrian asked.

It was a logical question, though I wasn't sure how it mattered.

"Yes, there were once many a long time ago. I'm afraid Themians don't like creatures that spew acid and attack on sight."

"Humanity wouldn't like them either," Adrian murmured.

Think, think, think! The only thing I brought with me is my mind.

All the great sages say 'the pen is mightier than the sword'. Unfortunately, in this case I was almost sure that we would need a fucking sword.

"Okay. Now, this tunneling system, is it a test?" I asked, pushing my fear for Tristan and Isolde to the side.

If they are alive, I need to live to find them.

"Yes, you will be tested all along the path to the underworld," Vika stated, releasing her elbows.

"It is not to determine our pureness of heart or any crap like that is it?" I hissed in frustration.

"Your heart's purity has already been determined. The tests are to determine your fortitude, your creative thinking, problem solving and the ability to overcome hardship," Vika must have brushed up on her underworld know-how since Alexandria.

"Are you fucking kidding me? For all the shit I went through as a kid, I need to be tested again? And for what? For hardship? Honestly, all this crap about fate and the all-knowing Universe, I don't think the Universe has been fucking paying attention," I retorted under my breath.

Vika cringed back and I immediately felt bad. This wasn't Vika's fault and I couldn't blame her for keeping to the back. She was a bookworm, not a fighter and I couldn't expect her to suddenly stand up and fight. It wasn't in her nature.

But survival should be, and I can't understand anyone who won't fight for that under any circumstance.

I hung my head for a moment to regain my composure and perspective on the situation. I couldn't let my emotions over the kids destroy my chance of finding them. Vika was an asset for knowledge, not dead weight and I had to think of her that way.

"I have an idea. Hera, I require you and your son," Adrian breathed low.

He glanced back at us to assure himself Hera had heard him.

"Whatever is necessary, I will do," Hera instantly replied then squeezed my hand.

"I need you to dreamwalk to your son and I need you to have him dreamwalk back to us. Hercules is going to kill this hydra. He ran around telling stories about killing one. Well, now he can pay his penance. Every one of his labors which he did or didn't do, he *will* do them now. Even if I have to transport his dumb ass everywhere I go," Adrian remarked.

I was taken aback by the anger, yet the justice of it wasn't lost on me.

"Oh, I agree. Lying is wrong and Hercules absolutely must pay for his lies. However, I am not sure that he will feel he's being punished. He's been caged on one planet for thousands of years. He may actually see this as a holiday," Hera remarked and I had to stifle a laugh.

"I don't care. He can view it anyway he wants to. Just get his ass down here!" Adrian retorted.

"It's really brilliant," I stated then tore the bottom of my dress, giving me a long strip of fabric to bind my breast with.

Hera sat down on the floor, assuming a lotus position of all things.

"Make sure he brings a big ass fucking sword. Oh, and a gun. Please," I breathed.

She tilted her head slightly up and peeked one eye open. "I wouldn't dream of asking him to bring anything else," she smiled.

Her body stilled. Her breathing slowed and she appeared to be asleep. Ten of the longest minutes of my life later, she opened her eyes and rolled her head around on her neck, stretching her arms out in front of her.

"He is coming. He's preparing. He will bring all the weapons necessary. He is going to dreamwalk through me. I will be the anchor." She took to her feet and tore the bottom of her dress from the knees down and wrapped the extra fabric around her waist.

I glanced over to Vika and her long dress. I cocked an eyebrow at her and she too tore the bottom half off and wound it around her waist.

"Note to self and to everybody else - don't let Hera die!" I remarked in a low tone.

The tunnel wasn't hot, but sweat still trickled down my face and neck. I used the back of my hand to push it away from my eyebrows. When I pulled my hand away, I expected to see smeared eyeliner, but other than sweat, there was nothing.

"I cannot participate," Vika said and backed away to the tunnel she'd emerged from.

The stone had already lowered, closing off that avenue of escape, but she pressed her back against it anyway.

"If you're not going to participate in protecting anyone or defending all of us, stay the hell out of my way," I hissed.

There is nothing worse than a spineless coward.

I had reached my limit with Vika and her wishy-washy nature.

The creature, the hydra, plopped down on its belly with its legs out to either side. Every so often, it flicked its tongues. It closed most of its eyes and kept the rest half open as if it was going to take a nap.

It gave me the heebie-jeebies just watching it. Its four legs resembled the stumpy feet of an Earth lizard. The long, thin necks moved like snakes, while the chameleon shaped heads carried translucent ears that fanned out on either side, enhancing its hearing. The fans around the ears folded open and closed as if breathing in sound and air at the same time.

"I bet you that thing would make a nice pair of shoes and a purse," I stated with a nervous giggle before gulping back my fears.

If it did anything to Issy and Tristan, becoming a pair of shoes and a purse was exactly what would happen after I kill it.

The fear rolling through me ramped up the air pressure in the cavern. I tried to pull back my power, but the rolling in my belly and the fear for the kids made it impossible to lower my threat level.

"I think it would make a pretty nice coat. That is if we have time to skin it," Adrian replied, making sure that the rest of us were behind him.

"Dammit!" I whispered.

I looked up, searching the darkness for a sign of the ceiling and sky. For a moment, I wanted to pray.

As if that could save my kids or myself.

"Hera," Adrian called in a low voice. "Your son's days of being a loudmouth and a liar are over." He waved one hand, urging all of us closer to the wall.

"I agree with you," Hera replied, pressing her body flat against the wall as we slowly moved deeper into the giant cavern.

The creature reared all of its heads, tasting the air. Two of the heads turned slightly and began flicking its tail. Others stared off into the darkness as if searching. Only two continued to stare at our end of the cavern.

Our steps carried us deeper into the gloom that had taken over the space. I glanced back to spy Vika, following at a distance.

"Are you ready to slay a Hydra?" Adrian mouthed.

I didn't notice anything about the Hydra's movements as threatening other than its presence in general, of course. But Adrian must have seen something I didn't. My heart clenched.

I don't know if Adrian can do this. What if he dies?

The quaking in my belly ramped up. Adrian handed me his extra dagger.

<Save the kids!>

I swallowed back the lump in my throat and blinked away the excessive moisture forming in my eyes.

<If I can.>

"Yes, I am," a voice said and the honey blond haired man who saved Issy materialized in front of Hera.

I finally took a good look at him. He was as big as a mountain. I'd always thought that Adrian was a big man with a long sleek swimmer's build at 6' foot 4". Adrian was muscular but not overdone.

This man was bigger than Arnold Schwarzenegger. He stood almost 7' tall and his shoulders were nothing more than a massive wall of flesh.

"Holy shit!" I looked over at Adrian. "He's huge!"

His hair carried a touch of ginger and it flowed down his back. His back was the only thing I could see. There were two swords cross slung to his back and he wore nothing more than a light piece of fabric held up by a belted leather kilt, while his leather sandals were cross tied and came up to mid-calf.

He pulled a one-handed broadsword from his back. In his other hand, he had a sickle shaped dagger. He turned to me and his blue eyes twinkled as his full lips curved into a smile.

"You are Sydney, are you not? We have not been properly introduced. I am Hercules," he stated without extending a hand.

For a moment, I didn't know what to say. I bit my lip and plowed ahead, "Ready to finally live up to your stories?" I sputtered.

"I like you. All business, no bullshit," he tossed his hair back out of his eyes.

"You learned to curse?" I remarked, changing my grip on my dagger to mirror his.

"Tobias is most informative. I find the rest of humanity's modern nomenclature enjoyable," he chuckled and moved to stand next to Adrian.

"Yeah, 'T' has that effect on people," I murmured, moving to Adrian's other side.

The creature was still busy cleaning and hadn't noticed Hercules' arrival and barely paid us any attention at all.

Hercules wasted no time, threw his head back and issued a booming laugh that ricocheted around the chamber.

All nine heads rose in unison and turned toward us. The hydra took to its feet, readjusted its stance and slowly ambled towards us, as if it was nothing more than an afternoon stroll.

"I guess a laugh is all it takes to challenge her." He pulled another long dagger from his leather waistband and tossed it at Adrian. who caught it in his off hand.

"In case it kills me, finish the job. Are you up for the challenge?" Hercules cocked an eyebrow at Adrian.

A dark smile moved over Adrian's face, "Yeah," he replied.

"Don't just stand there with the women. Come and be a man!"

The way Hercules said 'come and be a man' like he was talking to a child, wasn't lost on me. Being several thousand years old, makes anybody under 100 a child.

Adrian shifted the dagger from his left hand to the right. He turned the knife backwards in his grip and moved his arms in a smooth motion.

"I like that, nephew! That's a man's grip. You need to hold it out more. We are going to be stabbing and slashing."

Hercules' large hand readjusted Adrian's grip on the hilt. The muscles in Adrian's jaw worked overtime. He was irritated. His mind told me that he was terrified of failing and leaving me alone to protect the kids, wherever they were.

"The only blows we will be deflecting will be acid," he informed.

I gasped.

How do you deflect acid?

I had no idea what training Adrian might have had, but I was pretty sure it didn't involve dodging acid. Hercules turned back to me and smiled as if he'd heard my thoughts.

Without giving Adrian another glance, the Demigod strode forward with his sword held out to the side. He looked relaxed.

Maybe that was the whole idea?

The Hydra couldn't anticipate his moves because he wasn't telegraphing them.

With his sickle dagger, he waved Adrian further off to the side.

< The heads will come at us from different directions. You need to get behind it and distract as many as you can. Just remember - don't get hit by the acid or you'll probably be dead.> Hercules instructed, allowing all of us to hear.

"Thanks a lot, *Uncle!*"

The next few minutes stretched out like a freshly cooked piece of pasta. We waited for it to snap.

Four sets of eyes followed Hercules and three followed Adrian. One set continued to stare in the direction we intended to travel. One head stared at Hera and I with its tongue flicking in and out, tasting the air.

I don't care what Vika said. To this creature this is a game. She is toying with all of us.

Adrian moved along the cavern wall with slow and steady steps, bending his knees in readiness for an attack.

Hercules sheathed his sickle, took out another dagger and began flipping it around. For a moment, I was mesmerized by how perfectly balanced it was. He tossed it in the air and caught it easily. One of the heads became entranced by the flipping motion too. Hercules assessed the creature, watching the head bobbing. With one head watching the knife toss there was one less to notice Adrian and his slow creeping to outflank the monster.

One of the heads watching Adrian turned its attention to Hercules. Then Adrian did something I've never seen before. He put out his hand facing up and a ball of fire appeared. Hera sucked a breath through her teeth.

"I did not know Adrian could wield the forces," she exhaled and gripped my free arm.

"I didn't know either, but I do hope fire helps," I whispered.

My fingers tightened on my dagger. I had to force them to relax. Hera nodded her head and her strawberry curls swayed with the motion.

Finally, the head following the dagger grew bored. It decided to inspect the object of its desire. As it came within reach, Hercules quick as a flash chopped its head off with his sword hand. A second later, Adrian threw his fireball and burned the stump.

The eight remaining heads screeched in pain and all hell broke loose.

All eight heads sprayed acid in every direction. I pulled water from the puddles on the ground to deflect the bursts in our direction and Hera moved behind me for protection.

Adrian danced around the acid bursts, leaping and tumbling from one direction to the other.

Hercules dodged several blasts. Finally, Adrian made it around to the back side of the Hydra and quickly slashed one of its legs then another one.

The monster screeched in pain and anger, laying a new blast of acid in every direction. Hercules hacked one of the heads just as another spewed a fresh batch of acid his way. It gave Adrian just enough time to shift himself to the other side of the dangling head. Hercules yelped with a battle cry I'd never heard before and sliced the last of the heads away from the creature.

Adrian threw a fresh ball of fire to consume the base, cooking the flesh and releasing a noxious odor into the enclosed space. Hercules grabbed the head next to that stump and locked his arm around it, then tossed his sword to Adrian.

Adrian managed to dance between acid blasts back to the end of the Hydra's tail. One of the heads released a fresh round of acid at Adrian who ducked behind the beast. The acid washed over the creature's body, leaving it unscathed. Its hide was impervious to the acid.

The head Hercules held onto the beast as she thrashed back and forth in an attempt to free itself from the tightening grip on its neck. The head was unable to spray acid and its ear fans flexed, open and closed, as if desperate for air. The head was losing strength. On the downward, swing Hercules used all his weight to hasten its downward momentum. Hercules met the ground and a sickening snap filled the cavern. He released the now dead appendage and began slashing at the next head.

Adrian slashed a head clean off and burned the stump before tossing the sword back to his brother in arms. The creature's remaining heads screamed in anger. Hercules repeated the process on two more heads, leaving two more hanging lifeless. Adrian moved quickly to burn the stump of the next head to meet the ground as it rolled away.

The tail lashed around and just missed hitting Adrian who was slashing at it and throwing fireballs into the open wounds, causing the slash to burst open as the meat inside cooked and blistered. With every fireball the creature screamed in agony. The hydra lashed its tail, hitting Adrian full in the chest, slamming him against the far cavern wall.

I screamed and the pressure in the cavern reached a fever pitch. The lifeless heads rose in the air. I slapped them at the beast like a dodgeball game. I aimed for the burned stumps and the remaining heads.

Finally, there were only two left, both of which were bleeding from wounds Hercules had inflicted. Hercules moved in closer for the kill. He tossed his sword to Adrian who cleaved the tail of the Hydra which squirted green blood in every direction.

The creature flailed without its tail to counter-balance those heavy heads. Adrian threw the sword back to Hercules who then plunged it deep into the chest of the beast.

With its dying breath, one of the injured heads sprayed acid over Hercules' shoulder, melting his skin and muscles. He screamed in agony. The echo filled the cavern.

"Daughter of Poseidon, call for the water!" He yelled through clenched teeth.

I glanced around to see who he was talking to.

CHAPTER 17

SYDNEY

"You are the daughter of Poseidon, are you not?" he shouted at me through clenched teeth.

"No. I mean I don't know who my father was. My mother never told anybody. I don't know what you're talking about," I screeched, shaking my head.

"We can go over your lineage later. Now, bring forth the water, woman!" He shouted at me.

I stepped closer to the carcass of the Hydra where Hercules was on the ground, kneeling in agony. His skin was mostly gone down from one of his shoulders and arms. It was so bad the bones began to reveal themselves.

The power of water welled up inside me like a geyser as the pressure built. I called the life-giving liquid forth from the ground, pulling it from every crack and crevice. Water doused Hercules' body, washing the acid away.

"I don't have any Primordium," I remarked as the water receded. The hope in his eyes disappeared. He just stared off into the darkness and gritted his teeth.

"The injury isn't real. I can leave the dreamwalk and return unharmed," he said.

"Go back! Go back to Odyssey," Hera urged, tears filling her eyes at the site of her child's mutilated body.

For a moment, I felt terrible for dragging him down here. But deep down in my heart, I knew Adrian could never have killed that thing alone.

He squeezed his eyes closed. Wrinkles slowly formed and deepened on his face, until blood vessels rose in his neck. His skin turned red, his eyes bulged as he opened them.

"I can't leave," he said and his head turned to stare his mother down.

Hera ran a hand over his hair. She closed her eyes. Almost immediately, she began to shake. The color of her skin changed with the effort before she broke away, gasping for breath.

"I can't set him free. We are all trapped down here," she glanced around, assessing our surroundings.

She reached into her satchel and pulled out a small vial. "Primordium," she supplied then poured it over Hercules' wounds.

Almost instantly, the muscles began regrowing, knitting themselves back together. He threw his head back and let out a roar of excruciating pain. His body was shaking as the Primordium forced the regrowth. Strands of fiber reached out from the elbow to the shoulder bone, pulling tighter as more joined the mass that grew. His clavicle bone disappeared from view as fresh skin grew like the edge of a beach gaining sand.

Adrian rushed to Hercules' side who thrust his good arm into the air to fight off the agony. Adrian took his hand in his own and squeezed. Hercules' eyes locked on Adrian as his body shook. His screams echoed in the cavern. Adrian's biceps tightened with his hold on Hercules, making his arm's blood vessels swell. Adrian was shaking along with Hercules as if they shared an understanding of pain.

I turned away from the grizzly scene to watch the open space around us.

"Vika, watch our back!" I ordered.

Hercules roaring in pain will attract anything down here or alert them of our presence.

Panting, Hercules said, "I must go with you into the underworld. No one can fight fate, but I can defend it," he huffed as the last of the Primordium's work finished repairing the damage.

Hercules closed his eyes and leaned his head on Hera's breast. She pushed the hair back out of his face, then laid a tender kiss on his forehead.

My eyes darted up around the room, searching for Adrian.

"Did it get any acid on you?" I demanded.

"No, there's no acid. Hercules took the worst of it. If he hadn't taken that acid spray, he wouldn't have been able to stab the hydra in the heart," he admitted. "He would've missed his chance. We would be dead."

"No, nephew. You would have finished the job," Hercules stated in a whisper.

Adrian laughed, "Looked like you might die there for a minute."

"I wanted to for a moment. But I've got too much to live for," he chuckled, then pushed the sweat drenched hair out of his face, kissed his mother's hand and took to his feet.

No matter how many times I saw Primordium heal people, I still found it fascinating to see it do its work. Watching someone go from deformed and maimed to perfect health was like magic.

"So, what do we do now, Vika?"

She smiled her simple smile but didn't take the bait.

Too bad.

I really wanted to have it out with her. She knew these dangers were down and she never warned us. Instead, I moved my focus to Hercules.

"How would you know that I'm supposed to be Poseidon's daughter? My mother never told anyone who my father was," I asked.

"Do you not see?" Hercules asked, pulling his sword from the Hydra, wiping the blade off on the skin.

Then he slipped his sword back into the sheath strapped to his back and picked up one of the daggers off the ground. He pulled the skin tight away from the body and began skinning the creature.

"Yes? I see lots of things. But, obviously, you see something that goes beyond eyesight!" I replied, not liking the way things were going.

He turned to Hera, "Do you not see it either, Mother?" he pulled a blood-soaked arm back from the carcass and pointed his blade at me.

"I do not. All I see is a woman born of my blood, a woman who is obviously more than half Themian?" Hera replied, using her shawl to wipe from her face the blood left by the beast.

"You've known Poseidon your whole life, yet you cannot see. Perhaps it is a quality only meant for Demigods.

Maybe, we can see what you cannot," Hercules continued, skinning the beast while shrugging his shoulders.

<Listen to him, beautiful girl. He's making sense.>

I shook Adrian's advice off along with the idea that I was a demigod.

Hercules cut a chunk of meat from the carcass and tossed it at me. "You are half Themian. It is stamped upon you. Tell me, can you move earth?" he asked.

I caught the dripping mess.

<You wanted a pound of flesh.> Adrian snickered.

I threw him a dirty look.

"You mean like earthquakes, right?" I tossed the meat to the ground.

Adrian threw a fireball at it, cooking the meat before it hit the ground.

"Yes, causing earthquakes. Also, you can move objects and great amounts of water. Correct?" Hercules asked, folding the hide back on the Hydra, only cutting the portions he could get to.

"Yes, for decades," I huffed.

I glanced down the tunnel. All this talk of parentage stuck in my craw. I only wanted to push on. My nostrils flared as I thought of my kids alone out there.

"On the ocean, do you not find that you reach your destination faster than most boats, especially when you're in a hurry?" he continued to skin as he laid out his case.

"Yes. We always made great time when I captained. Now, can we get a move on? My kids are out there with no idea of what is down here," I barked.

This is neither the time nor the place for a conversation like this.

"I can move things through the air too. Anything else you want to know?" I waved Adrian and Vika to move on.

"But you cannot handle fire or bend it to your will?" Hercules continued and sliced the section of skin free of the Hydra. He then laid it open on the ground and smiled at Adrian.

Adrian lit the flesh on fire, burning it away, leaving only the hide behind. Hercules smirked and folded it up, sliced off two long strands and tied it in a roll before attaching it to his belt.

He patted the roll. "No sense letting good leather go to waste. We aren't on Homeworld 12 anymore," he flashed a blinding smile and moved to join the rest of us.

"No, I can't use fire. But lots of people can't. So, I'm good with wind and water. But that doesn't mean anything," I retorted, storming away.

"Can you dominate minds?" He asked.

I stopped dead in my tracks and turned to face him.

"Yes, I can," I said in a low voice.

It wasn't something I spoke about. Ever. Hera shook her head and turned away. She was pensive and began pacing.

"Hercules, yes, she has many of the characteristics of Poseidon. But that doesn't make her his child, or grandchild. Or even his great-grandchild, for that matter," she said, putting an end to the discussion. "All of his line ended before you were born. Apollo and Artemis saw to that."

"All of this is irrelevant. It doesn't matter who my father is. We're looking for a home and allies. Furthermore, while you're trying to figure out who my bio-dad is, my children are out there somewhere. My father is irrelevant." I grabbed Adrian's hand and continued, "Are you capable of walking and talking?"

A smile curled one side of his mouth. He looked at me as if he was seeing me for the first time.

"Lead on, my lady! Though, I'm sure your children are in no danger at the moment." He bowed as I passed him.

Adrian clapped Hercules on the shoulder as we passed and shook his head, making Hercules laugh out loud as if something passed between them.

"Thank you! That was probably the most dangerous fight I've ever had in my life," Adrian said and offered the dagger back.

"It is yours now, nephew. Keep it. You might have need of it again for this journey is not over. You will not want to be caught without a weapon to fight," Hercules replied.

I've come to learn men slapping each other on the back is a language, it says *'good job and thanks for saving my life'* or *'that was some funny stupid shit.'* Anyway, something like that.

As we headed further into the cavern, the gloom turned into darkness, so Adrian created a fireball to light our way.

"Out of curiosity, why are you calling me your nephew?" He asked with the fire lingering two feet above his hand as if it was a floating torch.

Hercules laughter reverberated across the walls. "We just killed a Hydra and you're worried about me calling you 'nephew'? You are the son of my brother, so what else can I call you," he asked.

"My father is not your brother," Adrian stated coolly.

"Apparently, your weak and feeble human side has just taken over."

Adrian bristled at Hercules jiving him. "You are of my brother Perseus' bloodline. This means that you are my nephew."

I hadn't thought about it much but it was kind of funny. I guess Hercules would be my 20,000 times great grandfather or uncle?

So, Adrian is in Perseus' line.

"Perseus was always handy with a sword and shield," Hercules murmured. "Your brother Tobias mentioned your new husband being handy with a sword," he directed his last statement at me.

I looked over at Adrian expectantly.

"I was on that island for a long time. Sparing is an excellent way to work out your aggression," he supplied as an answer.

"Are there any other tricks that you've learned?" I asked.

"Apollo and his friends, other than having a God-like complex, are adept with combat. Emily suggested I train to take my mind off my worries. I learned how to fight with a sword and various other combat disciplines," it was all Adrian offered.

I'll get those details later.

CHAPTER 18

ISOLDE

<Can you see what it is?> I whispered with my mind as fresh quivering shook my bones.

<It's some kind of pillar, maybe?> Tristan said in disbelief, then extinguished his fireball, plunging us into the darkness.

<Why would you put a large pillar in the middle of a cave?> I asked and immediately rolled my eyes at my stupidity.

To support the ceiling. Duuh!

Tristan snickered in my mind at me.

<I wish I could use my light. This walking around in the dark is ridiculous.> he murmured.

As if we'd crossed an invisible barrier, a blue glow slowly illuminated the space.

<That was convenient. How do you like my Godlike abilities now? I said let there be light and there it was.> Tristan released my hand and waved me behind him.

<Har, har> I replied.

The center of the room wasn't occupied by a pillar. It was actually a metallic Greek folly. The structure was held up with Doric columns, lacking the fluting the Earthly styles carried. The columns held up a dome that rose twenty-five feet into the air, touching the ceiling at its apex. The dome was made up of metallic fret work.

My mouth dried with the immense size of the structure. We both stopped at the base to study the strange building. The metal was like nothing I'd ever seen. The oily rainbow of petroleum frozen in place laced with orichalcum. However, it didn't glisten with crystals like the walls. The columns were set back from the edge by three steps. Between them, I could make out the shape of something standing in the center. Before Tristan could stop me, I took all three steps and stood just under the edge of the dome, flicking my middle finger against the surface of the nearest column. The metal released a deep *bong* of a solid member.

I sucked in air at the sight before me. The center of the folly was occupied by the statue of a man. He had short white curly hair and he stood with a staff in one hand while the other one was extended in front of him with the palm up.

At least he isn't typical Greek and stark raving naked. Thank God for that!

He wore a short-belted tunic and Themian style sandals. He appeared to be made of a white stone, because it wasn't marble or the crystalline material that permeates everything either. Nevertheless, every detail about him was immaculate and true to life.

I'd been drawn to an emotional thread in my mind. It was an emotion that could only have come from a person.

"Who do you suppose he is?" I mumbled as I moved over the ringed threshold on the floor.

"Obviously it's not a person. It's just a statue. The question is why is he here and also, what does he represent?" Tristan snapped his fingers and a flame roared to life in his hand.

He used the fresh light to scan the edges of the space. Other than the cavern we had come through, there was nowhere else to go. The tunnel ended here.

"I guess this is the end of the line," he remarked and turned back to me and the statue.

"Is there nothing on the walls or the columns?" I asked, unable to take my eyes off the remarkable creation before me.

"There is just more of that crystalline material. Judging from the size of the tunnels we almost drown in, there's no way they got all this down here that way. Maybe they levitated it," Tristan said and moved slowly around the room, humming a tune I'd never heard before.

"Stop thinking so two-dimensionally, Tristan," I scoffed, "Maybe, they shifted him down."

"Oh, yeah! Sometimes I forget that is my ability. Dumb," he laughed it off.

However, Tristan couldn't hide his need to be smart from me. How he could forget his new ability was beyond me.

"No, Tristan. You are one of the smartest people I know," I whispered and rubbed my hand up and down his arm.

"Sis, that's the nicest thing I think you ever said to me. Other than you saying I was your best friend."

He dipped his head and gave me a quiet smile. It reminded me of dad. Dad always dipped his head when he was embarrassed.

"You are my best friend, Tristan, and you are very smart."

I looked around and glanced back. He still had his head down and looked away sheepishly.

Tristan was my best friend. I mean twins are always best friends, right? I guess I hadn't told him how much I loved him and how much I appreciated him.

Everybody likes to hear that they're not being taken for granted.

I moved my attention back to the statue. It didn't have a pedestal and he was gazing off towards the direction of the tunnels.

I walked to the edge of the folly to examine the design in the metal work, hoping the positioning of the statue meant something.

"So far, everything has been intentional. Clearly, we're being led somewhere. So, there has to be a way out of this cavern and the statue could be positioned this way for a reason," Tristan stated.

"No, he doesn't. He could just be standing in here because we're supposed to do something. Then again, it could be completely irrelevant, I'm open to exploring all options," I shrugged.

Tristan could be so aggravating and right. While I examined the folly, I noticed there were no seams or cracks. There were no creases, no bubbles, no irregularities. Nothing at all.

This could mean anything and nothing.

The only thing of interest was that the statute did have his hand extended out, as if he was waiting for something.

My inspections ceased, as a roar cut the quiet of the underground space and echoed around the cavern. The agony of it rattled my teeth and quivered my insides.

I found I was screaming too.

CHAPTER 19

ISOLDE

The screaming ended with Tristan shaking me.

"What? What was that?" I asked, wrapping my arms around myself for comfort.

"I don't know, sis, but it was loud. We need to find our way out and quick." He pulled me to my feet, then took me behind one of the columns.

"What about mom?" I demanded as tears pricked my eyes.

The scream came from the direction we'd just come from. I glanced around the column into the darkness, searching the shadows for a sign. Yet, nothing formed out of the darkness. I gulped back my fears in an effort to appear brave to Tristan.

"Mom can take care of herself," my brother also darted a glance back the way we'd come from before moving back to the statue.

The scream had cleared my mind. The emotion we'd followed ended here.

"Tristan, remember when I said I was getting feelings from something?" I asked, studying the object in the center of the space.

My insides trembled over the implications of what I was about to say.

"Yeah. That's what we've been following in the dark. Your feelings," Tristan snickered.

I knew he was teasing me to take my mind off mom and the unknown, so I didn't rise to the bait.

"Yes, it ends here. Those emotions that I've been trying to shut out, they all end here," I whispered as if someone was listening.

"You think that thing's alive?" he pointed his index finger at the statue, incredulous of my statement.

"It's something. It's not a statue. Did you look at his eyebrows and hair?" I turned to assess Tristan's reaction. "Have you ever seen a carving with eyelashes?" I asked.

"That just makes it more realistic. Maybe they were applied later. Or maybe, Themians have a higher level of technology, enabling their carvings to be more authentic," he shrugged.

But he never stopped staring at the statue.

"No! I think he's alive," I said and the word '*alive*' echoed under the dome, repeating itself over and over.

Tristan finally tore his eyes away from the thing and stared me down.

"Who goes to sleep with their eyes open? They're white and creepy," Tristan grimaced and scrunched his shoulders up as a shiver ran down his spine.

"Are you going to touch him or should I?" I looked over at him with a half-smile.

Maybe if I do touch him, my feelings of trepidation will go away.

My hand closed, making a fist with my index finger extended.

I must look like a child, but I don't care.

My eyes were locked on to his face.

If he is alive, he should flinch or something.

I wasn't sure what part of him I wanted to touch. As I leaned forward, Tristan came and stood beside me. My breathing sped up as did my heart rate. Sweat formed under my arms. Just as I was about to touch him, Tristan's hand locked around mine, pulling me back.

"What'd you do that for?" I demanded in relief.

"I'll touch him. Whatever happens, it will happen to me. Dad said my job was to protect you and mom. He made me promise," Tristan whispered with a wrinkled brow and gritted his teeth.

"It's a statue or a person who's been standing still a long time. I doubt he's all that dangerous," I scoffed at him and raised my hand again.

Tristan slapped my hand away this time. "His mind is pretty dangerous though. He took control of you in the sanctuary. Remember?"

"Fine! Go ahead! You can touch him first. I really don't care," my mouth became dry as Tristan opened and closed his, extending his index finger.

"Do not touch him!" Hera ordered.

We both screeched, "I think I just jumped out of my skin! What do you mean '*don't touch him*'?" Tristan shouted and backed away.

"That is Charon," Hera replied.

"So?" I barked to cover my fright.

The name sounded familiar, yet I couldn't remember what they were talking about. I'd read so much recently that my brain was filled with tons of information. Sifting it around was like going to a filing cabinet using the Dewey decimal system to find a personnel file on a computer that's encrypted.

Both Tristan and I shouted, "Mom!"

Our mother moved to my side and I burrowed into her arms, thankful I could. Mom pulled Tristan in and kissed both of us on the forehead. Only then she spoke over my head.

"Charon, the boatman?" Mom asked.

Of course, my mother knows. She always knows everything.

"He will take you down the rivers and lead you to the entrance of the underworld," Vika supplied, keeping to the shadows.

Great!

"This is the guy we need to give two gold coins to?" I asked, stepping back from the creepy statue.

"Do we lay them over the eyes or something?" Mom asked.

She always went right to the bone, cutting away all the extra crap in the way.

I love that about her and hate it too.

"Not coins. Circles," Hera murmured while keeping an eye on my mother, who released both of us and looked down at her hand.

She kept rubbing one hand over her knuckles. Looking at each of us kids, she stepped back.

"I don't know if he would have understood." She stared at the rings on her finger for a few minutes, then she heaved a sigh, took her wedding bands off and separated the two rings.

Adrian shifted all the diamonds out of both and into the palm of his hands.

"Don't worry," he whispered in her ear, "We can have them remade. I am sure Gabriel would understand."

He opened her hand and poured the diamonds into her shaking palm. She looked down at the sparkling stones then up at Adrian. He nodded his head encouragingly to her. She bit her lip, then straightened her shoulders, flared her nostrils and closed her hand over the diamonds.

She slipped all the diamonds into a drawstring pouch Adrian handed her and cinched it shut, slipping it in between her breast.

"You're giving that creature the wedding ring daddy gave you?" I screeched before I could stop myself.

"Would you rather I gave him daddy's ring and not mine?" mom retorted with a catch in her throat.

I shook my head and looked away only to have my eyes land on Hercules. Tristan put his hand on my shoulder. I quickly glanced away to hide my anger.

"I can have another one made for me, but not Ga..." she murmured and choked before swallowing.

She locked her jaw and her eyes turned hard as her nostrils flared. Mom took two light steps to stand before Charon. Without touching him, she placed both rings in the palm of his extended hand. Instantly, his eyes cleared and became the vibrant blue Themians are so well known for.

His hair remained white, as color moved across him like a paint-soaked brush dipped in water, adding color to everything but his clothing.

We waited with baited breath until he lowered his chin and his gaze fell upon the rings. He immediately picked them up and placed them on his pinkie finger. Only then, his eyes shifted to take in the space.

That's when I noticed the bits of dirt clinging everywhere. His tunic had lost its whitened color with those small movements as dust drifted to the floor. At his feet laid a filthy dark cloak. He bent and slung it on his shoulders, raising the hood to cover the stark white curls, covering his pate.

Vika squeaked but no one spoke. His face didn't display even an iota of emotion. He was a statue come to life.

He turned the hand he had put the rings on and spread his fingers. A knowing smile scraped across his face as his eyes narrowed. Fretwork metallic panels shot up from the floor of the folly, closing us all in.

Fuck!

The lip I'd stepped over on the floor was the top of a cage panel, turning the folly into a prison.

I sucked in air as the entire structure snapped with an electrical charge. Soon, the snapping was replaced by a low hum.

Sparks flew as Hercules tossed a dagger at the cage walls, "Move away from the walls," he shouted.

Everyone took a step away from the walls. Vika began to whimper and crouched on the floor next to Hera, gripping the ripped edge of her chiton.

"It's a fucking Faraday Cage!" Mom shouted over the hum of the walls. "Why would there be a Faraday Cage down here?" She demanded.

The pressure around us grew and changed from normal space to the intense nothingness of the between, then grew.

It was more than I could bear. Both my ears popped. My skin was covered in icy cold needles, stabbing me everywhere. I squeezed my eyes shut and attempted to scream. A moment later, just as quickly as it came, it was gone and the air returned to the ambient temperature of a cave, damp and cold.

He had transported us to another cavern with water running through it. There, a vessel was tied to a wooden post. He looked from one of us to the others, meeting everyone's eyes, each in turn. All the while, he was pointing at the boat.

My mother lifted her head and grabbed Adrian's hand. I looked over at Tristan and he grabbed mine.

<Wherever we're going, we're going together.> Tristan remarked.

<We're always stronger together. > I replied numbly.

The boat was tethered to a wooden dock that extended into an underground river. The closer we came to it, the more the roar of the torrent grew. The channel did not appear very deep, but looks can and have deceived myself and others.

"This is Acheron, the river of sorrows," Charon announced in a voice devoid of emotion or inflection.

The only other sound around us was the tap of Charon's staff as he moved on the boat.

"This is as far as I go. If one of you would be so kind as to shift me back to the sanctuary, I wish you well on your journey," Vika stated in a quivering voice.

"You don't even know if we can shift you out!" Mom replied.

Her anger over Vika's craven request was apparent to everyone present.

"If we can get in, we can get out," Adrian supplied.

"Hopefully, by the time you return, I shall have all of Odyssey in order for you," she smiled tentatively, adding a nervous laugh to the end.

In a blink of an eye she was gone. However, it hadn't been Tristan shifting her. I glanced over to Adrian. He never even flinched.

Hera bit her lip in a reflection of mom as she stared at the empty space where Vika once was.

I searched the open space for our statuesque friend only to find him standing next to a viking style ship. Although it appeared wooden, it was not made out of old wood. It was made from some form of the crystalline technology used by the ancient Themians, only in dark brown tones. Many oars stuck out of the side of the boat through opening. They didn't extend into the interior, there were no handles to operate them.

Charon mounted the low dock. His staff rang hollow with each step he was taking towards the bobbing boat, indicating we should take a seat.

I gulped back my reservations. I climbed over the lip and sat down on one of the benches towards the middle. Tristan took the seat next to mine, while my mother and Adrian sat down with Hera and Hercules directly behind.

Charon boarded the ship like an automaton. He pushed off with his staff from the back of the boat. He also untied the mooring ropes, and we floated into the center of the raging torrent, moving swiftly away from the dock. He did not touch the rudder but moved it using his mind. Every oar shifted down into the water only to rise up again. The boat rowed all on its own. It was on automatic pilot.

Somehow, Charon is controlling it.

<So, the creepy guy can a row the boat with his mind?> I murmured to Tristan who snickered and squeezed my hand.

<Isolde, keep your thoughts to yourself. Now is not the time to be having a lot of chitter, chatter.> Mom ordered.

Like she is a great example of mind firewalls. She thinks louder than a megaphone at a rock concert.

At first, the white noise of the water comforted me. The rocking of the boat eased the stress of months away. I relaxed into the world I remembered from Calypso and the big blue ocean we used to call home.

I loved the water and everything about it. The little fish that used to fly on to the deck sometimes at night and the schools of Ono that rushed under the boat, just in time to be caught for dinner.

But this wasn't Calypso and nothing about this underground river was blue. The further down the tunnel we went, the more the raging built. The roar of the water ceased only to morph into moans. The screams of sorrow filled my ears and my body, tearing at my mind.

At first, I pushed the unnerving sound out of my mind. I knew how the water could play tricks on your mind.

Every sailor on Earth knows of the wiles of the sea.

Yet this sound worked its way inside my mental defenses and soon my fingernails dug into my hands. I glanced down to see I was bleeding. I tried to stop but all the crying voices filled me. I began scratching my own flesh, my arms and my legs as an attempt to block it all out. But I couldn't. I couldn't stop. The moaning and screaming, the anguish of every soul that has ever filled the Universe, filled this space and me.

CHAPTER 20

SYDNEY

They call it the river of misery, but to me, it seemed more like a raging torrent of insanity. Every which way I looked, there was either rock or water. The boat rocked, creating a trance like state, lulling your senses. Water has always worked to ease me, but this was different.

Hercules pulled closer to his mother, placing his arm over her shoulders.

As if Hera needs anyone to defend her.

His actions showed his love for her and it made me smile.

Isolde moved closer to her brother and Tristan braced his arm behind her back. The two of them were clinging to each other, just as when they were babies. Tristan murmured in her ear, but his words were lost to me in the voice of the river.

With one hand I reached for Adrian's hand and comfort, while my other one clutched the edge of the boat. I was too afraid to let go as we were pitching so violently. I was worried I'd be thrown out.

Tearing my eyes away from the water and stone, I examined the boat I've placed my life in. For a moment, I was angry. Angry because I'd got in a boat without checking its seaworthiness.

You're pushing too hard, too fast, Syd.

If what Hera told me was true, I couldn't push hard or fast enough.

My body rocked to the side with a violent pitch which was followed by a man's roar in pain.

"Don't get the water on you," Hercules yells over the raging torrent.

I glance over my shoulder. Hercules was holding one arm to his chest where blisters were already forming. The pained expression on his face told me there was so much more wrong here than the strange humming vibration of a forgotten river.

Hercules huffed through the pain, flaring his nostrils, then flipped his hair out of his face to meet my inquiring stare.

"The water is acid. Tell the others." He glanced beyond me to Isolde and Tristan. "And brace yourself with the pads at your feet. They are set there for the rowers."

I tilted my head in a *'thank you'* manner. There were indeed wooden pads to set your feet in and the moment I did so, the pitching was replaced by a gentle rolling. I shared the information with Adrian and Tristan, who also ceased to bob needlessly.

This must be how supplies feel when they're lashed down to a deck.

A drop of water landed on my thigh and burned through my tunic. I wanted to call the water and wash away the pain, but fear held me back.

What if the water I call is the acid-laced river? It will eat me alive and drown us all.

The river clawed at my senses, working its way into my psyche. The pressure grew as the ceiling closed in on us, compressing the bone vibrating sound.

Charon stepped down from the perch he'd been standing on at the back of the boat. The roof of the river cavern lowered until there was barely enough room to pass between the top of the bow and the ceiling of the cavern.

The deep humming joined the heavy pressure, squeezing my chest. Issy was hunched over twitching in time with the sound, while Tristan white-knuckled the bench. The vibration pounded into me. It worked as the bass of a subwoofer at a rock concert.

I wanted to grab my children and hold them but a deep dread engulfed me, shaking me down to the soft tissue in my joints. The image of monsters in the night began marching through my mind and the hypnotic sound played its evil dance with my memories.

A vision of my father's hate filled sneer played before me as the word *care* echoed in my mind. The slap of the belt whipped my body from side to side. I screamed from the remembered pain. I begged for my father to stop and prayed that God would save me. My body arched as each memory played over and over again.

Adrian's fear of waves washed over me only to join with my own memories and fears. The wave met my father and lifted him up to ride the crest. My fear of my father turned to terror as the wave crashed over me and I gasped for air.

My father turned into a gold hair man with Themian blue eyes. He was raging with manic joy as he pelted me with water and shells scraped from the sea bed.

My raw throat worked to scream as Adrian's memories of almost drowning took over my father beating me and the golden maniac.

My belly rolled and my chest compressed. I had to pant to breath. I screamed at my father, telling him that he didn't own me anymore. But he only stared down at me with hard blue eyes as the word 'care' echoed around us. A moment later, he morphed into the golden hair man and his head back to boom with mad laughter.

Fresh pain cleared the visions, pushing the hypnotism back. Water from the river burned into the back of my hand.

My eyes were just clear enough for me to make out the ceiling of the river.

It was a pocked honeycomb of holes, each one providing its own sound to the cornucopia of tonal beats.

Even the walls were dotted with holes, but the holes were nothing more than softer rock eaten away by the acidic river.

The movement of wind enabled the acoustics of a woodwind instrument, an underground Pan's pipes. The combination of sound and water was pure chance. Yet, its effects were the real wonder and problem.

I grabbed Adrian's chin with my freshly burned hand and forced him to look up at the ceiling.

"Do you see those holes?" I shouted over the din in the background.

He didn't answer, only gasped for air before stiffening in my arms. I squeezed his chin as hard as I could while shaking his head.

"Wake up! It's not real," I shouted again.

He gasped afresh for air, as if he was still in the water, drowning.

Glancing over my shoulder, to catch sight of Hera's sweat-covered face. She shouted something in a language I'd never heard before. She repeatedly called the word 'Jorhan', only to be joined by her son who called out to the same one.

Isolde was lying at the bottom of the boat, wailing in time with the river while her brother cried in Italian, "You can't die."

I didn't know who he was talking to, probably Gabriel. Tristan and Gabe always spoke Italian to each other.

Tears pricked my eyes at the thought of Gabe. I cradled Adrian's head to my chest and hoped the river would end soon.

I kissed Adrian's hair and rocked back and forth, murmuring, "This is what it really *means* to *care*."

<I care.> He whispered back.

<Look at the ceiling.> I replied.

I bit my lip and the pain kept the river from taking me over again.

"Yes. They must be working like some kind of an instrument," he stated and pulled away to get a better view.

He pressed the heel of his hand to his eyes, wiping the tears away. After several heavy deep breaths, he wrapped his arm around me and we clung to each other to keep the miserable river at bay.

"Den boreíte pankósmia kyriarchía tou Poseidóna," Hera shouted.

She then stood up as the ceiling rose, waving her fist in the air. The wind blasted fanning her hair away from her crazed face. Her entire body lifted and she floated in the air over the boat, following us. She screamed but the only name I could make out was Poseidon's.

The sound swirling around us gave me the heebie-jeebies. The ominous sound could have been just a trick of geology, and nothing more, but I couldn't shake the eerie rumbling beat. Finally, the cavern spread out and the hypnotic effect dissipated. Hera lowered down next to her son and slumped into his waiting arms.

A sandy beach lined one side of the cavern. I sighed with relief at the sight of not only land, but sand. I felt most at home near and on water. Since sand is part of the ocean, it has always grounded me. I was desperate to dig my feet into the salty granules.

Charon retook his position towering above us. His blue unseeing eyes stared straight. As he waved his hand, the boat moved out from the pull of the river. We were heading for a wooden stanchion embedded in the sand.

The bottom of our boat scraped the sand and I used my power to force it up on to dry sand. The ropes tied themselves to the stanchion and a plank slowly extended down onto the soft sand. Charon motioned for everyone to get out.

The desire to scramble out and leave the river behind was strong. I restrained myself and waited for everyone else to disembark before I set my feet on the gray particulates.

I surveyed our group. They all appeared wrung out, each sagged with weight of the emotions that had been extracted.

The vision of my father flashed before me. I gritted my teeth and scowled.

He can't hurt me. He's dead. Those memories belong in the past. I rule my life. Not the past and certainly not fate.

CHAPTER 21

HERA

Tristan laid down on the sand. His face was encrusted with salty tears, just as Hercules.

I swallowed back the words that lingered on the tip of my tongue. I haven't spoken Greek in many centuries and calling Jorhan's name still burned the back of my throat. I squeezed my eyes shut for a moment only to see Zeus snapping his body in half. The pressure from the river returned with a vengeance with the vision of Jorhan's body lying limp on the rocky river bank next to his village.

Zeus' wicked laugh beat at me. Zeus only killed him because of me. Because I loved him like a brother. Of all the humans I ever lived with, he was my favorite. The guilt ate at me.

It's just another burden I must bear.

I stifled the cry that desperately wanted to escape and closed my eyes to hide the pain.

The river of misery cannot change the past or bring back the dead. Jorhan is dead and I must live on.

My eyes adjusted to the gloom of the cavern when I opened them. The river flowed into a giant lake, spanning far across the cavern's high ceiling. The gray walls that surrounded us carried none of the telltale signs of crystalline tech. I sighed with relief.

Perhaps we can leave if we must.

Charon did not wait for us to get our bearings. His statuesque body continued to walk on a predetermined path, the tap of his staff leading us to a set location.

I faltered for a moment.

Do I really want to see this to the end? I am not a hero, nor am I a God.

I mentally shook myself. The future of my children and the hybrids mattered more than my feelings. My personal desires had not mattered since I chose to become a mother.

Adrian pulled Tristan to his feet, "Doesn't look as though our tour guide is going to be giving us time to rest," he chuckled and dusted himself off.

Tristan nodded his head, giving Adrian a deep serious look. I would never get over how much they look alike. Or how much they reminded me of Pursues. But that was to be expected.

Charon led us around the edge of the lake in a slow automaton fashion.

"How many rivers are there? In the underworld, I mean, and not the human version," Sydney asked.

She had removed her sandals to dig her feet into the gray granules lining the side of the subterranean lake. Her joy from the simple act brought a small smile to my face.

It was childlike behavior and it was unlike Sydney. She was always so in control and unwilling to let down her guard.

She closed her eyes and revealed in the moment before returning her shoes to her feet and ran off to catch up with Adrian.

Hercules too had moved ahead following Tristan and Isolde, leaving me alone with my thoughts. Hyperion's words echoed in my mind.

"If they catch you, they will kill you all."

A shiver ran down my back, shaking me out of my memory-soaked world.

My feet moved to catch up with my progeny.

"There are five rivers to the underworld —" Sydney was saying before I mingled in the discussion.

"...most of them intersect. But I do not know where or how or even if that part is true," I stated, glancing around to take in our surroundings. I made no comment on my actions in the boat.

The tightness around Isolde's lips told its own story. Reliving the worst moment of one's life in full view of others is truly the same as being naked. The only thing cloaking my past was a language barrier.

"There are indeed five and they do intersect. The Oracle was very specific about this part. The only thing of note amongst the listing is regarding the last one. Styx circles the underworld seven times," Issy remarked.

She was covered in a fine sheen of sweat and pasty, yet she had an absent stare devoid of emotions. And that frightened me.

"Our destination is Elysium. The underworld is merely a path to it," I intervened while working my hair back into some semblance of control.

"If so, defending ourselves against the guardians should not be an issue. After all, fate is on our side." Hercules pipped in with a wicked smile aimed at Issy.

She ignored him and kept staring at the water with a longing that worried me.

My first instinct was to ignore Hercules and his silly jabbing. He always liked to add a little joke everywhere to lighten the mood. Neither I or anyone else was interested in laughing, judging from the faces around us.

"Perhaps, we should question our guide?" I asked hoping Sydney or Adrian would take the lead.

No one answered the question or made a move to speak with Charon.

Time took on a new meaning in this subterranean world. The lapping of water on sand and the lack of light from a star, turned me around. I couldn't tell if we had walked for a few minutes or hours. My feet grew sore and the sand became pebbles and then rocks under my thin sandals.

Darkened alcoves pocked the cavern on our side. The further we traveled, the bigger they became. Each one was set just deep enough so I couldn't make out their true scope. On the other hand, many were just high enough I could duck into them.

Larger openings yawned like the mouth of the Hydra, dark and foreboding. Emotions battered me from my traveling companions. They too felt the apprehension in the air.

Sydney dropped back from the rest to walk beside me.

<I can't make this go any faster.> She remarked with frustration.

< As long as Odyssey keeps the stars between them and planet, they should be safe.> I returned to assure her.

< What about Vika? Adrian shifted her to the main sanctuary.> She mentally murmured.

< We cannot control Vika. Letting her go was the only way to show her we can be trusted. Hyperion will shield us for as long as he can. > I said, hoping that was the real truth.

In my heart I believed Vika didn't want to hurt us and would come with us. That her fear of us would keep her from revealing us to the High Council. Truth be told, I worried more about the failed acolytes of Pythos.

They left, but will they speak of the coming of the Fates? If so, what will Delphi's High Council do with that information?

I wanted to say more. However, there was nothing more to say. Our fears hung in the damp air around us like a fog not yet removed by a breeze.

I kept my eyes on the rocky ground, placing my feet one in front of the other, making sure each of my steps was solid so as not to twist an ankle. The soft blue light made the shadows darker, creating a false depth of field.

The crack of rock hitting rock whipped my attention from my footing. Instantly, my belly filled with the bubbling of a boiling pot.

In a cave near Tristan, golden orbs appeared, followed by the deep rumble of a growl. It echoed off the back of its cave and into ours. The sound could only have come from a large creature. The hair on my body rose to greet the anxiety and chaos the sound created.

<Get back!> I ordered our entire group.

Hercules moved in front of Tristan and Isolde before waving me behind him.

Four golden eyes blinked and moved closer to the mouth of the cave, as the tip of a large brown nose resolved itself out of the midnight blue darkness. The nostrils flared and puffed out warm moist air before its mouth lowered to reveal long gleaming white sharp teeth. Its lips quivered and a tongue licked out, while separating the jaws only to snap them back together.

For a moment, I stood frozen in fear.

The wind in the cavern picked up and I didn't know if it was me or Sydney. My weak grasp on the forces was only enough to move rocks, not aim them.

CHAPTER 22

SYDNEY

Pythia said that there would be guardians, yet as the giant two-headed dog slowly left the shadows of its lair, I wished she was wrong. I couldn't for the life of me, remember reading anything about a two-headed dog. Three-headed dog yes, but two-headed no.

"I've never heard of a two-headed dog, mom," Tristan remarked while gripping his dagger, turning his knuckles white.

The shaggy beast sported a gray and black with flecks of brown coat of fur, and it easily blended into the walls. From its soundless movements, it could have followed us from the beach, and we would have never known.

I shot Hercules a look of disdain for his hunting and tracking abilities. This was an epic fail to pay attention on all our parts, not just his. Somehow, I still felt he should have known.

"I, too, do not recall a two-headed dog monster," Hercules replied, motioning Adrian and Tristan to his side.

"I believe you were the one running around spouting about having killed Cerberus, the guardian of the underworld or whatever this thing is?" I said, throwing as much sarcasm as I could into my reply.

I should have noticed. I should have been watching our backs and not worrying about being discovered by a bunch of Themians who couldn't find this lake in 2 million years.

Odyssey can take care of themselves. I think. I hope... If we don't survive...

Hercules threw his head back and laughed. His long honey blond hair fell down his back in curls like soft and shiny silk.

Why do guys get all the great hair?

He scratched his chin "Awe. It's Cerberus' brother," he stated as if his pronouncement was really helpful, then shook his head.

"Okay, I call bullshit," Tristan announced.

"Thank you, Tristan. I call bullshit too," Issy said, taking Tristan's side, but remaining behind him.

"No, truly. Cerberus has a two-headed brother. Sure, you don't hear a lot about him. Most people would go crazy about a two-headed dog. But then you hear about the three-headed dog, which is Cerberus, and you won't give his brother Orthrus another thought."

What he said made sense. I rolled my eyes.

The loud-mouthed brute has a point. Another freak monster, with more than one head. I think this planet is fucked.

Orthrus shook one head and then the other one. His large ears flapped and dirt flew through the air. Saliva speckled the ground at his feet, making bits of rock and fur drift down from his underbelly and tail. His double nostrils flared and he snarled, letting fresh ropes of drool slip down the sides of his two mouths and coat his razor-sharp teeth. The dog moved its legs wide and flattened his heads.

"Are you saying that these creatures are immortal?" I asked the obvious question on everyone's mind.

I moved in step with the beast. He moved right and I went left. He was circling and we were bunching together. We were a perfect target.

"No, I only know the stories my mother told me," Hercules replied as the shaggy beast bared his teeth, releasing a new low growl.

The hair on my arm stood up with the echo that followed.

"No, they're not immortal," Hera said. "I don't know if two-headed dogs are endemic to Delphi. But they are not immortal and I never said Cerberus had a brother. Orthrus is the name of the bred."

Her eyes shifted back and forth as if wondering if there was anything else she could contribute. I bit my lip and turned my attention back to the dog.

"It doesn't matter now, does it, mother? Adrian, do you still have your daggers?" Hercules asked, waving him and Tristan to spread out.

"You know I do, *Uncle*," he said with a hint of sarcasm.

It took two steps back. "Now might be a good time to shift in a sword and a gun," I said. I never wanted a gun before, but now, oh man, I wish, I wish.

I'd shoot this motherfucker and be done with it.

"I don't even know where a sword is—" Adrian sputtered.

A moment later, a sword appeared in his hand. It was similar to the one Hercules already carried. A Roman-style broadsword, single-handed, with a rectangular-shaped pommel and a square quillion.

"Well, nephew, let's go kill the Orthrus beast," Hercules said.

Tristan and Adrian moved further out, arcing like the open arms of an old friend. Hercules took several shuffling steps towards the dog before Adrian blinked out and shifted behind the creature.

Orthrus snapped his jaws, creating a loud cracking sound. One of his heads turned to bark at Adrian who wasted no time chopping his tail off.

The stump pumped out blood, covering the smooth rocks on the ground. Orthrus howled with rage and reared its head, baring his teeth, brawling and gnashing as he whipped around to face Adrian.

Tristan shifted rocks like projectiles, smashing them into the heads. Isolde skittered away from her brother as the creature rounded to face Tristan. However, her sudden movements caught his attention and he leapt.

"Issy!" I screamed as my heart pounded through my rib cage.

Hercules rushed from behind and immediately slashed at Orthrus' lower back and haunches, cutting his legs and the leap in half. The dog landed hard, causing rocks to shoot in every direction.

Orthrus yelped in pain but kept moving, using his front legs to drag his way toward Isolde who was not more than four feet away.

The pressure around us grew with my fear. My first instinct was to pull the acid laced water from the lake, but I couldn't risk hitting anyone with it. So, I went with my next go to. I lifted rocks on the beach and flung them, hitting the dog in his eyes and nose.

Nothing seemed to stop him. He kept dragging his body forward.

Issy was locked with fear, shivering. Hercules continued his attack and stabbed the creature in the side. As it turned its head to snap at Hercules, Adrian drove his sword into the creature's neck, twisting it sideways before pulling it out and hacking at one of the heads.

Its jaw went slack and the head flopped over to hang limp, blood pumping from the gauges in its body.

The other head howled and growled in pain. The blood-spattered fur didn't hide what I saw in its eyes. The creature was mortally wounded and willing to kill whatever it could before it died.

The dog was within biting distance of Issy who wasn't moving. I grabbed more rocks, flinging them as hard as my heart beat.

"Issy, move! God Damn it!" I screamed.

Hercules rushed around Adrian and dove for Isolde's immobile form, smashing into the ground with Issy cradled in his arms. They rolled down the rocky slope, stopping just before the water's edge.

"Stabbed it in the chest, Adrian! You have to put him down. Now!" Hercules shouted.

Adrian took one more hack at the beast but couldn't remove his sword. It was caught in between two vertebras. He ripped his dagger out and stabbed it into the chest, turning it once again before he pulled it out. Blood gushed from the deep wound.

Tristan appeared by his side and stabbed it through an eye, pushing the blade in as far as it would go. Yet, the dog kept snapping and twisting his head in an effort to sink his teeth into something. The movement pulled the blade from Tristan's grasp. Orthrus' mouth searched for any piece of its attacker to tear apart.

Adrian continued pulling on the sword before freeing it. He quickly thrust into the chest of Orthrus and a high-pitched whine escaped. The creature slumped on his sword as Adrian pulled it back out of the creature's body, leaving it to fall lifeless onto the floor.

Hercules took three strides to the beast and cleaved the second head from its torso. What little blood was left, sprayed over his face. He then used his forearm to wipe his brow,

"Good job, nephew! You get the kill for this one. Wait till I tell Ares. Perseus will be most proud. I don't think it'll be regenerating," he huffed, patting Adrian on the shoulder, then leaned down to help Isolde to her feet.

She muttered a '*thank you*' but stood on shaky legs.

I didn't know what to do. The shock of it hung over me for a second. It had happened so fast and yet the world was still moving in slow motion.

The pressure in the air remained high. I opened and closed my eyes to blink. Then everything snapped back into place.

Issy was out of it. Tristan had a few scraps from sharp teeth and nothing more. Hera didn't have a spot on her. Hercules squatted down next to Isolde and whipped his sword off on the fur of the dead beast. Adrian was covered with blood up to his shoulders along with most of his face.

The rocks around me settled back to the ground as I breathed out the pent-up tension.

CHAPTER 23

ISOLDE

Mom quickly moved to wipe blood from Adrian's face.

I stood still. The fog from the river trip had turned me into a target and my fear had overcome me. I wanted to scream at myself. I'd stood there petrified and once again, Hercules had to save me from my own stupidity.

I pulled my shawl from my shoulders and began wiping Hercules face while he was still crouched on the ground. I took care to make sure our skin didn't touch. He stared up at me, but I did my best to not meet his inquiring stare.

When I'd touched him in the Biodome the vision of his life hadn't played. It didn't now either when he pulled me to the ground.

I don't know why.

I bit my lip. The memory of the blue flash lingered. He turned his head so I could wipe the blood near his hairline and the soft silky waves fell across my arm. For a moment, I wanted to run my fingers through his hair and see just how much there was and if it all felt like silk.

A slow smile pulled at his mouth and I found myself staring at his lips. I met his eyes and immediately pulled back.

He's a letch. I just know it.

I lay the shawl over his shoulder. "You can do the rest," I muttered.

"Thank you. What can I give to such a kind heart?" He asked.

I looked into his penetrating clear blue eyes with the dark rings. He was unlike anyone I knew. I wanted to cup his chin and hold his attention forever.

He had a half smile curling his lips and his eyes carried a glimmer of deviousness. I pulled my outstretched arm back. He turned his face and kissed my palm.

I sucked in a sharp breath, then squeezed my eyes closed for the vision that didn't come!

"What did you do that for?"

"I have no other way to repay your kindness but with a kiss," he replied low so only I could hear him.

My heart pounded in my rib cage and my mouth went dry.

It sounded like bullshit from a cheesy romance novel, but his lips were soft warm. Even though his lips hadn't caressed me, since it was a quick kiss, the spot where it touched me burned with the remembered contact.

He's like my 100,000 times great uncle or something. My gorgeous 100,000 times great uncle who keeps saving me.

< How romantic! > Tristan snickered.

< Shut it, Tristan! I don't see you romancing anybody. > I retorted

<Generally, there's no one around here for me to romance but you and that would be gross. > he returned, adding a mental yuck sound.

< You liked that Oracle chick. >

<I said she was good-looking. > He added.

<Nope. You said she was hot. >

Now it is my turn to snicker at him.

< She is hot for a Themian, but she's not a hybrid like us. Hercules is.> Tristan replied.

I didn't understand what he was getting at. Lots of hybrids lived with humans and Themians with hybrids.

What is the big deal about Hercules being one or not?

I glanced over at Hera. She held a thoughtful look as if gauging my reaction. On the other hand, mom was too busy wiping blood off of Adrian's face to notice Hercules kissing my hand. For once I was happy mom was so focused on Adrian.

She looked so happy.

Which was okay. My mother was allowed to be happy.

And Adrian did just slay a two-headed dog.

That was pretty awesome.

I watched Adrian staring at Tristan with pride. I couldn't say I blame him.

If my son had just helped me slay a giant two-headed dog, I think I'd be pretty proud too.

My father wasn't a weakling. He was just more of a boardroom guy.

I wonder what Dad would have done in this situation?

I pushed that into the background where stuff I needed to think about later lingered.

Charon waited further down the beach for us to catch up. Also, I had had enough talking for the moment. I glanced around and took in the terrain, looking for the next guardian or trouble. The last thing I wanted was to be caught off guard again.

A long narrow boat rose and fell in the water next to a makeshift dock. Charon indicated that we should board the glorified kayak.

Hera took her seat first, choosing to sit near Charon at the stern. Not wanting to throw the balance off, I chose the bow. Hercules took the seat right behind me.

It doesn't mean anything. I'm just being stupid.

There was a hot breath on my neck. "Hold on to the side rails. They will give you better balance. Also keep your feet on the planks in the bottom of the boat. They're angled to brace yourself."

His deep baritone voice gave me the shivers. Every hair on the back of my neck rose with the warm breath from his words.

You're just being silly, Isolde! Just because he's a good-looking guy... you're sort of, kind of related to him. I mean, not necessarily related to him. He's like, you know, your 50,000 great uncle.

I took a deep breath to calm my thoughts, it was no use, they kept coming.

To him I'm a stupid little girl who can't stay out of trouble.

Tristan shot me a raised eyebrow from the beach.

<He was helpful. >Tristan offered.

<Yeah, a little too helpful. Breathing down the back of my neck kind of helpful. > I retorted.

There was no way I was giving my brother more ammo to annoy me with.

< You don't mind it all that much. > he snickered.

< Mind your own business, Tristan. I don't need an arrogant liar breathing down the back of my neck to get his jollies, especially one that shows up late to the party. >

< Mom decided who came along. At least he didn't chicken out. He didn't flinch. When asked, he grabbed a sword and came to save our asses. Yours twice now. >

< Touché! He did join in the middle and saved my ass. > I replied.

<So, act like you appreciate it! I wouldn't have made it in time, Isolde. >

Tristan is just trying to help me see the big picture.

I was on edge. Everyone was and the littlest thing set me off.

Mom gets like this and I don't want to be her.

Nonetheless, I catch myself doing it anyway.

I did wish Tristan would just mind his own business. He tiptoed through my thoughts without my permission, all the time. I went into my mind and smashed the *Tristan* door between us shut.

There were lots of windows and doors in my mind. I kept most of them closed. I've always kept mom's and Tristan's open, but I've come to the conclusion that I needed to change that.

Hera — she wasn't a door but a window. She seemed able to open it at will. Though this aspect irritated me, she was non-intrusive and had never betrayed my secrets.

The next window I found was new. It had an empty plaque above it with no name. The many windows and doors in my mind, all came with names. That is if I cared to look. This was the first one not to have a name.

Or maybe I just didn't notice.

Before Tristan climbed in the boat, he cocked an eyebrow at me, mocking me, then blew me a kiss. I returned his sardonic stare with a small snarl.

The oars on the boat rose in unison and moved forward, then lowered into the water, making our little tiny boat burst forward. Charon stood at the rear with his unseeing blue eyes.

I didn't know what it was about him. He scared me. A lot.

Obviously, he's alive.

How, I couldn't fathom standing like a statue for a million plus years, doing nothing, seeing nothing, speaking to no one...

All that laid before us was a vast expanse of water as the shore drifted away. At first, it started soft, as a breeze through a window.

I half expected the fathomless whomping from the previous river to return. Instead, it was a low reedy sound, similar to the noise made by wooden wind chimes. The soft woody tones gained force, rising to a harsh metallic wailing.

My mom said it was just the pocks in the ceiling, a trick of geology, despite that I could hear it beyond my ears. The wailing clawed at my mind. It filled me with sorrow and suffering. I simply couldn't push it out. There were no mental doors or windows to close.

I placed both hands on my head, pressing the meat of my palm to my ear canal. I closed my eyes, hoping to close off my mind. Nothing was working. The boat shifted and my body quaked with it. The skin on my arms rose to greet the desperate sounds.

The wailing reminded me of the terrors from the many lives I'd witnessed. I was desperate to stop the noise. My belly ached with fear and I curled into a fetal position. The boat jolted with the water and I smashed against the railing.

Warm arms slid around my waist pulling me back. My body pressed against a rock-hard wall of muscle. The screaming wasn't just coming from the river. It was coming from me. It filled me, tearing me apart inside and out. The heat from the body holding me was the only thing keeping me anchored.

"Isolde, don't listen to the river. Listen to the sound of my voice. Don't let them overtake you," he murmured into my ear, his voice was low and filled with tension.

I whimpered with the screaming of the river which dug into my soul to tear out all the horrors, shred by shred.

Hercules never stopped talking. The baritone murmuring remained tickling the outer edge of my ear and it overtook the river's sorrow filled wails.

I understood then why he was such a great storyteller. Listening to the sound of his voice could entrance anyone, me being one of them. I could have believed anything he said. So lovely was the vibration of his vocal cords.

Eventually, the screaming stopped and my cramped muscles slowly released as I relaxed against him. Both his legs were braced against the wooden pads and I was curled up on his lap like a child. My senses returned and I released my ears.

Exhaustion swept over me.

Why am I the only one affected like this?

It didn't appear as if anybody else on the boat batted an eyelash. Only Adrian did seem a little worse for wear.

"Feeling better, Calla?" Hercules asked.

I tilted my head back and looked up into his eyes. His face was wrinkled with worry.

"You almost fell out of the boat. It's a terrible river to go for a swim in. Especially, when you're not capable of swimming," he offered the excuse.

I simply blinked back at him.

"Thank you," I faltered for what else to say. I didn't want to be ungrateful, like Tristan said. "May I take my seat now?"

"Now is not the time to be shifting seats. I think it's best if you stay on my lap until we're done." He pointed up at the ceiling, which was only a hand span from the top of his head.

"I'm sure I can wiggle over to my own seat," I replied, feeling uncomfortable with the way his arms cradled me in place.

"I haven't had a woman sit on my lap in a long time and I'm rather enjoying it. Sure, you won't stay?" he asked just before releasing my waist.

However, his hand lingered on my hip and gave it a little squeeze, making me squeak.

"I don't care if you did save me from being dipped in acid. Only an opportunist chauvinist pig would squeeze a girl's hinny just because she was close by."

"Forgive me, Calla, what is this word you used? Hinny? Does it mean bottom? Because I didn't squeeze your bottom, I squeezed your hip. Anyhow, I should not have taken advantage of you. I was wrong." He glanced down at his hands then back up at me.

"Thank you for saving me. Again. But I'm not your grabbing post. How could you not know what a hinny is? Yes, it's a bottom."

"I've been living on a Themian Homeworld for several thousand years. They don't use words such as 'hinny'. Actually, they don't use a lot of slang like Earth does. I'm rather enjoying it all. Your uncle Tobias certainly knows a great deal."

"I don't know my uncle Tobias. He's just a name on a piece of paper my mother showed me once."

"Well, then you're certainly missing out on a great guy. Too bad his wife didn't want to come with him and he has two small girls to care for. It's very sad for him." Hercules' smile turned down as he spoke about uncle T's girls.

"I didn't know his wife didn't come," I murmured.

"No, she announced that he and his children were freaks and left. It's okay, really. I have a feeling he'll meet a lovely young hybrid and make lots of beautiful babies."

"Why is making babies so important?" I squeaked.

I'd actually begun to soften before his baby remark.

He looked deep into my eyes and a twinkle along with a mischievous smile curved his lips.

"Having children is a byproduct, the making of them is the fun part. That's the part I'm most interested in." He leaned forward so our eyes were on the same level. The wicked smile left his face only to be replaced by an earnest interest. "What about you Isolde? Are you interested in the making or the having?"

My mouth went dry. I was still a virgin. I thought that was apparent.

Is he hitting on me? Why would he care whether I want to make babies or have them? Is this an ancient Greek pickup line?

"Whether I want to make babies or have them, is really no business of yours, *Uncle*," I retorted.

"Are you saving yourself for your mate?" He raised an eyebrow, mockingly.

"Whether I am or I'm not, it's private and none of your business. Thank you again for saving me, but now I think I'll get out, on my own."

He lifted his head and looked around as the boat had stopped and everyone else had disembarked.

"Well, I've wanted to get out of the boat for several minutes but you just wouldn't get off my lap so I wasn't going to be rude. But since you're ready, can I get out of the boat now?"

Ugh!

He was doing this on purpose.

Why is he flirting with me? What does he think every woman wants him? I hate aggravating men!

I quickly stood up and I lost my balance. I would have fallen over if it weren't for both his hands wrapped around my waist, righting me.

"Might want to be careful about your step there, Calla. Wouldn't want you to fall out of the boat," he remarked.

"I don't need your help, thank you."

I wanted to stomp my foot, but then I'd just looked like a child.

His amusement was apparent, he was clearly doing this to piss me off and it was working.

God dammit. I hate guys like that.

Tristan stood off to the side, barely containing his mirth.

<Stop laughing at me! I don't know what you think is funny, but it's not funny> I yelled.

<Oh, but it is very funny! Seriously, you're saying that you hate guys like him. Sis, you haven't met any guys like that before. > His laughter boomed in my mind.

<How would you know? >

<I've been with you since conception. You've never met anybody like him before. He's great. > Tristan kept laughing, but his face never revealed his mirth.

Other than the quivering muscles of his belly, no one would ever know he was laughing.

< Shut up, Tristan! > I snarled.

I just wanted Hercules to get away from me. Even Hera seemed amused. He was still holding my hand as I stepped over the edge of the boat. I snatched it back from him as soon as I was out.

"I told you. I don't need your help stepping out of a boat. I can do that just fine on my own, thank you."

"Whatever you say, Calla. I'm at your disposal," he demurred then smoothed his hair back out of his face, readjusting the sword on his back.

"You came along to help your mother. So why don't you help her?" I snapped.

"When she needs my help, I will be there. I'm a chivalrous man always trying to help a lady in distress."

"Really? The only distress here is you harassing me. Please, just leave me alone!" I shot back at him.

The look on my mother's face said she was amused too.

Fuck them all! Honestly are they all going to laugh at me? I almost fell out of the boat only to be saved by the big stupid brute, a 20,000-year-old misogynist wind bag, who is talking about making babies and having babies. Does he even know how old I am?

<You are 18. You're old enough, sis. >

<I'm having a private conversation here. One that you're not welcome to attend.> I rebuffed him.

< Then stop broadcasting so loud. Even mom can hear your internal conversations. That makes them not very private. > Tristan raised his eyebrows and rolled his eyes.

Charon walked away from the river, heading into a new tunnel. He was probably working our way to the next river.

I double-timed my pace to catch up and get away from all of them. Hera's mind pressed in.

< Isolde, Hercules doesn't mean any harm. He just likes to tease. It's part of his personality and charm. He does it to keep your mind off of all the trouble we face.>

<Does he hit on every woman he snatches from death?>

<Do you mean flirting or making advances towards? Because yes, he'll flirt with any available woman around him. He likes women. And they like him>

<Well, I for one, don't like him.> I retorted, wishing she would leave me alone.

She simply nodded her head, mentally backing away.

Like I want to just be another girl, in a long line of girls?

If what they're implying about him was true, he'd been sleeping with a long line of girls from the various bloodlines for thousands of years. I was not going to be another one of those girls.

He can go be a male slut with someone else, in some other bloodline.

My mother said the O'Dear's were from the girl's bloodline. Which meant that none of the boys had a part in my lineage. He could sleep with everybody else's bloodline, but leave ours alone. That also meant that I was like a 20,000 times great-granddaughter of his twin.

Creepy.

We came across a group of jagged rocks and my dress kept getting caught on them. I couldn't seem to hike my skirt up high enough to stop it. A second later, like a letch that you cannot escape from, he was right behind me.

"If you want, I can cut it off. Of course, not too short. I will leave you with your modesty. You can save the fabric for other things."

"Sure. You can use the fabric for a shirt," I said with my best bitchface smile.

He boomed out a laugh, "You're like a lioness. Taming you will take more effort than I think I have to muster. I have to conserve my strength for the various guardians down here. You have won, Calla. I will cover myself as you say and harass you no more."

I wasn't going to take the bait.

Herc can flirt all he wants. I have much bigger fish to fry.

CHAPTER 24

SYDNEY

<Adrian, did you notice what's going on with Issy and Hercules? What is that about?> I asked, unsure I really wanted the answer.

<He likes her.> Adrian mentally shrugged.

< She's too young for him.> I grumbled.

<Now who's being unreasonable? Is Emmaline too young for Ixis? How old is Ixis? A hundred thousand? Herc is ten thousand or so. He's been alone with his siblings. Themians are xenophobic. Give him a break. He did save her life.> Adrian chided, then ran his fingers up and down my arm.

He was trying to distract me and it raked me the wrong way.

<He could go for a different girl. The ship is full of them. Since when did you start calling him Herc?>

<The kids call him Herc.> Adrian replied with a smile.

I watched the way Hercules stared after my daughter. I didn't like it but I could see what he was looking at. She was young, impressionable, headstrong, and sassy as all get out.

What man wouldn't find that enticing?

Men always seem to like it when a woman tells them to fuck off. I threw a glance over at Adrian.

<When I told you to go away and leave me alone, did you like that?> I kicked a rock out of my path for no other reason than to keep my eyes off Adrian and his reaction.

<No, I found it intriguing. Beautiful girl, I'd known you my whole life. Then you told me you were not allowed to be friends with me and to forget about you. You had to know that was never gonna happen. I was never going to forget about you. You were my best friend.>

<Yeah, until your mom told you I wasn't and then suddenly, I was persona non grata.> I grumbled and worked not to cross my arms.

<I never forgot about you. I just couldn't figure out why you were telling me to fuck off. It didn't matter how many times you told me to go away. I wasn't going to.>

His fingers laced into mine. His hand swallowed mine and I drew comfort from it.

<Why? Because the two of us were mated? And because you could hear my voice even though I couldn't hear yours? >

<You were the most beautiful, smartest girl I knew. Girls threw themselves at me all the time, but you were the only one who told me to go away. You specifically said that you wanted nothing more than to be friends. Besides, being a major blow to a guy's ego when a beautiful girl says '*I don't like you for anything more than a friend*'. It also made me ask myself what would a guy, who wanted to be more than friends have to do to get your attention.>

The tip of his sword tapped a rock on the ground as he pulled me around to look at him. He stared at me for a moment before glancing around.

<What do you think is going on with those two?> I asked before I too searched the rocky walls and shadows for the next guardian. The adrenalin from the previous fights still flowed in my body making me shaky.

< I think he's looking at Issy and thinks, '*A beautiful smart girl told me to take a long walk off a short cliff.*' He's finally able to pick any girl available to him and the one that he wants doesn't want anything to do with him. No offense, but having a girl throw herself at you isn't nearly as interesting as a girl who tells you '*I see who and what you are and I'm not interested*'. Men are stupid animistic creatures. We automatically believe that everyone would be interested in what we have simply because we're pretty hot stuff.>

I snorted a laugh, then bit my lip to hold my mirth back. <You are gorgeous and smart and funny, but you honestly do you think you're so great that any woman should want you? > I demanded in disbelief.

< I don't want just any woman. But wouldn't you be kind of offended if the person you did want was like, '*Yeah, not interested. Next!*'?> He pulled me into his chest and forced me to look him in the eyes just like he had when he told me he loved me.

My breath caught in my throat as a new hormone raced through my veins. I swallowed and closed my eyes to push back the desire I still felt every time he held me.

< Okay, so you think this thing with Hercules isn't going to go away? > I demanded to cover the heat rushing over me.

< No. The way he stares after her, gives me the feeling that Hercules will be hanging around for the duration. Or until something happens to make him stop.> Adrian finished then released me.

The wicked smile on his face told me he knew exactly what he was doing.

Bastard!

< Wait! Something like what?> I asked, dreading the answer.

<A mating.>

I stepped back gobsmacked. The idea of my daughter being mated/married to anybody frightened me.

Okay. She was 18 and could make her own choices. But this wasn't the good old US of A. We weren't on a boat on planet Earth. We were on a different planet, in a different solar system, in a different galaxy.

Not to mention that at any minute we may start an intergalactic battle for our very survival.

Hercules was half human, a hybrid just like Isolde. The only difference was that Hercules was not immortal and Issy was.

Issy is immortal. I said it and so is Tristan.

I hadn't given myself a second to think about it. Nonetheless, there it was, right in front of me. I didn't want my children to go through what I did with Gabriel.

Whoever they end up with, will have to be immortal too.

It's not like I planned this. Hera said she kept her children alive. Yet, she never said she made them immortal.

Maybe I'm just being silly.

My feet kept pace with our group and I'd let my mind slip. I quickly took in our surroundings to assure myself there were no threats lurking in the dark blue shadows.

The Isolde issue will have to wait for another day.

We needed to get away from Themian space first and out of the underground maze of water.

After all, Isolde told him to go on...

I couldn't let go of the fact that the last man who tried to sweet talk her was also trying to rape and kill her and me.

Other than throwing her brother a lot of dirty looks.

Maybe it's just men in general she has a problem with.

I chanced a glance behind us and ran into Tristan's back. His arm was extended to stop all of us. I peeked around my son and caught my breath.

"What is that?" I whispered.

"The next Guardian?" Tristan replied as Issy slowly stepped backwards towards Hercules' outstretched arms.

When she reached his hand, he guided her around behind him to stand next to his mother.

"Khimera," he murmured.

The creature hardly looked like anything. It was all curled up on a large boulder, reminding me of a kitten with its furry body in a ball.

"You mean the goat, lion headed thingy?" Adrian remarked.

I didn't see a goat head, but the acid in my belly churned over and bubbled.

"Yeah. I do think it has a snake tail too," the reply came.

I glanced over at Adrian. The two men were locked in deep conversation mentally. Both of them had their knives and swords out.

"You guys can't go fight that thing?" I murmured.

The terror in my mind caused the rocks on the beach to shift and slip.

"What did you think we were going to do, Sydney? Where's your son? I wish to speak with Tristan," Hercules inquired.

I looked from Adrian to Hercules. Adrian waved his hand in a downward patting motion. He quietly attempted to still my terrified mind and the power I held there.

"Tristan, come! The men need to speak," Hercules called

I wanted to burst at the patriarchy of Y chromosome poisoning, but didn't.

Tristan was by their side in two steps, as Isolde gravitated towards Hera and I.

"Hera, what are they doing?" Issy asked.

"Hercules is devising a battle plan. The Khimera is crafty. It has the ability to breath out fire from one mouth and ice from the other."

"What can Tristan do? I mean other than teleporting," I asked in terror at the thought that my boy would be either frozen or burned to death.

My belly quivered at the idea of my boy becoming a block of ice.

"Tristan can make fire, mom. When we were in the first tunnel, he made a fireball and carried it with us so that we could see in the dark."

I scrunched my eyes closed. That was the last thing in the world I wanted to hear.

At least it's defensive.

I opened my eyes and looked at Isolde. She seemed excited about it.

"And you think this is a good thing?" I remarked while turning to bore holes in the back Hercules's head.

I'm sure he is going to get my family killed, if I don't.

"I have no defensive abilities except for maybe a mind attack. I can send emotions to people and confuse them. You can dominate their minds and move things around. You control water and the wind. Tristan can transport himself through time and space. I think the fact that he can control fire is awesome. Can you or Hera control fire?" Issy asked with bated breath.

Her eyes kept traveling to Hercules and her brother then the surrounding room and back to us.

"No, I cannot control fire. I can only draw on fire that is already present. I am good with wind and water but nothing like your mother. I can move myself with the wind. But I can't move other objects. Not unless I'm under great strain. I'm a dreamwalker," she stated as if that wasn't a weapon.

I knew better than to believe her. She could make you see whatever she wanted.

The men broke apart and fanned out in a large circle around the creature.

"You know I can't control fire. I am glad Tristan can and so can Adrian. Actually, it makes perfect sense. He inherited it," I said and glanced over at Tristan and Adrian, momentarily catching Adrian's eye.

He gave me a wink and then refocused back on Hercules and the positions they were moving into.

Charon stood with his back to the cavern wall like a statue made of white marble and frozen in time. The stark contrast against the gray/blue scale of the wall made it seem intentional, his unseeing eyes neither judging nor refereeing.

I do wonder. What if none of us survives this. Will he stand there forever, waiting for the next Fates?

<If you do not succeed, I will stand here forever. There can be no other Fates. There are only The Fates, Atropos > Charon answered.

<He speaks?> I remarked.

There was no reply.

CHAPTER 25

ISOLDE

I knew it had a name and that it was a monster in every sense of the word.

"I thought a Khimera was a thing that could change and blend into its environment or a genetic disorder."

Tristan's eyebrows shot up and he broke out into a smile. "Oh man, sis! You have got it wrong. What were you doing in that library?"

I scrunched up my nose on one side.

I hate it when he acts so omnipotent.

"I was looking for Elysium, not monsters. If you're so smart, what is it?"

He opened his mouth only to have Hera cut him off.

"It is the child of an Orthrus, a fearsome fire and ice breathing monster. She is fast and strong."

"She? That thing is a girl? Are you kidding me?" Fear gripped me.

We just killed her father.

"I hope she doesn't have a daddy complex, cause we just killed him," I said and moved back a step, hoping to get away from the soon to be angry monster.

"Girls don't take kindly to that," Hercules replied.

I pinched my lips and cocked an eyebrow at Herc. Boy, was he the king of the understatements?

"What else do we know about this thing?" My mom was always going for the upper hand anyway she could get it. "It's strong and..."

I regarded the creature. She reclined on a huge boulder. There was a glimpse of the river just beyond, but there was no way to pass or go around without disturbing her.

She had two heads. One was a goat or ram, while the other one was a lioness. The front paws were massive with black razor-sharp claws, protruding from the end of the shaggy fur covered pads. There had to be toes under all that fuzz, though there was no way to see them.

She lashed her tail high into the air. All the blood drained from my face. The tail was scaled, red, and horned with an articulated armor appearance to it. That wasn't what scared me. It had a halberd like spear on the end. As she slammed it down on the boulder, small sparks flew off in every direction as a portion of the stone broke off and crashed to the ground.

When Hera said Khimera was strong I didn't think she could break stone.

The motion had a cat like grace to it. It reminded me of the way an Earth cat would flick its tail in irritation, just before it decided to get up and —.

"Oh shit! She is going to move. Get ready!" Herc jumped in front of me with his scythe like dagger and short sword. He threw a few words at me. "Whatever happens, stay behind me or your brother," he ordered.

I bristled at him bossing me around. But he was right. I don't have any defensive abilities. I didn't want to cause a distraction again and find myself needing to be saved, so I moved further back.

"Adrian, Tristan, stand to the front."

<I only have a dagger.> Tristan screamed in my mind, yet everyone heard him.

Herc threw his scythe at Tristan. "Stick the pointy end into the bad monster."

Tristan shot him the look of '*go fuck yourself*'. <What a dick!>

<Tell me about it> I replied.

"Tristan, just shift in and out around her and stab where you can," Adrian offered.

Tristan has no training.

My hand covered my mouth to stop myself from biting my lip. Anxiety coiled around me, and my eyes darted from Tristan to Hercules and back.

Breath! As long as that thing doesn't crush their head they will live.

"Issy, I want you to send out fear to her, and only to her," Hercules instructed.

He must have overheard me talking to his mother.

"O-kay."

I reached inside to that moment when I thought I was alone and Jacques was going to rape me. I grabbed it and thrust it out like a bullet at Khimera. She reared her head back. Her eyes blazed with rage as she locked onto me.

Khimera was not just a large monster. She was massive. She was easily two times the size of an African elephant.

I couldn't quite place why the tail looked so strange and dangerous until the third head rose from behind the furry mane of the lion's head.

The red scale covered head embodied every human nightmare ever conjured in history. It sported a flicking forked tongue that curled as it exited its mouth to taste the air. The black faceted eyes gleamed in the dim blue light, while ribbed fans protruded from the sides of its head. Her snout was hooked at the end with elliptical nostrils where a minuscule wisp of smoke escaped.

The fear I threw out went from a memory to reality and it was quickly followed by panic. My breathing went shallow as my heart pounded into overdrive.

She yawned to reveal rows upon rows of dagger shaped teeth. She snapped her jaw shut and turned her malevolent gaze on us.

It was a fucking Dragon.

What could have made this thing?

It looked like three different animals got mixed up in a transporter accident.

And she is not the least bit concerned about us.

I was practically petrified with my legs locked in place. My mouth became dry instantly. I couldn't tear my eyes away from the monstrosity.

She leaned back into her haunches, which looked more like the feet of a bird, and stretched her front cat shaped paws. The lionesses mouth opened wide, while the goat snapped its jaws, creating a clicking noise that reverberated against the nearby pocked wall.

The horns on the goat were black and white. They were twisted, pointing straight into the air. Light gleaming off the raw sharp edges. The goat shifted its head back and forth, shaking its chin one way and the other, making its long beard trail across the top of the cat's head.

The dragon turned its eyes on us.

She clearly doesn't see us as a threat. We are just another inconvenient thing to play with.

The dragon settled on me. However much of an animal it appeared, it was clearly intelligent and knew I was sending out fear and she didn't like it.

A loud scream tore from its mouth, as the tail lashed back and forth a few more times cutting big swaths into the side of the boulder and part of the beach. That thing's tail is 30 to 40-foot-long. Forget the rest of its body.

"Does anybody know how to kill this thing?" I moaned with loathing.

My hands were shaking, as I ran them over my tunic to ease my fears. But the grimy fabric's texture did nothing for me. It only reinforced my panic. I was tired, hungry, dirty and now there was a dragon in front of us.

Herc tied his long hair up in a knot on his head. "Typical Themian rules, cut off its head and burn the stump," he supplied and shrugged his shoulders before rolling his head around.

He shook his arms to loosen the muscles and relaxed into a fighting stance.

"Cut off its head and burn the stump? Is that the best you could come up with?" Tristan yelled before shaking his head.

<There has to be a better way.> my brother murmured.

"Worked the last two times. Sydney, you have some amazing abilities? I will need you to join the fray. I don't think that your son and your mate are going to be enough for us. Not this time," Herc remarked, then began sucking in deep breaths of air to up his oxygen levels.

My mother narrowed her eyes at him. "I can move things, obviously, and you know, I control water and wind."

She left out her ability to find things or see through other's eyes.

Hera gasped. I glanced over at her sharply and she shook her head.

Now isn't the time for whatever conversation I want to have with her.

"Woman, I need you to push that thing around as much as you can. Pull water from the river and see if you can drown it. Do whatever you think you can do. Isolde, keep doing what you're doing. It's clearly pissing them off but it's distracting them too. The more distracted he is, the easier he'll be to beat."

"She. Easier she'll be to kill. It's female, not male," I retorted, letting my fear get the better of me.

He nodded his head and a smile spread across his face. "Point taken, Isolde. She will be easier to kill if she's distracted," he repeated.

Khimera moved slowly, padding closer. The fur on her feet made the movement soundless. Not even a pebble was dislodged. All the while she was flicking her tail.

I was waiting for her to stop and start cleaning one of her paws. I got the distinct feeling it was not only playing with us but that it was going to pounce on us.

"Tristan, can you hopscotch?" I asked.

A second later he was standing by me with his wicked little grin "Yeah!"

"If you can hopscotch in here so can Adrian," I informed him.

His smile slipped away with the realization of what could happen. He shifted back to his original position near Hercules and shared a look with Adrian.

A low rumbling sound filled the cavern as every hair on my body stood on end. The deep rumble was affecting everyone else in the same way.

The fear factor I was sending out wasn't enough.

Khimera threw the bone grinding sound around the space, filling the cavern. There was never another moment I was more terrified than now. The Nemeans were an overture. This was the whole opera, finale and all.

I took the feelings of terror I had and I wove them together like fabric. The sound along with all my fear and every drop of the horrors I now carried from all those other minds. I dredged deep into the memories of the judged ones and I created a fabric of panic. Then, I threw it.

"Wow, Isolde! What did you just do? It's petrifying," Tristan shouted over the roar.

"Everyone, shut me out! I can't stop now," I said and kept pushing.

I kept picturing it like a laser beam sitting on my head right into the Khimera's minds. The intense emotional blast pushed her back on her haunches. However, she regained her footing and began wiggling her weight between each of her back legs, getting ready to pounce.

The dragon puffed out her wings, rearing back. The tail was lashing so hard it dug great gouges in the floor, causing rocks to fly in every direction.

We were fighting on her turf and she was determined to crush us.

The goat screamed and half the beach turned to ice, stopping just in front of Adrian's fire wall. The goat breathed ice and a cold mist escaped from her nostrils.

Mom kept pushing Khimera's body, batting it this way and that. She pulled the creature forward onto the ice slick and Khimera's dragon head released a blast of fire at its feet. The heat pushed my hair back along with my body and I landed hard on the uneven ground. Tears formed in my eyes to cover for the heat, evaporating all my moisture away.

I quickly got back to my feet.

The ice slick was gone, leaving only puddles of water on the ground.

The low rumbling ceased and turned into a loud uproar. The lionesses reared back and the goat screamed in anger. Every muscle on her coiled just before a sudden release. She leapt into the air and a second later she unfurled her wings. She beat them twice, pushing a tremendous amount of air.

Hercules leaned into the wind and I followed suit. Khimera gilded back to the ground only steps away from Hercules.

I screamed.

Hercules was off balance. Before he could regain his footing, all three men shifted out and reappeared in a new position surrounding the monster.

Unfortunately, we couldn't take advantage of our new tactile position because she leapt into the air and shifted into the middle of us. With that, Hercules disappeared.

I screeched in shock before spotting him further down the beach. He blinked out and reappeared near me.

"That bitch shifted me!" He shouted to Adrian.

Oh my God! Khimera is a shifter!

<Holy Fuck, Batman!> Mom shouted.

Mom immediately pushed Khimera back with a force I'd never seen her able to wield before. The dragon reared back, puffing in shock, like a snake just before striking.

I chanced a peek at Hera. She didn't know what was going to happen.

"Get out of the way!" I shouted and dove after her.

I collided with her stomach. I wrapped both arms around her and we tumbled to the floor. The smell of burnt hair skimmed the back of my body as the flames blew over the top of me, singeing everything in its path.

I'd broken my concentration and the fear was gone. She had attacked Hera on purpose.

I hate monsters!

It intended to stop me. I felt the suddenly drenched water and heard my mother yelling, "Get off the ground and move! Move, ladies!"

Mom's voice broke me out of my daze.

Hercules had already begun slashing at the creature's side hindquarters, while Tristan blinked in and out desperately avoiding the Halberd-like tail as it lashed back and forth. The spike stabbed at Tristan, and Adrian threw fireballs on the fur. Nothing took.

"That thing is God damn fireproof!" Adrian yelled just before he shifted to a new location and tossed a fresh fire.

Water splashed my face, "Get your head in the game, Isolde, or you're gonna die!" Mom shouted.

Hera pulled the wind, forcing the creature back as my mother gave it a mental pushed. Each of them fought with what they had. I quickly retook my position and pulled the fear from my mind and tossed it like a fishing net.

She turned and took a swipe at me. I dove and rolled to the side.

Maybe my days on the boat haven't been such a bad thing.

Boat work had increased my reflexes and had given me stamina along with strength and agility.

Adrian appeared in front of me a moment later and threw a fireball. It didn't catch but it definitely burned.

The creature shrieked in anger as it curled its paw in on itself. Adrian took his sword and slashed its paws in several places. The Khimera shrieked again. Then, Adrian disappeared only to reappear a hundred yards down the beach.

He yelled a moment before shifting in next to me.

She unfurled her wings.

"Adrian, the wings! Stab them! That way she can't jump," Hercules shouted from the other side of the beast.

Adrian shifted from standing in front of me to suddenly standing next to the wings. He slashed the delicate membranes between the bones, shredding them.

The dragon turned its head and reared back before releasing a fresh blast of flames, but Adrian shifted to the other side quickly and slashed that wing too.

The tail came around, and he disappeared just as it entered the air where his chest would've been. My mother screamed. A second later, water from the river enveloped the entire creature in a giant bubble, quenching any errant flames.

Then I remembered something.

I know it's just human mythology but there has to be some kind of truth to it.

One of the heroes had killed Khimera in the Greek mythology. I couldn't remember which one it was, but he thrust a spear into its chest. It was something about Pegasus distracting the creature and fighting long enough for some hero to stab it in the chest.

I looked over at Hercules. "I think I know how to kill her. You need to stab her in the chest right between the two breastplates."

His eyebrows pinched together, but he nodded his head and moved in.

One paw right after the other swiped at him, just like a giant cat would do when playing with a mouse. He ducked underneath all but one from Khimera.

The paw landed in the center of his chest. He couldn't hold back and screamed with agony. I wove my fabric of fear and threw it out again. The dragon head immediately shifted her malevolent eyes to stare me down. She turned her head this way and that, allowing either eye to have its turn to study me.

Tristan shifted in and stabbed the goat's neck, which gurgled as icey blood poured from the neck wound.

The dragon lurched over to see what happened. However, the lion was not distracted in the least. She just kept yowling and hissing. With every step, the sound got 10 times louder and more terrifying than anything in the animal kingdom.

I strained to hold my net of fear together, keeping it wrapped tightly around Khimera and away from my family. She screamed at me before planting her front paws. She looked from me to Tristan, then lifted her hind legs and kicked Tristan across the beach.

I screamed Tristan's name.

In slow motion, the blow landed square in Tristan's chest before slamming him against the cavern wall. The lashing tail appeared inches from Tristan's chest. My brother's head lulled to the side.

My world shrunk down to the size of that moment and my brother. A second before the tip of the tail pierced his chest, it disappeared.

All three heads on the creature reared up and roared in agony. Adrian threw a fireball, burning the end of the tail. Hercules picked up the tip of the tail and impaled it on his sword. With a grim smile, he turned around. Using his powerful arms, he raised the sword like a spear and thrust it into the monster's chest.

Her scream was garbled, as the dragon had begun to spew fire every direction.

Mom threw up a wall of water between us and the flames. Adrian picked up Tristan's body and shifted behind the wall.

All the while, Hercules pulled his half-melted sword out of Khimera's chest and chopped off the head of the Dragon.

Adrian laid Tristan down and shifted back. He then threw a fireball to burn the stump.

The goat head spewed a fresh round of ice at random before slumping to the side. The chest wound pumped out a burning orange sludge that continued to melt the skin as it found its way to the ground.

"Tristan, Tristan!" I called over the lump in my throat.

Mom was openly sobbing. "This is my fault. If I had just settled for a Homeworld..." she cried.

I huffed to keep breathing. I couldn't hear Tristan's mind. I held his hand and rocked back and forth as mom clutched him to her chest.

There was blood on the back of his head. His eyes were open but they rolled around.

I looked up at Hera, "Don't you have any more Primordium?" I pleaded.

The pain raging in my chest was heavy and tight. I couldn't move. I was wielded in place. The scene of daddy dying played out before me. Mom was on the right, just like then, and I was on the left, but this time with Hercules taking Tristan's place next to me. A thick sob escaped and I melted next to my twin.

"I do but after that we only have one vial left. We won't have any more chances," Hera stated. She pushed her damp hair out of her face and rummaged around in her bag.

"I don't care," mom howled.

Hera pulled the vial from her bag. Her hand came back bloody. That was the last vial. The other one was broken. The

Primordium had leaked away, leaving a damp spot on the outside of the purse.

There weren't any chances after this.

After this we're on our own.

"It must've broken when I stopped the dragon from burning you," I muttered as additional tears flooded my vision and my nose began to run.

"It's my fault." I looked around at everyone there.

"It is not your fault, Isolde. Saving my mother was not a mistake. So, we lost the vial. We can still save your brother. And we learned shifting can be used as a weapon," Hercules returned.

I pushed my pain away to look at Adrian.

Adrian had changed a lot over the last few months. First, I saw him as the love of my mother's life, but also the interloper. And then, of course, Tristan's biological father. But now I could feel what he really is.

He loves us as much as my father did. He really does.

My mother took the vial from Hera's hand. She pulled the cork out for Tristan and poured it down my brother's throat. He moaned and groaned, then rolled over and shrieked.

I guess it hurts when bones knit themselves back together.

I held my hand over my mouth to hold back my crying. A large hand landed on my shoulder, but I couldn't tear my eyes away from Tristan's withering form.

"He will survive, Calla. He will learn from this and be stronger," Hercules whispered.

I nodded my head numbly, then I turned and buried my face in his chest.

Tristan got up and rubbed the back of his head. His hand came away with blood. There was no way to wash it off. I didn't trust the water of these rivers.

Tristan laughed, "Water, water everywhere, yet not a drop to drink."

At the sound of his voice, I left Hercules and hugged my brother to me fiercely. It was the most beautiful moment of my life.

I pulled back to look him in the eye and assure myself he was okay.

He laughed at me, "Don't worry Issy you're not going to get rid of me that easily. After all, I can go anywhere. When I'm sure that you can take care or yourself, then I'll rest in peace knowing someone else got this crap job."

I punched him in the shoulder. <Shut up, Tristan! >

He smiled and mentally chuckled. Mom quickly took over the hugging and petted Tristan's hair back from his face. Hercules offered her the torn fabric from my dress and she used it to wipe the blood from his face and head, then peppered his face with kisses and hugged him to her, murmuring incoherently.

"Alright, I'm okay. Mom! MOM!" Tristan protested.

She released him from her death hold but kept a hand on his shoulder. She patted it several times just to reassure herself.

Hercules judged the fight a success even though the creature was lying on its side, twitching in agony with black and orange blood spewing from its lioness head.

The hind legs of the creature kept kicking. Finally, Herc raised a sword and chopped off the Lionesses head and the thing stopped moving.

Adrian took Hercules sword and walked over to the goat head. In two blows, he cleaved off both horns, then cut strips of skin from the Hydra hide and wrapped it tightly around the base of each horn, turning it into a grip.

He turned the horns over in his hand, inspecting them before stabbing the Khimera several times. The horns pulled in and out easily with a sick sucking sound. It was an efficient killing tool.

"That's for trying to kill my family," he murmured.

He handed Hercules his damaged sword back. "I have my own weapons," he said.

Hercules threw his head back and laughed. He retrieved Adrian's only blade, tossing his damaged sword to the ground.

"Can I have the other dagger?" Tristan asked.

"If you can get up and wield one," Hercules replied.

"As it stands now, we are flying without a net so whatever we do from here on out, we better be at our best," Adrian stated and pulled my brother in for a hug, then quickly released him.

"Guess you just have to hope that being immortal would be enough. At least for those of us who are because I don't think Hercules is," Tristan replied.

I was staring at Hercules. A big smile broke over his face.

What an arrogant ass! Looking at him doesn't mean anything.

I turned away quickly.

"See anything you like, Calla?" Herc asked.

I just glanced over my shoulder, "Nope."

He laughed.

Charon waited further down the cavern, next to a rickety raft. I heaved a sigh.

Another guardian, another boat, another river.

CHAPTER 26

ISOLDE

The raft was nothing more than a wood-like composite, fitted together to form a floating platform. Stanchions rimmed the edge holding up a limp rope. It was tied to a mineral encrusted dock. The whole thing barely looked sea worthy.

Charon took up his position next to the rudder type paddle. He stared off into the blue gloom without a word.

I eyed mom and Tristan to gauge their reaction. Tristan shrugged and mom bit her lip. In the end, each of them deemed the raft safe, or safe enough, and tentatively boarded the thing.

I waited for Hera, Adrian and Hercules to join them before deciding whether or not it would sink.

"Are you going to take your place on the raft, Calla?" Hercules whispered.

His breath tingled down the back of my neck and I shivered.

"After you, Herc," I replied.

He didn't move and the heat from his body worked like a furness chasing the dampness of the cavern away.

"My job is to protect your rear," he replied and Tristan snicker.

<Tristan, so help me if you don't bud out, I'll tell everyone you prefer animals to girls.> I shouted.

<I do, just not sexually.> He chuckled and I mentally groaned.

When did sharing my mind with my brother become such a pain?

Hercules held his arm out, inviting me to board the bobbing platform. Gritting my teeth, I stepped on to the uneven surface.

The raft shifted with the added weight, pushing the far side up slightly out of the water. I thrust my arms out to counter balance, keeping my feet under me. Luckily, muscles have memories and all those years on the boat had taught my body how to move with the water.

Moving to one side, I chose a position to even the load. Hercules set one foot on the raft and the entire platform jolted. I had to grab the limp rope hanging at the sides to study myself. Herc lowered his full weight and the raft settled with the balance that was struck.

Without a word Charon worked the paddle/rudder.

I expected this river to drain into another one, instead Charon maneuvered us closer to the white noise of water falling.

The far side of the cavern was bathed in midnight blue shadows. Rocky outcroppings peppered the walls and other than the glassy surface of the water there was nowhere to go. The lake ended at the pebble covered beach. We could have walked to this area if there was a new tunnel. Suddenly, the rushing sound of water grew with no obvious source.

We collectively held our breath. Uncertainty clung to us as water clung to the paddle Charon used to move the raft, dipping it again and again, in and out of the water in a steady motion.

I found my hand covering my mouth, forcing my teeth to stop biting my lip. The deep scrape of rock against wood echoed against the cavern walls, making me gasp.

One edge of the raft pressed against the side of a giant circle in the water, shattering the illusion of glass.

There, at the edge of the water level, was the opening to a circular shaft. The water of the lake was barely high enough to slip over the lip. It gave the shaft the illusion of an infinity pool. If you didn't know it was there, you would have never seen it.

The lake poured over the edge and the shaft worked to angle the sound, perched as close to the edge as we were. The roar was almost deafening.

Charon wordlessly moved to the lip and stepped off the edge and my stomach dropped with him.

I released a scream before I realized he hadn't jumped to his death. A short distance below the lip, a ledge jutted into the shaft. Though water poured over the side, the acidic effects didn't burn away his clothes.

Hercules moved, shifting the raft with every step and throwing me off balance. I clung to the limp ropes to keep from being pitched over the side.

Adrian grabbed Herc's arm and brought him to a stop, "Are you sure you want to go first?" he murmured and his words barely registered above the roar of the water.

"I swore to protect my loved ones," was the only answer Hercules gave before leaping over the edge and landing firmly on the lower ledge.

He released a booming laugh and thrust his hands into the rushing water.

"The water is clean and free of pollutants," he yelled back at us.

Everything about this trip had been nothing but one test after another. There had got to be a catch.

Mental control, Issy! Get a grip on your brain. Fear of the unknown is irrational like giving yourself a broken arm just before you climb a mountain.

Adrian helped my mother off the raft, lifting her down to the ledge. Tristan jumped, his strong legs landing with ease as his knees absorbed the impact. Herc handed his mother down then offered his hand to me.

I was hanging back, resisting for some reason, something telling me not to go.

Do not cross this ledge. It's my Rubicon. The Rubicon is just another river I'll never see again.

"Something eating at you, Calla?" Hercules asked, staring at me while I bore holes into the narrow ledge.

"Yes," I swallowed to push the quivering in the throat away. I didn't want anything to change. "I'm scared," I whispered just low enough for the water to cover my answer.

"Fear is what will keep you alive, Calla. Don't stop living just because you're afraid," Herc replied.

As he leaned towards me, his arm extended in earnest. The fluttering in my belly overtook me and all the moisture in my body disappeared at once.

I glanced down at his hand, unsure what would happen if I touched him again. I've touched him before, but other than blue electricity, I'd never seen his life. I closed my eyes and prepared myself for the hit of adrenalin that usually comes with the memories. The flavor of ozone lingers on my tongue in anticipation.

The vision hit me in the belly like a baseball bat and all the oxygen in the cave disappeared with it.

*****

The cavern is filled with thousands of people, all filthy and exhausted. Children sniffle in the background, while parents smother cries.

Pythia stands on the top of the shaft, taking in every person here, none of which stand in water. The cavern is bone dry.

"Let this crossing of a figurative river be the beginning of a new life, as we Lethe or forget the old. Elysium and all that it stood for is on the other side of that figurative river. Let us leave it there. I have found a way to the surface and there is a fresh water spring there to sustain us. No longer will we be trapped at the entrance to the Underworld and all the nightmares it holds. We will travel these last few rivers, shedding our sorrow and misery along the way. We are traveling to the land of the living, where we, mortals, will live as all living things should. Free."

She stopped to take in the faces of her people.

A man came to stand at her side. It is the blond God from the Atlantis statue and Hera's vision. He stands tall next to Pythia and leans to whisper in her ear. His fierce demeanor reminds me of my mother, serious and like the shot from a gun focused only on his goals. He looked as if he would level mountains to achieve his desires.

Pythia listens to him for a moment before he turns away, and reaches down to grasp the muscled arm of another man. His body slowly leaves the shaft to reveal the red curly haired man from the statue in front of Pythos. A cruel smirk edges his lips as he gazes down at the mass of people crammed into the cavern. He slaps the blond man on the shoulder and nods his head as if taking in his domain.

Pythia speaks again, "The Fates!"

Her words echo down the shaft.

She looks at me and she mouths my name–Isolde.

*****

Reality snapped back into place. Large arms pulled me back from and the gapping shaft.

"Whoa, Calla! There are safer ways to reach the bottom," Herc chuckled.

I whipped my head to the side. He was close, too close. The ledge was narrow and Tristan was perched on a different outcropping across from us. There was nowhere to go.

Charon began handing out harnesses to everyone. Mom ran them under the falling water, rubbing the straps together to remove the grime, then she pulled on each and every connection joint to assure herself they were safe.

Once she was convinced, she handed one to me. I numbly stepped into the apparatus, folding my dress between my legs and pulled the straps up over the fabric before tightening the straps down. I slugged the rig over my shoulders and latched the shoulder straps.

I rolled my head on my shoulders to loosen up.

This will be no different than zip-lining.

The harness was similar, though I was sure that getting insurance for a two-million-year-old rig might have been a bit hard.

Tristan snorted at my mental bleed.

Herc double-checked Hera's gear, then mine. The adrenaline flaming in my system had no way to bleed off so my skin shivered.

"Don't worry, Calla! Themians build things to last." He gave me a tentative smile.

"I don't want to forget anything important," I mumbled.

"I could think of something you could forget that would make me very happy," Herc replied and his husky voice was barely above the roar of the water.

"And what is that?" I asked absently, mentally still chewing on my vision.

"You could forget that you don't like me."

Crossing my arms, I looked up at him. I didn't know why he got my hackles up, but he did.

"Or maybe you could forget to fuck with me. It should be pretty easy as I'm three seconds worth of your memory space," I said.

It came out sharp and I immediately regretted saying it so I bit my lip and then tried to stop myself with my hand.

"No, Isolde. You've become my whole world. I can't remember anything before you."

Men are so aggravating.

I stomped my foot. He flashed a toothy grin and stepped back off the ledge into the open air of the shaft.

"Herc!" I screeched.

He laughed as the cable attached to the side of the shaft got caught, stopping his free-fall.

"You're a grade A asshole!" I shouted at him.

"Really, Issy?" Mom scoffed.

Tristan howled with laughter and slapped his leg, creating enough friction for a flame. A fire ball blasted to life in his hand as he leapt for the center of the shaft. He slapped both hands together and pulled them apart, creating two flames glowing in each hand. He held his arms wide as he fell illuminating the shaft on his way down.

"Show off!" I screamed.

Hera and Mom repelled down the wall of the shaft as if they were taking a stroll.

"You comin, Issy?" Adrian asked while the cold water poured over the sides.

"What if the cable breaks?" I asked.

My arms shook with pent up fear and all the chemicals the body feeds you to enhance it.

"Why do you think your brother went first? If we have a problem, he'll shift you," Adrian gave me one of his quiet smiles along with a little squeeze to my hand. "Don't wait too long or your brother will shift you down and where's the fun in that?" He winked at me with a clicking sound from his mouth.

I rolled my eyes and stepped off the ledge.

The shaft was the same color as the Egyptian pyramids. That creamy yellow that spoke of heat and sun. Adrian's fireball was the only light I had to travel by and it grew more distant as time went on.

I never went inside the Great Pyramid at Giza to experience the baking heat and humidity. I read several books and watched documentaries about it but that was it. However, I knew that they used to close the pyramids sometimes if the humidity was too high.

I didn't understand why. It was just one of the many things I've read.

Here there was no humidity or salt tang in the air to denote the nearby desert.

The desert is here, but so many hundreds of feet of rock lay between us and the surface.

For a moment my throat closed with the idea we would die down here.

Why did I decide to do this?

I kept my hand on the cable locks, allowing it to open and close as this planet swallowed me. I gulped back that thought, hoping it would push the butterflies in my belly back too.

Hera and mom chattered back and forth deeper in the shaft. The lilt of mom's voice carried up to me. Tristan whooped and I smiled.

He must have found the bottom. I heaved a sigh.

There is a bottom.

I closed my eyes to thank God and picked up my pace. Adrian's light grew closer until I could make out the three-day old shadow on his face, a face that pulled into a smile as I passed him by.

CHAPTER 27

ISOLDE

The vision had shown me the one piece of the puzzle we didn't have. The rivers were all fake.

The names. Just that. They are just names.

All this water down here was added later by Pythia simply for show. She blocked the way back to the Underworld on purpose.

But why?

There must have been a reason, though without further information there would be no answers. Just more questions.

The water poured down the sides of the shaft, coating not just the wall but everything in its way. I didn't want to release the handbrake and go into free fall like Tristan. That left me with the only other choice available which was walking down the wall, getting soaked to the bone doing it.

The white fabric of my chiton clung to every curve of my body, leaving nothing for the imagination. I glanced up the shaft at my mother and watched the water part for her and Hera, leaving them dry with their dignity.

The shaft carried on deep into the planet. Unfortunately, the hope of a hot molten core to warm us never came to be. I shivered and my teeth chattered echoing in the shaft.

Keeping my eyes on the prize, every downward move took me closer to the end of the shaft and the glowing fireball that illuminated my brother's wicked grin.

My breath caught in my throat. For a moment, in the flickering light, he looked like that golden man with Pythia from my vision, the Atlantian God. Just as quickly, the flames changed, leaving only Tristan and his dorky smile.

I blinked several times to clear my mind.

I must be tired because I'm seeing things.

At last, I came to the end of the shaft and lowered into the new cavern. The water from the lake above poured around me like a curtain, creating a cylinder of liquid surrounding me with Tristan and Hercules at the bottom.

When my feet finally touched the ground, I was soaked to the bone. I clasped my arms in an effort to warm myself. The weight of fabric draped my shoulders and I glanced over to spy Herc. Hercules took the leftover rags from my dress off and put them on me.

His skin was dry and as warm as his smile.

"Thank you," I muttered.

Tristan elbowed me.

"Is that it? He gave you the shirt off his back, sis," he said, then began to dry my clothes with his heat-soaked hands.

<It wasn't a shirt. It's the bottom of my dress.> I roared.

<If you weren't so blind you would see it. Hercules likes you, dumb ass.> Tristan hissed.

<What? No! He's a loud-mouthed womanizer who's been lovin' and leavin' women for thousands of years. I will not become a notch on his belt.> I shouted back, shaking with rage.

Who in the fuck did Tristan think he is? I'm not getting involved with a manwhore. Why would he even suggest it?

I stopped shivering as soon as Tristan finished his dry-cleaning hands and handed Hercules back the fabric.

"Thank you. I'm good," I remarked.

He didn't say a thing, only unbuckled his shoulder harness and slung the fabric back over his shoulders, covering his muscles. The material wasn't long enough to reach his waist and left the six-pack he sported exposed. I quickly turned away to keep from sighing and to keep the fluttering the view brought in line.

God, that man is hotter than hell.

<Hades, sis. He's hotter than Hades. We are Themians.> Tristan snickered.

<Get the fuck out of my head, Trist. God! Can't a girl have five minutes alone without being harassed by some stupid man?> I shouted.

Tristan wiggled his finger in his ear and smirked at me.

"It is taking an awful long time to get where we're going," I murmured.

"I think you're just impatient, Isolde," mom called from above.

"We're being led by a guy who's been sitting in the same place for 2 million years. Next to him everyone is impatient," I retorted.

As if she had room to talk. Mom's mental bled was beginning to wear off on me.

Okay. Standing next to Charon, I was definitely impatient. Anybody who could sit around for a couple million years, waiting for *the Fates* to show up deserved a gold star for sure.

What if we hadn't made it?

We were obviously part of his journey, not that mom believed in the Fates to begin with.

"What happens to Charon if we don't make it?" I asked just to fill the time until everyone was on the ground.

"We are the Fates. There are no others," mom replied as her feet touched the uneven rocks next to me.

Hera quirked an eyebrow at her and hitched her mouth to the side.

"What? I asked him and that's what he said," mom remarked shrugging her shoulder.

"I haven't heard him say anything," Hera returned, unclipping her harness and letting it fall to the ground.

"It was in my mind," my mother replied.

Tristan quickly went to work drying Hera's clothes, while Adrian reached the ground and went to work on mom's shivering form.

"You were in his mind? What did you see there?" Tristan asked, directing it at me.

My whole body shivered with remembrance. "I saw stars. Trillion upon trillions of stars. Young, old, yellow, green, blue, and red. A myriad of colors. His mind was floating on a cosmic wave in the void."

My internal shuttering never stopped. What I had witnessed in his mind was a universe beyond my comprehension. I was there but not there, trapped but free at the same time. I shook my head and glanced at his milky blue unseeing eyes.

No one spoke. I wasn't even sure I could explain it any better. Adrian's explanation wasn't much different from mine. His psyche was lost in the ocean of space.

There was a light murmuring in the background, like when you hear your parents speak before you drift off to sleep. Just like that comfortable feeling of being cocooned, safe and secure.

Charon stepped through the wall of falling water that surrounded us and into the space beyond. For a moment, the taste of copper lined the air before disappearing as the water closed us off.

Tristan took my hand and pulled me through the curtain wall of water and into the cave beyond. I found I was weaving on my feet.

Every moment I stood there my limbs became heavier and my eyes drooped. I leaned up against one of the bigger boulders and slowly slid down the rock to sit on the ground. The lapping of the water against stone waves filled the background and it grew to a hypnotic level.

My eyes trailed around the cave and over to my mother as her eyes closed. Tristan slumped down into a boyish pose of utter exhaustion and Hera laid down next to Tristan, placing her head in his lap.

My brain registered it as strange, but I couldn't hold on to that thought. It slipped away along with a wisp of fog that hung over us. The sudden urge to yawn overtook me and just as I was about to close my eyes a foot nudged the side of my leg.

"Leave me alone! I'm going to sleep," I muttered through the lethargy and turned on my side to snuggle down into the rocky floor.

The heat of a body pulled me up as my eyes drifted down. I relaxed into the murmuring of the water. The warm body smelled of leather and sweat and limes. It was delicious. I smacked my lips and snuggled closer to the tempting scent. Pulling in deep breaths, I sighed with satisfaction as rough hands shook me.

"Calla, wake up! Isolde, don't go to sleep in here," Herc shouted at me.

All I could do was lick my lips. A callused finger pulled my eyelid open and my eyes and rolled around in my head. I tried to blink. I opened the other eye and glazed up at Hercules.

He was beautiful with honey blond hair like a mane. He stared down at me and a ridge of concern pushed up between his eyes.

A smile broke over my face, "Hercules, come sleep with me. Everybody's sleeping. You should sleep too," I muttered and yawned again.

He shook me violently and my head snapped back, forcing my eyes open. "Isolde, wake Tristan, Sydney, and my mother!" He yelled.

I could hear him but I couldn't make out what he was trying to say. My head lolled back as he picked me up. I wanted to tell him to lay me back on the ground. I just wanted to get back to sleep. I felt myself drifting back down into the deep recesses of the sleep world and I welcomed it.

"You should go to sleep too, Herc," I murmured.

Suddenly, I was awake and wet.

"Why am I wet?" I shouted.

Hercules hand patted the side of my face and then he kissed my forehead. "You're awake. Good! We have to wake everyone. This is Hypnos' cave. He'll knock you unconscious and take you to oblivion forever!"

"I don't remember reading anything about that," I sputtered.

I yawned again. Herc threw some more water on me. My eyes popped open.

"Stop throwing water on me!" I growled, pulling away from his comforting grasp.

He kissed my forehead again, "Don't forget on me."

"Forget? Forget what? That you threw water on me? Not a chance you Herc-ing jerk," I struggled out of his arms and pushed him away.

We were just outside a small cave tunnel. Water was falling inside like a curtain, blocking my view.

"Where is everyone else?" I demanded, then took a step back toward the watery wall.

Hercules grabbed my arm and pulled me back. "That is Hypnos' cave. Anyone who goes in there, goes to sleep. You can't go back," he ground out through his teeth.

"Why aren't you asleep, big shot?" I snapped.

"Because I'm already asleep on Odyssey. Whatever is knocking you out doesn't work on a dreamwalk. If I go to sleep here, I'll just wake up on the ship. Astral-projection aka dreamwalking means that if you go to sleep you just wake up," he replied and shook his head in frustration.

I glanced back at the wall of water. "The water works as a filter, keeping whatever makes you sleep inside?" I asked, then looked back at Herc for the answer.

"Exactly. I'll bring everyone out. The water will wash most of the sleep from them. You keep throwing water on then until they wake up."

"Yes," I replied and stepped away from the cave and into the cold water of another river.

Ugh!

"Yes, but don't get it from the river. I brought my water skin with me and so did my mother. You greenhorns didn't bring anything."

"Don't call me a greenhorn, Herc."

He flashed a look back over his shoulder at me with a teasing smile, "I could get used to that nickname."

"It means Herc-ing moron."

"I don't care what it means. You gave me a nickname. That means you must like me," he chuckled before disappearing into the watery wall.

I threw water directly in my mother and Adrian's faces. I actually stopped and watched for a few minutes just to get the satisfaction of viewing it.

Mom sat up and instantly her eyes flashed. Hercules flew across the room, landing on his backside.

"What are you throwing water on me for?" she demanded.

While she was holding Herc in place with her mind, I explained about the cave. She finally let him down but kept giving him the stink eye.

I poured some water in my hand and tapped it onto Tristan's face

<Tristan, wake up now!> I pushed as much mental energy to him as I could, screaming with my mind.

His eyes flashed open, "I hear you. I'm awake. Who could sleep through that?" he groaned and shook his head to clear the cobwebs. "I'm awake! You don't need to throw water in my face or scream in my mind. I heard everyone. I'm awake."

Hera seemed to be the smartest one of the bunch, "We have to get out of this cavern!" she stated.

Taking to her feet and dusting off her dress, she adjusted her tunic and breast bindings before smoothing her hair.

"Are we supposed to do something here?" Mom asked while gazing at the flow of the river before us.

It was the placid ease of undisturbed water. It was fed by the cave we just exited, but the main body erupted from under an outcropping in the far wall.

Hera closed her eyes, tilting her head back and shaking it. She opened her eyes and looked at me. "We're supposed to forget."

CHAPTER 28

Hera

My words poured like icy water down my back.

"You want us to drink the water and forget? Forget what?" Adrian asked.

Hearing him spearhead this issue was new. Adrian usually waited and weighted in once all the information was available.

"You have no fucking idea what we will forget. We could forget everything or just one little thing," Sydney scoffed.

She ran her hands through her hair, stopping at the wet tangles, twisting it up into a knot on her head.

"This isn't real. The rivers were never here. Pythia redirected the water to fill these tunnels and caves to hide the past," Isolde blurted out, then leaned against the cavern wall and tilted her head back.

"Isolde, we know about the river. But what makes you think she was hiding anything?" I asked.

Sydney and I both moved to her side. I believed we were the 'Fates'. There was too much evidence for there to be another answer. I was still taken aback how the three of us were gravitating to each other. From the moment we entered the same room, I was drawn to them.

"I had a vision before we went down the shaft. Pythia talked about crossing a figurative river and forgetting everything on the other side. But the upper cavern was dry." Her eyes stared out across the river as if across time, only to continue, "The blond guy from that statue in Atlantis was there and he talked to Pythia along with a red-haired man," Isolde said in an almost desperate manner.

Poseidon! He was there! He would know what Pythia had to hide.

But Tartarus was too far away to shift anyone from there and we were too far along to ask for help.

Besides, he would never help us.

"Who is the blond one?" Sydney demanded.

Adrian moved to stand behind her and began rubbing her shoulder. The rocks all around us rattled against each other.

"Poseidon. The blond Atlantian is Poseidon," I remarked absently.

Nevertheless, the red-haired man was of more concern. The only Elysian from the first landing with red hair was Anu. The man Ixis asked me to investigate. All the records said Anu died on Tartarus when they cleansed the planet.

Anu and his followers are gone. The Great Division ended their demented ideas.

As if hearing my thoughts, Isolde shivered and held herself. Her skin puckered. "Who was the red-haired man? There was a statue of him outside Pythos," she whispered.

Her dread spilled into the air and poisoned my own emotions. The taste of it soured the very zest for life.

"Anu, a brilliant Elysian. He led the members of the Anu-ites. They believed might makes right. He was the first to dominate minds. He told his followers the weaker minded of us should be dominated for the betterment of society as a whole."

I closed my eyes to force the pictures out of my mind. It did no good. The recorded vision of Anu's speeches played over and over again, his vile words infecting the power hungry and bitter.

"Anu incited a war. He wanted to dominate our new people. Themia stood against him."

I couldn't stop the visions that played in my mind and automatically pulled everyone into a dreamvision.

"Most of the people rallied behind Themia. She was our leader at the time. Pythia retreated to Pythos and chose to remain neutral. Poseidon led the battle on behalf of the High Council. During this time, Anu chose Tartarus as his first capital Homeworld. The Themians surrounded the world and killed as many as they could, before the planet was cleansed of all life," I stopped to take a breath and pushed the bitter flavor down my throat.

Tristan freely retched. His gagging noises and the flow of water were the only sounds around us.

"Mother, you must stop and release everyone from the dreamvision," Hercules ordered.

I coughed and shook my head. Our group visibly sagged. My eyes darted around the giant space, looking anywhere but my companions.

"None of that matters. This Aun guy and his merry band of assholes are dead right?" Sydney asked.

"Yes. I think that was who Pythia wanted to stop," I remarked as guilt ate me up inside. "I am sorry. I had not intended to take you into a dream vision."

"These things happen, Hera. Control of your powers is a daily battle," Adrian offered while rubbing Sydney's back.

Sydney stared me down with her hard as diamond blue eyes. She disliked anyone controlling her in any way.

What I had done was a violation.

"Where is Charon?" Sydney asked, crossing her arms, ignoring me and my mistakes.

Tristan spit on the ground and Hercules handed him a water skin. He proceeded to gargle and spit again.

"He crossed," my son said, reattached the water skin to his belt and pointed to the other side of the river.

"Adrian," Sydney smiled and he nodded to her.

The pressure in the air grew but the shift never took.

"It's not working," Adrian remarked then looked at his son.

The two shifters nodded and the pressure in the cavern grew again, unfortunately the cold of the shift never took hold.

Sydney huffed, "It's not working. I'll have to part the red sea," she drolled.

She thrust out her hand but nothing changed. The flow of the river continued on, unabated.

"Looks like we will have to swim it," Hercules laughed, then tied his sword to his scabbard. "Adrian, you may wish to affix your new weapons to something." He pulled the fabric from his shoulders and handed it to the man.

Adrian wrapped both horns and tied them to his back.

"What if we forget?" Isolde breathed.

"Then you won't remember and it won't matter," Hercules chuckled.

She shoved him unamused.

Without waiting for the rest of them, I entered the icy water. It climbed up my legs quickly as the bank dropped away. I pushed into the main flow, pumping my arms for forward movement. The flow was strong, but I had crossed many rivers in my life. I swam hard for the center of the river and used the push of the water to send me to the other side, being mindful to keep my head up. But mostly to keep the water out of my mouth.

I gained the bank just in time to catch a glimpse of Charon lowering his foot on my head.

"You must forget," he stated with his milky blue eyes devoid of emotions.

The water covered my head and I pressed my eyes shut desperate to keep the liquid from entering my body. My hands grabbed his foot desperate to push him off and reach the oxygen my body needed.

The pressure in my lungs grew and I had to make a choice — drown or drink.

The only thing I wish to remember is my children's faces.

And it all turned black.

CHAPTER 29

HERA

I floated in a world without form and no matter how hard I swatted at the mist, it never drifted away. I giggled to myself at the absurdity of it. I reached out to remember why it was absurd to find nothing.

Not even my name.

The muscles on my face pinched together as I searched for answers. In spite of that there were none to be found and the feeling that I needed to do something wouldn't go away.

I smoothed my chiton and patted my hair. These were things I understood about myself. My dress was right and my hair the color of spun honey with a touch of strawberry for depth. Though I hadn't looked in a mirror, I knew my eyes were blue and I was healthy.

The rest was blank and for the life of me I couldn't find the answers or even think of who would have them.

The white mist changed to a room filled with child sized furniture. The space filled me with peace. The anxiety of not knowing who I was eased with the familiarity of the place. I wandered out of the child's room, through the rest of the house and out the back door, heading for the gardens.

But the moment I set foot outside, the scene shifted from the green of the outside world to the white of a giant room.

I found myself seated in an amphitheater surrounded by thousands. I was close to the outer edge and low to the ground, facing the dais. Twelve men and women sat above the room with one man speaking. His words washed over me, covering me with his charisma, yet the meaning was lost. I enjoyed his orating ability and the inflection of his convictions. As to the reason for them, I could not say.

A rough hand pulled me from my seat, dragging me back through a door.

"Have you lost your mind?" The golden-haired man asked me. "If even one of them sees or hears you, they will track you back to your location and kill you," he whispered, terror quivering in his voice and body.

I stared up at him in wonder. He was beautiful and strong. I found I couldn't do anything but smile.

"You know me?" I asked hopefully, petting the cloth of my dress.

"Don't play games, Herathina! Now is not the time." He released my arm and ran his fingers through his hair before knotting it in a ponytail.

"Herathina. Is that my name?" I asked, taking his hand in my own.

This strange man carried such passion, unlike the rest of the people around us. He stopped moving and really looked at me.

"Come this way! The High Council is about to leave the citadel for their chambers. You need to be there."

He gripped my hand tighter and pulled me down long corridors and past arched doorways. Finally, we came to a mosaic. He glanced either direction down the hall and pressed his fingers into five tiles, pushing the wall in.

A section swung in, revealing a blue lite passage. He quickly pulled me in and pressed the mosaic back into place.

"The High Council knows you've entered Pythos. They think you will die there," he said, pulling me along.

I had so many questions, I didn't know what to ask first. So, I let him keep talking while I tripped along behind him.

"They are going to blow up the site and encase you in the underground tunnels."

"Why would they do that?" I asked, unsure how they could do it since I was here. "I'm here. They would kill themselves," a giggle escaped and I covered my mouth to stifle it.

The man stopped. "You aren't making any sense, Herathina. You are on Delphi, at Pythos," he growled. "Stop with the childish games. I can tell the difference between the real you and a dreamwalk. We are too old for tricks," he snapped.

I must have known him for a long time for him to snap like that. But for the life of me, I couldn't recall having met him or anyone else, ever.

We came to a junction and turned right, before coming to a stop in front of a recess with a bench seat.

The man waved his hand over the wall and a holo appeared. The holo revealed a room and the same people from the dais were seated around a table. One man stood towering over the others.

"They will cross the rivers and forget. If we blow up the sight now, all our problems go away. There will be no Fates, therefore the Titans cannot return," he stated and the room exploded in voices.

"You cannot destroy our most sacred sight. Pythia said that the Fates would arrive and they have. We must trust they will save us," a woman shouted over the rest.

"What about Poseidon? We could simply go to Tartarus and get rid of him. That would stop the prophecy from coming true," a man with reddish hair and an intertwined staff replied.

"Or maybe killing Poseidon is what brings it to fruition. Hermes, you are a messenger, not a thinker!" another man countered.

Hermes stared the man down as if his very eyes could kill the other.

I turned to my companion, "what are they talking about?" I whispered.

"You, Herathina. They are talking about you and your companions."

I tore my eyes from the screen to look at him. "But why? I don't even know who I am, let alone your name. I have no companions. I am here alone," I stated, the curiosity welling up inside me. It gave me such energy I only wanted to jump up and run for hours.

He patted my hand, and kissed my forehead. "You crossed the river of forgetfulness." His face pulled into a tight smile.

"I don't know. There was a white fog and now I'm here with you," I replied and returned his smile.

"I am your brother Hyperion. You are Herathina, though you now call yourself Hera. You need to leave this dreamwalk and get off Delphi," he stated.

The argument on the screen reached a new level and I turned to listen.

"You don't know how deep those rivers go. As a matter of fact, you have no idea what is down there. Everyone who has ever tried to go back has died. They will never come out. This conversation is a waste of time," one of the women shouted over the rest.

She stood up and turned to leave.

"They *are* the Fates," a voice carried over the others and the room quieted.

I held my breath, even though I couldn't say why.

"Herathina was identified as a Fate before she left for Terra by Poseidon himself. He said he would keep her under his watchful eye. That fell apart. Then, Athena claimed she would keep her on Terra indefinitely. She also failed. That was because Ixis interfered. How many times do we have to try and stop the Fates before we realize we can't?" The man asked, throwing his hands in the air.

The energy flowing under my skin began to crawl. They have been trying to keep me from something.

But why? What can I do that will be so dangerous?

"They will drink the water from Lethe and forget. I don't understand why you are so afraid? Gaea, Thoon, might I remind you that Pythia didn't see the Great Division coming! Who's to say she saw this correctly?" Hermes replied with a chuckle.

He leaned back in his seat and threw his feet up on the table. His tunic fell back barely covering his manhood but exposed his muscled legs and I giggled.

Hyperion elbowed me, "You don't like him," he remarked.

"I don't have to. He is just nice to look at," I replied.

Brother or not, I will look at what I want.

I smirked at him, turning back to the screen and the drama that was unfolding within.

"You didn't know Pythia and your arrogant statement proves it. I came here from Elysium with the other Titans. You have no idea what they are capable of. The Fates may drink from Lethe and forget, but the pool of Mnemosyne will let them remember. You should pray to the Lords of the Underworld that they don't find it," Gaea retorted.

Hyperion grabbed my hand and drug me away from the alcove, turning the screen off as we went.

"Where are we going?" I asked then glanced over my shoulder just to assure myself the holo no longer displayed the room. "That was just getting interesting," I mumbled. "Who are the Lords of the Underworld?"

"You need to go back to your body. I get it now." He stopped and clasped my face in his hands. "Herathina, you crossed Lethe and forgot everything."

My forehead scrunched to understand what he was saying. It made sense why I didn't know my own name and couldn't remember anything before the fog.

I must have forgotten, but what did I forget?

"But I don't know what you mean. Go back," I replied, feeling like a child who was being told to do her homework.

I didn't understand.

The dim passage faded away, leaving Hyperion and I back in the fog.

"I will open the way for you, but you must walk through."

He waved a hand and the fog to one side fell away. A cavern opened with a river running along one side. Six people were laying on the ground and I was one of them.

"How can I be here and there at the same time?" I asked.

I ran my hand over my dress. The other me was wearing a dirty ripped rag.

"Because you are asleep, sister. You dreamwalked me. You didn't forget completely. Lethe couldn't take me from you or you from me. We are twins, each sharing a piece of the other. Now, wake up and find the pool of Mnemosyne and remember," he hugged me and kissed my forehead, then pushed me toward the cavern.

I stepped over the edge and back to my body. I sat up from the ground. He was gone and so was the dream. For a moment, I wanted to cry for the loss. It was as if I'd lost a part of myself.

I gazed around the group of strangers and addressed the only one standing.

"Take me to the pool of Mnemosyne!" I ordered.

The man didn't move, only stared at the rocky walls lining our side of the cavern.

I took to my feet, stepping over my companions as Hyperion called them. Only one of the faces brought a flip to my pounding heart. It was a large man lying on the ground next to a young woman. His arms were wrapped around her in a protective manner.

A smile touched my lips and traveled through the rest of me, warming my soul. "They must be in love," I remarked. "What a strange place to take a nap."

They could not be comfortable lying on the small rocks. I shrugged and moved to face the standing man. His unseeing blue eyes stared through me into the empty space beyond.

I waved my hand in front of his face and snapped my fingers. He gave no indication of my actions or recognized my presences.

The people from the room said I was identified as a Fate.

Whatever that means.

I squared my shoulders to the frozen man and shouted, "I am a Fate! Tell me where the pool of Mnemosyne is."

The man blinked and for a moment looked at me.

"Only the Fates can discover the pool," he replied and the light behind his eyes quickly faded as he returned to staring at nothing.

Ugh!

I kicked a rock. It ricocheted off a large boulder, broke in two and cracked against two other rocks before clattering to a halt.

"Tell the man with the jackhammer in my head to shut up," one of the women said.

She glared up at me. Her eyes were bright and fierce.

"Apologies. I did not mean to disturb you," I returned.

She offered her hand and I took it, helping her to her feet. She rubbed her hand across her forehead and rolled her shoulders. "Who are you?" she demanded.

I was relieved I could answer that question.

"Herathina, but you may call me Hera. I am a Fate," I stated, then heaved a sigh as that was the last of the helpful information I carried.

"What does that mean?" She replied, taking in our little beach and all who occupied it. Then, she rolled her shoulders and stretched her back.

"I do not know. But it must be important. I overheard someone talking about me." I nodded my head in earnest.

She glanced around and pointed to the standing man. "Who? Him?"

I shook my head. "No, they were in a room. I saw them in a dream," I informed her.

Her mouth hitched to one side and her eyes narrowed.

"Who am I?" She asked.

My brow pulled down in frustration. Hyperion left that part out. He didn't tell me who my companions were. I huffed.

"That, I do not know. But I do know that we need to find the pool of Mnemosyne. That will help us remember," I assured her, nodding my head.

She snorted, "Did you see that in your dream too?" She rolled her eyes and turned away from me.

"Yes. I mean no. My brother told me to find it," I replied.

I smoothed the rag covering my body as if that would clean the dingy fabric. The act eased my emotions and gave me confidence to face this woman.

She moved past me and shook one of the men on the ground before moving to the next person.

"Get up!" She shouted.

Each in turn yawned and sat up, wide eyed and confused.

A blond man with piercing blue eyes smiled at her and said "Beautiful girl!"

The woman smirked and ignored him. "We need to find a dreamy pool of water," she threw a glance at me then turned back to the group.

Most of them didn't react. However, the young girl took to her feet and came to my side and gripped my hand. I returned the act, happy to have someone to reassure me.

Three men stretched and yawned but offered nothing in the way of information.

"We have forgotten," I stated to fill the uncomfortable silence. "Hyperion said we must leave this place."

"Slow down, Skippy! Is the frozen guy over there Hyperion?" The fierce woman asked, hooking her thumb at the unseeing man.

"No, Hyperion is my brother. I talked to him in a dream," I replied.

Finding the words to explain was difficult.

"What does this dreamy pool do that I should find it with such urgency?" The large man asked.

"Do you know who you are?" I inquired.

Everyone shook their heads.

"The pool will give us back our memories. Hyperion said that we need to find it and get off Delphi. I don't know what Delphi is, but the people I overheard said they would blow it up to get rid of us."

I wasn't doing a good job of explaining and I wanted to start over. I shook my head. Pressure grew in my belly at my inability to make them understand.

"If the pool will make me remember, let's find it," the fierce woman said. "Where is it?"

"Next to a white poplar tree," the unseeing man stated.

My head whipped around to stare at the strange man. He didn't utter another word nor did he bother to look at anyone. It was as if he spoke to the rocks on the beach.

"Fan out and look for that tree!" The clear-eyed man ordered.

I turned around and headed away from my companions. The rocks on the beach slipped away under my feet to skitter across one another. Other than the sound of footsteps and flowing water, all remained deathly quiet.

I walked hundreds of feet until I came to the cavern wall where the water disappeared under the rocks and the gray stony beach ended. I turned around and placed my back against the cavern wall.

On the other side of the river there was a tunnel leading away from it. Our side of the river was covered with nothing more than boulders and pebbles with no way out.

I rushed down the beach back to my group with my idea.

CHAPTER 30

HERCULES

The woman with the dream ran toward me, her face bright with hope.

She came to a skittering halt and almost fell. I caught her before she tumbled to the ground.

"We have to cross the river. There is nothing on this side. It must be over there," she huffed, gulping for air.

"What if it isn't there?" The young woman asked.

"There are no trees here. Look around. There is nothing a tree could grow in. It's just rock. We need to find soil, dirt, terra," the first woman replied.

I rubbed the bristles on my chin and pushed my hair out of my face. She had a point. I couldn't deny it. No tree could grow down here, not without light and soil to sustain it.

"I'll go," the fierce woman snapped.

She pulled her loose hair back from her face, twisting it up into a knot on her head.

The man who called her beautiful intervened, "No, I'll go."

I chuckled under my breath, "None of us knows who is best suited for this." I pulled the sword from its scabbard on my back to inspect the blade. "I believe I am a warrior. Let me fulfill my purpose."

Before they could argue on the matter I thrust the blade back into the scabbard and leapt into the river.

The cold water filled my ears and tickled the hairs in my nose. The cool of it lowered my body temperature, keeping my muscles from overheating with each pull.

I worked my legs and arms until my hand slapped against stone. I pulled out of the water unable to remember why I needed to be there.

The people on the other side screamed and waved their arms. The meaning of their garbled words were lost to the roar of the moving water.

I sat down to catch my breath and loosened the water pouch at my waist. I pulled the stopper and took a long pull on the water and swished it around in my mouth.

I closed my eyes and pushed the remaining river water from my eyes, then swallowed.

I opened my eyes to see the world and every memory of my life slammed down on me. All the storied I told on Terra, the vision of my father's head rolling across the citadel floor as his blood poured from the stump onto the white crystalline composite, thousands of years trapped on Homeworld 12, Hebe crying over Jorhan's mangled body, the Nemean Lyons, and Isolde.

I looked down at the water skin and threw my head back and laughed.

I waved at everyone on the other side, took to my feet and walked into the entrance to Hypnos' cave.

The water poured over me, washing what was left of Lethe from my body. The frigid cold of it sank into my bones, freezing the very marrow. Instead of shivering over the lost warmth, I made for the far side of the cave and the long dead tree there.

I couldn't tell what kind of tree it was. It appeared so ancient. Its roots were buried in a pot. The tree was stunted and leaning to one side as if it had been set down and forgotten. The trunk was white with death and age.

The woody feel of bark had long since fled the poor plant, leaving only the petrified smoothness of stone. I ran a finger down a branch to where it met the trunk and marveled.

Was it carried here from Elysium?

The cave was barren of anything else, except for the shallow stone basin I'd seen before. I had filled my water skin and drained most of the water before. However, it was once again full.

I scratched my head over the mystery, wondering over the hows and whys of it. Cupping my hand, I brought a drink to my lips and sucked the refreshing beverage from my fingers, then stared down at my reflection.

For a moment, all I could see was my own face and the blue glowing light that surrounded the small pool. I shifted my weight from one foot to the other and blocked out the glare over the water. The bottom of the pool came into focus as did the infinity symbol.

Everyone caulked me up as a buffoon, but I could be clever, in my own way.

It's an infinity pool. Of course. It heals all wounds.

I barked out a laugh and filled my water skin, took to my feet and did what I should have done the moment we entered this cave. I examined it. The walls were smooth while the ceiling and floor were covered in stalagmites and stalactites. The water from the shaft saturated the ceiling and dripped down, forming the various pillars and the light mist in the air.

Whatever has put everyone to sleep must be in the mist.

The mist in the air wasn't thick like a naturally formed waterfall mist. It was light and dewy. I went back to the infinity pool and squatted down next to it and waited. I wasn't sure what for, but there was more to this cave than met the eye.

I didn't need to wait long. Adrian burst through the water curtain into the cave. He took two steps and pointed his index finger at me before his eyes lowered as did his body.

I watched in fascination as the infinity pool dispersed a fine mist into the air. The pool was the source of the sleep agent, not the cave.

I took the water skin hanging from Adrian's belt off and filled it from the pool. Then, I heaved him up over my shoulder and carried him out.

The cold water washed the sleep agent away along with what little heat I had stored up. I shivered as I laid Adrian's body on the stony beach and patted his cheek to wake up.

His eyes fluttered open, "What happened?" he mumbled.

"Here, drink this and I'll explain the rest," I pressed a water skin to his lips.

He took a long gulp and sat up.

"Charon!" was the only thing he said.

I smirked at him and nodded my head before squatting on the ground next to him. I crossed my hands in front of me as I rested my arms on my knees.

"Yes, he made sure we all forgot," I replied and patted his shoulder.

"I should kill him before Sydney does," he laughed, then squeezed the water from his hair and stood up to wring his tunic out.

"It might be a kind death, but it's not up to us. The Fates must decide that," I returned and chuckled. "Where are the horns?" I asked.

His back was bare. I glanced across the river. There was a pile of filthy rags on the beach.

"I didn't want to be weighted down," Adrian replied. "I guess we're lucky there aren't any guardians here."

"Don't speak too soon, you will tempt fate," I jeered and elbowed him.

Adrian snorted, "My wife wants to kill everything down here, don't tempt her." he laughed. "Let's go back!"

I handed him his water skin and we both swam across the river, making sure to keep our heads above the water. I made the edge of the bank with my memories intact and handed my water skin to my mother.

She gave me a sheepish smile and took a small sip before passing it to Isolde.

Part of me wanted to keep her from drinking it, but that was not how you win the heart of a woman. So, I waited for everyone to regain their memories and the barrage of questions that would most assuredly come with it.

Sydney took one gulp, then stalked over to Charon and slapped his face.

"You bastard!" She shouted.

Adrian pulled her away, but that didn't stop her voice from tearing into him.

"What in the ever lasting fuck did you need to push us under for?"

Charon didn't reply, only stared off into the cavern wall at the few boulders piled there.

CHAPTER 31

ISOLDE

"Where was the pool?" Hera asked, looking from Adrian to Hercules.

"In Hypnos' cave. None of you would have reached it," Herc replied and dipped his head before he tilted it back, proud to be the solution and not the problem.

I smirked at him. "If you weren't asleep already, we'd still be in that cave."

His smile grew and stepped closer to me. "Yes, Calla. That is correct."

His deep stare pulled me in twelve different directions at once and I turned away from him.

He too looked away and spoke to his mother. "It was an Infinity pool, maybe the first one ever made. The pool is the source of the sleep drug. Every time the air pressure in the cave changes, it disperses the drug. Adrian hit the floor before he could get a word out."

"Only a dreamwalker could get out," I mumbled.

His toothy smile widened, "I guess it was fate for me to be here."

My mom groaned, "Enough with the fate crap! We got lucky you came along. That's it."

"Really, mom? After the statues, the tunnels, Charon and your rings...all of that and you're still in doubt?" I demanded, placing my hands on my hips.

I didn't always stand up to my mother but I'd had enough. Her doubting Thomas-blather was getting on my nerves.

"I don't do predetermination. I can't. I'm not wired that way, Issy. I question everything," she replied and mirrored my stance.

"Occam's razor," Tristan shouted. We both stopped and turned to him. "The simplest answer is the right one."

Mom laughed, "Don't you go and use scientific theories, that by the way I taught you, to hang me with!"

Tristan never broke a smile or flinched, "Stop being unreasonable, Mom! It doesn't have to make sense to be right."

She only gave him a wan smile, then moved her focus to Charon, "Where to now, boat-boy?"

"The way forward is blocked," Charon replied.

"Where is '*the way*'? How did the people get here to begin with?" Mom asked and bit her lip.

His hand pointed to the pile of rubble he had been staring at. My heart stopped beating for a moment.

"What? We have to go through the rocks? We need to move the rocks?" Mom demanded.

I glanced over at Tristan. Adrian blinked at me with wide-eyed innocence, while Hercules simply stood with his legs wide and his arms crossed. As if he was ready to do whatever he was told, but had no idea what that was.

We moved forward as a group to inspect the rocks. The closer I got the more it resembled a rock slide. The rocks had not come from the ceiling. There were no stalactites, stalagmites or any loose rocks at all. The stone was a different color than the rest of the stones lying around.

Pythia. She must have placed them here. But why? Also, why are all the roads blocked? Who was she trying to stop from reaching whatever is down here?

Those were questions that could only be answered by moving forward. I couldn't move those rocks. Tristan and Adrian couldn't use their abilities.

Maybe Hercules could push a few to the side.

I shot him a look. He stood with his arms crossed and one hand rubbing his chin. His biceps were huge as was his back.

He threw that Lyon off me like it was made of paper.

"Do you think you could move one or two of these big boulders?" I asked.

He gave me a toothy grin and stepped to the closest stone. He then crouched down and placed his shoulder against an enclave in the rock, flexed his leg muscles and pushed with all his might.

Smaller rocks from above tumbled down, peppering Herc's back and hair. The big stone barely budged and Hercules eased it back into place.

"I don't think I'm strong enough to move it on my own," he replied and took a drink of water.

"The family that plays together —" Tristan mumbled.

"We should move some of the smaller debris from above, then try to move the larger stones," Adrian said, then began climbing the pile and pushing smaller rocks to the side with his foot.

Tristan joined him. Hercules moved the smaller rocks from around the base of the pile and mom and I helped him. All this time, Hera was inspecting the cavern wall to one side of the pile.

"I don't think we need to move all of them. Just enough to open whatever passageway is buried here," she remarked and began tossing rocks behind her, creating a small landslide.

"Mother, you'll bring the pile down on you. Move back and let me do that for you," Hercules barked, then gently moved his mother away from the rock pile.

I rubbed the sweat out of my eyes with the back of my hand. Adrian focused on the rocks closest to the wall and pushed them away from where Hercules worked. They slowly worked to ease the blockage away and the arched outline of a tunnel came into view.

The entrance was clearly man made. The walls had no crystalline structure. There was a blue glowing light all around and some depressions that could have been symbols. Babylonian, Sumerian maybe. Nevertheless, it was a hodgepodge. It was as if it had all been one language, that later separated into many.

Maybe that's the answer. Maybe it was really just one language. If we were on Earth and gathered all three of those languages together, would they spell out something very different than what we think?

That was an idea for another time since none of us was ever going back to Earth.

After several hours of lifting and moving rocks of all variety, we ended up being thirsty and sore. My hands were covered in little cuts and scraps.

"Hercules, what did you do on Themian Homeworld 12 for all those years?" I asked.

I plopped down on the rocky ground without thinking about whether any of them had sharp edges or not.

"Not a lot. Pretty much just sitting around waiting for something to happen. They said we weren't smart enough to have a job," he shrugged, "and going to the library for a couple thousand years is okay but after a while you become bored. Themians really are very xenophobic. More so than I'm sure you can even imagine. The High Council tried to make sure we were as isolated as possible. They didn't want us mixing with the main population. So, we were secluded to certain areas of the city. We were allowed to go to the library but only during certain hours. That was usually when it was closed to the public. We weren't allowed to go out in public, to restaurants or performances. We had to have things delivered. It's like being a prisoner in a really nice prison. Tobias actually described it as Club Med or Club Fed. I don't remember which one he used," he laughed.

We all started laughing, "He probably said Club Fed. That's in reference to a resort on Earth called Club Med. It's supposed to be swanky. Club Fed is a prison that is supposed to be like that resort. You can play golf while being in jail," I snickered and shook my head at his blunder.

"What is this golf?" he asked in confusion.

Tristan looked like he was about to die laughing, smacking his hand against his chest a few times in a fit, "Only the most boring game ever invented by a Scotsman," he choked.

"I thought the Scots were good people?" Hercules replied confused as to the joke. He pushed his hair out of his face and frowned at Tristan.

"They are. They just invented the most boring game ever, that's all. Now you want a real exciting sport? Well that's surfing. It was invented by the Hawaiians. You can die surfing. You can't die playing golf unless it's from a heart attack or boredom."

Hercules guffawed, "I want to learn about surfing. Any sport that can kill you is the one for me."

"You're gonna love it. It's right up your alley, dangerous with lots of bragging rights," Tristan replied and Adrian nodded his head in agreement with my brother.

Mom rolled her eyes. She didn't understand why you would want to do anything that could kill you. And yet, here we were, looking for the underworld and having almost died several times.

She has a different level of danger meter from the rest of us.

"One more push and I think we can punch through," Adrian remarked, then moved to the last big boulder blocking our way.

Hercules chose his spot and Tristan moved in next to him.

Mom, Hera and I stepped away in case anything went wrong. The guys heaved with all their might puffing. The sound of skittering rocks echoed against the cavern wall and down the tunnel. The stone rolled over, leaving a three-foot space between the stone and the tunnel.

The passage was bathed in the pale blue light. Rather than catch their breath, all three men entered the tunnel. I pulled from mom's grasp and followed my twin.

Every cavern and tunnel down here was lined with the crystalline material. The eerie blue light was the kind you expect to be accompanied by angels, ghosts or some ethereal being. It washed over everything and it was indistinct. I never identified exactly where the glow emanated from but it was there, permeating everything surrounding us.

I found it depressing. I longed for the bright light of any star.

I would prefer a yellow star just because I'm part human and that's what I'm familiar with. Yet, at this point in time I'll take a red star, anything.

Nothing had prepared me for what was at the end of the passage. It wasn't just another cavern. It was massive and stretched out for miles. The center was filled with another rock.

The smooth massive rock that was bathed in a brighter blue sat in the middle of the cavern and my heart fell into my feet, then jumped to my throat and stopped. The smooth rock filling the space wasn't a rock at all.

One of things I liked and hated about Themian technology was how it resembled nature so closely it was hard to distinguish.

"Is this what I think it is?" I asked and chanced a glance at Hercules.

His mouth hung open loosely and his eyes were the size of saucers. I glanced around to see where Charon had gone. The creepy guy was nowhere in sight.

"Where's Charon? Has anybody seen him?" I asked and pulled my lip from between my teeth.

"He went around the side of the machine," Hera stated.

I whipped my head around the look at her.

She said 'machine'.

"What machine?" I sputtered.

"This is a spaceship," Hera remarked without a hint of fear, only wonder.

"Are you shitting me? What spaceship? This is a spaceship?" Mom demanded pointing at the sooth surface of the machine.

"This is Prometheus," Hera replied and smiled, then covered her mouth with her hand and laughed.

I shook my head.

Like I'm supposed to know who Prometheus is?

"Prometheus that died?" I asked, hoping I was wrong and this wasn't a robot.

"No, Issy. Prometheus is the first spaceship. The one that brought all of the Themians here from Elysium," Hercules said, "This is the first ship built for shifting."

Adrian reached out to run his fingers along the hull, "There's still energy in it. I can feel it vibrating inside."

I put my hand out to touch it but I didn't see or feel anything different.

"I think we need to find Charon," I muttered and mom nodded her head in agreement.

"Isolde, you, Tristan and Hercules go left. Adrian, Hera and I will go this way," my mother ordered, pushing a stray strand of hair out of her face and tucking it behind her ear.

"Tristan and I can go by ourselves. We don't need a babysitter," I remarked with a grumble.

"He's not there to babysit you, Isolde. Hercules is older than you are and has been around Themian culture longer than you have. We're taking Hera for the same reason. Stop thinking it's all about you. It isn't. Sometimes you can be so self-centered. Please grow up!." Mom snapped and turned to head the opposite direction.

Wow, now I really feel like an asshole.

I glanced at her sheepishly. Herc had a smirk on his face like he enjoyed every moment of my mother's dressdown.

Jerk!

CHAPTER 32

ISOLDE

The shape of the ship was a smooth curve and it emanated its own version of a blue glow. It reminded me of my mother's blue dream and the sapphire ocean. The shade was an indescribable hue. My inability to find the right color was not a new feeling. I wasn't even sure the feeling was mine.

I still haven't figured out whether the crystalline material was a stone or metal.

Maybe the answer is simply — yes.

I wandered on while Tristan and Hercules fell behind, talking quietly amongst themselves about whatever boys talk about. I'd learned to block Tristan out a long time ago. However, the deep timber of Hercules' voice was harder to block. It rattled my nerves.

Up ahead, Charon stood stock still with his milky blue eyes, staring sightlessly into a black opening on the side of the machine.

"Herc, Tristan, come quick!"

The sound of rocks crushing under feet as they dashed over was my only notice they were even listening to me.

A moment later, the pressure around us changed and with-it Mom, Adrian and Hera appeared.

"This must be one of the small entrances to the spaceship," Hera, the ever obvious, stated.

<All answers are inside.> Charon announced in his toneless eerie fashion.

He danced the verge of creepy, representing the epitome dissociative.

Why is he always so cryptic? 'Your answers are inside'. Where did we get this guy? Oh yeah, in a cavern underground.

The opening was a black maw and intimidating. I somehow expected the interior of the ship to be lit up. Instead, it was pregnant with a dark inky blackness. It made me shiver.

"Charon, if the answers are inside, lead the way," Mom ordered.

He didn't budge an inch. I looked over at my mother.

"It was worth a try," she shrugged and Adrian lit a fireball in his hand while gesturing my mother forward with his other hand.

She stepped through the opening and the fire light revealed the pressure seals of an airlock door.

I bit my lip. This ship was closer technology wise to humans than Themians. I was expecting something Star Trek, but this was definitely more Star Wars.

Tristan and I hung back, while Hercules and Hera stepped through the airlock door ahead of us.

Tristan lit up a fireball, "We made it this far." He urged me ahead of him and I complied. He threw me a big toothy grin as I passed him by.

Hercules and his gleaming hair were all I could see. His giant body blocked everything else. The interior walls lacked the smooth crystalline of modern Themian technology. They reflected a myriad of colors much like the rest. However, there was something about this version that was clearly alien. All the other crystalline structures were made of lighter colors, making the space bright. This was dark gunmetal blue with streaks like blackened veins spreading out in a spider web like pattern.

Part of me saw Charon as the spider leading us to his web. I pushed that image back into the box of fanciful notions where it belonged.

I glanced back at Tristan. There was a shadow wavering behind him and a squeak escaped my lips.

Hercules hand grabbed me around the waist and pushed me behind him as he brandished his dagger.

"Whoa, it's just Charon. He's following us, dude," Tristan said.

My brother planted his hand squarely in the center of Herc's chest, holding him back. Hercules released a heavy breath then turned around. His eyes bored down on me and with the light behind him, his face was lost in shadows.

His voice dropped, "Stay in front of me, Isolde. I don't want anything to happen to you."

Why does he care whether something happens to me? Take your male chivalry, patriarchy bullshit and shove it up your ass.

<Nice! Why don't you just tell him to fuck off? > Tristan demanded.

<If he tried listening, then maybe I wouldn't have to! He doesn't understand what the term 'fuck off' means.>

<Or maybe, there is nothing you can say that will make him go away. Maybe, he wants you to choke on his love for you. >

<Shut up, Tristan!> I glowered.

I turned around and started down the hallway, apologetically brushing past Hera. I needed to put space between me and Mr. Possessive.

The Hall came to a nexus and branched off in a myriad of different directions. This ship wasn't shaped like Atlantis or Odyssey. It was more like a big globe or a perfect sphere.

That explains why I couldn't figure out what it was when I first saw it. I was only seeing a small portion of the whole ship.

"Hera, is Prometheus a sphere?" I asked without stopping.

"The data chip said it was the shape of a heavenly body," she replied.

Her exact answer raked over my already exposed nerves. Hercules had filleted the flesh covering them back and now everything was hurting.

"A sphere is a circle, a three-dimensional object in space," I retorted.

"Most heavenly bodies are indeed in the shape of the sphere. Though, they are not truly round. Most are an uneven pocked sphere, due to meteor impacts and erosion from what every liquid is on the surface," Hera's lack of ability to give a straight and definitive answer was just adding to my problems.

Odyssey was massive. Even though I'd never seen it from the outside, I understood this. Walking from the shifting room to the biodome or the laboratories was a 15 minutes jaunt or more. And that at a relatively rapid pace.

Here, I couldn't gauge the size.

Odyssey has the ability to hold at least 5 million souls, not that we are anywhere near capacity.

But this ship seems like it was capable of carrying an entire civilization.

"Can you tell us anything else about this rust bucket?" Mom inquired.

Hera faltered, "I can tell you it brought a great deal of the Elysium population with it. They later became Themians. Yet, I don't know what the female to male population was at the time. The early records are spotty at best."

"You said this ship was designed specifically to be maneuvered by a shifter. Are there no engines?" Adrian asked.

Part of me hoped Charon would finally snap out of his iRobot funk and talk to us and fill us in on the digs of the ship.

"As I've said, the information is spotty. Some of it was degraded or missing. Intentionally, I think. It was of a new design, specifically for a shifter."

I trailed my hand across the wall, following the black veins embedded there. They were slightly raised and the texture was satisfying to my senses.

"So, it's safe to say that all of your ships might be based upon this design?" Mom asked and stopped walking.

I was sandwiched between the two of them and the air crackled around the three of us.

"That would be a logical assumption. However, we've made many technological advances."

"Is it safe to say at least that the design of all shifting rooms are similar?" Adrian asked for clarification.

"Yes, all shifting rooms are at the very top of the ship, to see the sky or stars whichever you wish, to allow the shifters to align themselves." Hera's face was half in the shadows from the flickering flame of Adrian's fire.

Mom shifted on her feet, allowing the light to reach the whole of her face which now carried a knowing smile.

As a group we all looked up, for the shifting room that must have been over our heads somewhere.

"All the hallways we've traveled were horizontal. We need a vertical way up or down. The shifting room is going to be at the top or at the bottom. We are clearly in the middle. It goes without saying that although space is a three-dimensional place, and the ship was built in a three-dimensional fashion, it would've landed with a two-dimensional idea," Adrian explained.

My mother had been suspiciously quiet during the entire exchange.

I never trust my mother's silence, because she's thinking and whatever she's thinking usually means trouble.

She would produce a cockamamie idea or outlandish plan that we would have to deal with.

I think she's crazy.

I stopped. Whatever answers we needed were confined inside Charon. So, I turned around and started walking back towards Tristan and the ferryman.

"Where are you going, Calla? That's the wrong way. Everyone else is heading in the other direction," Herc asked then moved in step with me.

"I don't care where everybody else is heading. I want to see where Charon is supposed to lead us," I remarked.

Tristan's light threw his shadow over us as he turned around. "He's gone!" Tristan shouted.

"Where did we lose him? Wherever he is, we need to go there," Hercules growled.

"This is my specialty," I gritted out my reply.

Contacting that place inside where I was able to reach the emotions around me was like falling down a well. I braced myself. The hit of adrenalin came and I swayed on my feet. My heart crashed around in my chest like an angry bird on a smartphone. My stomach dipped as the vision of Charon being a spider ricocheted back into my mind. He was attached to a thread of spider silk that led away from us.

Someone clasp my hand as I headed off, following the silken thread. My eyes were open now. They didn't need to be closed anymore. I could see in real time where I needed to go.

I barely registered Tristan and the fireball light behind me. I didn't need the light, only the thread. We walked through great rooms and passed halls lined with doors, while view ports gave us a glimpse of the cavern beyond. We passed the mashed-up writing that labeled doors and compartments.

Hercules ran his fingers across some of the words. I barely noticed since I was so focused on pulling the thread that was leading to Charon.

We came to some port windows that looked down at a massive space with three smaller ships. The passage opened into a giant lab, filled with tables and machines. There were hundreds of work stations.

Following the thread, I wove my way around the tables and chairs before the thread disappeared into an alcove and the ceiling.

I pulled out of the trance and closed my eyes to ease my heart rate back to normal, then glanced down at the hand I was holding. I expected it to be Tristan's but it was Hercules'. Everyone else was standing behind us.

Hercules and I were inside the alcove and he was too close for my taste. The wall slid shut, closing us off. I released a scream, banging my hands against that doorway.

"What the hell?" I screamed before the inertia of gravity pressing down on me dropped my stomach to the floor.

I gazed at Hercules. He was still holding my hand. I wrestled my fingers out of his grasp.

"Do you mind? We're not dating."

Heat rolled over my skin.

His eyebrows drew together and his lips turned down into a deep frown, "I'm sorry. I was just being supportive."

I smirked at him, "You can be supportive by standing in front of me before this door opens."

< Nice one! > Tristan was eavesdropping,

< No one asked you.>

<Sorry, but you're being a grade A royal bitch. Hercules was just trying to protect you. I couldn't hold your hand and keep the fire from going out. We needed to make sure you didn't wander off. You went into a daze.>

<I'll say something to him later.> I mumbled.

<Stop being a shit, Issy. Apologize now!> Tristan retorted.

I didn't know Hercules and I felt like he was constantly trying to hook up with me. The feeling of him seeing right into my soul clawed at me. I had seen enough souls to know I didn't want anyone looking at mine.

Hercules positioned himself between me and the door with his dagger at the ready. The elevator traveled for miles.

Humanity hasn't started to build on this level.

This spaceship was big enough to go to another planet with all they would need. It encompassed miles and was over 2 million years old.

I swallowed back the fear and awe that climbed my insides. I closed my eyes. The scent of the man in front of me overwhelmed the small space. I flashed my eyes open and tilted my head up to stare at the curved ceiling.

The pressure of movement slowed and the door swished open. Hercules held his body rigid, with knees bent and one arm raised while the other was lowered. Every one of his muscles was tightly coiled so he could strike.

For a guy who had spent several thousand years stuck in an apartment, not being allowed to interact with other people he is in really fucking great shape.

He slowly inched out to the hall with me trying to peek around his shoulder.

"It looks like a hallway. Stay right behind me. Don't grab any of my clothing. Just in case I need to battle something, I don't want to accidentally hurt you. Stay behind me, but not too close," his instructions came out clipped.

I wasn't some kind of a moron. After watching him fight, there was no way I would stand inside his sword reach.

We inched our way down the dark hall. There was a light source at the end. The closer we got to the light, the more of black spiderweb veins I could make out. The light was the source of everything.

I gulped, hoping my dry mouth would somehow grow wet. Fear changes your physiology and the adrenaline that flooded my system to find Charon got a fresh dose. My hands shook with the natural reaction.

I ran my finger over the surface and the black raised veins pulsed.

Maybe the ship is alive or maybe it still has energy.

We were almost at the light source and Hercules turned his head slightly.

"I'm going inside. You stay here. Press yourself against the wall and watch our backs. Keep an eye on the end of the hallway," he whispered.

"If something happens, I'm sorry for being a bitch all the time." I replied.

He gave me a long lingering gaze. Then, he does his dance into the room, blocking the light and blanketing me in darkness.

His large frame shifted out of the way to reveal Charon standing next to a pedestal with an orb, in the middle of two seats.

The orb is the light source.

< I can only be saved by the Fates. I must be judged. > Charon said.

CHAPTER 33

ISOLDE

Great! Another one of these wackos wants to be judged!

I deftly didn't want to see everything this guy had ever seen. Especially, in the last million years or so, when he stood there in the dark.

That sounds really exciting.

I mentally rolled my eyes. A moment later Tristan's hand landed on my shoulder. I glanced over at him

<How did you get here? >

<The picture in your mind. This is twin powers united.> He chuckled without releasing a sound.

< I don't know if I can do this. > I gulped back the terror, lining my throat and mind.

Hera came and stood beside me, "Be careful what you ask for, Charon. You may not receive the desired outcome."

< I will receive Fate. >

"Is it just me, or is it kind of cheesy that he keeps being so ominous? *'It's the coming of the Fates',*" I couldn't hold my snark back. It covered the fear I was barely holding at bay.

"Isolde, now is not the time for your facetious levity," my mother said.

I hate it when she's right.

Hercules had worked his way around the room, "It's just him." He indicated Charon. "Also, the bridge appears to be relatively safe."

I followed my mother into the room. Tristan trailed behind, while Hera with Adrian brought up the rear.

In unison Hera, mom and I moved into position in front of Charon in a row and I was locked in place.

I don't believe in fate. I don't believe in fate. I don't care what the prophecy says. I don't believe in fate. My life is not predetermined.

I couldn't decide if it was mom saying it or me. I was desperate to turn my head and look at her but I was frozen. The only free thing in the room was my mind. I tried to contact Tristan but the contact came back blank like it hit a wall of nothing.

Charon presented himself to Hera. She laid her hand on his left shoulder and the only words that escaped her lips were, "You have completed your task. You may move forward."

Fresh dread bled into my belly. He moved to stand before me and a new wave of adrenaline jetted into my system. My heart turned over in my chest as I watched my hand rest on his right shoulder and the replay began.

*****

Life on Elysium is beautiful. It's a world bathed in blue. The planet is lined in goldenseal dew. Everything Elysium did appears to be perfectly glorious. Beautiful majestic waterfalls are surrounded by cool mountain rivers.

Tropical beaches dot the oceans and connect beauty to perfection everywhere.

It is a dream world of plenty, yet he was never satisfied.

Charon is different and he's in love.

He is a nymph geneticist working on the forced mutation of longevity, using genetic materials from other species. His people have become apathetic, lazy, lounging around, producing nothing and doing nothing.

Charon is disgusted by their inaction. Charon's wife becomes sick.

Most of their sciences were forgotten or left behind.

He petitions to study his wife's illness for a cure, believing it is possible. The Lords of the Underworld deny his petition.

He begins speaking out against the government. He gains followers, one of them, a man named Anu. They work together to find a cure, however the Lords of the Underworld destroy his work and try to imprison him.

Charon's wife dies.

He and his followers create a spaceship and set out into the cosmos outside the reaches of the planet and the evil of the Lords of the Underworld.

Elysium has ceased exploring the cosmos many thousands of years before. Space travel is only used to remove criminals and trash. He continues his genetic research and somehow, he and Anu come up with a gene therapy. He injects himself with it and several of his followers. He has created a genetic anomaly that changes the way the brain waves worked. It allows him to become a shifter.

He convinces everyone that believed in him, millions of people, to build Prometheus and find another planet to inhabit.

Prometheus launches into the spatial void and Charon announces he is ready to make the first shift, but in a grand jester, he injects everyone with his gene therapy, changing them all. Then he shifts.

*****

The information overload was too much for me.

I was forced to relive every moment by myself. The pain of watching his wife wither away and die ate at me.

Daddy died the same way.

They just faded into a shallow shell of a being.

Then, I saw what had gone wrong. I understood why his mind was frozen and the terror that came with it.

*****

The awakening of every mind, all at once, fills my head with loud petrifying screaming mid-shift. I grip my ears in an attempt to protect my mind from the onslaught, but I lose my way.

We are in between and the full impact of our folly lays waste to all my plans. I scratch at the walls of subspace desperate for a way out. I can't find the proper exit.

Anu's voice rises above the rest.

<Take any path you find.> He screams.

I aim for the brightest star. The space around us pops and the flavor of burned air meets my body. I stare at the ship and all my companions through the blurred skin of subspace. I beat my hands on the walls but they won't budge. I am trapped in-between.

The ship drifts away yet I remain.

~ 478 ~

*****

Suddenly it was all clear in my head.

That's why the shift failed. That's why they hadn't made it to the planet. Only the power of the Oracle had saved them.

His arrogance had done this to millions of people and yet I could identify with why he'd done it. He was disgusted by what Elysium had become, lazy, living purely for the moment, the emotion, the decadence of their society. They did nothing to further themselves.

I had to judge him. His arrogance and his power-hungry nature disgusted me, but I could understand why he was so unhappy. Would I really want to live somewhere, where all was perfect, but nothing ever changed?

Nobody strives for anything better than what was already there. Like a bump on a log?

Like Themia.

I made my choice. "You have been judged," I stated.

Let my mother sort him out.

He stepped in front of my mother. Her eyes had gone from the crystalline blue to milky white. He trembled, standing before her. It was an actual show of emotion. I was surprised. My mother placed her hand on his forehead and his whole body went into convulsions. Sweat formed a thin film over his skin. It was a sheen reflecting the light from the orb.

"Shifters, come to me!" Mom ordered.

Both Adrian and Tristan step to my mother and place their hands on her shoulder. Suddenly, I was released from my trance, as was Hera.

I reached out to join my twin, but Hercules snatched my hand.

"Don't touch any of them, Isolde! They're making a transfer," Hera said.

"What are you talking about?"

"Charon's is being judged. I don't know what your mother can do, but she's transferring his knowledge to your brother and his father," she supplied.

"She can do that?" I whispered.

"You are the Fates. You can do anything," Hercules returned.

I whipped my head back to look at him. Fear coiled to my belly.

We have the power to change anyone's fate but our own?

CHAPTER 34

SYDNEY

The terrified look of disgust on Isolde's face as she judged Charon tore my heart out. She released him with a whimper. Her body shuddered and her hand shook as she lowered it to her side.

The milky blue eyes of the ferryman changed the moment he faced me. They turned fiery red. I was the enemy and it was time to do battle.

I don't believe in fate. I don't believe our lives are predetermined.

I couldn't get used to the idea that there was nothing I could do. That every choice I've ever made was decided long ago and even if I was thinking I was changing it, the truth is I was always destined to make that choice. My stomach rolled with the anger of inevitability.

The Bible spews out its religion prophecy, stealing our free will. Apparently humanity learned it from the Themians, who got it from Pythia.

No, they will not steal mine.

I hated that my hand rose of its volition and that I was helpless to stop it. The rage that came after my father began beating me rose up as a wall to protect and defend me. The power it gave me was a cudgel. I wielded it, gripped tightly. My palm barely met his damp skin before our private war began.

His mind was strong. Charon had millions of years to accumulate his defenses. He's cloaked himself in stars, hiding behind nebulas and flinging asteroids at me.

Being a fate meant choosing life or death for someone. I couldn't do that without seeing inside his mind. I searched his face and the cosmos for chinks in his armor, mental weakness.

As always, his weakness was what drove him here and what brought him to stand before me. His voice whispered in the background, telling me of his sorrows and begging for forgiveness.

Should I forgive the fact he misled millions of people? Or the fact that he left everyone else behind to flounder? He took his people to a universe and left them adrift. Is genetically manipulating oneself to become more wrong?

I didn't believe in God but I didn't believe in playing God either.

I moved around inside his mind back and forth. I was dodging his walls of protection. However, every time I was able to see a chink, it seemed to fill as quickly as I could identify it.

He's desperate. I can hear his heart beating ripping through his chest. He's filled with fear and determination.

"Charon, you will submit to me!" I growled as my body trembled.

He never spoke out loud as if his vocal cords had been damaged and he was incapable of using them from atrophy.

The trembling, I felt wasn't me at all. It was him. I zipped around in his mind like a roller coaster, pulling 4G's. I was mentally scanning for a small opening. I just needed a sliver of a space in his defensive universe. In a matter of seconds, thousands of systems flashed past me in my desperate search.

But the fabric of the universe is not perfect. It is torn in ways the human mind can't imagine.

Having traversed the stars, I was not tied to humanities ideas. The tear in his mental universe wasn't a tear at all, but a small shining diamond floating in his star laden psyche.

I snatched the shining rock and finally reached inside to see the ache and pain, the suffering. The reason for his entire existence wasn't just to be better or to rule or to dominate. It was his complete and utter disgust for the complacency of his people. Their complacency had caused them to stop seeking scientific excellence, not move forward. His people lived, breathed, loved, reproduced and died. That was the whole of their existence.

His wife's illness was nothing more than a catalyst along with the refusal to look for a cure that led to his metamorphosis. The way his entire culture had atrophied into decadence fueled his rage.

Charon was like me. He understood that knowledge is power. He reopened all the old libraries and educated himself. All for the love of a woman.

<Not just any woman. My wife. She was beautiful and vibrant and they let her die. No one even tried. They simply said that because she had the sickness that she should die.>

The vision of a dark-haired woman, dancing on a pink sand beach and beckoning to me flooded my mind. There was an undying love layered with awe.

I understood that kind of love and what it could drive you to do. Part of me wanted to pull back and let him be.

<They said I should make her comfortable. They wouldn't even give her drugs to ease her pain. There was nothing I could do. I was neither fast enough or smart enough.>

The vision of his wife wilting away in his arms ripped my chest into a thousand pieces as agony burned me.

<She died in my arms and they did nothing. All of them live in a world where they would let a beautiful creature such

as my wife die simply because they were too lazy to learn or try.> He mourned.

<All civilizations require growth of some kind to maintain themselves. Laziness and complacency are no excuse. So, you engineered all of this.> I replied, swallowing back my personal experiences.

<Yes, I engineered it all for her, so what happened to her would never happen again. I didn't wish to live in a society that wouldn't stand up and say 'Enough! We can be better'.> He shouted.

The vision of all the people he experimented on before he reached his cure washed over me like a tsunami. I drowned in the spilt blood. He and his compatriots used thousands of men and women, creating misshaped children and allowing them to die so they could try again. His compatriot Anu seemed to enjoy the bloodletting and sheer torture of their victims.

I wanted to find the catalysis for the gene therapy, but it wasn't there. Charon hadn't made the breakthrough. Anu did and the knowledge of that miracle died with him.

<You will surrender all your knowledge. You will give it willingly. You will not make me force it from you, or I will

take it and when I'm done, I will end you. You have a choice. You can die or you can live with us. I will wipe all your memories, so you won't remember anything of her or your life before.>

It was the only choice. He was too dangerous to mingle with the hybrids or the Themians on his own.

< I will submit.> he replied.

Those were his only words, yet the tone was not one of submission. It was a move on a chess board. He believed he could beat me.

He can believe whatever he wants for the next few minutes and then it will all be mine.

I pulled Adrian and Tristan to me, as if they were Knights on my galactic chess board.

< Prepare yourselves. > I ordered.

Their hands lightly touched my shoulders like sentinels.

The only site my eyes held were Charon's visions in my mind. His impressive knowledge of the Universe rivaled my wildest dreams. Shifting through the immense amount of information was a Herculean task. I snickered to myself.

Adrian and Tristan only needed shifter related information. I created baskets in my mind. One for shifting, one for genetics, and one for everything else. Only Hera and Marilyn could implement any scientific understanding. I packaged it up like a mental UPS box and smacked a label on it for later.

As for Charon's memories of his wife and the life he led before the shift, I crumpled them up like a ball and tossed them into the proverbial trash can to be recycled.

I was starting to get the hang of this judgment thing. If I treated the mind I dominated like a computer screen, pulling up what I wanted and tossing the rest in the trash, the job became easier. I could quickly determine whether they were worth saving or too far gone for redemption.

It sickened me, but if I didn't make a choice, we would be locked in this mental limbo for eternity.

Make a choice or one will be made for you, not necessarily the one you want.

"Where am I?" Charon asked.

I'd hollowed him out like a gourd for water. "You are on Prometheus," I replied, desperate to hold back the gore that pooled in the back of my throat.

His head whipped around, studying his surroundings before settling back on me.

"I don't remember boarding a ship," he mused, then ran his fingers through his grimy hair.

Bits of dust and dirt drifted down like dandruff. The flakes landed on the floor and his shoulders.

I ignored his first question and moved on to testing him. "Where are you from?"

"I'm from Elysium," he replied, shaking his head.

"How old are you?" I demanded.

It was not as if I knew that answer, but I was sure that I could retrieve it from my mental data banks.

"207."

"Do you know your name?" I asked and bit my lip.

His eyes shifted back and forth searching the room for answers.

With his brows knitted together he replied, "No, I don't know who I am. I don't know my name. I can't remember." He stared up at me bewildered. "I know how old I am, my favorite food, my preferred color. Yet, I don't know my name!"

"Ron. Your name is Ron," I supplied for ease.

It was a variation of Charon and no one else needed to know his real name.

He stepped back, finding one of the seats in the room, then he plopped gently down. He was covered in dirt and probably needed a shower from standing in a cave for 2 million years.

I glanced around the shifting room. Tristan and Adrian both stood facing each other with their eyes locked open. Their mental chatter raged in the background, but I ignored it. Whatever they were talking about was their business and they could handle it. I had complete faith that Adrian would take care of any and all issues that needed to be dealt with.

Witnessing Hercules possessive demeanor towards Isolde brought more disturbing questions to mind that I didn't wish to voice at this time. I was more worried about Tristan and his mind. The mega dump of galactic information with every visual of the cosmos that Charon had ever encountered could short circuit his brain.

"So, what do we do now?" Issy demanded. She moved to touch her brother, but pulled her hand back at the last moment. His mind was now a minefield of Charon's star charts.

"We have to wait for Adrian and Tristan to come out of their information hangover. What did you see inside his mind, Isolde?" I asked.

"I saw a sad man who was power hungry and desperate to find out anything he could to improve himself. Apathetic with everything that was happening on his world, he gathered together like-minded people and left. I saw that his arrogance constantly overestimated his abilities and kind of screwed himself." She squeezed her eyes closed, then ran a hand over her forehead.

"Yes, but he made the jump and everything should have worked out perfectly," Hera mumbled, then glanced over at 'Ron'.

"It's simple, Hera. Just before they made the shift, he gave everybody the gene therapy. There was an agreement.

That's why everybody followed him like he was the leader of the Branch Dravidians," I replied with a sigh.

"Okay, but what did that have to do with messing up his shift?" Hercules asked, as he ran a finger along the console in front of the pilot's seat and rubbed it with his thumb.

"He'd only actually given the top brass of his group the gene therapy before. None of them were telepathic. However, the moment everybody else got the gene therapy, suddenly they were all telepathic and a myriad of voices, emotions, everything poured into him as he made the shift. It created confusion and caused him to shift to the wrong place," Isolde sniffled.

I couldn't imagine the terror that flowed through him and into Issy.

"Okay, so they didn't end up where they were supposed to. Who cares? Where were they going and where did they come from?" I scoffed.

After all I've seen of Elysium, do we still want to go there?

The only answer I could conjure was 'Yes'.

My mind was working a mile a minute. I wanted to listen in on Adrian and Tristan but math had never been my strong suit. Unless, of course, it had anything to do with money. When it came to higher computations of physics and sorry my brain just shut itself off.

The only thing I could think that explained the difference between a jump and a shift was alternate reality.

"He comes from an alternate reality. They all come from an alternate reality. That's why they call that a shift. Because they'd shifted realities. That was kind of what he was planning on doing the whole time. He said he wasn't making a jump. He said that he was making a shift," I looked from Adrian to Tristan.

Adrian and Tristan were both acting strange as if they were the same person operating in unison.

"The only reason they didn't land where they intended to was because of the disruption of the minds. Charon should've waited to administer the gene therapy until after the shift. His plan all along was to go to a different dimension." I stated.

"So, the multiple reality theory is true? There's not just one reality, but an infinite number based on an infinite number of choices at any one moment in time and dates?" Issy asked.

It gave me the feeling that she had talked about this kind of crap before.

"Yes, Isolde," the way Adrian said 'Isolde' was withdrawn, emotionally vacant.

I placed my hand on his shoulder and his facial features softened lightly, only to return to the vacant clear blue stare.

"Isolde, speak to your brother in his mind," I instructed.

<Adrian, snap out of it! > I barked.

<This will pass. Do not worry, beautiful girl.>

<What is going on in there? > I huffed in frustration.

<Charon's mind has been drifting through time and space for the last 2 million years trapped in a place between. We have to find our way through the cosmos back to ourselves. Charon was not able to do it in 2 million years because he was alone and had no point of reference. Tristan and I are both drifting together. We have a point of reference

— you. Distracting us will only make the process take longer
>

I heaved a sigh of relief and glanced at Issy.

"All Tristan said was something about trying to find his way back to us. Which is bizarre since they're standing right here," Issy scoffed and sneered at her brother in disbelief.

Hercules moved to her side to rub her shoulders and she sagged into the comfort he offered.

"Yeah. Adrian said the same thing. They know where they're going. I guess it won't take him long if you believe what they're saying."

The entire time Hera's eyes drifted from one face to the other, quietly observing. She was doing that scientistic thing where she was studying us. It was ominous and I didn't like it.

"Hera, stop studying the human creature! There isn't one here. We are all part Themian," I snapped.

"What if Charon didn't just shift them from one reality to another? What if he shifted them through space and time at the same time, not just jumping from one dimension to another but jumping back in time from one dimension to another?" Issy asked, pulling on her lower lip.

"We will have answers to those questions as soon as Adrian and Tristan snap out of their mind meld and somehow get back here," I retorted.

Time dragged on and I'd lost my ability to wait patiently for the answers I longed for. Those days passed away the day I left my father's house.

I will never sit quietly by, waiting.

Action was the only answer I understood any more, and I needed action.

Adrian and Tristan stepped towards the pedestal. In unison, both placed their hands on the orb. The interior of the spaceship lit up with a vibrant blue-white light, blinding me after being in the dim glow. The black spider veins disappeared and turned into glowing blue arteries, fueling power to the ship. The internal systems whirred and hummed, making everything blue.

The floor shifted underneath us and I stumbled briefly before righting myself by pressing my hand against the wall. The sudden light disorientated me.

A voice echoed around the room. "New crew members recognized. State your name."

I glanced at Hera. She raised her shoulders and shook her head.

"Sydney Rhiannon O'Dear," I supplied.

"Noted, Sydney Rhiannon O'Dear. Please state your designation."

<Leader!> Hera offered.

"Leader and one of the Fates," I barked, then bit my lip at the volume of my reply.

"Does 'leader' equate to commander?"

"Yes."

"Are you replacing commander Charon?"

"Yes, commander Charon has retired," I retorted.

He will never command anything other than a dinner plate if I can help it.

"Greetings, commander O'Dear. I sense there are other life forms on board. Please identify, along with your designation."

Adrian and Tristan both removed their hands from the orb. "Adrian Mitchell Shipman," Adrian said then winked at me.

I heaved a sigh of relief.

If he's talking, he's not lost in space.

"Designation."

"Pilot."

"Are you replacing Charon?" The ship inquired.

"Yes."

"Identity confirmed. You have been logged into our databases."

"Herathina, otherwise known as Hera," I turned to take in her answer, "designation scientist and one of the Fates."

"Please, define your field of study?"

"The mind."

"Next designation please."

"Tristan Thomas Cosimo, designation pilot."

"Are you replacing Adrian Shipman?"

"No, secondary pilot," Tristan puffed his chest out with pride.

"Adrian Mitchell Shipman. New designation - primary pilot. Next name and designation.

"Isolde Rhiannon Cosimo, designation a Fate and empath."

"Accepted, Isolde Rhiannon Cosimo, empath and one of the Fates."

"Name and designation, please."

"Hercules, son of Zeus and Hera, designation hero," Hercules stated and the room groaned.

CHAPTER 35

SYDNEY

Honestly, couldn't he think of anything else to say?

I shot a glance at Hercules and caught Tristan smirking as if it was actually funny. He raised his hands in surrender, "What? Everybody thinks he's a hero anyway. It's funny!"

"Hercules, son of Zeus and Hera, the same Hera that is present?" The ship asked.

"Yes," Herc replied, his super hero smile holding more teeth than a dentist office.

"Unrecognized designation 'Hero'. Please define."

"Warrior, defender of the weak, savior of the innocent," Issy groaned out.

He crossed his arms, putting his hands under each bicep, forcing them to bulge.

It's the sexy man stance.

He must've learned that over several thousands of years. With both his legs planted in a wide stance, he appeared daunting.

Do they teach this at hero college or is he just born with it?

All questions I didn't want to chase down a rabbit hole and waste my time.

"My son, Hercules, defender of the innocent. I like that," Hera murmured.

The cheesy shit eating grin on his face widened, "That's the first nice thing you've actually said to me, Isolde. Thank you. I'd like to think I only ever defended the weak and innocent," He winked at her.

Why can't he leave well enough alone?

She was just describing what a hero was for the computer.

"The ship is powered up and we have control. Where to, now? Tristan asked.

Adrian's fingers flashed over the controls on the console, then he placed one hand on the orb.

"We have to get out of this cavern and it's not going to be as easy as you think. We can't shift out of this cavern. The walls are shielded." His hand turned the orb clockwise and the lights on the console changed color. "The Elysiums lived on this ship for years until they were able to make their way out of the caverns. The tunnels were created by them. That's why they all have a laser-like smooth feel. Also, that's why there are no stalagmites or stalactites," he stopped talking for a moment only to continue, "The rivers were way points. Charon didn't bring the ship down with the manual controls. He remembers the trip but not how they did it, therefore we can't shift out. We will have to fly." His fingers stilled over the controls as he rotated to face us.

"That doesn't sound all that difficult," I replied to reassure the group as well as myself. "I mean, you have Charon's memories, so I'm sure you know how to fly the ship,"

I gulped before asking the next question, "Now, what's the catch?"

"There are underground vents or tunnels that gas escapes through," Adrian glanced down at the flooring then back up.

Uncertainty bled through our connection. I wanted to search his mind for the source, but held myself in check.

"We could follow the tunnels until we can either find an exit or shift out!" I suggested.

"I don't know, mom. After the shift, Charon stood here like a statue on this ship until they actually dug the tunnels. Then, they shoved him into that cavern. There is no one alive today who was there for the trip down. Even if there was someone, they might not remember. Lethe would strip all those memories away," Issy's argument was sound.

However, my gut was telling me that '*if there's a way in, there has to be a way out*'.

2 million years is nothing in geological time.

"That is not true," Hera said, "Some of the first still live. They remember. The primordium gave back all that Lethe took. Poseidon would remember."

I shivered at the thought and shrugged Hera's statement away. I had bigger fish to fry, "Do the engines still work?" I asked, injecting as much command into my voice as possible.

"Would you like to execute a ship wide systems analysis?" Prometheus inquired.

"Yes," I whispered.

Whirring filled the space as different panels flashed, displaying symbols I couldn't identify. Rumbling and groaning issued from deep within the ship, which made me internally groan right along with the ship.

"Prometheus?" Hera spoke and I jumped at the sound of her voice.

"Yes."

"Are the Bio-domes inside the ship still viable?" She asked.

Holy fuck on a stick.

I held my breath.

"There is still life inside the Bio-domes. However, I cannot guarantee safe progress through any of them. The ecosystems have fully integrated and taken over the areas. Without proper maintenance it has become wild in the extreme. But oxygen production is at optimal."

I sucked in air as every person in the room looked at Hercules. A giant grin spread over his rugged features.

"Are there any other living creatures on this ship other than ourselves?" Hercules asked, then tapped his nose.

"Yes. The wildlife within the Dio-domes and two Elysians," Prometheus returned.

We don't have time for this.

"Where are these Elysians?" Hera demanded, then smoothed the grimy fabric of her dress.

"Secured in preservation containers, located in the storage section of the shifting room."

"Who are they?" I asked a bit too quickly.

I just wanted to see the next obstacle and be on our way.

"Information unknown. No name or designation was applied to them."

"When were they put into the preservation canisters?" I retorted.

Two people in a storage closet could be a problem. I bit my lip.

But not as much as Hera's curiosity.

"Just after landing."

Oh boy! That's a pickle.

I looked over at Hera. She'd already stepped in front of a section of the wall near the doors, looking for some indication of how to open the closet.

"Hera, do your people have preservation technology?" I asked.

Part of me hoped she knew something, while another part of me wished the whole thing would go away.

"No, we don't need to place anyone in stasis ever. I'm assuming that stasis would be for long-term space travel. We travel space instantaneously. As far as I know, if someone is ill and you are incapable of curing them," she tilted her head from side to side, "putting them in a stasis chamber might help prolong their life. The infinity pools made this technology irrelevant," she concluded.

"Humanity hasn't figured it out yet," Issy murmured.

The ship rumbled then jolted left and right. The sound of an engine straining hummed deep in the structure. Who could blame them? Sitting still for 2 million years, every working part must have been dry as a bone.

"Systems analysis complete. All systems are in an adequate working order. Do you wish to start the main engines?"

I froze for a moment.

What if I blow the ship up, killing all of us?

"Syd, do we wish to start the main engines?" Adrian asked.

"Prometheus, what is the status of the hull's integrity?" Hercules interjected.

I threw him a grateful smile.

"Hull integrity cannot be gauged until the hatches are secure."

"How many open hatches are there?" Hercules continued.

"There are approximately three open and one cargo bay door," Prometheus supplied.

In a second, Hercules was up and out the door in a flash, yelling.

"Direct me to each hatch and the cargo bay with the shortest travel time."

I looked from Issy, to the doorway and back. She lowered her head and followed him out the door, picking up her pace as she went.

"Please secure all hatches and make sure your trays tables are in their upright position. We are going to move this rust bucket," I stated with a dry laugh and took a deep breath.

Part of me wanted to cross myself for good measure just in case we all died. The other part of me stomped down on the crossing and screamed *'Gods aren't real, you fool! Push the damn button!'*

After twenty minutes, Prometheus announced, "Acknowledged. All hatches secured."

I looked around the room. Adrian and Tristan didn't have eyes for anything but the blinking lights and touch pads.

"Is there anything else anybody can think of, besides closing the doors?" I asked. No one responded, so I took a breath.

"Prometheus, fire up the main engines! Let's hope the ship doesn't explode."

Adrian spoke up, "Don't worry. If something goes wrong, we will be out of here fast enough to survive."

"Computer, what is the status of the engines?" I demanded without taking my eyes off the various blinking lights.

The vibration inside the ship grew, but none of it was earth shattering. It felt like the resound pedal on a piano once it has been depressed. It was a light humming barely noticeable, somewhere in the background.

"The engines are functioning within tolerable parameters. They will be ready for liftoff and 2.3 kritos."

I glanced around the shifting room, hoping someone knew what the hell a kritos was. Instead of answers, I was met with silence and view ports. They were similar to the windows on the space-shuttle, all facing the front with the added windows overhead. It created an unimpeded view of the roof of the cavern.

This was designed to shift or pilot the ship. It was meant to be flown like any other type of spacecraft. And yet, it was a perfect sphere.

I glanced from left to right. Hera was still fiddling with the back wall, desperate to try and open the panels for the stasis chamber.

"Hera, whoever or whatever it is in those chambers is still alive and waited this long. They can wait a little longer."

"Whoever is in there is an original Elysium. They will remember everything about Elysium," she huffed, still searching for the release mechanism.

"You don't know that. Whatever they remember is irrelevant right now. We need to get this ship out of this cave system and into space. Leaving them in there a few more days or even a week isn't going to hurt them. We can wake them up later," I widened my eyes at her to emphasize the urgency of our predicament.

Her eyebrows pulled together as her eyes filled with pain. She wanted to help them.

Isolde moved to her side. Placing a hand on her shoulder, she whispered something in her ear.

I know sometimes I come across as cold, but they've been in there for 2 million years. What's a couple more days?

"Engines at optimal levels." the ship stated.

Adrian and Tristan sat in the only two seats in the room.

"Prometheus, are there more chairs?" I asked.

"The shifting room was designed for the captain and the pilot alone. If you require more seating, you shall have to use a viewing chamber."

Well, that answers that. I ain't leaving.

The pedestal holding the orb embedded itself into the console. Tristan and Adrian placed their hands on an orb. The entire ship groaned. After that, just like pulling the cork out of a bottle, we popped free of the ground, swaying side to side and hovered.

The front view ports turned into giant digital displays with a map of the various tunnels that gave us access, not only to this chamber but our entire trip down. It also revealed a way out.

"Do you really think you can maneuver us all the way through? It looks like a giant maze," I demanded, moving to stand behind Adrian's chair and digging my fingers into the headrest.

"Hey, if Lando Calrissian could do it, why can't we?" Tristan asked, then chuckled.

"Mom, it's not any different than trying to make your way through a reef without a depth finder. Only in this case, we have proximity alarms. We can do this," Issy joined her brother in her youthful belief that we could survive anything.

This is insane.

The ship was millions of years old and we were trusting that it was not going to fall apart even if it were to rub against a few rocks.

What if one of the tunnels isn't big enough? Or what if there are cave-ins? What if we get close to the top and the rest of the ascent is blocked?

"Prometheus, is there any way to scan our path and see if we're capable of traversing these tunnels?"

"Scanning now." The holographic image in front of us began displaying the scan results and after maybe a kilometer it halted. "Unable to do a complete scan."

"Why are you unable to complete the scan?" I asked, trying not to sound like I was on the verge of tears.

"There's been a cave-in. The tunnel is impassible. We must discover a new trajectory."

"Are there any weapons on board capable of opening a tunnel wall?" Hercules interjected.

"No, the ship was not designed for warfare."

"There's your answer, Herc," my daughter stated.

"It's now or never, Isolde. We will deal with the block when we get there and either Tristan or Adrian are going to shift as much rock as they possibly can back to this cavern or wherever the fuck they can shove it," I grumbled.

Sweat formed under my arms. All I could think was *'we can do this'*.

"Do we know for sure that that's the way we're supposed to be going?" Issy asked, pointing at the hologram.

"It's the original path of the ship," I replied.

"The original path of the ship or not, what if we can go around it and maybe even shift out of this whole cavern? Would it not be worth it to us?" Adrian asked.

"Just because there's a cave-in doesn't mean that the crystalline matter that stops us from using our abilities outside the confines of this space has disappeared. It could still be there."

There are no guarantees we can do anything.

<Stay the course.>

<Of course, beautiful girl.>

The ship moved into the tunnel above us, threading its way. Every now and again, something scraped on the outer hull and Adrian cringed. We bumped into rocks and the vibration flowed into my feet and up to my teeth. The ship was massive but it was like a tuning fork. We could feel everything, as if it was designed to funnel it all into this room.

"We've reached the end of the tunnel," the computer was really starting to get on my nerves.

"Prometheus, continue scanning surrounding areas. Search for alternate routes!"

Tristan's eyes took on a faraway gaze. A big chunk of the rock wall in front of us suddenly disappeared. Bit by bit, it was eaten away like an invisible monster munching down stone.

"My scans indicate we are very close to breaking through to the other side. However, the temperature within the next tunnel has risen significantly and my readings indicate there may indeed be a fire or lava burning on the other side," the ship's computer informed us.

Wouldn't that be fucking great! Lava?

"Prometheus, is there any way you can define what's on the other side? I would prefer not to take a couple million-year-old ship into magma," I scoffed and held my breath for the reply.

"Prometheus was designed to withstand thousands of degrees Kelvin. There should be no problem being engulfed in magma or any other type of superheated product."

"Great. No problem with lava. Will it cook everyone inside?" I demanded for clarification.

The ship would be fine but I needed everyone on board to make it too.

"My systems indicate there would be minimal damage to the ship and its interior residents."

Minimal damage! I hate it when they use terms like that.

Computers always say things like minimal or maximum.

But what does that mean? The maximum life capacity of the ship being several million and minimal killing means basically the five people on board. Or max being five and minimum killing two?

I bit my lip, "Tristan, break through!"

"Well, here goes nothing," Issy murmured.

The rock disappeared and a scorching umber liquid engulfed most of the view ports.

"The Phlegethon River of Fire," Charon announced

My head whipped around. I'd just wiped his memory.

There's no fracking way he could even know where we are or what we're doing.

"What did you just say?" I demanded.

"I didn't say anything. I swear. I didn't speak," Ron replied in a frightened voice and moved to the back wall near the door.

CHAPTER 36

SYDNEY

"Mom, nobody spoke," Issy said.

"Are you sure? I thought I heard someone."

I could swear to God that I heard Charon say something.

If he didn't say it, where did it come?

"Sydney, no one spoke."

I can't be hearing things. I'm not crazy. I'm not going to buy into the crazy.

My attention was drawn away from the supposed voice that I had or hadn't heard because the glowing spot of lava on the view port grew bigger. Slowly, clumps of rotten glowing rock oozed down. The last time I witnessed something like this was at the lava flows of Kilauea. All that liquid stone was glowing molasses.

"Do you want me to keep moving the rock, mom?" Tristan's voice drew me away from the mesmerizing view.

"Well at least we now know the river of fires isn't fire at all. It's molten lava. How the hell did they get this ship down here?" I remarked.

"We may never know, Syd. Right now, the question is 'can we get the ship out'?" Adrian intervened.

"Yes, let's get this show on the road. Prometheus, can the ship survive the lava flow?" I growled out over my gnashing teeth.

"Affirmative."

Well, the ship can survive. Hopefully, we don't die inside it.

The last section of rock Tristan removed caused the entire ship to jolt back with the force of the magma flow. There were no more walls defining our travel, only heat. We were just flotsam on a giant river, trying to push back against the flow.

I thought that the human stories of Greek mythology described a river with fire floating on top, nevertheless that too was just someone's imagination. The truth was so much more terrifying. Their stories could never compare to reality. The temperature in the entire shifting room grew. Sweat slicked my back, coating my body and even the space between my fingers. I pushed droplets from my brows back into my hairline to keep the salt laced moisture from blinding me.

Prometheus said the ship could withstand the heat. Notwithstanding I wasn't sure everything was fully shielded for the heat.

Maybe this river hadn't been here at all when they first arrived.

It didn't matter. Now, we had to deal with it.

"We need to get out of the main flow if we can."

Adrian and Tristan maneuvered their controls forward in unison and the ship strained against the pressure.

One thing was for sure. There was no way we were ever going to be able to go back to the cavern. Even if we wanted to, it would be filled with lava by now.

It won't even exist.

There was only one way out and we were on it.

The vibrations in the ship grew and the engines powered up to move us forward through this viscous fluid. Time slowed with the lack of visibility and the waking heat that baked into us.

But then, like blowing a golf ball through a hoes, the ship burst forward and to the right as the flow changed.

"Are we in a pinball machine?" I shouted.

"No, the lava flows are just dragging us all over the place. You need to hold onto something and don't sit down. That's not going to save you. I think it's gonna be a bumpy ride," Adrian returned.

I moved forward and gripped the back of his seat so hard that my knuckles turned white. It gave me a better view of his console and the holographic map. Hera in turn stood behind Tristan.

I was glad to see she'd stepped away from the wall panels. I glanced behind me and spied Hercules. He'd braced himself into the frame, surrounding the door. A frown crossed my features that I couldn't wipe away. He had one arm wrapped tight around Isolde's waist.

That's interesting.

Tearing my attention away from them, I returned my focus to the screens and the front viewing panels. Glancing between the controls a holographic image revealed we were rising rapidly with pressure building behind us.

"Prometheus, are we inside a volcano?" I asked.

"Negative. We are in a horizontal lava tube."

"Is there any way you can use your sensors to determine where we will come out on the surface of the planet?" Hera asked.

"Negative. My sensors cannot penetrate the molten rock."

We were being pushed, hopefully towards the surface – blind. The force of the flow kept jolting us, left and right, up and down. Several times I thought I was going to fall. Then the gravity shifted and we weren't heading horizontal anymore.

"Sydney, stand by the door with Hercules. You too, Hera or you're going to fall," as soon as the words were out of Adrian's mouth, the full pressure of the gravity change hit me.

I was hanging by the back of Adrian's chair. There was no breeze here to slow my dissent and Hera was hanging by one hand.

"Tristan, shift us to the wall!" I yelled.

The room changed and suddenly I was standing on the wall with Isolde laying on top of Hercules, looking straight up at me. Her honey blond hair covered his entire chest, fanning out in every direction. I took two steps and crouched down to push it out of his face.

"Thank you! I thought I was going to suffocate with all that hair going down my throat," he chuckled.

I gave him a halfcocked smile "We O'Dear girls are known for our hair."

I tilted my head back to get a better look at the view screens and the holographic display, then I decided I might as well sit down and lay back and enjoy the ride. I couldn't do anything about it. I laid down next Isolde and Hercules, interlocking my arm through Issy's.

"Do you have a nice firm grip on the door frame, Hercules? I'm afraid we might dislocate your shoulder if the ship yanks us around too much," I asked to reassure myself more than to check his needs.

"Don't worry, lady. You are in good hands," Hercules blustered.

Isolde internally groaned and rolled her eyes. "Really? You're like some old timey movie. What do you think you are? A superhero, Herc?" she moaned.

"I like the sound of that very much. Superhero. Nothing tops DemiGod," he mumbled as a smile warmed his face on top of the heat in the room.

Isolde elbowed him in the stomach.

I don't know why he goes to so much trouble, when all she does is hurt and admonish him. He's either got a bad or he's too stupid to realize when a woman wants him to go away.

According to the display, we were about to reach the green section any moment.

"We're about 2 miles from the surface and we should be in the green. But we're still inside the lava flow. What do you want to do?" Adrian asked in his cool voice.

"Can you shift us?" I asked.

Adrian and Tristan locked eyes and the ship rumbled. We were there but we weren't. They turned back to the view-screen. "No, this lava flow is an ability blocker."

The pressure holding me in place changed and my lock on Issy's arm became the pull on an elastic cord. As the ship rolled over, we were being rolled around like a beach ball. With each jerk and bounce, the ship moved to right itself.

"The densest portion of our mass is at the bottom of the ship and we automatically write ourselves so the weight is down. The force of gravity is playing with us," Adrian supplied to quiet my squeaks every time the ship rocked and rolled tossing me around.

Hera wasn't doing any better.

The jarring around us reached a new high. We weren't just some bubble floating in liquid. We were inside a tunnel filled with lava and our screens were covered with it.

I'm such a moron.

Of course we couldn't shift. We were covered in the liquid that prevented it.

"The entire ship's covered in lava. Is there any way to get it off?"

"I'm getting redline signals all across the boards," Adrian informed me as he was shaking his head.

"Prometheus, are we losing hull integrity?" I shouted, praying I was wrong.

"There have been several breaches in the hull and lava has entered the ship. I have sealed off bulkheads in those areas. However, we have taken on additional weight. It is slowing our ascent. Also, the main engines are off-line."

Even with the pounding heat, my blood ran cold.

"Do a system wide analysis. We need to know how much damage we've sustained."

"Confirmed. System wide analysis underway."

Hera's hands gripping mine. I hadn't even realized she did so. I turned my head and looked into her terrified eyes.

"Don't worry. We're going to get out of this one way or another," I assured her and myself.

"How? The ship is covered completely in lava and the lava blocks our abilities. When we reach the surface, we won't be able to go anywhere or do anything without exiting the ship. The engines are off line. We won't be able to remove the lava until it cools. That could take days or weeks," she faltered as beads of sweat rolled down her hairline into her ears.

I smiled at her, "You know how resourceful humans are, right?"

She tentatively returned my smile. "Yes, but you're not human."

"Part of me is or was. One thing I do know, we never give up. We always find a way," I nodded my head to reassure her, then I turned my eyes back to the screen and it struck me.

The whole ship is covered.

But what if...

"Prometheus, is the entire surface of the ship covered in this molten lava?"

"There is a small portion above and behind the shifting room that is not covered. The friction from colliding with one of the rock walls has removed it."

I didn't hear the reply. Molten lava, liquid rock.

Liquid.

"YES!" That was all I needed to know.

I heard a dry laugh from Hercules.

"Are you up to something, Daughter of Poseidon?" he asked.

Yes, yes, I am!

I reached deep inside for my power.

You always have to find it and it is never easy. It's not on the surface of the sandbox. It is something you have to dig for.

And that was what I did. There was water here on this planet somewhere and I knew that if I could just make contact with my ability to control water and the ability to control liquid, I could control molten lava.

Because in the end, it is nothing more than liquid.

I pulled at my power. I could feel it flowing through me. Every muscle in my stomach bunched as lights exploded in my mind. With that, I pushed the lava back from the surface of our ship.

My body shook with my exertions. The sound of my own screaming filled my ears.

"Keep going, Sydney! I can see out of one of the windows," Adrian urged me on.

I pushed it back. All of it. It was water and earth blended together. Controlling them both was easier than I thought it would be.

An ocean or a river. It doesn't matter what state it is in. It all travels through its various stages from liquid to gas, to solid.

Maybe I am a daughter of Poseidon.

It didn't matter. It was a liquid and I could move it.

I pictured the views screen in front of us and I pushed the liquid rock away as gravity pressed down.

"Sydney, what are you doing?" Hera shouted.

I couldn't pay attention to what they were saying. We were pulling at least 4Gs and gaining and I could feel the push back of every single one of them. My skin sunk back into my frame, holding my body in place, while my cheeks plastered back into my skull. My eyes were held open against the push of gravity and ready to pop if we were to go just a little bit harder. The closer we got to the surface, the heavier the gravity became. We breached the surface and shot out like a bullet from a gun, only with liquid propelling us.

We were rising up in the air, and I couldn't keep the momentum going.

I'm not a teleporter.

"Adrian, shift us! Now!" I screamed.

The heavy pressure from the shift popped my ears as the cold filled my joints. We were intangible, every moment changing, altering. The reality of Delphi and the non-reality of Delphi. Then, suddenly, we were in normal space. The cold black void clothed us, cooling our overheated world and blanketing us in stars.

My body floated up from the wall. Isolde's arm was still interlocked with mine. She anchored me in place. My gaze followed my other arm to the hand I still held firmly — Hera. I smiled at her.

The three of us, the fates, had passed through fire and come out together.

"You are amazing. I could feel the energy. I have never known anyone to be able to control the forces like that," Hercules sputtered.

"Yeah, mom! That was awesome. I could feel you moving us though lava and around the rocks," Tristan said.

A smile burst on my face. I glanced down at what should have been the floor of the shifting room to hide my embarrassment.

"Adrian, where are we?" I asked, using the question as cover.

The screen sputtered and was instantly covered with a three-dimensional image of Ixis and Emmaline.

"Don't just stand there with your mouth hanging wide-open. Are you gonna tell me how in the hell you found that ship?" She shouted.

I burst out laughing, "Good to see you too, Emmaline."

"Would you like to explain why the whole of your ship is glowing like a briquette at a BBQ?"

"You'd be glowing too if you just popped out of a river of fire," I replied while everyone chuckled.

"Are you pullin my leg? A river fire, honestly?" Emmaline patted the spit curls lining her face in disbelief.

"No, Emmaline. I'm not pulling your leg. It was a river fire all right."

"A river of fire... It was lava for God sakes," Issy yelled.

"That explains why the whole of your ship is glowing," she glowered at us.

"I'll bet we're the hottest sphere you've ever seen, huh Emmaline?" Tristan snickered.

"You are. That young man..." Ixis visibly stiffened "who is the man on the bridge?"

"This is Cha — Ron," I supplied, stumbling over my explanation.

"You mean Charon the first shifter?" Ixis asked

"Yes."

"Ixis, I have a ton to tell you. We have the star charts we need. Tristan, Sydney and I will be transferring to your ship," Adrian intervened, putting an end to the very public conversation.

CHAPTER 37

ISOLDE

< You comin, sis?> Tristan asked while wagging his eyebrows.

"I'm going to stay here," I announced and detached myself from Hercules' vice like grip.

"I'll stay too. After all, you might need some muscle. We have no idea what's on this ship," he still had his hands around my waist and righted me before I fell.

My eyes rolled as they glanced over to land on Hercules, "Really? Muscle?" I groaned.

Herc just smirked at me and shrugged, "Somebody's got to be the strong warrior hero in this quest."

I shook my head. His arrogance knew no bounds.

I mean, honestly, he is gorgeous and strong and totally the hero type, the real Hercules, but he doesn't need to keep rubbing it in.

< He's attracted to you. >

< Shut up, Tristan! I don't care that you did mind meld with the oldest shifter in the known universe, stay out of my love life. >

All he did was snicker off to the side, like he knew something I didn't.

He was always lording his additional three minutes of life over me.

Three minutes is definitely not enough extra life experience to run around acting like an intellectual elitist.

"I don't think we should take the ship any further until the hull is fixed and we're certain that all the systems work adequately," Hercules changed gears so fast it could give you whiplash.

He stepped away from the bulkhead and stretched his arms to loosen up.

"I agree with that and I'm exhausted. I don't know about you guys, but I would really like to find a warm meal, a cot and just lay my head down," Adrian stifled a yawn, stood up and stretched.

"I don't think we need to fix anything just yet. Why don't we go back to Odyssey and sleep in our own damn bed?" Mom groaned while itching the dried sweat in the creases of her neck.

"Mother, why don't you go with them? Isolde and I will remain on board of Prometheus to watch over her and defend her," Hercules urged his mother.

"And why exactly am I staying on the ship with you?" I demanded, moving away from him to stand closer to my brother.

"If we have a problem you can contact your brother for any quick moving. He'll be here to save us," he replied.

"And if I don't want to stay here, you can contact your mother. She has the ability to get a shift. It would still achieve your goal. This way, you can stay by yourself," I returned even though I hated the fact that what he was saying made so much more sense than what I was saying.

"Hercules' idea is the best one. The two of you stay. If there is an issue, Tristan or myself are more likely to hear you than Hera. We will get there faster. Nobody wants to play telepathic telephone," Adrian interceded.

Is that even a thing? Telepathic telephone?

Taking a deep breath, my chest raised and lowered as an "O-kay" escaped my lips.

I should stay. I'm the better conduit. The less people we have to bother to make something happen, the better. I hate it when he's right. Why does he have to be so freaking smart?

"I'll stay," I slid my eyes over to Herc and shot him an evil 'die by a thousand fleas' stare. "Does this mean I have to stay in the shifting room or can I go and find quarters?" I asked.

I uncrossed my arms. I didn't even realize I'd crossed them.

"No one says you have to sleep in the same room, but I wouldn't wander too far from the shifting room, though. Prometheus, please notify Isolde and Hercules of any changes in the ships. If possible, notify anyone on board of Odyssey. I'm turning over commands of Prometheus to Hercules," mom replied and ran her hand over her eyes.

She looked like shit. Moving all that lava had really taken the strength out of her.

"Hercules? Why would you turn over the whole ship to him?" I practically yelled, then covered my mouth to keep from biting my lip.

"Because he is the oldest and the most mature of the two of you," my mother's reply came.

I highly doubt he's more mature than I am.

"Hercules is more familiar with Themian technology than you are, since he lived around them for thousands of years," Hera remarked.

God, I hate it when she points out the obvious. I just hate everything. I've got to be tired.

I know my whole stance gave away the fact that I was completely pissed off. I didn't want to be under his command for anything.

"He's not in command of me," I grumbled.

Hercules stood to the side with his legs spread wide and his arms crossed. He always put his hands under his biceps, which made them look 10 times bigger than they were.

As if he really needs any help in that department.

The man looked like he'd been drinking steroids since the moment of his inception. It was really the smirk. He knew exactly how it was gonna play out before I did.

"Orders confirmed. Acting captain is Hercules."

I wanted to slap the smirk off his face and watch it hit the floor, then pour acid on it, until the skin bubbled and crisped before melting away into the bulkhead.

"Don't worry, Isolde. I won't order you around too much. After all, a good leader, leads by example."

I actually caught myself before I stomped my foot on the floor. I really, really didn't like him.

Mom kissed me on the cheek as Adrian shifted the three of them over to Odyssey.

Hercules leaned back, resting his backside on one of the pilots' chairs, then casually tossed one ankle over the top of the other, giving me one of his big shit eating grins. "Now, that I've finally got you alone, what should we do?"

"I'm not doing anything with you, Herc," I poked him in the chest. "I'm going to look for quarters to sleep in. I'm tired. It's been a long week. I'm not even sure how long we were down there. And, frankly you annoy me."

"By annoy, you mean, I make you feel something," he winked at me, "Prometheus, please bring up the schematic of the ship. Show me where all the quarters are. Preferably, quarters that are closest to the shifting room."

"Request confirmed, acting Captain Hercules."

Ugh! Why does it have to say acting Captain Hercules? It's like putting salt on a wound or something.

We both turned towards the holographic display. Right down the hallway there were four quarters. I didn't bother to say a damn thing to him. I simply turned around and walked through the door, heading in the direction of potential rest.

About 150 feet away from the shifting room was the first door. I pushed it open and immediately entered the room.

It was a large space with a massive bed that could fit four or five people. Everything was decorated in that deep Carnelian blue.

Everywhere I go, this color is there.

As I was about to step into the room, a warm breath tickled the back of my neck.

I closed my eyes.

Great! It's Hercules.

It had to be. The only other lifeforms on this ship were in cryo-sleep.

"Isolde Rhiannon O'dear Cosimo, you have entered the commander's chambers. I'm afraid I must ask you to leave," the ship announced.

It's the first bedroom I came to. I don't give a crap whose room it is.

I heaved a sigh.

"Do any of the chambers on this floor belong to anyone else that I should know about, Prometheus?"

"The next chamber belongs to the pilot." The ship relied.

"Well, in that case I can take it because the pilot is my mother's husband and I think he'll be sleeping in the commander's chambers," I scoffed.

Hercules breathed, "He's referring to your brother. Take the room after."

"Thanks a lot, good to know I'm relegated to number three," I remarked and quickly ambled down the hall.

"Don't be so uptight, Calla. Go to sleep. I can stay in the shifting room."

He headed back to the shifting room.

I turned around and came face to face with Charon. I'd forgotten completely about him and he really didn't seem to remember anything.

"Are you sure you want to stay on the ship Cha — Ron? I could have my brother shift you over to Odyssey. You could talk to other people, interact and make friends," I supplied, too wherry to think of anything else to say.

"I don't think I'd be very good at that. I'm not a social person. Although, I don't remember that about myself. I just know. Prometheus appears like the perfect getaway," his words rang in my mind. They had an eerie resemblance to his original get-away trip from Elysium.

"Why don't you go find some quarters of your own and I'll see you in about eight hours?" I offered him a weak smile.

"Goodnight, Isolde! It was lovely meeting you. Hercules is a lucky male."

I whirled around and glared at him "What are you talking about? Lucky male? Hercules is not my guy and I certainly don't belong to him," I barked.

Charon — Ron raised his hands, "No? Forgive me. I was mistaken then. I thought you were mated."

"Nope! Sorry. not mated," I retorted.

My face heated, then it ran down my body. I must have blushed right into my toe nails.

"Oh, forgive my mistake. I hope I didn't embarrass you. I can see how much he adores you," Ron sputtered, "I thought there was a closer relationship there. After all, the energy that's transferred between the two of you is..."

His eyes lit up for the first time since mom had wiped his memories.

I narrowed my eyes, "What do you mean 'the energy transferred between the two of us'?"

"I can see personal energy matter and the energy transfer between your mother and Adrian is similar to the one between you and Hercules. I thought perhaps since they were mated, you and Hercules are mates also. I must be mistaken. Please forgive me. I'll just find quarters and get some rest. Good night, Isolde," Charon — Ron dipped his head and wandered down the hallway.

Are you kidding me? That wipe must have turned his brain to goo.

In the back of my mind I could hear Tristan howling laughing and being obnoxious.

Why do brothers have to be so irritating?

My feelings were none of his business. I was so tired of him listening in on my conversations.

<By the way, Tristan, Charon's comment are private. >

<Close the doors in your mind and I won't be listening.
>

<I can't do that. It just feels wrong. > I mumbled.

<Well, then suffer the consequences of me knowing everything about you and vice versa.>

< There's nothing interesting to know about you, Tristan! You are the most boring boy ever.> I retorted.

More laughter came back.

The room was much smaller and cramps compared to the quarters on Odyssey. The quarters were relatively boring and everything was white. That suited me just fine. I figured out the door locking mechanism. I was asleep before my head ever hit the pillow.

I was dreaming again.

*****

I'm standing with Mom and Hera on either side of me. Hera is no longer holding my hand. Now, she is at a giant loom. But the loom doesn't hold fabric. Instead, its strands appear to be stars. She has a basket filled with twinkling light.

As the shuttle slides through the loom, she reaches her hand slowly into the basket and pulls out one of the balls of light.

She works it in her hand, like silly putty rolling it into a ball, then slowly rolling it out into a thin cord that she stretches. She attaches one end of the light to the shuttle, then winds it up.

The spun thread resembles fiber-optics and yet it's infused with a blue light. She slides the shuttle through and then works the pedals of the loom, locking the threaded light in place. She's creating the fabric of the universe.

She's no longer weaving for a person but the cosmos. The fabric has stars, gaseous giants, planets and comets, others are dead rocks. Moons and various livable worlds dot the woven universe. Every few moments she adds a new thread. It is fascinating.

To my right, my mother smiles and says, "Don't worry! We will mend it all."

*****

Suddenly, I was awake.

CHAPTER 38

ISOLDE

"Wake up, Isolde! Everyone is here and it's time to go,"

"What time is it?" I kept opening and closing my eyes to blink back the dream.

A warm hand cupped my cheek and I turned into it. It was strong and rough like a sailor's hand. Daddy's hands felt that way from all those years working the ropes on the boat. A light musky scent filled in the air. I turned onto my side. I didn't want to get up. If this was a dream and my dad was sitting there petting my face, then I wanted it to last.

The deep voice came again, "It's time to get up. We have things to do."

I grunted and wiggled a little bit too, "I don't want to get up, dad. I'll just lay here and listen to your voice for a while. I love the sound of your voice."

A chuckle followed my comment and my eyes shot open. That was not my father's laugh.

"How did you get my room? I locked the door!" I shouted, quickly taking in the blanket coverage and gripping the seam edge while pulling.

"Sorry, I don't mean to invade your privacy. You have to get up. They're going to shift the ships in 15 minutes and I know you don't want to miss it. You've been asleep for 34 hours," Hercules replied. His permanent smirk was gone.

"And the answer of how you got in my room sitting on my bed, watching me?" I asked, clutching the covers to my chin.

"As acting Captain, I can have any door unlocked for any reason. I'm not touching you. I'm trying to wake you up. Don't make it sound nefarious when it's not," he returned.

I gripped the covers at my chin tighter. I'd taken all my clothes off before I got into bed. Everything I'd worn was nothing more than filthy rags. I cleared my throat.

"Can you please leave? I will join you on the bridge presently"

"Certainly, but your mother will send me back if you don't move quickly," he said and took to his feet.

"My mother sent you??"

My mother would never send him to my room.

"Yes, she told me to open the door," with that he strode to the door as it whooshed open at a touch and he was gone.

Now I feel like a jerk. Why does this keep happening?

<Because you're constantly jumping to conclusions without getting all of the information.>

<Shut up, Tristan! And stop eavesdropping! It's obnoxious.>

He just laughed at me.

I shot out of bed.

Who wants a strange man in their bedroom while they're naked? My mother sent him. Ugh!

The only clothes I had was my toga from Delphi which was filthy and smelled less than fresh.

<Tristan, if I let you eavesdrop for the next 24 hours, will you please ship me over a new outfit? I don't want to wear the dirty toga again.>

<Certainly. I could shift you over a new outfit. That is of course, if I hadn't already done that. Look on the counter in the bathroom. > his smile bled through our connection.

<I love you, but forget that I said you could eavesdrop for the next 24 hours. > I blew him a mental kiss on the cheek.

<Thank you, but you can't renege on an agreement! It just so happens that me being thoughtful paid off. This being said, eavesdropping shall commence in five minutes. >

< Fucker!>

At least Tristan was sensible. He sent over a pair of jeans, a T-shirt and a nice pair of tennis shoes. I wasn't going on another adventure dressed like Helen of Troy.

I marched down the hall towards the shifting room only no one was there except Hercules.

"I thought everyone would be here. I needed to get up because I didn't want to miss what?" I quirked an eyebrow at him.

"I wasn't lying. They will be here in a couple of minutes. Your brother is moving Odyssey."

"When you came into my room, were you snooping around?" I asked and stared down at the floor to hide the stain crawling over my skin.

"What you really want to know is if you were drooling in your sleep. No! Were you exposed? No! You weren't snoring either. Does that answer all your questions? What kind of a man do you think I am, Isolde?"

I glanced up at him and he ran his hand over the scruff on his chin. "Yes, I may have a pretty high opinion of myself and my abilities, but I'm not a letch or a libertine. I would never take advantage of a woman who is sleeping and defenseless. Nor would I use it as an excuse to lear at her or feel her... " he broke off at a loss for words, then turned away from me.

Now, I feel like crap. Why do I keep putting my foot in my mouth?

Tristan laughed in the back of my mind. I said he could listen in the next 24 hours and I fucked that up too.

<The five minutes aren't up, Tristan.>

<Sorry I started early, couldn't wait >

I pushed Tristan's mental hooting to the back of my mind.

"I'm sorry. I wasn't trying to imply that you were a letch. I just didn't want to be embarrassed if you saw something or I was doing something awful," I mumbled while twisting my fingers together.

"Isolde, even if I did see something or if you were doing something awful, do you really think I would tell you or anyone else?" He whipped around to stare me down with his hard-sapphire blue eyes which were so like my mom's.

My heart rate picked up under his intense stare, "I don't know. I was scared. And no. I guess...I didn't really think that."

"Excellent! So now I have permission to tell somebody that you are laying there completely exposed when I walked in?" His serious face curved into a wicked smile.

"What?" I demanded, then I punched him in the chest and he howled with laughter.

"I'm just joking. You looked like an angel sleeping, covered up with all your sheets. It was the first time you were ever nice to me." The naughty gleam in his eyes melted away to a shy smile.

"I was?" I asked, pulling my head back a bit, raising my eyebrows in shock.

"Yes, you said you liked the sound of my voice. That's the nicest thing you've ever said to me," he was serious.

I wasn't talking about him, but I couldn't tell him the truth.

It would be mean.

"Your voice was soothing. It was a nice way to be awakened," I mumbled as a small smile tickled the corners of my lips.

"That is the second nice thing you've said about me. Thank you, Calla," he whispered and the low sound sent shivers over my skin.

"My name isn't Calla. It's Isolde," I replied to cover the feelings he was churning up in me.

"Not to me. To me you are Calla."

He moved closer and reached out to cup my cheek. The shy smile on Herc's face had disappeared only to be replaced by a hot intense one.

Part of me was being pulled toward this man and the emotions, but I stepped back. "Okay, Herc. You can't run around renaming people."

"You renamed me. My name isn't Herc. It's Hercules. I'm going with my new name, can't you go with yours?" He asked and stepped forward.

He's right. I gave him a nickname and he returned the favor.

"Alright. I guess you can call me Calla. I don't have to like it."

He looked down at the floor, then back up at me. He gave me a one-sided smile with both of his hands on the top of the pilot's chair and leaned forward. "Oh, but I think you'll like it," he whispered.

My mother and Adrian chose that moment to shift everyone in and thank God for that. I didn't know where this conversation was going and I was afraid to find out.

CHAPTER 39

Hera

The bright shifting room on Odyssey was a relief from the slate blue of Prometheus and the glowing veins flowing all over the walls.

Sydney was already deep in conversation with Emmaline and Ixis. I hated to be the bearer of bad news but it couldn't wait one moment longer.

"Sydney, I need to speak to you," I stated loud enough for the entire room to hear.

Every voice died as the room came to a standstill.

"O-kay," she stared back at me with wide expectant eyes.

"Alone!"

A second later we were both in my chambers.

"We are all tired. Can't this wait?" She asked, rubbing her hand across her forehead.

"When we crossed Lethe, I dreamwalked my brother," I started then faltered.

Where to start and how to explain?

"Yeah, you told us. So what?" She scoffed then plopped down on the recliner with a huff.

I started telling her everything from the beginning and didn't stop until the moment when Hyperion ended the dreamwalk.

"Fuck!" she mumbled and tilted her head back to rest it against the back of the recliner.

"Getting off Delphi is good, but we left Vika there. And every failed Acolyte from Pythos knows the Fates have arrived. The High Council will have a fleet here within days. We need to leave. Now!" I said then took a seat myself.

"I guess we owe your brother big time," she remarked.

She began unwrapping the fabric she'd used to bind her breast and dropped it on the seat next to her.

"Ixis stole this ship," she mused, shaking her head in disbelief.

"I can't blame him. We would have done the same thing, if we were in his position," I replied.

Sydney tilted her head forward to take me in. I stared back at her as if the act alone would provide us with the answers we need.

"They knew who you were all along and they were going to keep you on Earth until you died," she remarked. "It's diabolical. What are they so afraid of? We both read the Prophecies of Pythia. They didn't sound too *'end of the world'* to me. What are we missing?" She asked with a yawn, as her eyes grew heavier every moment.

"Gaea was there. She didn't seem as frightened as the rest. But she knew Pythia. I do know someone who would be able to answer our questions," I stopped to take a breath.

What to do about Poseidon had eaten at me from the moment we left Earth.

"We could go to Tartarus and free Poseidon," I offered.

Sydney began violently shaking her head. "No fucking way. I read what he really did. Not the human bullshit. That man is a tyrant. I will not pick him up and give him parole for information. No way!" She got to her feet. "They don't know where we are going or how to get there. Nothing Vika says can hurt us. So, what if they get a bunch of ships to Delphi in a few days? We aren't there," she smiled and ran her hands over her hair.

"We aren't? But..."

"Emmaline moved the ship after we were gone for more than a day. Adrian shifted us right here. We didn't tell anyone for security reasons. They can't find us for now," she finished, came over and planted a kiss on my cheek. "Now, get some sleep."

A second later she was gone, leaving only the scent of ozone.

CHAPTER 40

SYDNEY

It's amazing how efficient the brain works after a good night's sleep. Over the almost two days we'd been back, I'd only managed to steal 18 hours of sleep, but it was enough to recharge.

All the neurons in my brain fired at full capacity and you notice things you might have overlooked before. My arrival on the deck in the shifting room of Prometheus was apparently not too late.

I think Adrian's timing is improving for everything.

I smiled to myself.

Hercules was leaning towards my daughter in a rather provocative fashion. He had a smile on his face as if he was ready to pounce and devour her.

If Gabe was here, I'm sure he would have commented on the situation with a bat or some other weapon.

Adrian just smiled and shook his head. He knew something although why he didn't tell me I could not understand. Adrian had always been able to keep secrets from me. I could pry, but part of the fun was figuring out what he was holding back.

Isolde lunged at me, forcing a giant hug on me as if we hadn't seen each other in weeks.

"Oh, mom, I'm so glad you're here. Although I did sleep pretty good, I could still sleep another solar week," she remarked with a smile.

She seemed refreshed. Her hair was damp from a shower and she'd managed to change into her old jeans and a T-shirt. I held her for the brief moment. She gripped me and I breathed in the clean scent of her half dry hair. I could live a lifetime in that scent. She released me and the reality of our situation returned with a vengeance.

"We agreed to start scanning the databases of Prometheus. We need to find Styx. We're not done yet," I stated since she should know this.

That wasn't the only reason I was here. Hera's revelation brought on a new sense of urgency. If she could reach Hyperion, he could reach her. He could find us.

What if they dominate him and he betrays his sister and us?

I didn't know anything about Hyperion other than the fact that he had children.

If he's anything like his sister, he will turn the universe inside out to save them.

I couldn't allow that. The only thing keeping us safe at this point was being two steps ahead of everyone else.

Adrian took his seat in the pilot chair and tilted his head back to gaze at me, "Commander, you're in charge. What do you want to do?"

The double meaning wasn't lost on me, yet I ignored his playful teasing.

"Prometheus, do you have any visuals of the actual trip to Delphi?"

"Yes, commander. Would you prefer a video or stills?"

I glanced down at Adrian. He still wore the Themian style tunic. I guessed that after all the years he'd spent on Alethea, he'd grow accustomed to the style.

"Still shots, please," he replied.

The holo-displays were peppered with thousands of pictures from everywhere. Some were filled with stars of varying colors, while others were nothing but blinding light. One was a void with a glowing ribbon in the distance.

"Prometheus, can you give us the exact coordinates for the beginning of Styx?"

All the screens went blank and a seven-digit number of some kind appeared. It was a numbering system I didn't recognize.

Adrian boomed out laughing, his shoulders raising and lowering with each and every burst.

"What are you laughing about?" I demanded.

"The computer's just as literal as you are, only to the extreme. You asked where the river Styx began, and he gave you the coordinates — a seven-digit number." Tears leaked from the corners of Adrian's eyes as he tried to breath around each word.

"It's not very funny. Actually, it's kind of irritating. That is when it comes to a computer," I huffed.

Adrian's laughter was infectious and snickering carried around the room until we were all laughing.

When Adrian finally caught his breath, he shook his head, "Why don't you let me ask the questions, beautiful girl and you can tell me what to do," he winked and I rolled my eyes.

"Fine!" I snarled to hold back the laugh lodged in the back of my throat.

With amusement still coloring his speech Adrian started, "Prometheus, please display a holographic image of our position in space versus Styx and the closest point to the ship's last known contact with Styx, along with the entire journey taken by Prometheus."

That's what I said. Why couldn't the computer figure that out?

Holographic images appeared in front of us. The dots of light were so small it removed any concept of how many light-years across the actual image was. I couldn't wrap my mind around where Delphi was and where the stars began.

All I could grasp was a giant white strip of light against the black velvet background of the cosmos and a green line marking the spaceship's journey.

"Prometheus, what is that?" I asked and pointed to the twisted thread of light on the star chart?

"That, Commander, is Styx, the ribbon of hate, also known as the Oath keeper."

A sharp intake of breath came from behind me. Hera eyes were the size of saucers. "You've heard me swear on Styx, have you not?" She asked, her attention remaining locked on the holo-display.

"Yeah, sure. All the Themians do it. The Greeks and Romans did also," I remarked.

"Yes, but the humans swear on the river. Themians swear by its light," she replied, as her hands worked over the fabric of her dress, smoothing the cloth.

I tilted my head to the side. "Really?" I didn't see the difference. "So, what's the big deal?" I asked with my brow pulled down.

"I never thought that by swearing by the light of Styx, we were swearing on a ribbon of stars," she replied.

Her eyes met mine briefly then returned to the holo-display.

"River... a river of stars," I remarked.

It fits!

I liked the term.

"They thought it was a ribbon of stars on the first shift?"

"I don't know," she replied absently, "maybe they just called it a ribbon and somebody thought it sounded similar to river. Time and language can change many things."

"Yeah, but why would they name it the ribbon of hate? I mean, it doesn't look hateful to me. It's beautiful, almost magical and it spans the cosmos, creating a strand of light. It's amazing. A brighter milky way."

"I don't know why they call it the ribbon of hate," Hera muttered

"We have to follow it to reach Elysium," I replied.

Everyone faced the holo-display with an intoxicating aura of excitement. The only thing that kept running through my mind was the fact that stars create gravity.

So, what's a river worth creating?

"Prometheus, can you display the visuals in chronological reverse order?" Adrian asked.

"Working."

1000's of different images, one overlaying another, crowded the view ports. I'd never seen technology like this before. It was nothing like Odyssey.

A lot of the computer usage had been dispensed with over the centuries. But when this ship was built the Elysium didn't have mental powers. It was easier to send a picture from one mind to another versus pulling it up on the computer.

This is what going back in time millions of years gets you.

Go back several million years for humanity and you get a whole lot of nothing. Maybe, some cave drawings or a fish crawling out of the primordial soup.

"Please bring the closest picture of Styx to the forefront," I ordered and found I was gripping the headrest of Adrian's chair with white knuckles again.

Working in reverse was going to be a little mind wrapping.

"This is the most recent and last picture taken of Styx's closest position to us," the computer's hollow voice informed us.

"How far away is that?" Adrian inquired while placing his hand on the orb.

"At our current speed and course, we can be at this location in 9.12 pritos. It is approximately 7 star years away," the computer's answer rolled around in my head as I converted the number to English.

I closed my eyes to compute.

That means *19.12 years.*

"Are you kidding me? Of course, we are not going to use this speed to get there. Adrian can you send this picture to Tristan and Ixis?"

"You know I can, beautiful girl. Synchronizing now." Adrian's eyes took on a faraway gaze.

It must be what he looks like when he's talking to me.

I could hear the background buzzing between him and Tristan. It was just something I kind of pushed out of the way. As much as I loved the two of them, listening to mathematical computations or discussions of what exact position in the picture we should be focusing on, didn't light my fire.

I was aware that I could be really impatient. It was a very human failing, yet I saw it mostly as part of our charm.

"We are ready, *beautiful girl.*"

I opened my mind. It was time to tell everyone what we were up to. This wasn't the last shift we were ever to make, but the first shift into the unknown part of this journey. This shift was different. After traveling the other rivers, I understood how little we knew about what we'd gotten ourselves into. We have no idea what to expect.

<As most of you are well aware, myself and the rest of the command crew have been desperately searching through databases and libraries, looking for a Homeworld. So far, we haven't found anything that we felt would be adequate for us. More so, we've also been looking for something else — allies. Space is a very large place and at this moment in time we are alone in it. Humanity is not ready for us and the Themians have made it more than clear that they have no desire to be our friends.>

I kept the part about them hunting us between Hera and I. There was no need to scare the crap out of everyone just because the High Council wanted us all dead.

<If we want to survive in space, we need to create alliances. As I've said, we haven't yet found the Homeworld we are looking for. This shift will put us on our way. I don't know what we will find at the end of this shift because there may be another 50 after it. But I do know that this is the first step on that journey. The place we're going is Elysium. It's the original Themian Homeworld. I know you're all probably laughing and saying that's Greek mythology. You've already discovered the Greek Gods are real and so are the Demigods. So, why wouldn't Elysium be real? The impossible has

become possible. We will be the first hybrids to ever see Elysium.> I took a breath.

I'm doing the right thing. I know it.

<I don't know about you, but I have the explorer spirit. It's in my heart. It's part of my life and it's not something I can control or stop. This being said, we're jumping to the river Styx. It's not a traditional river. It's a river of stars, also called the 'oath keeper'. I swear now that no matter what happens, I will keep you safe and I will find us all a home, even if it costs me my last dying breath.> I stopped for a moment to allow people to take it all in. <We're going to be doing several shifts in a row. If something about the shifts is too much for you go to the laboratories and see Melinda. She'll do everything she can to make you more comfortable.>

Even if it means putting you to sleep.

I couldn't think only about my kids. This was for the kids. For all of them.

<As many of you know, Odyssey now has a sister ship, Prometheus. I don't know what shape she's in. That's why I haven't moved anyone to Prometheus yet. We discovered her while looking for Elysium. She's fully functional but she's pretty old so for now we're keeping everyone on Odyssey. The

new captain of Odyssey in my stead is Emmaline and first mate is Ixis, your pilot. I will be in constant contact with Emmaline and Tristan at all times. If there's any doubt or any worries whatsoever about your safety, Odyssey will shift away and Prometheus will continue on. We feel that finding Elysium will bring us not only allies but perhaps a Homeworld or place we can call home until we find one. Now, prepare yourselves for the shift. You have 10 minutes.>

"Was that any good?" I asked, biting my lip.

"Yeah, mom. I thought it was great," Issy replied.

"Perhaps we can have Emmaline explain in depth exactly what we've been up to," Adrian remarked.

"I believe your explanation was good but it will churn up a lot of questions. Emmaline should meet with the council members. We don't want them all assuming something strange or different. Once they understand we're going to Elysium, they'll realize we're going to the underworld. Not everyone is going to be comfortable with that," Hera said and took the empty seat normally occupied by Tristan.

"I know not everyone is going to be comfortable with this choice. Once we reach the entrance of the underworld, we leave Odyssey behind," I stated without taking my eyes from the cosmos beyond the holo-display.

Tristan would stay behind with Odyssey and Isolde would come with me. I blinked back the tears that threatened. It was the right choice to split them up. I shouldn't risk both my children and everyone else.

"I think it's a good idea, beautiful girl. There is no reason to risk our entire population," Adrian added, even though. his jaw snapped shut on his own words.

He didn't want to leave our son behind, but he would never disagree with me in front of anyone else.

"So, we just leave Tristan?" Issy demanded, "...and the rest behind? What if we die?" She grabbed my arm to turn me around, but I held firm.

"This was meant to be," I replied and pressed my lips flat.

"You hate this shit, mom! You despise the idea that our lives are predetermined and there's nothing we can do about it or that somebody else is making our choices for us somehow," she was beginning to shout.

Hercules reached to pull her back, but she shrugged him off.

"Yeah, truthfully whether I like it or not, something tells me that what we're doing now *is* predetermined. That we're meant to do it." I turned with a cold stare, "It's just like one of those little brain teasers that I always dumped on you and your brother. There is only one right answer."

"This isn't a Rubik's cube," she yelled.

I laughed at her. "I know that better than you."

"You don't just get to move the pieces around until you finally solve the puzzle," Issy continued screaming at me.

"And there are no redos," Adrian interjected, trying to be helpful.

"I know, Adrian. That's why I'm saying leave Odyssey behind. They can jump with us to the end but once we reach the entrance to the underworld, they can't go with us. They need to stay." I pushed the sleeves of my shirt up to my elbow.

It was getting hot in here and I didn't think it had anything to do with the temperature.

"I agree with Sydney. Leaving Odyssey behind is the best choice," Hera said, then moved her focus to her son, "Hercules, you should transfer back to Odyssey. We only need a shifter. There is no reason to endanger you."

"No!" Adrian cut in, "Hercules stays here by my side. What if there's another creature to fight?"

I was surprised. I didn't think he was worried about running into another dark creature.

"Thank you, nephew! I'd be proud to stand by your side in battle. How am I supposed to be a hero if I don't continue on the quest?" he shrugged and winked at Issy.

Issy rolled her eyes. I actually thought he was just a clown. A very old, very good-looking one, but a clown nevertheless. All he needed was a red rubber nose, some big floppy's shoes and a few bean bags to start juggling.

A smile burst across Adrian's face as he tried to stifle a laugh.

<Stop laughing! You weren't supposed to see that. >

<Sorry, but you sent a very vivid picture and the idea of Hercules, dancing a jig and dressed up as a clown, juggling bean bags is hysterical. >

<At least I only made him a clown.>

<Yeah, he looked really happy. However, I'm not sure he'd be as amused by your vision if he saw it. > Adrian mentally chuckled.

I double checked all my mental walls to make sure I hadn't been broadcasting anything, although Hera did quirk an eyebrow at me.

She has very long ears.

"Adrian, one thing before we go and I'll leave you to concentrate. Can we have a couple more chairs installed in this cockpit?" I asked angry with myself for not thinking of it hours ago.

"Not without proper supplies," he returned, then glanced around the space, turning back to his console.

"Don't worry. I'll make sure they're properly attached to the deck," Hercules offered.

He seemed quite in earnest of his comments. Issy issued a general air of annoyance at anything he said. Part of me felt bad for the guy.

Adrian focused his eyes into the distance at the one image Prometheus displayed. He was in conversation with Tristan and Ixis. Suddenly the mental chatter ceased.

"Shifting now!" he announced mentally and out loud for our entire population.

The pressure changed all around and that cold feeling of non-space enveloped me and the ship. Every time Prometheus shifted, she gave off a glow, as if the ship itself felt the energy change. Its pressure and mass adjusted. For a moment, it was a cold terror which was followed by a pop. We were so close to the river, all you could see were the stars.

The hull creaked and my eyes darted around the room.

"What is going on?" my insides quivered with my uncertainty.

"You're right about the gravity. There are so many stars here, it's pulling us in a million different directions all at once," Adrian confirmed.

<Mom, I'm having problems maintaining our location. > Tristan said.

"Prometheus, display the next picture in line!"

How in the hell did they make it down this river using just the sub light engines?

"Displaying image."

<Brace yourselves! This is gonna be rough.> I shouted at our population.

My eyes darted over to Adrian but he was entirely consumed with focusing on the image before him. Our location on the main star chart turned from green to red.

"Shifting now!"

This time the view port was almost completely filled with the stars and the creaking of the hull grew more intense. The ship swayed under my feet. It was as if the ship was a wash cloth wiping the kitchen counter.

My grip on Adrian's chair increased. Hera belted into the secondary pilot chair, while Hercules had already braced himself back in the door frame. His one free arm was locked around Isolde's waist.

<Ixis, send over three chairs!> I ordered.

Three chairs appeared in the cockpit, taking up space on either side of the door. Issy immediately sat down as the ship was rattling and jerking. Various bulkheads groaned and popped.

I took the nearest seat and stared Hercules down, "You said you could attach them to the deck. I think you need to do it now! I'll help you find a way."

Hercules darted out of the room without a word.

"Prometheus, give us the next image with every shift. We need a new image immediately with no delays," I stated.

I smoothed the shorts I'd tossed on and gripped the armrests.

"Understood," the ship's voice replied.

Immediately a new image appeared, "Adrian, take us to the new way point. God damn it!" I shouted.

He nodded his head, "Shifting now!"

The pressure changed around us again, building up in my ears. My head was pounding, from the added pressure I couldn't release.

<Melinda, I think you're going to need to start passing out, drugs or something>

< I'm already on it > she snapped.

<Emmaline, have everybody strap themselves down as much as possible. It's going to get really rough and I don't know how long it's going to take.>

< I gotcha. We're takin' care of it. You take care of your ship. I'll take care mine.>

Just like Emmaline to find a way to be snotty.

"Shifting now!" Adrian announced.

I braced myself for the next shift, holding my breath for the pressure change. The splitting inside my head became more of a vice pressing all around my cranium. I looked at the holographic map. The green line was long and only a small fraction of it was now red.

I can understand now why they called it the ribbon of hate.

They must have hated every moment they were here.

Can you imagine being on this river for years?

I placed my fingers over my nose, squeezing it tight as I blew air out through my ears in an effort to displace the built-up air and break the pressure seal inside my head. The relief was short lived. The lost pressure was replaced with a wave of nausea.

"Is there any way we can make this easier?" I asked as I panted through my next breath.

"Sorry, beautiful girl, there is nothing I can do about the gravity or how it affects a shift."

I glanced over as Issy jumped up and down in her seat and pointed her toes while pushing her hands out before her.

"Tristan did something when we were in the caves. I asked if there was a way he could cut down on the pressure of the shifts. We were hopscotching through the caves, and he said that there was. He created a bubble around us so the pressure wouldn't affect us. I don't know how he did it, but whatever he did it worked," she smiled then blew her ears out.

<I'm on it, beautiful girl!>

The computer displayed the newest image, but we hadn't jumped. Tristan was trying to explain something to Adrian.

All I could think was *please don't let my head explode*. I couldn't imagine what everybody else's head was feeling like, but their cries of anguish found a way through my mental walls and ate at me.

"We are going to give this a try," Adrian announced and the pressure change of the shift came.

It was more like your first dunk underwater, slightly uncomfortable but as the liquid fills your ears you get acclimated and it's over.

<How was that?> Tristan inquired.

"A lot better," I said, "Tristan, you're brilliant. I'm so thankful I didn't drown you the day you broke the spinnaker and pissed me off so bad," I finished and smiled over at Issy.

"I'll remind him," Issy giggled.

"Shifting now!"

The pressure on my mind sank into the background. However, the gravitational pull in the groaning of the ship's bulkheads rushed to the forefront.

There has to be some way to create some kind of field to displace the gravity.

The physics of our situation left my mouth dry. I was not a scientist.

Five jumps later, the groaning in the bulkheads had changed to whining. At times, a keening sound echoed from deep inside the structure of the ship, depending upon how close we were to the various stars and how strong the gravitational pulls were.

I know gravity depends upon size and mass and 1 million other mathematical equations that I just can't wrap my head around.

Talk about trading stocks and how many points you gained, your yearly dividend payment, what looks ripe for a short, was one thing. But talking about calculus, trigonometry and figuring out the gravitational pull of a planet, that was way out of my league.

Not my fucking bag.

<Is anyone an astrophysicist or mathematician, astronomer? Hell, I'll take a palm reader with tarot cards at this point. I think we need one.>

I stared at the holo-display and the length of the green line versus the red. I closed my eyes for a moment and pushed the deep weariness away.

<There's some guy who's been pounding at the door to the shifting room for the last 20 minutes telling me I need to let him in. > Tristan offered.

<Find out what he wants. >

<He says his name is Dr. Michelson and that he is a mathematician and has a degree in physics and astrophysics. He also says gravity might actually pull our ships apart.>

CHAPTER 41

SYDNEY

<He's a professor of astrophysics?> I asked.

<That's what he claims.> Tristan replied.

<Have Ixis send him over after the next jump.>

<Well, this guy apparently has already had some Primordium. That's a good sign. Right?>

"Shifting now!"

A man appeared and if I didn't know any better, I would have thought it was Val Kilmer. He was tall with whitish blond hair, piercing icy blue eyes and an arrogant smile, all wrapped up in a tweed jacket while gripping a pipe.

His eyes grew wide as he looked around the room, "I'm Professor Michelson," he mumbled, "I've been trying to get into the shifting room on Odyssey for the last 20 minutes. We need to stop shifting. Please, let me re-examine your course projections. With the type of gravity running through this star field, these ships are water balloons in space just waiting to pop," he cringed at a keening sound that burped up from the lower decks.

"Designation please!"

"Not now, Prometheus! Designate him as Professor Michelson - Navigator."

"Designation recognized. Welcome, Professor Michelson."

I rolled my eyes and pointed to the holo-display.

"Ignore her! Check out the holo map over there," I instructed.

He moved closer to the console and Hera left her seat to give him better access.

"That's our course projection. If you can pick a better one, go for it."

"I'll do my best. I have no desire to become stardust" he laughed at his own joke, yet I didn't find it funny.

The professor glanced up at the bulkhead as a new groan joined the chorus of others, then snapped back to the map. He started manipulating something on the main console. The entire holo-map rotated. I couldn't figure out how to turn the damn thing around.

Mr. Astrophysicist came and hello!

Suddenly, he was able to manipulate a three-dimensional map that I couldn't figure out.

Note to self: Sydney, you should have looked for better help before you started jumping through space and time.

<Your internal monologue is distracting me, beautiful girl.>

I bit my lip. <Oh! Sorry. >

"As I understand it from the other hybrids that I've spoken to, all you need is an image in your mind to go anywhere. You don't even necessarily have to have been there before. Correct?"

He ran his hand over his head, then stopped to stare at it in surprise as if he hadn't expected hair to be there. After that, he returned to the holo, enlarging and shrinking the display all along the green line.

"Thank you! We already know that. Can you give us something useful?" I demanded.

This guy was nothing like Professor Glover. This guy was an egghead. It was as if it was all still a simulation to him.

He exhibited a sheepish look and raised his shoulders, "Sorry! I'm used to teaching. Up until we left Earth, it was all relative." His smile was on the edge of awkward.

"Okay, we don't need any more teaching. What I do need is a hell of a lot of doing. Can you do?" I asked desperate to keep my voice down and keep my cool.

"You're not skipping far enough along and there are some places that clearly have a lower gravitational pull than others, places where the stars are smaller and not as close together."

"Prometheus, redirect our shifting points to wherever Michelson indicates," I ordered.

"Acknowledged."

<Do you know how to send, professor? > I mentally asked with no comeback.

"Michelson, are you able to send telepathically?" I repeated.

"No. I've only had a few drops of primordium. Melinda told me on my last visit with her that it might take a bit more considering my age."

Hera stifled a snicker.

"Considering your age? How old are you?" Issy breathed.

She leaned forward in her chair.

"On my last annual, I was 93," he said and a bright smile ran across his face.

"When was the last time you actually taught astrophysics?" my eyebrows rose to the ceiling in disbelief.

"Oh well, I haven't actually given any lectures in about eight years. However, I have been avidly working on some of my own formulas in my spare time of retirement. The enforced boredom of space travel and, of course, talking to Ixis has been most enlightening. I was actually going to request a laboratory of my own that I might continue on with my work. After all, I have several million years to catch up on," he remarked.

The holo map continued its ever-changing size and shape as he chose which point to skip.

"I need a point," I glanced over at Michelson and he pointed to a spot on the map.

"Prometheus, pull the picture of that location," Adrian instructed the ship.

"Affirmative!"

The newest visual appeared a moment later, "Shifting now!"

The groaning and moaning of the ship's hull decrease instantly. Michelson immediately pointed to a new location. "Might I have some paper and pencil?" he asked and glanced around the room.

<Ixis, paper pencil? Please! >

Paper and pencil appeared in front of Michelson, "Excellent, I will say! We hybrids are most helpful with these abilities."

He rubbed his hands together and immediately began to scribble on the paper,

"Shifting now!"

The pressure changed and that feeling of being underwater presented itself, followed by a pop. The next thing I knew, we were at the new location.

Michelson looked up from his writing, "Oh yes. On to the next way point."

"Affirmative!"

"Now, I don't know if any of you have been paying attention but the holographic image in front of me seems to be in the shape of a spiral and –"

"Can you get to the point," I cut him off, "before we shift again?"

"Yes, yes. Of course. Right now it seems we're circling. If you zoom this three-dimensional map out, we're spiraling or circling around a specific point." He continued to shrink the image down smaller and smaller.

It began to look exactly like a corkscrew. We were spiraling around a specific point in space. It only looked like a river from the right point of view.

Everything's about point of view, isn't it?

"Okay, is there any way to jump across the spiral?" I asked.

A straight line is faster than a curve.

"Well, that's what I wanted to say. Yes, we can jump further along. A lot further along and it would cut down on a lot of the forces. Also, we're on the inside of the turns and not the outside, therefore the pressure is much stronger than the outer sections. But seeing as we have no way of knowing what the outer sections look like, we can't alter to that course."

He scratched his head again, pulling his hand away in surprise then quirking a little smile and putting his hand back.

"Can you just pick a spot now? We need to get out of here. Tristan just told me they're having serious problems in the outer rings on Odyssey," Adrian informed us.

I left my seat and indicated to Hera to take it. She immediately buckled in and leaned her head back.

He pointed to the next location, "Here."

I looked at the curve of the river.

Rivers naturally don't run in a straight line. Nothing does.

"And it circles on this point how many times?" I glanced at Issy, whose eyes grew.

Hera grabbed my hand.

"Well, that is kind of where I was going. I didn't want you to think that I was pulling your leg given where we are headed. But there is only one place Styx leads and it circles that place seven times. That's the Underworld. Sound familiar?" Michelson asked.

I shot a look at Hera. Her eyebrows were raised and she gave her head a slight nod, "That is how the story goes. The river Styx circles the underworld seven times," she confirmed.

"All the great mythologies agree on that. However, most failed to mention Oceana," he replied and gazed at me for a split second, then looked to Adrian.

A moment later, the professor ducked his head and went back to writing down numbers and calculations on his paper.

"Oceana? The river that circles the entire known universe, the underworld and living world?" Issy asked.

She'd spent more time in the library and she never mentioned Oceana.

"The library said there were only five rivers," Hera pressed her lips flat with her objection.

"Did you see the other rivers?" He asked and turned to face us as the next shift took over.

As soon as I shook off the underwater feeling, I moved my jaw around a few times to see if I could pop my ears. One gave but the other didn't.

"Yes, we saw them. We can talk about them later. Now get to the point," I barked as the ship whined and jolted.

I steadied myself by gripping Adrian's headrest again. However uncomfortable standing was, the movement of the ship reminded me of the ocean. All those years standing at the wheel steering the boat had prepared me for this.

"Well, yes, Oceana is a swift moving river that encompasses the entire known universe, underworld. Everything. And I do believe that you must traverse it in order to reach hell," he pointed to a few more places on the holo-map, then waited for me to reply.

"Did you say hell? Really?" Issy scoffed at the man.

I mentally nudged her to stop.

"Yes, hell. The underworld. They are both the same. You know, the place where souls are tortured for eternity. You have to pass it and also Cerberus in order to reach our destination," he leaned forward, placing both elbows on his knees and clasped his hands.

I pursed my lips and nodded. He returned my hard gaze with a wan smile.

"You got the destination right. Anything else you might want to share? If so, you better do it now," I replied.

I mentally held my breath hoping there wasn't another shoe to drop. We hadn't lost anyone yet—.

He pointed to four spots on the chart in order. The four images popped up on the display panel in front of Adrian.

"Shifting now!" Adrian's voice was tight.

Everyone was getting tired of this. The time on my watch had barely changed. It read two hours. That was until I read the date. It was a new day.

Adrian and Tristan have been at this for 27 hours.

Isolde sagged in her chair.

"Why don't you go rest, sweetheart? There's nothing for you to do."

"Yes, Isolde you should rest. You look exhausted," Herc agreed with me.

"Thanks, Herc, but I don't need to take a little nappy-poo. I'm not a child," she retorted.

I cocked an eyebrow at Issy. She was so tichy towards Hercules. I thought he was just being sweet. I mean, an arrogant clown but sweet.

"Would you like me to come in and tuck you into bed? You could listen to the sound of my voice. You said you liked it so much," he gave her a toothy grin.

"You're funny! Ha, ha! Mom, next time send anybody but him," she barked.

The pressure changed from a new shift. It hardly bothered me and Adrian hadn't announced this one.

The population of Odyssey has to be exhausted.

I wondered how many people Melinda had to drug.

The professor wrote down a bunch more numbers and proceeded to do some calculations. He pointed at 12 more spots on the chart and 12 more visuals popped up.

"Why don't we just skip all 12 of those and go to the very last one?" I asked.

Adrian's mental connection was pulling energy from me and I was wilting fast.

"I can't jump that far. Sorry."

"Why don't we have Ixis do the jump? I mean, after all, if he can move an entire planet, why can't he move two spaceships all at once?" I didn't know if my logic was flawed or not.

The bone deep exhaustion ate at me. Adding in Adrian's and I was a walking space zombie.

<I would not risk every life on every ship just to get there faster. > Ixis informed me.

It was more of a mental slap. I took it. Ixis knew his shit.

A kraft of hot coffee appeared on the bridge and I placed one cup in Adrian's hand and the next in Michelson's. Hera was out cold in her chair. I settled down in Issy's seat to sip the ambrosia and braced myself for the next shift.

Even weakened Adrian was hyper focused. He said he couldn't break his concentration long enough for anything other than coffee. I kept the study supply topping off his cup every few hours.

Suddenly, alarms went off everywhere. As the cold of subspace pulled back, the blue veins lining the walls pulsed.

"Alert! We've skipped a way point. Commander, your pilot is violating his orders," the ship informed me.

My head jerked up from the light cat nap I'd slipped into. Adrian lifted his shoulders and shot me a quick glance with something of an innocent smile.

"Sorry, beautiful girl! I wanted to tell you what our plan was. We didn't know if it would work. Tristan and I have been shifting simultaneously. We brought Ixis into the shift and were able to skip a jump point. We can cut the shifts in half."

I was wide awake. Prometheus's alarms wailed, pushing all thought of sleep into the background.

"Did you do this for me?" I asked terrified.

The '*what ifs*' of the situation rushed through my mind like the adrenaline did my body.

"For you, beautiful girl, I'd do anything, but risk your life."

I kissed him on his forehead as his eyes glazed over and stared at the next holo image.

Hercules had somehow managed to bolt each one of the chairs to the floor. The sleep my body had been so desperate for a few minutes before was gone. I took to my feet again, riveting myself to the same spot. The images changed and the ship moved in and out of subspace. I offered Michelson and Adrian coffee. I looked at my watch and another day had slipped by. I went and sat in one of the chairs and closed my eyes for a moment.

At least, I thought it was a moment because when I opened them again, the ship faced a distant cluster of stars, all swirling at us.

Styx.

It was a hateful river of gravity and light.

The Oracle must have been out of her mind swearing she would find them a home somehow. Only an unwavering belief in her premonitions would have convinced everyone to follow her.

And yet, I am sitting here after giving the same promise. I must be every bit as stupid as she was.

Rubbing my eyes, I looked around and realized I was alone. There wasn't another soul in the shifting room. Standing up, I recalled Isolde said something about there being quarters further down the hallway. I went in search of a bed.

Wherever we were, obviously no one thought we were in danger or someone would have been on watch. The door slid silently open and I followed the blue veins down the hallway to the first door. It opened and I found Adrian laying on a giant blue bed. He looked peaceful, like he did when he was a little boy. For a moment, I had a flash of the two of us jumping up and down on his bed in his parents' house.

Before all of this was possible.

We were just children and the joy of seeing how high you could jump or break the bed was all that existed.

A lump formed in my throat.

Am I really doing the right thing by taking all these people into the great unknown?

It was just a prophecy that said I was some great fate and I judged people. It should have said that I cut the thread of their life. That I dominate people, then decide who should live and who should die.

They were evil. The ones I killed.

I tried to justify my actions.

When fate takes over, I don't have a choice. I have to judge them. If I don't, I'll be trapped with them for eternity.

*****

The vice like pressure of multiple shifts tightens around my chest. All I can see are the bodies of the judged laying on the stone floor of Pythos. The pools of blood cover the stones filling the cracks and seams. The copper scented liquid leaked from an acolyte and touched my sandals.

The vacant eyes of the acolytes stare into a future they will never have. The scent of dead cooking flesh surrounds me and I gag on the cloying sweet smell. It's the smell of human meat – cooking.

The scene changes. Instead of Pythos, I stand in a great Citadel that once held millions. The benches hold bodies lying everywhere and the stench is here. The unseeing eyes are of Themians.

I tear my wet eyes from the carnage to discover the source of the smell. Smoke rises all around me as do rubble and crystalline stone chunks. My throat thickens with my anguish over the loss of life.

A blond man in the distance calls to me. His arm is extended as he beckons me. His stance is imposing. The set of his shoulders reminds me of the statue in Atlantis.

He shouts, "I am not your true enemy, but he will be here soon!" His lips pull back into a wicked smile.

Poseidon.

*****

I stumbled and right myself against the bulkhead. Blinking back the vision, I gulped to clear my throat of the smokey taste of death.

Shaking it away, I pushed it back.

Whatever that was, I can't deal with it right now.

There was no point. It just weakened you. I needed to stick to my resolve.

I will never see another Themian Homeworld. It wasn't a vision, it was just tired me.

I let the door slide closed and walked to the next room. I silently peeked in to see Hera curled up on a bed. Her honey blonde hair fanned out behind her. She looked like an angel. I backed out of the room and let the door slide closed and move on to the third door.

Isolde slept in her bed and right next to it was a chair with a giant beast of a man. His head leaned back and his hair trailed down his torso. Hercules releases a light snoring sound. His hand was on hers.

Seeing the two of them sleeping, I thought it looked right.

A year ago, if I'd found a man in my daughter's bedroom, I'd freak out on her. Or on both of them.

But Hercules has already proven he is willing to protect her.

What they were doing looked fairly innocent. I backed out into the hallway and returned to Adrian. Crawling into the blue bed, I hurt from sleeping in a chair. I curled up next to him, tucking my legs in behind his. I put one arm around his chest, resting my hand gently on his peck and sleep overwhelmed me.

CHAPTER 42

SYDNEY

Awakening, I found I was alone.

I guess Adrian got up and went to go seek food or a restroom.

I was not even sure where that was on this ship. Of course, there had to be a restroom. Thousands of people on the same space ship had to take a leak somewhere.

My questions about where he'd gone were soon answered as part of the wall slid into a hidden pocket. Adrian was clothed in a towel wrapped around his waist. He carried a second towel rubbing it through his hair.

"You're awake. I missed you. We could have shared a shower."

A naughty glint infected his eyes. Showering was the last thing in the world he had on his mind.

"Sharing shower with you would be the opposite of getting clean," I replied and stretched, "It would just be getting dirtier with water." I popped up, "I'm going to take my clean shower now, thank you very much. I take it you found the washroom?"

"Yeah, it was actually pretty funny. I had to ask Hera where it was. She said to look to my right and all I could see was a wall. Since nothing here is activated by a bracelet, I actually had to figure out which portion of the wall to touch and release the door. I felt like Marcel Marceau, miming my way to the bathroom," he gave me a crooked smile.

I laughed lightly as I jumped off the bed and scampered past him. He reached out to grab anything, but I smacked his hand away.

"I'm sorry, but I haven't showered in days. And whatever it is that you have in mind, is going to have to wait," I ordered with fake dignity.

"Oh yes. I remember. Business first. Always. Don't worry, I can wait until you're tired and can't fight me off anymore," he laughed, then threw me a kiss and dropped his towel.

"Did that work for you recently?" I retorted and averted my eyes.

"No, I was too tired to fight you off," he returned then pulled on his Themian kilt and belted a leather one over the top.

I cocked an eyebrow at him.

"Is there a war on, I should know about?"

"Life is a battle. Be prepared," he replied.

With that, I walked through the door and allowed it to slide shut behind me. Whatever he had in mind, it would have to die on the vine. I had to see where this river of stars had led us.

The warm water from the shower poring over me felt glorious. A shower wasn't about getting the dirt off. It was a luxury. A place I could retreat to and become one with the liquid. I could pull the water from the pipes and bend it to my will. However, allowing the utter chaos of water to engulf me and run amuck, eased my weary soul, pulling tension away and freeing me. A freedom I hadn't felt days.

The shower I'd taken on Odyssey had seemed like a month ago. When I finally opened my eyes and pulled myself back to the real world and all the obstacles in it, I noticed a symbol on the wall. It was strangely Sumerian-ish.

Sumerian always reminded me of a line of pennant flags on a battlefield with the breeze, all pulling them in different directions. They were nothing more than triangles.

I waved my hand over the symbol and a syrupy substance dispensed from the wall. It quickly formed bubbles.

Shampoo, soap or whatever an Elysian calls soap or shampoo?

I didn't really care as long as it created a lather and removed dirt. That was all that was necessary in my world.

I stepped out of the shower with fresh eyes and examined my surroundings.

The bathroom resembled a giant empty metal box with symbols on the wall. All you needed to do was wave your hand in front of the correct collection and the space would alter itself to the configuration. Took me 15 minutes to figure out which one was the shower, counter, toilet, sink, some kind of a hairdryer. A reflective surface appeared and disappeared when you stood in front of the sink.

Cubbyholes projected from the walls, acting like drawers. It was efficient and kept everything tidy. If you wanted to clean the room, all you needed was a hose, if it wasn't already self-cleaning.

Comparing them, Odyssey resembled more of the modern-day earth style bathrooms. Many of the fixtures were stationary. After about 40 minutes in the bathroom, I determined I should probably emerge and face this new world and whatever problems were in it.

A change of my clothes from Odyssey laid on the bed. A smile pulled at my lips.

Adrian is perfect, sometimes.

<Thank you. I'd like to think I'm perfect>

<Eavesdropping is rude > I remarked.

<I know, but when you're talking about me, is it really eavesdropping or is it just joining the conversation? >

<Go back to whatever it is you're doing and if it's food, make sure there's enough for me too, please >

<Of course, beautiful girl. >

I pulled on the jeans he'd left and the tank top, then emerged from the captain's quarters, heading towards the shifting room.

Maybe I should have our resident astrophysicist expert, Professor Michelson, look into finding someone to help Prometheus be more sentient.

If both ships had an innate sense of self-preservation instead of constantly having to have someone babysit them on watch, it could keep us from spreading ourselves too thin.

"Good morning, beautiful girl! I have something here that resembles coffee. Would you like some of it?" Adrian asked and kissed me on the cheek.

"Now that is the silliest question I've ever heard. I'd like a 5 gallon bucket of it," I remarked and several chuckles rolled around the room.

Isolde stood with her arms crossed, staring at Hercules. Her face was as unreadable as her handwriting. On the other hand, Hercules looked unbelievably rested considering he'd slept sitting up.

Hera was perfect. If I didn't know she was an alien, I would've mistaken her for a Goddess myself.

Professor Michelson crouched over the console, examining star charts. A holo-image floated over his head and somehow it was vaguely familiar. I'd seen the corkscrew circles a few days ago, and it reminded me of something I'd seen on earth.

It wasn't a true corkscrew. The spiral grew wider towards the outer edges.

"Do you see what I'm seeing?" Michelson whispered to no one in particular.

"No, but there is something familiar, yet I don't know what it is," I replied and tucked my hands into the back pockets of my jeans.

"Really? Something mom actually doesn't know?" Issy scoffed, "A useless piece of information? You're like a wealth of useless knowledge. I don't know why you didn't go on Jeopardy or one of those television shows and win several million dollars?" She giggled at her smartass remark.

I glanced over at Issy and gave her a dirty look. She was right.

I am a wealth of useless information. I am kind of an insufferable know it all.

Even so, I didn't know what I was looking at. At least, I couldn't recall. I shook my head several times, trying to shake off the feeling of powerlessness.

"So, what am I looking at?" I finally asked to kill the feeling of having the answer on the tip of my tongue unable to scrape it off.

"The golden ratio," professor Michaelson replied with awe.

I raised my eyebrows and shook my head, "I'm sorry, it doesn't ring a bell."

"The golden ratio? The perfect spiral? The Fibonacci sequence?" He asked, staring at me and then everyone else in the room.

Shaking my head, I still had nothing. I'd heard of it, but didn't know what it was.

"It's a mathematical equation. You can use it to create a perfect spiral. It is used in architecture and art if you look closely," Adrian supplied.

He'd wanted to study engineering and architecture before the island.

"Actually, it is called the Nix progression," Hera said as she moved closer to the holo-image staring at the nautilus shaped spiral of stars.

I cocked an eyebrow and I darted a glance at Professor Michelson. He smiled brightly, "So, it is older than human existence. Excellent!" He took out a little notebook and wrote something down.

"What does this have to do with where we are going?" I wanted to push ahead.

The entrance to the underworld was supposed to be here. I didn't care about a math equation.

"It's a perfect example of mathematics, which shows this was intentional. It couldn't have just accidentally appeared! The entire cosmos runs on rules. There are certain ones that can be bent but there are a lot that cannot be broken," Michelson remarked.

"I have powers and abilities that allow me to break the rules all the time and defy gravity. How do you explain that?" I asked.

I sat in one of the chairs and took a sip of my coffee. The smoky flavor transported me to a heavenly place for a moment.

"Exactly! Somehow our genetic abilities allow us to break mathematics rules. In doing so, I think we created the river of stars," he stared out the window in awe.

I shifted my attention away from Michelson and my coffee. Michelson turned the ship away from Styx and suddenly the perfect spiral made sense.

We were facing three stars, each a different color, red, green, and yellow. They were positioned like the points of a triangle.

They were creating a massive amount of gravitational pull, more than three stars should. I glanced around the shifting room to find confirmation that we were far enough outside the gravity well not to have it alter our trajectory. There was no way for me to confirm my fears.

I bit my lip.

What is it?

A voice in my mind loudly announced '*Cerberus, Guardian of the underworld.*'

I looked around. The voice sounded like Charon but he wasn't even in the cockpit.

"Did anybody else hear a voice?" I asked as I whipped around to search for its source.

"No, beautiful girl. You heard a voice?"

I must have seemed desperate, darting from one face to the other, searching for any recognition of sound, I nodded my head numbly.

"Yes, I heard a voice"

"What did it say?" Isolde asked.

"It said '*Cerberus Guardian of the underworld*'."

"These are dog stars. It makes perfect sense. A three-headed dog - three stars. You heard a voice in your head say '*Cerberus, Guardian of the underworld*'?" Hera asked and moved to my side.

Charon entered the shifting room. His eyes were bright with glee.

"The three-headed dog star, Cerberus."

Every head in the room swiveled to stare him down. Air moved over my tongue, my mouth must've been hanging open.

"You've seen these before?" I whispered.

This can't be happening, I wiped him.

"Yes, but we tried to stay away from them. The center is a black hole. It is Oceana."

The End

KILLING GODS V

UNDERWORLD

Everyone thinks entering a blackhole is suicide, but that's not what will kill you, its what's on the other side.

https://amzn.to/3m8CLCj

If you've enjoyed what you've read here please give it a little

love and leave a review or feel free to follow me on Amazon

Or send me an email slmason1889@gmail.com or follow me

on Instagram @s.l.mason_author

For the most up to date information on the Killing Gods

Universe or These Hallowed Hills visit:

Quickquillpublishing.com